KILLA CITY

A JOHN MILTON THRILLER

MARK DAWSON

PROLOGUE
SEVERAL WEEKS EARLIER

Oklahoma State Highway 15, an hour and a half south of Dodge City, Kansas. The heartland. They had been on the road for more than six hours, a steady procession over worn asphalt, between fields of harvested wheat and corn and then empty scrubland that was marked by a few copses of trees.

Gianluca Monteverde had stared out of the window the whole time, hardly speaking a word. He had tried to strike up a conversation with Sal twice: the first time when a police cruiser passed them an hour outside Kansas City and then, to his relief, carried on its way without showing them any interest; the second time after the radio reported a storm front coming in from the west. Sal had told him to be quiet both times, and Luca had taken the hint. He had spent the last hour staring through the streaked windshield of the decades-old grey Chevy Impala like time wasn't passing. The atmosphere was heavy and tense, and Luca hated it.

Sal had said that Luca would be doing all the driving, and he had known not to argue. Salvatore Provenzano was Bobby Whitesox's go-to guy, the enforcer who was dispatched whenever Bobby had a job that required a certain kind of man to carry it off. He had an explosive and unpredictable temper and was as ruthless as Kansas was flat. Luca knew not to cross him, even on the small things.

They had driven southwest, crossing into Oklahoma just before dawn. The highway felt empty, just the odd early-morning commuter from Oklahoma City or Tulsa, together with infrequent eighteen-wheelers and other commercial vehicles that rumbled in the opposite direction. The police cruiser had been the only sign that the law was around.

The towns between KC and their destination were tiny collections of two- and three-bedroom 1950s bungalows and colonials that flashed past them in a blur. There were occasional red-and-white motels with sedans parked outside and the odd grain elevator, corrugated steel creaking in the breeze. But that was it. It was unremarkable, mile after mile after mile of it. Luca wondered why anyone would live in places like these. Other than the occasional oil derrick pumping up and down in the distance, he could see no economic reason why a person would choose this as their home. It was just fields and the odd patch of woods or scrubland.

"Remind me," Sal said. "What are we looking for?"

"A rusted fifty-gallon drum," Luca replied, keeping his irritation at being asked for the second time out of his voice. "I know, Sal."

"And then?"

He kept his fingertips pressed lightly to the worn grey vinyl of the steering wheel. "And then I turn right and follow the first gravel road for four miles to the crossroads, then hang another right when we see the red mailbox."

Sal grunted his satisfaction and withdrew the pistol he wore in a speed holster attached to his belt. Luca looked over at the weapon and felt a twinge of nerves. He had always figured that someone was going to wing him eventually, and that the odds were that his number would be up early, just like his younger brother, Patrizio. But he never brought up his reservations, and certainly not in front of someone like Sal.

Everyone said he was born with ice in his veins. The story was that Bobby Whitesox had visited Calabria for a meeting with the 'Ndrangheta in the early 2000s and had been impressed with the quietly imposing soldier who had been deputed to act as his protection during the stay. Luca had heard that Bobby and the Italians had consummated an arrangement to work jointly on the importing of Colombian heroin and cocaine into the country and, as a part of the deal, Bobby had requested that Sal come to Kansas City to work for him. That was years ago, before Luca had become involved in the family, but he had heard all the stories. Sal was an old-school Mafioso, and his life was underpinned by unquestioning loyalty to his boss. Luca would never have been so gauche as to ask him about the jobs he had done at Bobby's request, but he knew of half a dozen men that he had killed, together with the rumours of at least the same again.

There was one killing, in particular, that stood out. Sal had been there when Patrizio had been shot at Gambino's Pork Store, and had been there the next day when Bobby had taken revenge on the street crew who had been responsible. Sal had led the ambush near Saint Luke's. It was the Thirty-Third Street Aztecas, and Sal had shot two of them and then chased the third into the kids' playground at Roanoke Park and shot him, too.

THE RADIO in the car was tuned to KAHE 95.5 FM, and Blondie's 'One Way or Another' was playing. Patrick O'Connor put the binoculars to his eyes and adjusted the focus. He had noticed a cloud of dust on the horizon, but as the image clarified, he saw that it was a large truck and not the Ford Econoline that they were waiting for.

"Anything?"

Patrick lowered the binoculars and turned to his brother. He shook his head. "Not yet."

Kenny was sitting on the hood of the car that they had driven out here. "How much longer?"

"I don't know. Bird said the meet was set for eight." He checked his watch. "It's not half-past yet. Probably going to be here for another hour."

"You trust him?"

"Who?"

"Bird. You know he's basically incompetent."

"I know. But he serves a purpose."

Kenny stretched. "I told you we didn't need to get up so early. I could've had another half hour in bed."

"And you know what Da used to say."

"Better three hours too soon than a minute late," Kenny muttered. "I know. I'm just bored."

The two of them were twins. Patrick was the older by five minutes and took pleasure in reminding Kenny of that fact whenever his brother questioned his decisions. In truth, though, dissent was unusual. Kenny wasn't a leader and knew that it was one of his limitations; he didn't have the mind for it, nor was it something in which he was interested. He had been content to follow Patrick's lead ever since they had been youngsters in Clondalkin. Their parents had always said that Patrick had been born with the brains while Kenny got the muscle. The twins trusted each other implicitly, and the combination of their talents—together with a ruthlessness that they both shared—had served them well in life. It had brought them here, from Dublin to Missouri, and they were going to need every last scrap of moxie to pull themselves out of the mess into which they had been pitched.

The DJ on the radio faded down Blondie and cut to the weatherman.

"We're just giving you advance warning of a line of severe storms that are passing through Ford County. We got reports of severe thunderstorms and possible tornados. Sixty-to-seventy-mile-an-hour winds and dime- and nickel-sized hail. The front is moving quickly and is not expected to stick around for long, but you'll need to take it easy on the morning commute."

Patrick looked over at the horizon. There was a bank of black and grey clouds at the fuzzy margin where the ground met the sky.

"Shit," he said.

"You think they'll still come?"

"They're not gonna leave it at the farm. They'll come. Check the gun."

"I checked it."

"Check it again."

Kenny slid off the hood and went around to the trunk. They had brought a Barrett REC7 carbine with them, together with plenty of ammunition. Kenny had picked the gun up from a middleman whom he had used before. He had told Patrick—over and over and *over* again—that he had used one to take out four British soldiers at checkpoints across South Armagh. Kenny had served in a Real IRA squad operating out of Dromintee and had amassed something of a reputation; indeed, the screensaver on his phone was a picture that had been taken in Crossmaglen, showing a man with a gun and the legend 'Sniper at Work.' This particular gun was clean. Not that that would matter. Kenny would dump it in the smelter at the plant on Guinotte Street once they were done.

Bird had told them that the pickup was due to take place at the old farm three miles to the west. Patrick had considered lying in wait there, but had decided that the guys who made the run from Vegas would complicate things. Better to wait until the wops had collected the van, and then hit them out here, on the road, miles from anyone.

He listened to the metallic *click* as Kenny depressed the magazine catch button and the *clunk* as he pulled the magazine down.

"It's fine," his twin said. "You get down there to those rocks when we see them, let them get close, and then step out into the road and stop them. I'll pick them off from here. You still okay with that?"

"What else are we going to do? Let them go? What do you think Bobby would do if he finds out what we've done?"

"I'm not complaining," his brother said with a grin. "Just checking you've still got the bollocks to go through with it."

"Don't worry about me," Patrick said.

Patrick had always prided himself on his sagacity, but he had made a stupid mistake that had put them both in danger. Losing Bobby Whitesox's money was the dumbest thing that he had ever allowed to happen. Fixing the problem required them to do something that was perhaps even more stupid, but he was fresh out of ideas. It was this or a bullet in the back of the head and burial in a shallow grave.

Patrick put the glasses to his eyes again.

He scanned the horizon. There was still no sign of them.

He checked his watch: seven forty-five.

THEY PASSED another red-and-white motel near the tiny town of Gage, with two cars parked out front but no other signs of life. Then it was more empty fields of sagebrush and wild grass for five or six minutes and a set of railway tracks to their right. The road followed the tracks for hundreds of miles, but they hadn't seen a train. The sky was clear, with just wisps of cottony white clouds. The notion of a storm would seem absurd anywhere else in the world.

Not in Kansas and Oklahoma. Luca knew better.

He spotted the rusty barrel a half mile before they reached it. The sun had been up for less than an hour, but it was bright enough to see the turnoff.

Luca turned the wheel, and the car's tyres sank slightly into loose gravel as they pulled onto the unmarked side road. The vehicle fishtailed a little, and he backed off the accelerator to avoid a disdainful look from Sal. The sedan approached the crossroads, and he turned the car to the right. A tin Quonset hut appeared a mile or so ahead on the left. That had to be the place. The building grew as they approached until it was the size of a small factory. Just beyond it sat a dilapidated house with white paint peeling off its warped wooden siding. Three trucks were parked in front of it; three were parked beyond it. The red mailbox, just a dented tin container atop a rotting wooden post, sat just outside a five-foot-high barbed-wire fence.

They followed the driveway for another fifty yards before Luca stepped on the brakes.

"Nice and easy," Sal said. "Money makes men do crazy things, and this is a lot of money."

A figure appeared in the old home's doorway. Luca checked his watch. It was just after seven fifty in the morning. Luca saw tattoos on the man's bare arms and down his neck. He was broad shouldered, and the dark glasses he was wearing obscured his eyes.

"That's Tony Giancana," Sal said.

Luca knew that the Mafia in Vegas had retreated from the casino business after the cost of running the resorts became too steep, even for them, but they were still there: construction, food and beverage, the sex industry, garbage collection and taxis. They maintained their connections on the Strip, and Giancana was the point of contact between the head of the Tropicana's *Folies Bergère* show who ran the skimming operation and the outfits that profited from it. The Colombo family was responsible for the Vegas side of the operation, and Bobby laundered the money. Luca and Sal would drive it back to Vegas and Irish Ray would clean it, remitting the funds to two shell companies in the Caymans. It was a smooth and well-oiled operation that had worked without incident for the last eighteen months.

Giancana nodded at them as he lifted the gate.

Sal wound down the window. "Hey," he said.

Giancana pointed ahead. "By the tin hut."

Luca stepped gently on the gas, the gravel crunching under the Chevy's tyres. He pulled it halfway past the Quonset, then turned and slotted it so that it faced the tin building.

"Keep it tight," Sal reminded him as they unbuckled.

They climbed out of the car. Giancana was walking back towards them, crossing the hard-packed mud and yellowed, dead grass. Two more men came out of the house: a shorter guy with a patchy beard and a man with a shotgun resting over his shoulder. The shorter guy moved confidently; he had a thick gold chain around his neck, and the sun sparkled off it as it swung from side to side.

Sal pointed to the man with the gun. "What the fuck, Tony?"

Giancana shrugged. "Can't be too careful."

"Tell him to put it away or we go back to Kansas. You can explain why you have to make another run."

Giancana smirked, turned to the house, and wagged a finger. The man with the shotgun stared at Sal, who stared right back at him. The man lowered the shotgun and propped it up against the wall, leaving it within reach in case it turned out that he might need it.

"*Vaffanculo,* Tony—what are you thinking? We're on the same team."

"Don't get your panties in a bunch, Sal. He's put it down."

Sal paused, and Luca saw the tendons in his neck knotting and bulging. He had seen that before, and knew it was often a prelude to a detonation of temper.

He kept a lid on it. "Is it ready to go?"

Giancana nodded towards the shed. "Inside."

They followed the man across the parking area to the hut's metal back door. He punched in a six-digit code on an adjacent panel. Luca memorised it, just in case, and followed Giancana and Sal inside. The hut had been divided by a long central wall into two sides. The right side had been closed off as offices. A door with an inset square of glass led inside. To the left was a long open garage area, with a couple of dirt bikes and an old ride-on mower parked by the wall. About forty yards away, at the other end of the hut, a van sat in front of the roll-up metal door.

"You did it like you were asked?"

Giancana nodded. "Took a week to open it up, then put it back together."

"Is the best way," he said. "We do it like this in Naples."

"Easier to hide it in a box."

"Easier to find it, too. Keys?"

"In the ignition."

"Gas?"

"All the way to the top. You're good to go."

The man who had been toting the shotgun went over to the roller door and hauled the chain to open it.

Sal turned to Giancana and pointed to the man at the door. "Tell him that if he comes out this way again, I take a pair of bolt-cutters and snip off his fingers. He gets to walk away today because I got some respect for your boss, and I can only think that he's got no idea that such a *cafone* is working for him. You hear me?"

Giancana stared at Sal and, for a moment, Luca thought he was going to be stupid enough to argue.

He wasn't; instead, he nodded. "Next month, then."

Sal turned to Luca and pointed to the van. "Let's go."

LUCA DROVE the van out of the farm and picked up Highway 15, retracing their steps back towards Dodge City.

"*Figlio di puttana*," Sal spat.

"What?"

"Bringing a shotgun. I should have capped him. What was he thinking?"

"I know," Luca said, appeasing him in the hope that he might relax a little.

"It is a lack of respect," he said.

Luca was about to make another conciliatory reply when he saw a car in the mirror. It was a police cruiser, and it was accelerating hard.

"We got company," he said.

Sal looked in his mirror. "Take it easy. You know the story. We just delivered some air conditioning units. Now we're going back to KC."

The cruiser was right on their tail. It stayed there for a solid minute before it pulled out and sped around them, accelerating into the distance.

"Weird," Luca said.

Sal shrugged. "It's gone now. Forget it."

The drive to Kansas City was six and a half hours, maybe seven if they hit traffic. Luca was supposed to pick up his idiot nephew from school that afternoon, and it looked like he would be there in time. Francesco had started playing in a band, and he was all talk about how they were going to make it, how they were going to use music to get out of the city. It was all bullshit. Luca had told Franny that, too—that it was a pipe dream and things like that didn't happen to kids like him. Luca had been decent at baseball when he was growing up, but, although he was good, he had known that he wasn't good enough. He could have tried to find a spot in the minor leagues, but there was no money in that, and you couldn't get anywhere in this world without a little paper. He had known that he would eventually find his way into Bobby's crew, just like his father had before him. There had been no point in fighting it, so he didn't. He was doing good now: good money, good prospects, and, despite runs like today's out to West Bumblefuck, the work was pretty easy. He wasn't about to complain.

Sal tapped him on the arm and then pointed out to the west.

Luca looked.

The storm front had come out of nowhere, and it wasn't far off. The long grass in the surrounding meadows began to rustle and bend. The van was buffeted, wind slamming into it, pushing it a half foot sideways each time.

"Shit," Luca swore.

"We should've had the radio on," Sal said.

"You said you didn't want to—"

"They would have given a warning."

Luca looked sideways again and saw that the horizon had disappeared. A wall of dust was closing in on them. It reached from the ground all the way to the clouds, a seething brown mass that stretched for miles.

"Stop," Sal said. "Pull over."

Luca stood on the brakes and edged the van over to the side of the road. They were next to a big hackberry, its boughs shaking violently in the wind. Luca looked out of the windshield and saw a red-tailed hawk overhead, the bird already struggling to stay aloft.

Sal took two pre-rolled joints from his pocket and offered one to Luca. "Close the air vents," he said. "We ride it out."

PATRICK AND KENNY were up on a raised bluff, and they had a good view of the landscape below them. They had chosen the spot so that they would get plenty of notice when Bobby Whitesox's guys were on the way with the money, but the vantage point also allowed them a grandstand view of the storm as it blew in from the southwest.

Kenny pointed. "You see that?"

Patrick raised the glasses, picked out the ribbon of asphalt, and followed it back. The black storm occluded his view, but he saw two vehicles picked out against the acceler-ating darkness. The first was a van—hard to make out the model and make from this distance, but black, like they had been told to expect—and the second was a black and white police cruiser. The cruiser pulled out and passed the van, speeding away from it as it headed towards them.

"Is that it?"

Patrick concentrated on the van, adjusting the focus a little until it was as clear as he could make it. He had been told that the money would be moved in a Ford Econoline, and the van certainly *could* have been a Ford.

"Patrick?"

"I think so."

"So get down to the road."

Patrick pulled up the scarf he was wearing around his neck so that it covered his nose and mouth. Kenny took the carbine and lay down with it, sighting the road. Patrick started to pick his way down the loose scree trail that led to the asphalt fifty feet below. He heard a tremendous boom of thunder. He looked up, but he didn't need the binoculars to see as the storm rushed up behind the van and then swallowed it.

He stopped and called back, "Can you still see it?"

"No," Kenny shouted.

Patrick felt the first fat drops of rain. He cursed. There was nothing they could do if they couldn't see the van. Deciding that it made more sense to wait out the storm in the car, he turned around and started to clamber back up the slope.

LUCA TOOK a toke on the joint as the storm rolled over them. The roar was guttural, pebbles and rocks picked up by the wind and tossed against the side of the van. Hail lashed down, thundering against the roof and the windshield. The van shook, its wheels tipping up off the ground, first on one side and then on the other, rocking them violently like a cradle about to flip. A golf ball–sized piece of hail crashed into the windshield and cracked it, the glass spiderwebbing around the point of impact.

"*Andare a puttane!*" Sal swore.

They sheltered there for fifteen minutes, and at last, the storm began to lift in stages: the wind dropped, the hail turned to rain, and then, finally, the rain stopped. The Econoline's cab smelled strongly of dope as Luca looked out. The windshield was cracked in three places and covered in a thin layer of hail.

He flicked on the wipers and waited for them to clear the debris away, wet smears arcing across the glass.

"Shit."

The view ahead was clear enough for them to see the flashing red lights. Gianluca saw the police cruiser that had passed them. It had stopped in the road, half turned across it to block the way ahead.

Luca turned to Sal. "What do we do?"

Sal shrugged. "We take it easy. It's probably nothing."

"What if it isn't?"

"Come on, Luca. What are they going to find? Nothing. Have you checked it out? They did a good job in Vegas. It's a work of art. You wouldn't know anything was here unless you knew where to look. We're good. We got nothing to worry about."

PART I

1

The snow started to fall somewhere between Denver and Lincoln. John Milton had decided that he would take advantage of the empty seat next to him to stretch out and get some sleep. The sky had been dark and foreboding as they rolled through Colorado, but now, as he awoke to the never-ending fields of Kansas, fat flakes were piling down from the clouds. The light was almost all gone, and he had to check that it was mid-morning, as he had expected. The bus's wipers squeaked as they swept back and forth, clearing the windshield so that the driver could peer ahead as far as the high beams would allow.

The Greyhound from Oakland had taken two days to reach Kansas City. Milton could have taken a plane, but had decided against it for two reasons: first, he wanted to limit the number of times that he had to present himself for official inspection. He had reason to suspect that London was looking for him again, and, with that in mind, he preferred the anonymity of the road. Second, going cross-country was a far better way to enjoy America than to look down at it from the air. These so-called flyover states—Utah, Colorado, Missouri—were the heartland of America, and Milton wanted to enjoy them properly.

There were just a handful of other passengers on the bus now. Milton had watched them all get on, and, from force of habit, had remembered their stations of origin and details that he would be able to recall later: the army veteran with the Vietnam patches on his denim jacket who had boarded at Avenal; the single mother and her teenage son who had joined at Salt Lake City and had bickered ever since; the old man on the other side of the aisle from him who had embarked at Cheyenne, Wyoming, ate a single square of Hershey chocolate every half hour, and drank from a dinged-up Thermos.

Milton felt the old man's eyes on him now.

He looked over at him and raised his eyebrows. "Brutal weather."

"They've been forecasting it for a week," the old man said. He tapped the iPad that he had on his lap. "You know the heaviest snow we ever had in KC?"

"I don't," Milton admitted.

"Twelve inches, all the way back in sixty-two. They're saying we might get nine today." He gestured at Milton. "You ain't really dressed for the weather."

"I might have to get myself a winter coat."

"Your accent—Australian?"

Milton smiled. "I get that sometimes. English."

The old man reached down to anchor himself as the bus rolled around a bend.

"Where you been before here?" he said when the bus had straightened up again.

"Sorry?"

"Before you got on the bus. You've got colour in your face, and I know you didn't get it from here."

"Oh—Colombia."

"Holiday?"

"I wish," Milton said. "Business."

He looked away, watching the landscape roll by. The sky was a leaden vault for as far as he could see, and the clouds looked like they had settled in for the long haul.

THE GREYHOUND PULLED into the station and slid into one of the empty bays. The driver called out that they had reached their destination and switched off the engine. Milton waited for the old man to struggle up from his seat and stand. He followed him into the aisle and offered to help him with retrieving his bag from the overhead locker.

"Thank you," the old man said. "That's good of you."

Milton opened the locker and fetched down the old man's leather case. "Here you go."

"Much obliged."

Milton reached back into the locker and took out the rucksack that he had bought in Medellín. He was travelling light, as was his preference: a change of clothes, a couple of books and a bag of basic toiletries.

The old man started down the aisle and Milton followed. There was a queue at the exit as the driver helped an elderly lady descend the steps.

"Enjoy the city," the old man said. "It ain't what it once was, but, then again, there ain't much that is anymore, is there?"

Milton disembarked. The snow was falling heavily now, and little drifts were already gathering against the walls of the station building. He slung his rucksack over his shoulder and crossed to the other side of the street. He had arrived in plenty of Greyhound stations during his visits to the United States, and this one looked like so many of the others. Troost Avenue was in an industrial part of town with wide roads and low-slung warehouses. He could see that it was not the sort of place in which a traveller would have been encouraged to linger should he or she arrive after dark.

Milton checked his watch. It was midday. The area was not that busy, with just a single Mack truck lumbering along the snow-covered road. He checked his phone and retrieved the address that Ziggy Penn had located for him. Kansas City Fresh was located in Gladstone, ten miles to the north. Milton opened the Uber app. The wait for the first car was ten minutes. He chose the cheapest option and went into the waiting room, where he found an empty bench and sat down.

2

Milton asked the driver to take him to the nearest Walmart so that he could pick up clothes that would be more appropriate for the weather: a heavyweight jacket with a fur hood, a pair of leather gloves, and zippered tactical work boots that were both waterproof and slip resistant. He paid the cashier from his small reserve of cash and ordered another Uber.

He bought a coffee and a Danish while he waited and flipped through a copy of *USA Today* that had been left on the café table. The front pages were taken up with domestic politics, but on page four there was a report of a raid on the El Centro drug cartel, which operated from a stronghold in the rainforest outside Medellín. The raid, according to the report, had been a joint operation between the United States and Colombian militaries, with support from the FBI. Anonymous sources were suggesting that the leadership of the cartel had been impacted and the narcotics business disrupted. Milton folded the paper and put it aside. The story was no more than a sketch of what had happened and omitted most of the details. There was no mention that

British intelligence was involved or that the cartel was protected by both MI6 and the CIA. There was certainly no mention that Group Fifteen had been responsible for the assassination of the US ambassador, a killing at the behest of a faction within the CIA that wanted to shore up the cartel against pressure from the DEA and FBI.

Milton's activity in Colombia had damaged the Group's plan, and he was concerned that it had put him back in their crosshairs. He had enjoyed an amnesty of sorts since the death of the previous Control, and he suspected that the state of affairs might have changed, and not in his favour. That was the reason for his trip to Missouri. He had a connection here who might be able to find out.

THE DRIVER DROPPED Milton opposite his destination. The road here was wide, with two lanes in each direction, and businesses set out in generous plots of land on either side. Kansas City Fresh was located on Seventieth Street, a cul-de-sac that served Flex Fitness on the right and a long, low-slung industrial building on the left. The snow was still falling heavily, and some of the vans had been festooned with an inch of it on their roofs.

There was a food truck parked at the top of the street. Milton ordered a black coffee and waited next to the vehicle, just watching. A number of white delivery vans had been slotted up against the long building, each emblazoned with the blue water drop that was the logo of Kansas City Fresh. A line of private cars was squeezed in between the vans and the trees at the end of the street. The building itself was accessed by way of a number of roller doors, many of which were open so that the business's staff could load the vans with bottled water from inside. A radio was playing country music, the song vying with the shouts and calls of the men who were tending the trucks.

Milton double-checked the details that Ziggy had sent. Milton had been surprised when he had suggested that his old acquaintance could be found in Missouri. He had been *so* surprised, in fact, that he had asked Ziggy to confirm that his information was correct. He had expected that he would be making a trip to England, to the sort of Home Counties dormitory village that attracted commuters who wanted a little bucolic charm at the end of their working days. But Ziggy had verified his research and confirmed that it was accurate.

Milton was a little nervous. The man he had come to see knew more about him than most, and seeing him again risked dusting off old memories that Milton would have preferred to keep locked away. He sipped his coffee and watched as one of the vans pulled out. The newly opened space allowed Milton a better view of the next van down the line. A man in blue overalls was wrestling large bottles of water from a pallet behind the van onto its loading ramp. Milton paused and observed him until he was sure this was the man he had come to see. He dropped the unfinished coffee into an open trash can, slung his rucksack over his shoulder, and crunched through the snow as he made his way towards the loading dock.

The man either didn't notice him or, if he did, was too busy to pay him much attention. The bottles looked heavy, and Milton could see that he had an issue with his right leg that made it more difficult for him to haul the bottles off the ground. Each bottle elicited a grunt of effort, and the man was sweating despite the frigid air.

Milton reached the van and stopped.

The man manhandled the final bottle into the van, secured them all with a fabric tie, and slammed the doors. He reached for a walking stick that he had propped against the wall of the building and made his way around to the driver's side.

"Hello," Milton said.

The man paused. "Can I help you?" he said in an unmistakable English accent.

"I hope so."

The man's eyes went wide and his mouth dropped open.

"Long time, no see," Milton said.

"Jesus…"

Milton offered his hand. "Hello, Tanner. Could I have a word?"

3

"Jesus," Tanner said again.

"I'm sorry to surprise you like this."

Tanner swallowed. Milton could see that his bewilderment was receding and that wariness was taking its place.

"I probably should've told you I was coming," Milton said.

"That might have been an idea."

"Sorry about that."

"What do you want?"

"I need to talk to you."

Tanner looked reluctant. Milton wasn't surprised. *He* would have been circumspect had the roles been reversed.

"Please? It won't take long."

Tanner looked over to the warehouse and then back to Milton. His brow was furrowed, and Milton guessed that he was working out what it would be sensible to do. He had anticipated hesitation, perhaps even diffidence or hostility, but he was prepared to stay in town until Tanner heard him out. But the uncomfortable moment did not last long.

Tanner shook his head and chuckled. "Sorry to seem so unfriendly. It's just that you are probably the last person I ever expected to see again. You gave me a shock."

Milton shrugged. "Truthfully? I didn't know if you'd speak to me if I called ahead."

"So you thought you'd just turn up and give me a heart attack?"

He said it with a smile, and Milton could tell that the conversation he wanted would be possible.

"Hop in," Tanner said, tapping his hand against the side of the van. "I've got a delivery to make. We can talk on the way."

TANNER PUT the van into reverse and backed out of the lot. He swung the wheel, put the engine into drive, and slotted into a gap in the traffic. Milton waited for him to begin the conversation. Small talk felt pointless. The two of them had always been civil, but it would have been an exaggeration to say that there was anything between them beyond professional respect. Milton had thought carefully about the people he could approach for help to understand the situation that he might now be in. Tanner was the best option he had been able to come up with; indeed, he was probably the *only* option.

Tanner drove slowly and carefully through the snow. There was still a good amount of traffic on the road, and it would have been easy to slide across the compacted ice. He slowed for a stop light, then turned and looked across the cabin at Milton.

"How'd you find me?"

"I have a contact who used to work for Group Two. He does little pieces of work for me now and again."

"Let me guess—Ziggy Penn?"

There was no point in pretending otherwise. "Yes," he said. "How do you know?"

"Back when I was in London—when Control was looking for you—we always suspected that he was involved. He was out by then, too, but we knew he would've left backdoors that he could exploit."

"He used one of them to track you down," Milton said.

"I doubt it was all that difficult. It's not like I've made any effort to hide. I'm not like you and the others. I wasn't much more than a paper-pusher. No one's coming after me." He paused, then shook his head a little diffidently. "Well—not until today, anyway."

The lights changed and Tanner pulled out. He had been the aide-de-camp to Control and had, in that capacity, been responsible for the liaison between the agents in the field and the man responsible for their orders. Control and Tanner had been diametrically different in character: Control was irritable and cold, dispassionately distributing his red-ribboned files to the agents who carried out the instructions contained within; Tanner had more humanity, and, where Control never showed warmth, it was not unusual for Tanner to leaven his grim instructions with good humour.

Milton indicated the truck. "This is your business?"

"It is now. It belonged to my wife's father. She took it over when he died."

"I didn't even know you were married."

"I'm glad there's a limit to Penn's research."

"Does she work with you?"

"Not anymore. She died last year. Cancer."

"Shit. I'm sorry."

"It is what it is," he said. "It's been a tough couple of years. I got out of London after Control was killed. Whitehall found out what he had been doing, the whole mess that Beatrix Rose kicked up, and anyone could see that they wanted to sweep everyone out and start again. I'd been looking for a reason to quit, and that was that. I sold my flat and came over here. They'd just finished the probate on my father-in-law's estate, and the business was going to fail unless someone took it on. We thought we'd make a go of it. Then she got sick and I carried on myself. I was going to sell it, but it turns out that I kind of enjoy it. It's a change from what I used to do."

He glanced over as he said that, as if watching for a reaction.

"It's certainly different," Milton said.

Tanner stopped for another light. He looked over again. "What do you want, Milton?"

Milton sighed. "Long story."

"But you need my help?"

"Just to talk. About London. And about the Group."

Tanner shook his head. "I've been off the reservation almost as long as you. I'm not sure I'll be able to offer much you can't sort yourself."

"But you didn't burn your bridges."

"Well—not like you."

"You still have contacts?"

He drove on. "Some. Why? What do you want to know?"

"The last I heard, the Group had been shut down. Now I'm hearing that it's up and running again."

"And what would that have to do with you?"

Milton glanced out of the window, his thoughts flicking

to the jungles of Antioquia and the streets of Medellín. "I think they might be looking for me again."

"Why would they do that? There was an amnesty when Pope took over."

"I *may* have inadvertently put my nose in their business."

"Not the best idea."

"No."

They were up on North Congress Avenue. Tanner flicked the indicator and turned onto a service road that led to a row of businesses. Milton saw two two-storey warehouse buildings, both finished in white cladding with orange and black horizontal stripes serving as decoration. There was a large parking lot serving the buildings, but not many cars.

"We're going there," Tanner said, pointing to the snow-laden sign outside the left-hand building that announced KELLY'S – SINCE 1987.

"What is it?"

"Jack Kelly runs an auction business—he sells cars. He's been taking his water from us for years. Got a couple of bottles to change. Fifteen-minute job."

Tanner parked alongside a tall flagpole with a Stars and Stripes cracking in the breeze. He switched off the engine and turned to look at Milton.

"So," he said. "What do you want to know?"

"Is the Group looking for me?"

"Do you think they might be?"

"I think it's possible. I'll need to give you a little context."

"Fire away."

"I was in Medellín before I came here."

"Why on earth would you go to a place like that?"

"A friend was murdered by a cartel hitman," Milton said, careful not to reveal more than was necessary. "I decided that was unacceptable and that I was going to show them that actions have consequences. The Group had three agents working with the cartel. I'm not entirely sure why, but it looks as if the leadership was being protected."

"And?"

"And not protected very well. I don't think what happened would have pleased London—let's leave it at that."

"So you want to know *how* displeased they are?"

Milton nodded. "Are they coming for me again? Do I need to be careful? I have no beef with them. I'm quite happy to go my own way, but it would be good to know if that's something I can do without looking over my shoulder every five minutes."

"All right," Tanner said. "There's someone I can call—I might be able to get a steer. How do I reach you?"

"I'll give you my number."

Tanner tapped it into his phone. "How long are you in town?"

"I'm in no rush," Milton said. "I was thinking about picking up a road trip I started before Colombia. I bought a GTO in Oakland. I was going to drive it coast to coast."

"What year?"

"The car? 1969. Cortez silver with a vinyl top. Ram Air cam, roller rockers, Edelbrock intake—she was a real beauty."

Tanner whistled. "Nice."

"It was," Milton said.

"Past tense?"

"I put my nose in something else," he said with a rueful smile. "Ended up losing the car in Las Vegas. It's probably in a police pound somewhere by now."

"Well," Tanner said, "speaking of police pounds, you

might be in luck." He pointed a finger out of the windshield. "Jack has auctions two times a week—Tuesdays and Thursdays. He gets a lot of his stuff from the police. Some nice vehicles at very competitive prices. You should check it out —there's one this afternoon."

Milton looked out at the warehouse. A large parking lot could be seen between the two buildings, guarded by a metal fence. Milton could see half of a set of bleachers and a podium with a lectern and microphone, most likely where the auctioneer would conduct proceedings.

"Come on," Tanner said. "Give me a hand with the water in the back and I'll introduce you."

4

They unbuckled their belts and got out of the van. Tanner opened the rear doors and muscled one of the bottles to the lip of the load space where he could get his arms around it. Milton knew that Tanner had lost a leg during his military service, but he didn't want to insult him by asking if he could manage. He had obviously been managing just fine for years, and Milton would just be patronising him if he offered to carry both bottles. Instead, he wrapped his arms around the second bottle and lifted it out of the van, closing the doors with his shoulder.

"Heavier than they look," Tanner said.

"What is it—five gallons?"

Tanner nodded. "Weighs about forty pounds."

They set off through the snow, Milton matching Tanner's more laboured pace.

"It's quiet," Milton said, indicating the other cars that were parked in the lot.

"The crowd depends on how much Jack advertises. Today, though, with the weather? You never know, you might see something you like the look of—I doubt there'll be many here today."

They carried the bottles through a gate in the fence and into the auction yard. It was a simple empty lot with the dais that Milton had seen from outside and bleachers with capacity for a couple of hundred attendees. A man in a winter coat was sweeping the snow off the bleachers with a broom. At the back of the lot, fifty yards away, sat a four-bay garage building, about the same size as a car dealership. Milton scanned the handful of people waiting for the auction to start: a bored teenager in cargo pants and a puffer jacket, hands in his pockets; a couple of guys in branded jackets; a woman with a designer clutch purse.

"In here," Tanner said, nodding to an office area facing the yard.

Milton followed him inside. There was a water dispenser inside the office. Tanner lowered the full bottle and told Milton to do the same. He lifted the empty bottle straight up from the cooler and took out a rag to wipe around the rim so that he could dry it off and clean away any debris. Milton grabbed the neck of the full bottle with his left hand and placed his right beneath it. Tanner unscrewed the cap from the neck, and Milton lifted it, tipping it at a forty-five-degree angle to start the flow of water. Tanner secured it to the base.

"Got help today, David?"

They turned. An older man was in the doorway. He had a crown of sparse red hair around a pale bald head and wore a dark T-shirt that said 'Support Our Troops' in huge red, white and blue letters.

"Just a friend. John—this is Jack Kelly. Jack—this is John. I used to work with him in London."

"Two Limeys at my auction," Kelly said. "Not something I see every day."

"John might be looking for a car," Tanner said.

Kelly cocked an eyebrow. "What kind of car?"

"He had a GTO. He's thinking something similar."

The older man smiled. "You like muscle cars?"

"I do."

"You could be in luck."

Milton raised his hands to slow Kelly down. "I doubt I could afford anything like that today."

"You might be surprised," Kelly said. He went over to a desk, picked up a sheet of paper, and brought it over. "These are on the slate for today. Might be one on there that lights your fire—very nice 1969 Oldsmobile 442. No reserve, either. If you asked me to guess, I'd say she goes between twenty-five and thirty."

Milton doubted that he would be able to afford the car, but he was interested enough to stick around and see.

"I've got to get back," Tanner said to him. "Mollie's expecting me."

"Mollie?"

"My daughter," he said.

"You haven't met her yet?" Kelly said. "You're in for a treat. She's a firecracker."

"And thirty years younger than you, Jack."

Kelly grinned. "I got to get started. See you outside, John." He grabbed a thick winter coat, slipped it on, and then shook Tanner's hand. "See you later. Thanks for the water."

He made his way through the office to the yard.

Tanner grabbed the empty bottle and hoisted it up until it was balanced on his shoulder. "I'll make that call to London for you," he said. "I'll let you know if I find anything out."

5

M ilton looked down at the single page that Kelly had given him. It was neatly split into two columns of thumbnail-sized pictures of cars with adjacent copy. One of the pictures caught his attention. It was tiny and blurry, shadows obscuring the front angle. The description read, '1969 Oldsmobile 442, 89,000 miles on rebuilt block, excellent condition. No reserve.'

He was definitely tempted. The fact that it had no reserve was encouraging, but that didn't mean it was going to go for a price that was in his range. A car like that had no business being sold at a place like this and, assuming that the local dealers and collectors were savvy, he knew that the price would climb precipitously.

Milton wasn't flush with cash, either. He had given most of what was left of the money he had taken from the Russos to charity, saving just enough for a ticket to the United States and then subsistence for six months. He had reserved twenty-five grand to buy a cheap set of wheels in the event that he decided to continue his road trip. Driving a muscle car across the States was a bucket-list item, and it had been curtailed when he had been foolish enough to offer a ride to Jessica Russo. The money was in his rucksack. He doubted it would be enough for the Olds—whatever Kelly might have said—but that didn't stop him entertaining the hope that he might be wrong.

The snow had stopped when Milton walked over to the bleachers. He picked up a paddle that he guessed was used to signal a bid, and made his way along the empty benches just as Kelly leaned towards the microphone.

"Seats, please, ladies and gents. I think we're just about ready to get going."

Milton scanned the crowd. There were perhaps two dozen others with him. Most looked uninterested. He guessed that the men in branded jackets were commercial buyers, looking for stock that they could sell on. The lady with the clutch purse was a bit incongruous, but there was a Porsche Cayenne coming up that would be a good fit for a soccer mom with the finances to go big. The kid in the puffer jacket had taken the seat along from him. He was the hardest one to place. What might he be looking for? A first car, perhaps? He looked barely old enough to drive. He was bracing himself with a hand on each knee, his expression apprehensive.

"Okay, folks," Kelly said. "Thanks for coming out in this weather, but at least it's stopped. Let's get this underway."

The roar of a powerful engine could be heard from the garage building to Milton's right. A roller door clattered upwards, and a black pickup truck rolled out, printing its tracks on the fresh snow.

"We're kicking things off with lot number thirty-two-forty-two, a 2013 Chevrolet Silverado LTZ crew-cab full-sized pickup."

The bidding was fast and pointed, going up a thousand

at a time, then five hundred, until Kelly finally slammed the gavel down.

"Sold! To Tom Stafford from Stafford's Used Cars... How are you doing today? Sold for twenty-two thousand, five hundred dollars. A reminder, ladies and gentlemen, that all purchases must be settled up at the office."

The truck rolled behind the dais and down the slope towards the parking lot. Milton watched as the driver carefully parked it in one of the reserved spots along the lot's back fence. The buyer—the dealer named Tom—shook hands with the man he had been sitting next to and went to the office to pay.

The Olds was the last car of the afternoon. Nothing before it held much interest for Milton. There was a Mini Clubman with low mileage that Kelly said had been used as a demonstrator. Next was a Cadillac that was going for next to nothing, followed by a yellow 1970 Volkswagen Minibus. The woman with the purse bid on the Cayenne, just as Milton had expected, but she lost out to one of the professional buyers and stalked off muttering obscenities into her phone. There was one more vehicle before the muscle car. Milton noticed the teenager fretting with his catalogue with nervous fingers. He hadn't bid on anything yet.

The vehicle in question pulled out of the garage and parked where it could be inspected. It was a Ford van that looked as if it must be twenty or even thirty years old. The van was painted black, but the front panel on the driver's side was white; it looked as if it had been replaced without the owner going to the trouble of spraying it to match the rest of the vehicle.

"Moving right along," Kelly said. "The next-to-last lot is number four-seven-seven-three: a 1990 Ford Econoline E-150 van, in black. The bodywork needs a little attention, but the engine is in good condition—it's a good, reliable workhorse. This is a police auction of proceeds of crime and, as such, is offered with no reserve but also no warranty or limitation. The van has 122,000 miles on its original engine and a new front windshield, just installed. Who'll start the bidding on this van at a thousand dollars?"

No one raised their paddle. Milton watched the teen. He had started to raise his hand before he hesitated and held back. Smart. There was no reserve on the van and no reason to jump in at the first offer.

Kelly tried again. "Come on now, folks. I understand people being edgy about this one, but it's a great vehicle and a fantastic value. Do I see a thousand dollars?"

No one bid.

"You guys are *killing* me," Kelly said. "Do I hear five hundred to open? Come on now, folks, that's a steal of a deal. Five hundred to open on this—"

"Five hundred!" the teenager called out, waving the paddle a little too enthusiastically. "Sorry," he added more quietly as every head in the crowd turned his way. "Five hundred."

6

P atrick O'Connor swerved the car into the nearest available space, killed the engine, and got out.

"I told you to *check*," he said. "What did I say? I said you should check what time the auction started so we could be here in plenty of time."

Kenny got out, too. "I *did* check. Frank said they'd had it moved to three."

"So why does it say two thirty on the sign?"

"I don't know."

Patrick hurried away, aiming the key fob behind him and blipping the locks. Kenny followed. "And why has the auction already started?"

"I don't know. Maybe Frank made a mistake."

"Maybe, *Kenneth*, you made a mistake when you were speaking to him."

"Piss off," Kenny muttered. He hated it when he was referred to by his full name; it was a sore point that Patrick had exploited ever since they were kids in Clondalkin.

"I can't trust you to do anything," he said. "*Anything.*"

Detective Frank Bird had called last night with the news

that the van was being sold at auction today. It had been impossible to get at it while it was impounded, and Patrick had been worried that it would divulge its secrets if it was given a thorough inspection. He had consoled himself with the fact that there was no need for the van to be examined in any great detail. Bird had explained what had happened: the police suspected that the van had been used to move the bodies of a triple homicide five years earlier. The case had remained unsolved, but, incredibly, the Vegas crew had continued to use the vehicle. The police had run a routine check after coming across the van on the road outside Parsons and had seen that it had been flagged on the system. Bobby's men had been driving it, and, although they had been absolved of any responsibility, the van was too hot to be reclaimed.

Patrick knew that Bobby Whitesox would just send someone to buy the van when it was auctioned, so he had been clever. Bird had found a clerk who worked at Kelly's and, for the sake of a five-hundred-dollar bribe, she had arranged for the van to be put up for sale today, five days before the Wednesday slot for when it had originally been listed. Bobby would never know; by the time his men made it to the lot next week, the van would have already been sold.

To Patrick.

But that required them to be on time for the sale, and, because he had trusted his *idiot* brother, it looked like it was going to be tight.

7

Milton saw movement near the concessions. Two men were arguing with the old woman who was in charge of the gate that allowed access to the auction area.

"Any advance on five hundred?"

Milton kept his eye on the altercation.

"Five hundred, then."

Two men: the one in front was shorter and wiry, and the one at the back was big. They were still remonstrating with the woman. The man in front gesticulated angrily, pointing down to the van and then to Kelly. The woman was resolute and was refusing to let them enter.

"Once, twice... sold!" Milton looked back as Kelly slammed down the palm-sized gavel. "Five hundred bucks is a steal. Great work, son. Remember to stop by the office to pay."

Milton turned back to the dispute. The men stared over at the dais where Kelly had just shaken the teenager's hand. The man who had been arguing with the woman leaned in to his partner and gestured at the teen.

The staff member who had driven the Econoline out of the garage got back inside and moved it towards the parking lot. The young man was grinning as he wandered off to pay. The two men had left the woman and were making their way around to the office. Milton could just see them around the side of the bleachers. They were heading to where the van had been parked.

Milton felt a prickle of apprehension. Something wasn't right. It looked as if the men had wanted to bid on a vehicle in the auction and, from the fact that they had gone around to the office now, it looked as if they were here for the van. Milton assumed that they were going to wait for the boy. He looked over to where the kid had been sitting and saw a little flash of orange against the white of the snow beneath the plastic bench. Milton shuffled across and collected it. It was a plastic guitar pick. *Sonny's Music Exchange* was printed in a white graphic on one side.

There was a screech of feedback as Kelly leaned in to the microphone again. "This is our final vehicle of the day, ladies and gentlemen, and a fine one at that. We got a pristine 1969 Olds 442. It's a great driver's car, well used and well cared for, with 89,000 miles on a rebuilt engine. Recent additions include shocks, struts, front and rear brakes and new glass. The body is immaculate, although at some point she's been repainted from candy red to navy blue and white. It's a great muscle car, and we're going to open this no-reserve auction for it at fifteen thousand dollars. Do I hear fifteen?"

Ouch, Milton thought. It wouldn't take much action to move the car out of his budget.

He looked back at the offices. The boy had paid for the van. A member of staff gave him the keys and then looked over the teenager's head to where the vehicle was waiting.

The man had a look of almost parental worry. The boy moved off towards the parking lot. Milton got up to give himself a better view. The two men were waiting for him. Milton felt the familiar intuitive frisson that tickled his spine.

The driver revved the big block on the Olds 442. It rumbled and purred.

"Listen to that, folks," Kelly said. "Do I got fifteen?"

"Fifteen," a man said, raising his paddle.

"Fifteen thousand to Gary from Gateway Classic Cars."

The young man was nearly at the van. The man in the office was staring at him, as if waiting for a crash that he knew was about to happen. Milton bit his lip. Maybe his read of the angry man at the entrance was off, he thought half-heartedly. Even if it wasn't, did he *really* want to get involved? He thought of Jessica Russo. Just like the situation with her, anything that might happen to the young man here was none of his business. He looked back to the gleaming Oldsmobile. He had twenty-five thousand to spend on a car. The Olds would do him just fine if he could get it beneath that price. The boy was none of his business. He needed to stay in his lane.

He raised his paddle.

Kelly pointed the gavel at Milton. "Sixteen thousand to the English gentleman who is probably questioning the good sense in coming to Missouri in the winter. Thank you, sir."

Milton looked back again. The young man had stopped walking. Was he pointing to himself? He was talking to the two men, but it was too far away for Milton to be able to hear anything.

"Seventeen thousand to Gateway Classics. Do I hear eighteen?"

Milton raised the paddle again.

"Eighteen thousand to my English friend. Do I hear nineteen?"

Milton couldn't concentrate on the auction. He turned his head again, unable to ignore the kid. The boy was holding both hands wide, as if to say that he couldn't answer a question. The shorter of the two men stabbed a finger into his chest.

"Nineteen thousand to Bob from Scanlon's Auto and RV. Thank you, Bob."

Damn it. Milton couldn't ignore what was going on. He got up and laid down his paddle, signalling to Kelly that he wasn't going to bid any higher. It was moot; the bidder from Gateway Classics quickly pushed the price all the way to twenty-five, and then the man from Scanlon's Auto indicated that he would go to thirty.

Milton walked quickly towards the lot. He reached the gate in the fence, and, from there, he could see the boy attempting to get into the van's cab. The two men blocked his way. Milton could see them better from here. The short one wore his hair buzzed to his scalp. He was dressed in a parka and black trousers. The second man wore a padded leather jacket and had a face that suggested both lazy hostility and incipient violence. He had thick ears and a nose that was bulbous and flat to his face.

Milton took out his phone and took a series of photographs of them as he closed in. The bigger of the pair held out his right hand towards the boy and wagged a finger, then reached down with his left hand to open one side of his coat.

He was showing the boy something.

Milton knew what it was.

A gun.

Milton crunched quickly through the snow. He hurried through the gate, pushing past a young couple heading the other way. The two men had not noticed him. The shorter of the two was still remonstrating with the kid. His partner was close behind, both of them trapping the kid against the side of the van.

Milton slowed to a brisk walk. "Excuse me."

They turned in unison.

"Can I help?" Milton said.

The shorter man frowned. "What?"

"Can I help you?"

The man smiled, feigning civility, and shook his head. "We got this covered, thanks." He spoke in a broad Irish accent.

"I couldn't help noticing that the three of you seemed to be arguing."

"Don't you worry yourself," the man said. "All under control."

"You were shouting at him—he's only a kid. Maybe I can help smooth it out."

"Didn't you hear me, pal? I said we don't need no help."

Milton held his ground. He looked over at the kid; his eyes were wide with fear, but Milton could see a little gratitude there, too. He couldn't have been older than sixteen. He was badly out of his depth, and it looked as if he was relieved that someone else was involved.

Milton smiled at the two men. "Like I said—he's young. Whatever it is you're arguing about, just take it easy."

The bigger man with the flattened nose glanced around to ensure that no one else was paying them attention.

"I asked you nicely," the shorter man said coldly, "so now I'm telling you not so nicely. Just fuck off, all right? I don't like people who put their noses into places where they don't belong."

Milton recognised what had just happened, because it had happened so many times before: he had arrived at a junction where whatever he decided would have ramifications for his future. He could apologise, turn away, and return to the conclusion of the auction. He could leave the kid to deal with whatever situation it was that he had fallen into. But Milton knew himself well enough by now to know that that was not an option. He was drawn to situations like this—to people who needed his help—like a moth was drawn to a flame. If anything, his recent excursion to Colombia had increased his distaste for bullies, not lowered it.

These two were bullies. He wasn't going anywhere.

"I could do that," he said calmly, "but it'd make me feel bad for leaving this poor kid to deal with a pair of Neanderthals like you. So I'm going to put this nice and simply so that you can get it into your thick skulls—you need to let the boy go about his business. If you wanted the van, you were too late. He bought it. It's his. Get over it and get out of his way."

The big man raised his hands as if he was preparing to shove Milton, but he never got the chance. Milton pivoted on his right heel so that he was side on and locked up the man's right arm. He stomped down with the heel of his boot, scraping the hard rubber down the man's tibia. It was painful rather than damaging; the man grunted and stumbled to the side. His hand went to his waistband, fumbling a pistol out of a clip-on holster that he wore on his belt. Milton kicked him, knocking the sidearm from the man's grasp. It clattered against the asphalt.

Milton was facing away from the shorter man. He felt a hand on his shoulder and fired his elbow straight back into the man's face. The hand slipped off, and the man stumbled back.

The bigger man was up again and took the chance to swing a right hook. Milton raised his left arm to block it and then drove his knee up between the man's legs. His eyes rolled back in his head and he reeled away, bouncing off the side of the van as he tried to keep himself upright, both hands cupping his damaged groin.

The shorter man was backing away. Milton's elbow had crunched into his nose, and blood was running freely out of both nostrils. He had both hands raised in surrender, but Milton paid no attention to that. He closed the distance to him with three quick paces and slapped away a half-hearted jab. He drove a hard left-handed body shot into the man's ribs to lower his guard and then drilled him with a right cross. The punch caught the man on the chin and knocked him to the ground.

Milton turned. The van's engine rumbled, and it jerked out of the space. The kid had slipped into the cab during the mêlée, and now the van shot out of the lot, the shocks cradling it as it bounced over the kerb. It turned left onto the road, slid across a patch of hard snow, and then disappeared.

A police siren blared loudly, perhaps a block away.

That was quick. Time to go.

Milton crossed the lot, walked between the trees on the verge that separated it from North Congress Road, and turned quickly to the right. A police car swung off the street and into the lot.

Milton kept walking.

9

Enzo Pizzolato kept both shaking hands clamped to the oversized steering wheel and his eyes on the traffic. It was heavy, but not bumper to bumper. He guessed that it was commuters heading home, people trying to beat the dinner rush; maybe someone had crashed in the snow and caused a jam. He had driven a van only one time before, when he was working at De Moura's Bakery. He had only just got his licence back then, and it had been a challenge to go from the car in which he had learned to a larger vehicle. That Chevrolet had been cumbersome and heavy, but, at the same time, modern and stable. This big Ford was difficult. The engine was powerful and the steering was loose and inaccurate; it took a half block of braking before he felt confident that he was not going to steer it into the parked cars next to the sidewalk. The snow didn't help at all.

Enzo had been nearly overwhelmed by anxiety after the conclusion of the auction. He had used the counting and muscle-tension techniques that Dr. Sadler had taught him to calm down. Anxiety was just one consequence of his autism; it was also one of the most difficult for him to control. He was still tense now, and he tried to slow his breathing. The men had been frightening; not just the ones who had tried to jack his ride, but the other guy who had come to his aid. Enzo had been about to give the van up, the five hundred bucks that he had paid for it notwithstanding. He had lived in KC long enough to know that when someone tried to take your wheels, the best thing to do was run. But then the third guy had interrupted the other two, they had started to fight, and, without thinking about what he was doing, Enzo had pulled himself into the cab, started the engine and fled.

He drummed his fingers on the wheel. Why had they come after him? It was probably the money. They must've gotten to the auction late and seen him win the van super cheap, figured they could take it and the rest of the cash that he hadn't spent.

At least that confrontation was behind him, but he knew that another was coming: he was going to have to face his mother. Getting her to agree that he needed a vehicle at all had been tough, but he had done it. He'd argued that he needed a car to use while he was working. That way, he suggested, he would be able to get better jobs than those that were available in the neighbourhood without bussing halfway across the city. He would be able to earn back that thousand and then add to it. It would be an investment. That had been the plan. He had promised her that he would buy a decent second-hand car. The Mini Clubman that had been up a few lots before the van would have been *exactly* what she had in mind.

Her agreeing to him having any vehicle at all had not been a small decision. She worked two jobs, plus part-time hours at a third. Money was tight, and Enzo had done his best to contribute to the thousand bucks that she said was his absolute maximum budget. He had his own part-time job and a fledgling bedroom business building hand-wired guitar amplifiers; he had sold a few amps to help get the cash together, but they took a long time to make, and there was only so much that he could charge for them.

He knew that he was going to have to tell his mom about the two thugs. He was reluctant, because she hated conflict. His father had been a member of Nicholas Civella's outfit back in the day, before he did his time. Enzo's mother used her husband's life—and death—as examples of how not to live. Getting into trouble like this was not going to make her happy.

At least she wouldn't be home until after six. That would give him a little time to come up with an excuse for what had happened. He was going to need a plausible explanation as to why he had bought that van and what had gone down afterwards. He was a good distance away from the lot now, and he could feel his pulse slowing down to a regular beat. The anxiety faded with each slow, deep breath. He wasn't worried about the two men. They'd just been opportunists. Petty crooks looking at an easy score. They were history now. He thought about their accents: Irish, he thought. The guy who had helped him had sounded English. What were the odds of that? Two Irish guys and an English guy at the same time in a place like that. They had to be tourists or some such shit.

Didn't matter.

If there was one thing that Enzo knew, it was that tourists didn't venture where he was going. The guidebooks made it pretty clear: you went into East KC at your own risk.

The light changed and he stepped gently on the gas. The van rumbled forward.

10

Milton had used his phone to book a room at the Crowne Plaza while he was travelling to the city aboard the Greyhound. It was downtown, on Wyandotte Street, and he took a cab there from Kelly's lot. He kept an eye out of the back window to ensure that he wasn't being followed—either by the two men that he had put on the ground or by the police—but, once he was a couple of blocks away and there was no sign of anything suspicious, he allowed himself to relax.

"How you doing?" the driver said to him.

"I'm good," Milton said.

"You new in town?"

"Why?"

"The accent."

"That's right."

"What you doing here?"

"Just visiting an old friend."

He didn't elaborate, and, after another failed attempt to encourage conversation, the driver got the message and let him be.

Milton held his breath as he looked out of the window. He had allowed himself to sink back into his old self during his crusade against the cartel. He had needed to access those old traits that he had tried so hard to submerge after his exit from the Group: the ruthlessness, the amorality, the pitilessness. He was dismayed by how easy it had been, like pulling on an old, comfortable pair of shoes. He had first used alcohol to drown that part of his personality and his memories of the things that he had done, and when that had stopped working, he had found peace in the Rooms. The Fellowship required that alcoholics who wanted to resist the next drink needed to make amends for the things that they had done. Since Milton had killed many of the people to whom he would have been expected to apologise, he had made a bargain with himself: he would help those people who faced odds that they would not have been able to beat alone. His own well-being was secondary. His purpose was to find those in need and bring them succour, with the hope that eventually he might be able to balance out the evil in him with virtue.

Had he followed his own precepts recently? He didn't know that he had. And although he had known that he would need to summon his demons in order to give him a chance of staying alive in the Antioquian rainforest, the ease with which they had been revived was frightening. He wasn't cured; he knew now that he never would be. He still had not been to a meeting for weeks, relying instead upon miles and miles of running and a second-hand copy of the Big Book that he had found in an English-language bookshop on Avenida Poblado in Medellín. That was a poor substitute for what he really needed. He would find a meeting as soon as he could.

His phone buzzed. He picked it up. It was Tanner.

"Hi," Milton said.

"You okay?"

"I'm fine. Why?"

"Jack Kelly just called me."

There was no point in being coy. "And told you about the nonsense at the auction?"

"He said you were in a fight."

"It was nothing."

"Really?"

"Really."

"The police turned up."

"I'd made my exit by then."

"What happened?"

"There was a kid. He'd just bought a van, and the two guys looked like they were trying to take it off him. I didn't think that was fair, so I stopped them."

"Why would you do something like that?"

"Because it was the right thing to do, Tanner."

Milton heard chuckling.

"What?" Milton said.

"The idea of you with a conscience is not something I would have thought was possible from... well, from *before*."

"That was a long time ago. I'm not the same as I was then."

"Obviously. But you're okay?"

"It was just two thugs," Milton said. "I gave them each a little love tap, and that was that. I'm telling you—it was nothing."

The cab reached Wyandotte Street, and the driver slowed for the turning that would bring them up to the entrance of the hotel.

"Look," Tanner said. "I was thinking. Why don't we have dinner tonight?"

"Have you spoken to London?"

"I haven't got much for you now, but there are some bits and pieces you might find useful, and I'm expecting more. I'll tell you about it over some food. Sound good?"

"It does."

"Excellent. Barbecue okay? KC's famous for it."

"Perfect."

"I'll meet you at Arthur Bryant's on Brooklyn Avenue. Eight?"

Milton said that was fine.

"Good. I'll see you there."

11

Patrick and Kenny O'Connor retreated to the bar that Patrick's investment company owned on Main Street. It was closed until the evening and they had it to themselves. Patrick went into the bathroom at the back of the bar and checked his reflection in the mirror. His face was already showing the signs of an impressive bruise. His eye socket was blackening, and there were still dribbles of blood from his nostrils. He opened his mouth and used his finger to probe inside, finding a loose flap of skin where he had bitten down. He touched his nose, gently manipulating it until he was sure that it wasn't broken.

"No, no, no, no," he said to himself. "I'm not having it. I'm not going down there, getting my arse handed to me by some bugger. That ain't happening, it just ain't. No way. No, no, no—no fucking way."

He ran the tap with cold water, cupped his hands, and doused his face. The water stung a little and, when he looked back down into the basin, he saw that it was now stained a light red.

He looked back at his reflection. "Who's got the balls to

do something like that? Who? Someone who don't have the first idea what they're getting themselves into, that's bloody who."

"You okay?" Kenny called through the closed door.

"I'm fine."

"You're talking to yourself."

"Go get me a drink."

He pulled the plug so that the water could drain, swiped a towel to dry himself, and went back into the bar.

Kenny had taken down a bottle of Bushmills and two glasses. He poured two measures and gave one of the glasses to Patrick.

"What just happened?" he said.

"I don't know," Patrick snapped, taking the glass.

"Who *was* that?"

"I don't know, Kenny. I have no idea."

"You think he was with the kid?"

"No," he said, irritated as usual with his brother's sluggish speed of thought, always three or four moves behind him. "You were there too, right? You saw the way the kid looked at him. He was as scared of him as he was of us." He sipped the whiskey, wincing as the alcohol ran against the cut in his mouth. "I tell you what, though, Kenneth. We're gonna find out who he was, and when we do, he's gonna wish he hadn't done what he did, I swear to God."

"What about the van?"

"We've gotta find it. Unless you got an idea where else we can get our hands on five million. Do you?"

"No," Kenny said, flinching at his brother's sharp tongue. "Course I don't."

"No," he said. "Course you don't. Just like you never have any ideas about anything. No ambition, no ideas, no *nothing*. I got to sort this out myself because I'm fucking sure I'm not going to get any help if I sit here and drink this drink and wait for you to come up with a solution."

"That's not fair, Paddy."

Patrick could have said more, but, looking at his brother's wounded expression, he drowned his bitterness by sinking the rest of the whiskey. He put his glass on the counter and indicated that Kenny should pour another.

It had been this way from the time they were kids. Patrick had got the brains, taking after his mother, and Kenny had got the muscle. His brother was a follower, not a leader. Their dad had been involved in Irish Republican politics, and Kenny had followed his example and taken up arms with the paramilitaries. Patrick was more of a pragmatist; he had sympathy for the Republican cause, but not enough that he was prepared to dedicate his life to it. He rationalised his decision not to enlist by suggesting that he would be able to do more good by making himself rich. Their father had been disappointed that both his sons had not signed up, but Patrick had countered his criticism with the promise that he would buy the bullets so that his brother could fire them.

Kenny poured another two fingers into each of their glasses.

"This is what we're gonna do," Patrick said. "Jack Kelly will have a record of who he sold that van to, right?"

"Right."

"So we're gonna go back there tonight, break into his office, and see what we can find."

12

Arthur Bryant's was obviously a very popular destination. Milton stepped out of the cab and looked at the queue that snaked out of the front door and down Brooklyn Avenue. He asked a couple if the line was for those who wanted to get a table; they said that it wasn't, that you just ordered when you got to the counter and then crossed your fingers that you could find somewhere to sit.

"You eaten here before?" the woman asked him.

"Never," he said.

"You're lucky—best place in town, bar none. Get the slaw and thank me later."

Milton was about to go to the back of the queue when he heard a whistle and then the sound of his name. He turned and saw Tanner standing near the front. He said goodbye to the couple to whom he had been talking and went up to where Tanner was waiting.

"Evening," he said. "Find it okay?"

"No problem."

"You still eat meat, right?"

"Why wouldn't I?"

"This new conscience you seem to have developed—just checking you haven't given it up."

"I haven't," Milton said with a smile.

"Good. This wouldn't be the place for that. Been here for eighty years. You're only a few blocks to Eighteenth and Vine—you got jazz clubs and bars down there, one of the more interesting parts of the city. My wife and I used to go and see a show and then come here for a late dinner. It was the first place she took me when I came out here."

They reached the front of the line and were funnelled into the restaurant. Milton looked around: it was a classic old-style barbecue joint with a brick pit and a large smoker visible in the back. The queue proceeded along a cafeteria-style line to where the orders were taken and money handed over. The atmosphere was heady: Milton could smell the cooked meat and the smoke from the ovens.

"Can we deal with business first?" Tanner said.

"Shall we wait until we've sat down?"

"Mollie's coming. We were due to have dinner tonight, and I thought we might as well just add you rather than cancel. If she found out I came here without her, I'd never hear the last of it, but we can't talk about this when she's here."

Milton said that was fine. They shuffled along a few steps.

"So," Tanner said, lowering his voice, "I called a friend who still works for our former employer. He confirmed it— the Group has been put back together, and it's operating as if nothing ever changed."

"What about Control—who is he?"

"Who is *she*," Tanner corrected.

"Really?" Milton said.

"I know. There was definitely a glass ceiling then, but times change."

"You know her background?"

"Not a thing," he said. "She's extremely secretive. My friend said that she's worked in intelligence for years, but that she's kept a very low profile."

"A name?"

"I'm afraid not."

They shuffled closer to the front of the queue.

"What about me?" Milton asked.

"I'm working on that. My friend believes that there *is* a file out for you. He said it's been out for a while. He said it may have gone back to something that happened in Manila —ring any bells?"

Milton remembered Manila very well indeed. He had found himself pitted against an arms dealer who had been supplying local customers. "I had a run-in with someone who might have had connections."

"He did," Tanner said. "That's when the file was first generated, but it had a restriction on it. No action to be taken."

"And now the restriction's been lifted?"

"That's what I heard."

Milton was about to reply, but they were nearly at the front of the line, and he still hadn't chosen what he wanted to eat. The choice was limited: pork, beef brisket, ribs, sausage, chicken, smoked turkey and ham. Milton ordered a pulled-pork sandwich with potato salad, coleslaw and baked beans. He took his plate and was about to pay when Tanner interceded, handing over two twenties and waving the change away.

They took their food to one of the white Formica tables and sat down. The place had a diner vibe: the chairs had red vinyl covers, and the walls were covered with photos of the well-known people who had dined at the restaurant over the course of its life.

Tanner deposited a plate that was laden with meats and sat down.

"What's that?" Milton asked.

"Combination plate," he said. "Beef brisket, pulled pork and burnt ends. You ever try them?"

Milton shook his head.

"It's a KC delicacy. They chop up the meat from the thinner sections of the barbecue cuts that overcook, then they smoke it and serve it in a sweet and savoury sauce." He gestured down to the plate. "Try a bit."

Milton did, forking a morsel and putting it into his mouth. It almost dissolved on his tongue.

"Good?"

"Very."

It was good, and so was his sandwich. The pork had been slathered in a sauce that was tangy while still tasting strongly of tomato.

"You got anything else?"

"My friend's putting feelers out. He says he has a contact in the Group who might be able to give us a bit more. He said he'd try to get back to me in the next couple of days— are you thinking of staying in town?"

"I can," Milton said. "Like I said—I don't have anywhere else I need to be."

"That's settled, then. I'll call you when I have more."

Milton took a bite and then set the sandwich down, wiping his fingers with a paper napkin. "It's good."

"I know," Tanner replied. He took a bite of his brisket. "So what about this afternoon? You want to tell me what happened?"

"There's not much more to say. A teenage boy bought a van, and it looked like two guys were trying to take it. One of them flashed a gun. They were bullying him, Tanner, and I hate bullies."

"That conscience again," he said. "It'll be the death of you."

"I got a picture of them."

Milton pulled out his phone. The shot was grainy, but the two men could just be made out. Tanner looked at the picture, shrugged, then passed the phone back across the table.

"What happened to the kid?"

"He drove away," Milton said. "But he would've left his details on the paperwork. I doubt he'd be that hard to find."

Tanner loaded his fork with slaw and inserted it into his mouth. He watched Milton while he chewed, then swallowed. "Why do you care?"

Milton shrugged. "I think he's going to need help."

"Right," he said slowly. "And that has what exactly to do with you? You're not thinking of wading in?"

Milton stared down at the plate and his half-eaten sandwich. Was he? He knew that he would be lying to himself if he said he could just ignore it.

"Milton?"

He zoned back in. "I try to live my life in a certain way these days. I've done some things I regret. You know that—it's why I quit. I've been trying to make up for them. I tried in London, and it didn't go so well. I was arrogant. I thought it would be easy, and it's not. But I've kept on at it. I got better. I told myself that I wouldn't turn away if someone needed me. It doesn't matter what they're facing—if they need help, I'm there. And that kid needed help. And I think he still might."

Tanner laid his cutlery on the plate. "I'm not going to tell you what to do, because I know you can look after yourself. But if you were looking for friendly advice? I'd say there's no percentage getting mixed up in things here."

"He was a pudgy teenager. He had no way to defend himself. It wasn't fair."

"Maybe," he said. "But this is a dangerous town. It always has been. It's smarter now, but that's all surface. There are neighbourhoods here that look like they've been gentrified —you got artisanal coffee, hipster stores, house prices going up—but you poke around a bit and you'll see it's still rotten beneath."

"That's the same everywhere."

"Maybe," he said. "But there are guys here who you wouldn't want to cross. You…"

Tanner's attention flicked up, a smile broke across his face, and he raised a hand. Milton turned his head and saw a young woman who had just come inside.

"That's my daughter," he said.

"Remind me of her name?"

"Mollie. You'll like her."

13

M ollie Tanner ordered beef brisket and a mound of bright green pickle chips and brought her plate over to the table. Milton guessed that she was in her mid-twenties. She had a bright, open face—very different from her father's more reserved expression—and a head of natural brown curls. She was wearing a beat-up parka, an old grey Kansas State T-shirt, and jeans.

Milton got up as she approached.

"You must be John," she said, leaning in to give him a quick, firm hug. "Dad says you two go way back."

"We used to work together," Milton said.

Tanner shared a quick glance with Milton. "I don't get to talk about the old days all that much."

Milton wondered how much Tanner had told his daughter about what his old job had entailed. Anyone who worked for the Firm had to sign the Official Secrets Act, but they had all known that the consequences of breaking confidences would go beyond mere legal difficulties. Restrictions on what could and could not be said extended to anyone beyond the Firm, including family. Tanner had always been professional and discreet to a fault; Milton doubted that he had told his daughter very much at all, and decided that he would err on the side of caution and respond with generalities if she asked anything of their shared history.

Mollie took off her coat and draped it over the back of an empty chair.

Milton sat down. "So," he said, "how long have you been in the States?"

"Just over fifteen years," Mollie replied. "I was in England until I was eight. Mom and Dad separated, and I came over here with Mom."

"That was just after I started to work for the government," Tanner explained. "Elsa was from Springfield. We decided it made more sense for her to bring Mollie with her. We'd always stayed in touch, and I came over as often as I could so that I could see Mollie."

"Every summer," Mollie said, laying her hand over her father's. "We used to go to the Ozarks."

Tanner smiled at the memory. "Elsa had her cancer diagnosis just as I was thinking about quitting. Mollie was still in school, and I knew Elsa was going to need help. I decided to move over here permanently." He mopped up the last smear of sauce with a hunk of bread. "No more work. The thing that had led to us breaking up was gone, and we ended up getting back together. When she died, I decided that I'd stay. The business was doing okay again by that point—someone had to keep it going, and I figured it might as well be me."

Mollie smiled warmly at her father. It was clear that she loved him. Milton smiled, too, but it was reflexive. He felt the usual stab of regret that he would never have a relationship like theirs. He had long since given up the idea that he might be able to have a family and had, for the most part, come to terms with it. There were times like this, though, when remorse would stalk him, and he would find himself wondering what his life might have been like if he had taken a different course. He had studied law at university; what might have happened if he had decided to follow a career as a barrister or a solicitor rather than enlisting in the army? What if he had shunned Control's suave approach and his offer to join the Group? His experience would have been unrecognisable from the life that he had since lived.

He would have had a family. A wife and children. A home.

Normality.

He dismissed the thought as quickly as it had arrived. It was foolishness. There was no profit in thinking like that. He had made his bed, long ago, and now he had to lie in it.

"I was going to ask you something," Tanner said to his daughter. "John got into an altercation today."

"It was nothing," Milton said, brushing it off.

Tanner waved his objection off. "Mollie's a reporter at the *Star*. On the crime desk. She might be able to help."

"An *altercation?*" she said. "I'm intrigued."

"There were a couple of thugs at Jack Kelly's auction," Tanner explained. "John said they were bullying a kid who'd just bought a vehicle. He got a picture—I wonder if you might recognise them?"

Milton took out his phone again and woke the screen. He opened the pictures and waited as she swiped right, examining them one at a time.

"Do you?" Tanner asked.

"I do," she said. "It's the O'Connor brothers. The big guy is Kenneth O'Connor. The other one is Patrick."

Milton took his phone back. "What can you tell me?"

"They're notorious. Patrick's the brains. The word is that he launders money for the local criminals. He's much too clever to have ever been charged with anything, but everyone knows. He has an investment business. He poses as an angel investor, tries to find businesses that have fallen on hard times, and then lends them the money to stay afloat. He jacks up the interest so that they can't make the payments, and then he forecloses. He looks for the classic laundering businesses—cash businesses, the kinds of places where it's tough to see where the money is coming from. You know—bars, laundromats, nail parlours. I think he owns the driving range out in Northland. He gets rid of the owners, takes over the businesses, and then runs money through them."

"And his brother?"

"Kenny? He's nasty. There was a case a year or two ago. Assault. This guy with a hair salon on Hardesty Avenue got involved with the O'Connors and defaulted on his loan. He didn't like the terms that Patrick was offering, so Kenny went to see him. Tossed him out of a first-floor window. Broke both his legs, his pelvis... The guy wouldn't press charges."

She took out her own phone and opened an internet browser. She navigated to the newspaper's site and tapped out a search. She scanned the results and gave a nod of satisfaction.

"Here," she said, sliding the phone across the table. "The local underworld's all pretty incestuous. The word is that O'Connor washes the money of a number of other scumbags. We ran a story last month on local organised crime. One of the detectives I interviewed said O'Connor's been working with Bobby Romano."

"Italian?"

She nodded. "Old-school Mafia. It's nothing like it used to be in the sixties, but there are still a couple of dozen made men. It's Bobby's crew. They call him Bobby Whitesox on account of the fact that he wears these white tube socks with everything, even his suits. He must be in his seventies now, with younger guys all jostling to take his place when he's gone, but he's stone-cold ruthless and not ready to hang it up. The police think he's been running scams in Vegas, but they've never been able to pin anything on him. A guy like that is going to have a ton of money that he needs to clean, and—if the story is to be believed—he has Patrick O'Connor do that for him." She paused, a wary look on her face. "Your altercation with the boys? What was it? Verbal?"

"Not entirely."

"He means he put them both on their arses," Tanner said.

"*Right*," she said, drawing the word out. "Listen, John—I know we only just met, but I hope you don't mind if I give you a little advice. You don't want to go anywhere near either of the O'Connors. And you *definitely* don't want to go near any of the guys they work with, Bobby Whitesox especially."

Milton smiled. "Thanks. I don't intend to."

"And that goes for you, too, Pop."

Tanner held up his hands. "Yes, ma'am."

Milton picked up his sandwich and resumed eating. He wasn't prepared to forget about the kid. The more he thought about it, the more likely it seemed that there was something about the van that the two men wanted. The fact that the kid had managed to get away with it was one thing, but it didn't mean that he was in the clear. He would be easy to find. Milton had not settled on a course of action yet, but he knew himself well enough to know that he was going to have to do a little nosing around, if only to make sure that the kid was okay. He didn't *intend* to see the brothers again, but he knew that might not be a choice that was his to make.

If the kid was in trouble, the decision on whether or not to act would be taken out of his hands.

14

Connie Pizzolato sat in an old fold-up chair on the back porch of their modest, rented two-bedroom townhouse in Blue Hills. It was cold, but at least the snow had stopped. She stared at the van, trying to determine what to make of her son this time. The vehicle was parked in the corner of their backyard. It was getting late, and a tall street lamp adjacent to a telephone pole in the alley cast a healthy glow, sparking off the van's black paint. The vehicle had been washed, but, in some ways, that just accentuated the state of the bodywork. She could see the scads of rust around the inner fender and across the rocker panel, and the whole driver's side panel was the wrong colour, obviously fitted after the van had been in an accident. She wondered how bad that accident had been, whether there had been any other damage that the panel was hiding, whether the vehicle was even fit to drive.

She sighed and wondered *what* Enzo had been thinking.

Five hundred dollars was a lot of money. Connie had said he could buy a car. She could justify that to herself: it meant Enzo would be more flexible and looked good to employers. But this van? It was old and big enough that she was nervous at the thought of her son behind the wheel, especially when the roads were as treacherous as they were now. He had explained to her that it would help him with work, but she knew him well enough to know that there was another reason he had chosen it over a more sensible option. Enzo's band was his life. The van would give him a way to move their gear around. They were playing in the final of the Battle of the Bands in a week; it would make it easier to get their gear there. Maybe they would be able to play gigs after that; she was sure that had been at the fore-front of his mind.

She sighed, her breath clouding in front of her face. She couldn't dispute his talent. He was good, light years beyond the party-trick tunes her husband had been able to pull off. He could play songs by his heroes: Stevie Ray Vaughan, Kid Ramos, Little Patrick Ybarra, Albert Collins, Jimmie Vaughan and Lonnie Mack. What was more, he had taught himself. They had never had enough money for him to have lessons. His father had taught him to play 'Sweet Home Chicago' and 'Mustang Sally,' and that was all the encouragement that he had needed. He would spend hours on the internet reading about blues artists, and then weeks picking out note after note from old songs on YouTube until he knew them all by heart, his fingers flying deftly across the fretboard of his second guitar, a second-hand Fender Stratocaster. They couldn't afford to replace the old solid-state amplifier that he had found in a pawnshop with the type of tube amp he said that he needed to get his 'tone,' and so, undeterred, Enzo had learned to build them for himself. By then, of course, Connie had already known that he was prodigiously gifted. His condition presented chal-lenges, but when he wanted to do well—when he was engaged and interested—his intelligence almost frightened her.

Enzo had eventually skipped a grade, and then another, graduating high school at seventeen with college credit from night classes. Scholarship offers came in. She had tried to persuade him to take a full ride to Kansas State, with his tuition and housing covered. Enzo said no. He thought bigger than she did and wanted to go to the Massachusetts Institute of Technology to learn robotics.

She found it dizzying. Whenever he talked in detail on a subject that he loved, his condition often rendered him immune to the embarrassment that his listeners displayed at not understanding him. He would go on and on as if ignoring their discomfort might make it go away, as if he was trying to lend them some of his smarts. He was gifted intellectually like many kids on the spectrum, but, countering that, he was challenged when it came to his emotions. Dr. Sadler had explained it all to her after he had been diagnosed: his condition was not a disability; it simply presented him with a different set of strengths and weaknesses than was normal for most people. For example, he might have been poor with others, but give him a soldering iron and an analog circuit board... well, *that* came as second nature to him.

Connie remembered their discussion after dinner as she had tried to make him see the good sense in the option of Kansas State. She had described MIT as an unrealistic pipe dream and then had sat dumb as Enzo had gone into an hour-long disquisition on how artificial intelligence could either save or damn the world, and also that he had to study it in Boston. She had allowed herself to be persuaded, even if that meant waiting. MIT offered a partial ride if Enzo would accept a lesser prize based on cultural diversity together with a scholarship to cover additional expenses. Or, they said, he could wait one more year, at which point he would be their leading candidate to have his tuition and residence fully covered.

She had been terrified at the gambit, but accepted that he could sometimes see the way ahead more clearly than others. He had sugared the pill by pledging to work non-stop, to save enough money that she could come with him and share a place until she was able to find work. More than anything, Enzo had said, he wanted his mother to be there too. If he had to deliver flowers all week, play bars every night, and build amplifiers until his fingers fell off, that was what he would do. As far as he was concerned, they would both make it to Boston.

The screen door creaked open behind her, then quickly swung shut. Enzo walked up and handed her a cold bottle of Coors Light.

"So, Mama, what do you think?"

"I don't know, Enzo."

"I know it's not a car."

"It's definitely not a car."

"I can advertise myself as a delivery person for more than just flowers now. Maybe I could apply to be a delivery driver for Amazon. They're always hiring."

She took a sip from the cold beer, then reached up over her shoulder to grasp his hand. "I understand the principle, *pippolo*. But I also know that's a thirty-year-old van that's obviously been in an accident and is covered in rust. I'm just hoping it's still on the road by winter."

He shook his head, unconvinced. "It was a bargain. Five hundred bucks, Mama. It would've gone for more, but no one else was bidding. I got it well below its real value. I checked. There's this thing called the Blue Book—"

"I know what the Blue Book is, Enzo. And the price *is* relevant."

"It's not, because—"

"Not because of the price you paid," she said, correcting his presumption, "but because of the price they listed it at. Auction houses have the lower-priced items starting closer to what they're really worth. They have to do that, because the house takes a chunk off the top. That way the owner still makes something. It's not as much of a bargain as you think it is."

Enzo was not always as smart as he thought. Connie had been gifted as a child, too, though not to her son's degree. The difference in their upbringing had been stark: her father had beaten humility into her with a leather belt. She was not about to repeat that method, but Enzo did need to learn that humbleness and modesty were values worth having.

He looked surprised, perhaps at her suggestion but, more likely, at himself for not thinking of it. "Oh."

"Yeah," she said, squeezing his hand. "You didn't win that van because you were cleverer than everyone else. You won it because no one else wanted it."

Enzo did not like the suggestion. "No," he protested. "That's not it... There *were* others."

"Other bidders?"

He paused, and she sensed his reluctance.

"Enzo? Other bidders?"

"Not exactly."

"So?"

"These two guys. They came late—I'd already bought it by then."

"You didn't mention that."

He shrugged. "Didn't seem important."

She could see he was holding something back. Enzo was a brilliant child, but not the world's most convincing actor. And a mother *knew*.

"What happened?"

"Nothing," he protested. "Come on, Mom. You're making me feel bad for buying it."

Connie felt a swell of guilt. She knew that he had said that to manipulate her, but she didn't mind. He did make good choices, at least most of the time. And she wasn't even sure the van *was* a bad choice; plus, he *did* have a point with how he could use it to make deliveries. After all, they were going to need all the money they could get. Any funds that he could contribute would be welcome, even if that wasn't essential. She would find the cash.

If there was one thing Connie knew about her time on Earth, it was that when she left it, her boy would be successful. He was already someone special. He would have the life he deserved, no matter what she had to sacrifice to make it happen.

15

T he rest of the evening passed pleasantly enough. They decamped to a bar across the road, and Milton enjoyed an orange juice and lemonade while Tanner and Mollie drank bottles of local craft beer from Boulevard and KC Bier. There was no more talk of London, nor the fracas with the O'Connor brothers; instead, Mollie regaled them both with tales of her misadventures in online dating. One unfortunate experience involved a date with a man during which he'd seen his father leaving the restaurant with a woman who was not his mother. She suggested that the mood had been killed more or less immediately.

"That's awful," Milton said.

"That's nothing," she said, necking her beer. "I can trump it."

"My God," Tanner said, making a show of putting his head in his hands.

"This guy I saw last week? He asked if I'd ever dated anyone I worked with, then said he still works with his ex-wife. He told me how hard it was to see her every day and how much he hopes they'll get back together."

"And you asked him why he was dating you?"

"I did. He said he was trying to date others so it might take the shine off her, but it never worked. I left after the appetizers."

"Remind me never to do online dating," Tanner said.

Mollie looked across the table at Milton. "What about you?"

"Dating?" Milton finished his drink. "Not my thing."

"You don't date?"

"I move around a lot. I'm not really interested in settling down."

"You don't get lonely?"

He thought about that for a moment. "Not really. I like my own company."

"What John is trying to say is that he doesn't like people."

"No," Milton protested. "That's not—"

"I'm kidding," Tanner said.

"You should get yourself a profile," she said. "Put it online and see who bites. You never know—you might find someone who persuades you that you could stay in one place for a while."

Milton knew that he was dreadful at reading interest from women, and didn't know if she was flirting with him or not. She was much younger than him, and, although she was attractive, the thought of dating Tanner's daughter was so preposterous that he immediately put it out of mind.

"Stop hassling him," Tanner said. "Come on—you'll give him false hope. Look at him."

"I am looking at him," she said, giving Milton a very obvious wink.

The conversation moved on to a discussion of the local music scene. Mollie took Milton's email and said that she would send him a list of the best venues to visit while he was here. He thanked her and waited another thirty minutes before he decided that it was time to leave. He told them both that he was flagging after his day of travel. Tanner offered to drive him to his hotel, but Milton said that he was full and that he would benefit from a little exercise before turning in for the night.

"Thanks," he said. "I had fun."

"The food?"

"Not shabby," he said.

Mollie stood up and came over to kiss him on the cheek. "It was lovely to meet you."

"Likewise."

She took her purse out of her bag, opened it, and pulled out a card. "I'll have a look around and see what I can find out about the O'Connor brothers when I'm next in the office. If there's anything else you'd like me to check, just give me a call. But—seriously—be careful with them. They're bad news."

"Understood," Milton said, catching her father's eye for a moment.

She had no idea that Milton was bad news, too, and he saw no reason for her to be educated about that; he could tell that Tanner would rather she remained ignorant to it, too.

Mollie's phone rang and she motioned that she had to take it. Milton smiled and nodded and started for the door. Tanner followed alongside him.

"I'm sorry," Tanner said.

"Why?"

"Winding you up."

"Don't be daft," Milton said. "She's great."

"She is." He smiled. "I'm lucky. It wasn't always like that. She hated me when I split up with her mum."

Milton took his jacket from the cloakroom and looked outside. Fresh snow had fallen while they were inside, and another flurry was starting. He pulled the jacket on.

"Sure you don't want a lift?"

"I'm fine," Milton said. "You'll let me know if you find out anything else about the Group?"

"I will. He said he'd call me tomorrow."

"Thanks."

"Can I ask—what are you going to do if London *is* after you again?"

Milton paused for a moment. He hadn't given it much thought. "I'm not sure."

"You'll hide?"

Would he? The last time the Group had been after him had been an ordeal, and Control's death—and his replacement by Pope—had been a relief. Running was one option. The other was to face them down. The former would be tiring, a constant exercise in vigilance and perpetual motion; the latter, on the other hand, promised clarity, but also a good chance that he would be captured or killed.

"John?"

"The last thing I want is a confrontation. It was bad enough last time, and I'm older now. I'll hit the road again. They won't find me."

"I'm sorry," Tanner said. "What a mess."

"Forget it. It's not your problem. Just find out what you can. Maybe there's another way."

"I'll call you," he said. "Sleep well."

They shook hands, and Tanner went back to the table, where Mollie was still talking on her phone. Milton zipped his jacket all the way to the top, opened the door, and stepped out into the frigid cold of a Missouri winter.

MILTON WAS CHILLED to the bone by the time he made it back to the hotel. His jacket was decent, but too cheap to withstand the sub-zero blast as he walked from the restaurant. He went through into the bathroom and ran the bath, then returned to the bedroom to grab the Steinbeck novel that he had been reading. He laid the book on the side of the bath and stripped off, lowering himself into the hot water and luxuriating for a moment, allowing it to soothe the aches and pains that were a constant reminder of the misadventures that he had suffered over the course of his career and then during the years that had followed.

He picked up the novel. It was *East of Eden* and told the story of two families in the Salinas Valley, the Trasks and the Hamiltons, and the interwoven stories that bound them together. There were themes within it that were familiar to him: depravity and love, man's capacity for self-destruction, guilt and freedom. It had felt fresh and relevant the first time that he had read it, years ago when he was sheltering from Iraqi mortars in the desert. It still felt fresh today; even though the context of his own life had changed, the words had become even more apposite.

He searched for his place, and the guitar pick that he had been using for a bookmark dropped down into the water. He fished it out. It reminded him of the kid and the van and the O'Connor brothers. He looked at the logo on the back of the pick and then laid it down on the side of the bath.

In the morning, he decided, he would see where it might lead him.

16

T anner let himself into his house, locked the door behind him, and made his way into the lounge. He had remained in their home after his wife had moved into the hospice, and had stayed on after she had passed away. It wasn't as if they had lived there together for long, not as if the place was haunted by the shared memories of a long marriage. It was a solid house, in a solid neighbourhood, and Tanner saw no reason to uproot himself and find somewhere new. It helped that Mollie had been pleased that he had kept it, too. It had given her an anchor during difficult times.

He had a bottle of Macallan in the kitchen, and he had been thinking about how much he wanted a glass of it as he had made his way home. The whisky had been drawn from sherry-seasoned oak butts and was classed as a rare cask edition; it had cost him nearly three hundred bucks to have it shipped from Speyside. He pulled out the reusable cork top and poured out a large measure, added a little spring water, and took it through into the lounge.

He sat down in his armchair and worked off his shoe.

His stump was aching, and he was looking forward to taking the prosthetic off and getting into bed. He knew that he couldn't do that quite yet, though.

He had to deal with Milton first.

It had been a dreadful shock to see him at the warehouse that afternoon. Tanner had recognised him at once, of course, but the sheer incongruence of him being there had taken a long moment to process. He hadn't seen Milton for years, ever since he'd gone AWOL after the botched job in the French Alps; that mishap had left a local gendarme dead and the child of his targets left alive as a witness to what had happened. Tanner had had sympathy for Milton's position; the intelligence had been poor, the planning slipshod, and the thought of what the standard operating procedure required him to do with regard to the child was not something that Tanner would have been able to stomach, either. Control had not had the same tolerance, and his patience had been tested by Milton's request to stand down from the Group, and then exhausted entirely as Milton went AWOL.

Tanner had been involved in the operations that followed to capture him, none of which had been successful. Control's attitude had hardened over time, and finding Milton had become something of a crusade for him. Tanner thought that the matter had been brought to a conclusion with Control's murder, and had put it out of his mind.

But now he found that he was caught in an almost impossible situation. He had spoken to his contact that afternoon and had confirmed that the new Control had made it a priority to bring Milton to heel. There had been a number of instances where Milton had—unwittingly, perhaps—acted against the interests of the Firm. The decision had been made to reopen his file, and active measures were underway to find him.

Tanner now had to measure his reluctance to betray Milton against the damage that would follow were the Group to discover that he knew where Milton was and had failed to report it. Tanner knew what Milton had been capable of when he was a serving operative, and, although it seemed that he had mellowed with the passing of time, he had looked into Milton's cold blue eyes and recognised the same lack of emotion that he remembered from before. Milton was a killer; his capacity for murder would always be there.

But what of the new Control? Tanner had been told that she was as stony-hearted as Harry Mackintosh, her predecessor before Pope, and the Control for whom Tanner had worked. She was reputedly driven by a pitiless determination to restore the Group to the position it had once occupied before Mackintosh had brought it down with his perfidy. Tanner knew that the afternoon's call would have been reported and logged, and questions would be asked of him eventually: most particularly, what had prompted his enquiry about Milton? Dots would be joined and conclusions reached. They would find the truth, and, when they did, Tanner knew that he would suffer. His pension would be stopped, but it might not end there. He had seen enough red-ribboned files in his time and feared that his own name might end up on one of them, handed to one of twelve agents who would seal his fate.

The equation was simple. He had to balance the betrayal of a dangerous man against deceiving an organisation that would have no truck with his moral prevarication.

There were risks on both sides, but one felt more perilous than the other. Milton would not be able to hurt him or Mollie if he was out of the way.

Tanner's throat was sandpaper dry. He took a sip of

whisky, swilled it in his mouth for a moment, then swallowed it down.

He picked up his phone and dialled the London number that he recalled even after all this time.

"Global Logistics," the operator said. "How can I direct your call?"

PART II

17

Patrick O'Connor was outside the butcher's at five minutes to eight. Gambino's Pork Store was on the corner of Eighth and Central, next to the Phoenix Jazz Club. He parked the car in the lot on the other side of the junction, closed and locked the door, and made his way back to the entrance. The story was that Johnny Gambino had lost the business to Bobby Whitesox when he couldn't make the payments on his gambling debts. That had been sometime in the seventies, and Bobby had owned it ever since. Johnny's son ran it as an operating business, and, as far as Patrick could tell, it was viable. But Patrick knew that Bobby didn't keep it because of its balance sheet. He kept it because it had nostalgic value. His father had worked for Johnny Senior in the fifties and, or so the story went, the room in the back had been the venue for Bobby's first murder.

The store was already open for business, and there was a customer at the counter, picking out sausages and chops. Patrick saw that Johnny Junior had just prepared the day's veal Parmesan sandwiches, and the rumbling of his stomach reminded him that he had skipped breakfast. It was hunger, he told himself, and not the apprehension that he usually felt when he was summoned for a meeting here. There was a plain door at the side of the store. Patrick knocked and, after a long moment, it opened. Salvatore Provenzano, the enforcer from Calabria who had been given to Bobby by the 'Ndrangheta years ago, stood just inside.

"Is he here?" Patrick asked.

Sal nodded. "Inside. Go through."

There was no frisking for a piece or a wire. Why would there be? Patrick had been working with Bobby for months and, besides, no one would be dumb enough to do something that might tick him off. Bobby was infamous for his temper, and stories of what he had done to those who had riled him were well known.

The large space beyond the door was used as a store-room. The plain white walls had been decorated with vintage shots of entertainers from the fifties and sixties, many of whom had been mobbed up. There were shots of Sinatra, Dean Martin and Sammy Davis Jr. More recent photographs were of famous—and infamous—local clientele who had visited the store. There were politicians, sportsmen, and entertainers, all happy to bathe in the reflected glory of a much-loved local establishment and happy to ignore the open secret that the place had been inextricably tied to the Mafia for decades.

There was a table at one end of the room. Bobby was sitting at it, eating a plate of Johnny Junior's *capicola*.

"Hey," Bobby said. He jabbed his fork at the empty chair on the other side of the table. "Take a load off."

"Thanks," Patrick said, sitting down.

"How you doing?"

"Doing fine," Patrick said. He always found Bobby's

jollity a little forced, especially when set against the depravity of which he knew he was capable.

"You tried this before?" he asked, tapping the fork against the half-eaten slices of meat.

"I haven't."

"It's good," he said. "Johnny has a rule—the only pigs he'll use are the big ones, eight months old and at least three hundred pounds, ones from the south of Italy when he can get them. It's all about the ratio of fat to muscle. You want thirty percent fat and seventy percent lean so it's moist and tender even after you've cured it. Just like this." He used the fork to cut off a corner and slotted it into his mouth. "Look at me—here I am going on about my breakfast and I ain't even had the decency to offer you any. You want some?"

"No, thanks," Patrick said.

"You sure? There's plenty more behind the counter. Not a problem to get you a plate."

"I'm fine, Bobby," he said. "Thanks anyway."

"Suit yourself."

Bobby cut off another triangle of meat and chewed on it, staring at Patrick as he did so. His motive was transparent: he was trying to put him on edge, confuse him with pleasantries even as Patrick knew that he had been summoned here to be bollocked. The act was unnecessary. Patrick knew Bobby was a dangerous player, and he would never have been foolish enough as to not take him seriously. And he was already nervous.

"How can I help you, Bobby?"

He finished the meat and laid his fork on the plate. "I have a question."

"Fire away."

"How much money did I give you last month?"

"Ten million."

"That's right. Ten million. Not chicken feed, is it?"

"Oh no," he said. "It isn't—not at all."

"And when did I tell you I needed clean money in my account?"

"You wanted half by next week."

"Right. Half by next week and the other half a month after that. I looked at the Cayman account last night to see how much money you'd transferred to me. You know how much I found?"

"Two and a half."

"Two and a half. I did a couple sums, Patrick. You had four weeks to clean the first five. That runs out next week. So, in fifty per cent of the time I gave you, you've only managed to clean twenty-five percent of what you promised." He stared hard at Patrick, all of his affability abruptly replaced by a cold, hard edge. "You're behind schedule. What's happened to my cash?"

Patrick nodded, trying to disguise the fact that his heart was hammering in his chest. "I told you, Bobby."

"Tell me again. Explain *exactly* what's going on."

"It's not easy—ten million is a lot."

"That's why I doubled your fee."

"Right," he said. "Okay. The structures I have at the moment can't move that much money that quickly, so I had to expand. I found a nail bar on Delaware and the spa on Campbell, and I had to get lawyers involved in the paperwork to bring them into the mix. It took longer than I thought."

Bobby shrugged and spread his hands. "How's this my problem?"

"I ran the first two and a half through the existing structure. The next two and a half is being moved now. It might be a day or two late, but it's going through. It'll get there—you have my word."

"I know I do," Bobby said. "You enter into a contract like that, with as much money as this, and it goes without saying that I have your word."

Patrick heard the door open and became aware that the hatchet-faced Sal was standing behind him. He could feel his presence as a scratching between his shoulder blades and knew that, if Bobby gave him the signal, he would have a garrotte around his neck before he could do a thing about it. Patrick was aware of the other benefits to owning a butcher's store; there were plenty of stories of people who had crossed Bobby being brought here to be dismembered and disposed of. He felt a droplet of sweat running slowly down the centre of his back.

"I'm worried," Bobby said.

"There's no need to be."

"I heard that the arcade was robbed. One of the cops I got on the payroll said that three guys forced their way in and turned the place over. Is that right?"

"There was a break-in," Patrick said, speaking carefully.

"How much did they take?"

"The money from the machines," he said. "That and the day's float. Nothing else."

"You sure?"

Patrick held Bobby's eye. "I'm sure."

"I know you sometimes keep money there. Did you?"

"None of yours, Bobby."

The thieves had made off with more than just the day's takings and the float. They had ignored all of that, in fact, and directed their attention to breaking into the storeroom where Patrick and Kenneth had stashed the ten million dollars that Bobby had provided. It had been beneath the floorboards and inside the wall partitions, and they had torn the room apart to get at it. Patrick didn't have to think back too hard to recall the empty feeling in the pit of his stomach when he had arrived at the arcade the next morning.

"Ten million," Bobby said. "That's huge. If something happens to it... well, you know how I'm gonna react to that, right? I'm going to be very upset, Patrick. Very fucking upset."

"I know. Your money is safe and sound. You'll see the next payment by the end of the week."

"Two point five by Friday, Patrick. *This* week, not next. And the rest by the end of the month." He paused and, for a moment, the atmosphere was heavy with tension and the unsaid threat of what would happen if they were back here in a week and the money still hadn't been moved. Bobby held the silence for another beat, and then his face broke into a warm and open smile. "You sure I can't tempt you with some meat? I could have Johnny Junior wrap you up a parcel."

18

Detective Frank Bird sat in the passenger seat of the 2012 Crown Victoria. They were across the street from the office on Petticoat Lane where Patrick O'Connor conducted his business.

He looked at his watch and tutted.

His partner, Detective David Nicol, was in the driver's seat, buffing his nails with an emery board. "What's got your goat?"

"He said nine, didn't he?"

"He did."

"So he's ten minutes late. You know how I feel about tardiness."

"From long and bitter experience."

"So where is he?"

"I don't know, Frank. Maybe it's something illegal."

Bird gave him the finger. He was older than Nicol, and, despite the fact that they had been partners for three years, he still didn't like his sassy mouth. But Bird knew that he was right. O'Connor's contributions to their 'retirement' funds meant that the Dubliner got a pass from the KCPD's Gang Task Force and its two senior detectives.

"He's not going to be happy when he sees what we got for him," Bird said.

"That's what happens when you trust a goombah like Bobby Whitesox," Nicol offered, leaning back and then reaching down to retrieve a Styrofoam cup of coffee from the centre console. He took a sip, put the cup down, then went back to manicuring his right hand. "We can tell him how fucked up he is, just so long as he knows it's not our job to fix it. Because I'm telling you—there isn't enough money in the world for me to get my nose in Bobby's business."

Bird nodded. He was experienced enough to remember the last big operation against the mob in the city. The feds had indicted four men for running a multimillion-dollar internet gambling scheme. There were just a handful of made men left now, and Bobby was the most venerable. The KC mob used to have a significant interest in Vegas, but the casinos had been torn away from them, and now they made do with less remunerative and less glamorous fare: loan sharking, drugs, extortion, prostitution. There was also serious competition from the gangs that ran parts of the city: Los Tiburones in the upper west side, the Hilltop Crips around Truman Road, the Click Clack Gang from Twenty-Seventh to Emanuel Cleaver Boulevard, and the bikers and white supremacists. The old-school gangsters had to fight hard to hold onto what they had, but, regardless, it didn't mean that times were hard; Bird had heard a rumour that Bobby was worth north of fifty million.

Bird saw motion ahead of them. O'Connor's Lincoln Continental slid into an empty space next to the kerb opposite the building.

"There he is," he said.

19

There was a brass plaque on the wall next to the door that led into the office. It announced DUBLIN INVESTMENTS, INC, and Bird knew that Patrick made sure that his secretary buffed it up with EZ Brite for five minutes every morning. He knew enough about O'Connor's business to be amused by the ostentatiousness, but, on the other hand, he had to admit that it was the kind of neat little touch that might snag an unwary business owner who was looking for money. That was O'Connor's MO: he looked for distressed businesses and offered them the injection of funds that would keep the wolves from the door.

The trouble was, Patrick—backed by his psychotic brother, Kenneth—was a much hungrier predator than those the business owners were seeking to evade. The deals he offered looked equitable; he asked for a small shareholding in the company and charged a reasonable rate of interest, pegged around the level that would be charged by a commercial bank. But, once he was installed, O'Connor would make sure that the company's business withered and died. Suppliers would decide not to work with the business anymore, and customers would mysteriously take their trade elsewhere. The brothers were behind the sabotage, parasites that damaged their hosts until the loans defaulted and the owner was happy to transfer all of the equity in return for being able to walk away.

That was when the companies were repurposed as vehicles for money laundering.

You could look at all the little tasteless flourishes—the brass plaque, the sharp suits that Patrick wore, the Lincoln —and you could laugh, but there was no arguing with Patrick's success. He had been ripping people off for years; the combination of his flannel and Kenneth's muscle had proven to be very effective.

Bird stomped through the snow, reached the door, pulled it back, and held it open for Nicol to go inside. He followed. The office was small but well appointed: a leather couch, a table with a selection of pretentious magazines, a coffee machine that was chugging quietly as the water was brought up to temperature.

O'Connor's secretary, Sonya, was sitting behind the desk and regarded them both with professional suspicion.

"We're here to see Mr. O'Connor," Nicol said.

"Is he expecting you?"

"No. But he'll want to see us. Tell him it's Bird and Nicol."

The woman turned her head away from them, tapped a button on an intercom, and spoke quietly into the microphone that she wore on a headset. Bird paced the small reception area. He picked up one of the magazines—a glossy paean to consumerism and excess—flicked through it and then dropped it back on the table again. He paced some more.

"Relax," Nicol muttered to him.

"I don't like to be kept waiting."

The secretary cleared her throat. "Mr. O'Connor will see you—down the corridor on the left."

The two detectives followed her directions, passing a small kitchen and a bathroom until they reached the end of the corridor. There was an office to one side and, opposite it, a conference room. Patrick O'Connor was inside.

"Shut the door," he said when they joined him.

Nicol did.

"Where have you two been?"

"We've been busy," Bird said.

"You want to remember which side your bread is buttered. I've been calling you. I don't expect to be ignored."

Bird was used to O'Connor's grumbling. He seemed to be of the opinion that he could treat them with disrespect just because he had them on his payroll. Bird had promised himself that he would disabuse O'Connor of that misconception when the time was right. For now, though, he would let it ride. The money was good enough for him to hold his tongue.

"Frank's right," Nicol said. "We *have* been busy. And we have something you'll want to see. It took a lot of effort and a decent chunk of change, but we got it. Show him."

Bird took out his phone and selected a video clip that he had emailed to himself earlier that morning. He handed the phone to O'Connor.

"What am I looking at?"

"That's the security camera across the road from the arcade."

"Yeah," O'Connor said. "I see."

"Hit play."

O'Connor tapped the screen. Bird watched as the footage played, and saw the colour drain out of his face.

"No fucking way—is that who I think it is?"

Bird reached back and collected the phone. O'Connor had paused the footage so that one of the three men who had pulled up outside the arcade was looking up into the camera. All three of them were wearing their ski masks, but this one man had pulled his up so that he could scrub at an itch on the side of his face. He had pulled back enough of the mask for the camera to pick up the tattoo of a scorpion on his neck.

Bird tapped his finger against the screen. "The only man I know with a tattoo of a scorpion on his neck is Severo Addario."

"Mother*fucker*. I knew it. I *knew* it."

O'Connor had told them both that he had suspected Bobby's involvement in the heist, but now he had proof. Bird found it difficult to share his outrage. Bobby Whitesox had given O'Connor millions of dollars to launder, and then had rolled him and stolen it back again. As a result, O'Connor had been busy trying to steal the money from Bobby to pay off the amount that he had lost. The two of them were like vipers. It was funny when you thought about it.

O'Connor clenched his fist and looked, for a moment, as if he was going to strike the wall. He took a moment to compose himself before he spoke. "He wants my business. He wants to hold a debt over me. He knows that I'll have to work for free to pay him back for the money I lost."

"You got to admire his stones," Nicol said.

"No, I don't." He crashed his fist against the desk. "*Jaysus*."

Bird held his tongue as O'Connor composed himself.

"What happened with the auction?" he said after a moment.

"We got it moved up for you, like you asked."

"What time did you say it was happening?"

"Two thirty."

"You're sure about that?"

"I'm sure. Why?"

"Because Kenny said you told him it was three."

"No," he said. "I said two thirty."

"I don't know who it was," he said, "but *someone* fucked up. By the time we got there, the vehicle we wanted had already been sold. I need you to help me find it."

"All right," Nicol said, taking a pad of paper from the desk and a pen from the pot sitting next to it. "What are we looking for?"

"A Ford Econoline van," he said. "Registration DE8 Y2A. Black with a white panel on the driver's side."

"And why are we looking for it?"

"It doesn't matter why—all you need to know is that I want it, and there's a twenty-five-grand bonus if you can find it for me."

Bird's ears pricked up. "What else you got?"

"Some kid bought it from Kelly for five hundred bucks. We tried to buy it off him and he said no. We got a little heavier and then some guy rode in to the rescue. The kid drove it away before we could stop him."

"You know who he is?"

O'Connor shook his head. "I broke into Kelly's office last night for a look around, but there's no paperwork—at least nothing I could find."

"Fine," Bird said. "We'll run the plate through DMV and find out who registers it."

"How long will that take?"

"He'll need to report the sale to DMV within three days?" Bird suggested.

"No," Nicol said. "Five."

"That long?" O'Connor said.

"Might be quicker, but that's how long he's got." Nicol shrugged. "DMV can be slow to update, too. We'll keep checking."

"What about the kid?" Bird said. "Can you give us a description?"

"Sixteen, seventeen. He was wearing cargo pants and a puffer jacket."

"Got anything else?"

"He was just another kid. And we got distracted when the guy got involved."

"All right," Bird said, knowing that they were going to get precisely nowhere with a description as skimpy as that. "What about the guy?"

"Six feet tall, dark hair, a scar on his face." He drew a line from the side of his mouth to his ear. "And he had really blue eyes. Unnaturally blue. Spoke in an English accent, too. Tanned."

That was a little better, Bird thought. There might be something to go on there.

"Here's what we'll do," Nicol said. "We'll go and have a nose around at Kelly's. Maybe someone reported what happened. He's probably got security cameras there, too. We'll take a look and see what we can find. And, in the meantime, we'll keep an eye out with DMV. We'll get something; it's just a question of when."

"Make it sooner rather than later," O'Connor said. "If you can get me that van by Wednesday, I'll make it thirty thousand."

BIRD AND NICOL reconvened inside their car.

"What's that all about?" Nicol said.

"Beats me."

"Why would he want a van?"

"I don't know," Bird said. "But I bet it's worth a whole lot more than thirty grand."

"All those vehicles at the auction were police impounds, right?"

"As far as I know."

"So there's gonna be a paper trail for all of them. What do you say we roll by the pound and see what we can find?"

"Can't see the harm in it."

Bird started the engine and pulled out.

20

T he five-litre Mustang from the Hertz near the hotel had an engine that rumbled and thundered just a little when Milton tapped the gas. It made the drive to north Kansas City that much more enjoyable. The roads had been treated overnight, the asphalt a little more reliable, with slushy residue shoved off to the sides. Downtown skyscrapers gave way to low-rise retail outlets and industrial parks, and the traffic began to thin. There were more trucks and fewer cars.

Milton had been thinking about the boy all morning. If the men who had been at the auction were bad news, as Mollie Tanner believed, then he doubted that they would give up easily. He tried to anticipate what they might do. Their first gambit would be to get a line on the kid through official contacts—a friendly cop or a registry clerk who could run the van's plate. If that didn't work, Milton guessed that they would nose around the auction house in the hope that they could sniff something out.

Either way would take time, and Milton knew that he had a head start.

He had dropped the plastic guitar pick into the change holder by the Mustang's stick. It had been a simple enough task to find out what he had needed to know: he'd Googled "Sonny's Music Exchange" and "Kansas City" and had been rewarded with a single hit. He had visited the store's website and had the route mapped out on his phone. Sonny's was just a few blocks off East Tenth Avenue. It was a single-storey building sandwiched between a pair of coffee shops. Milton slowed the Mustang, waiting for a spot while a car that had been parked at the kerb pulled out. He slotted the car into the space, killed the engine, and looked out. The store had two large windows on either side of the door, and the displays in the windows made it clear to which clientele the business was aiming to appeal. There were nine guitars in the window on the left, each one standing on one of three raised tiers. There were amplifiers in the window on the right, smaller combo amps that were stacked on top of larger units. A poster stuck to the inside of the glass advertised a Battle of the Bands contest at the Nelson-Atkins Museum of Art in a week's time.

Milton got out of the Mustang and closed the door. He looked left and right and saw nothing to suggest that the men who had been harassing the boy were here before him. The sidewalk had been cleared of snow, with handfuls of orange grit scattered across it. Milton pushed open the fading and chipped teal front door. A traditional 'Open' sign with regular business hours underneath it hung at waist height. A bell rang as the door swung closed behind him.

Milton undid his coat, grateful for the warmth after the cold outside. The room was the size of a small gym. The hardwood floors consisted of two-inch planks, marking it out as an older building. The floor was stained, scratched and chipped beyond any sign of its better days. On either side of the room were narrow rectangular glass cabinets that ran the length of both walls. On the left was the counter, from behind which three clerks helped customers with requests and purchases. A technician was discussing a repair with someone. In the centre of the room were two drum displays. A large teen, perhaps five ten and two hundred and fifty pounds, was seated behind the bigger kit. He had a dark complexion and frizzy yellow hair that looked as if it came from a bottle. A potential buyer was listening as the kid explained the benefits of the drumheads produced by Evans and Remo. Another kid was trying out an amp near the back of the store, picking out what his lack of fluidity suggested was one of the few songs that he actually knew. The tortured effort was evidently pleasing to him, but his awkward playing made Milton wince. He tried to place it and settled on Led Zeppelin's 'Over the Hills and Far Away.'

"Yeah," a male voice to his left suggested. "He's sort of new to it."

Milton turned. One of the clerks was leaning forward, his elbows on the counter. He was small-boned, with ginger hair and freckled skin. "Can I help you?"

Milton scanned the wall behind the young man. "You must have hundreds of guitars."

The clerk nodded. "We might be small, but we're one of the best in KC. Not that that's saying much, mind you."

"Why's that? Most people buying online?"

"You got that right. It might cost a little more here, but we make up for it with the service. Are you looking for yourself?"

"I'm looking for someone who plays, actually." Milton flashed a friendly smile and retrieved the pick from his pocket, placing it on the counter. "He's really good. I meant to talk to him about hiring his band, but we got interrupted and he took off. But he dropped this."

The clerk took it and held it up. "That's one of ours," he said. "We sell about a thousand of them a month, though— they're five for a buck. Can you maybe narrow it down some?"

Milton ran through his memory of what had happened and, in particular, what he remembered of the teenager. "Seventeen, eighteen years old. He had the start of a moustache. Black winter coat and cargo pants. I spoke to him after he finished, and we got talking. He said he'd just bought a van at an auction, and he was going to use that to deliver his band's gear to gigs."

The clerk's eyes widened. "One of the guys on the floor was saying his guitar player just bought a van. I mean, the bar band community isn't the biggest, so even if it's *not* the same guy, he could probably find the guy you're looking for." The clerk looked past Milton, towards the drum display. The rotund clerk who'd been helping the boy earlier was gone. The clerk looked up at the clock and tutted. "I think you just missed him. Hey! Mike!"

The clerk by the amplifiers nodded his way. "What do you need?"

"Where's Aldo?"

Mike shrugged. "He left. His shift was done at noon."

Milton glanced at the clock. It was quarter past twelve.

The clerk behind the desk turned back and shrugged. "Sorry, dude. Maybe tomorrow?"

"Would you have a number where I could reach him?"

He shook his head. "I can't give something like that out."

"He's usually at North KC Junior High after his shift is done," Mike said as he walked by, a two-speaker amplifier in tweed Tolex suspended by its leather handle. "It's back across the river. You just take Independence and head east. His band practises there."

The ginger-haired clerk gave him a withering look. "We're not supposed to share personal information."

Mike set the amp down. "You think he wouldn't be *more* annoyed if he found out he could've booked a gig and you didn't pass it on?"

"I guess."

"That's why nobody wants you in their band, goober," Mike said. "That and—oh yeah—the fact you *suck.*"

"The school," Milton said, wanting to get moving. "Do you know where I could find him?"

Mike nodded. "There's a storage building attached to the gym. They do sets and shit for drama, and that's where they let the kids rehearse. You'll probably find him there."

21

I t took Milton ten minutes to find the school. He parked the Mustang outside the main fence, at the side of the road. He saw the gym: it was accommodated within a building the size of a supermarket, with a second floor added for good measure. Milton climbed out of the car and shut the heavy door with a firm shove.

He heard the sound of bass and snare drums as he made his way to the building. He could hear a steady, deeper beat that was followed by two quick ones, like the syncopation of an old Chicago blues song. It was muffled, coming from inside. He heard the other instruments: the steady strumming of a rhythm guitar and then the free association as a player began to solo.

Milton liked his music and had eclectic taste. He recognised the beat and tried to remember what it was that they called it. A shuffle, he thought. Like 'Sweet Home Chicago.' He wasn't the biggest blues fan, but he had always admired great guitarists regardless of the type of music they played, from Johnny Marr to Gary Moore to Jimmy Page.

He followed the exterior of the gym wall to the back

door. Someone had propped it open with a wedge and, as he got closer, he knew that whoever was picking out the solo was special. The notes flowed out in rapid-fire tempo, quick, then slow, then quick again. The guitarist alternated between double and triple time, then stabbed a note and held it, the clear tone throbbing in the early afternoon air.

Milton reached the door and looked into the building. The soloist had his eyes closed, his fingers flying across the frets. He had his head down, his black bangs obscuring his face, but Milton recognised him. It was the kid from the auction. The bassist and drummer were talented, too, keeping perfect time behind the boy, the drummer hammering on his skins and the bassist laying down thick licks in perfect time. Milton recognised the song: it was 'Killing Floor,' a version of the song made famous by Hendrix.

Then the kid began to sing. "Lord knows… I should have been gone!" He bellowed the lines, yowling about the woman who had left him, "right on that killing floor." He flew back into a solo, with chords drenched in distortion cutting over the beat and single notes hammered out in an angry frenzy. The song drew to a close. The drummer hammered out a short solo that led the lead guitar back in, then the bass, riffing heavily on the last chord before they crashed into the conclusion in perfect unison.

Milton realised that his mouth had fallen open. He was surprised. The boy wasn't just a guitarist; he was *incredible*. Milton had heard his fair share of Clapton wannabes over the years, but he had never heard anyone that fast, that accurate and that soulful. Milton stayed where he was as they played 'Dead Flowers' by the Rolling Stones. The kid took another solo, soaring and fluid, inventive and with a slight country twang.

They were just coming to the end of the song when the bass player's phone rang. He was smaller than the other two, lithe and with an obvious athleticism that the drummer and guitarist did not share. He answered it, said a few words, then ended the call.

"Yo," he called out to the others, "we gotta get out of here, head next door. Coach got some kids in early."

The singer frowned. "And?"

"And he needs us, Enzo."

"We got the Battle in a week," the singer complained. "We're not ready."

"So we practise again tomorrow," the drummer said.

"I guess."

The kid's name was Enzo. That was progress. Milton knew that he couldn't stay here forever; he doubted that a stranger on school property without a good excuse to be there would be treated sympathetically. He supposed that he could wait outside the front doors, but he had no idea how long the kids would be, and a man sitting in a car outside a school wasn't a great look, either.

He wondered whether there was another way. Milton strolled back down the block and leaned against the rental. He took out his phone and dialled Tanner.

"It's me," he said.

"All right?"

"I'm good," he said.

"What's up?"

"I got the impression that Mollie is well connected."

"She is. If she doesn't know a person, she'll know someone who does."

"Could you ask her if she knows anyone at North KC Junior High?"

Tanner chuckled. "I don't need to ask her. I can help you with that."

"You know it?"

"They do work with vulnerable kids. We sponsored their football team last year. The coach there is a man called Julio Fernández. He's a good guy—works with the hard cases. The poor kids with parents who are on drugs or in the gangs. Fernández's got an after-school program for them that has won awards."

"Can you do me a favour and give him a call? I'd like to talk to him."

He paused. "This wouldn't be about tracking down that kid from yesterday, would it?"

"I can't ignore him, Tanner. I think he's in danger."

"There are disputes like that every day in Kansas City. In *any* big city. I mean, even if you're right and it was just some bad guys seeing an opportunity to rip the kid off, who says the kid even wants your help?"

"Wanting it and needing it are two different things."

"You can't save every kid who gets mixed up with lowlifes."

"I know," Milton thought, recalling the mess that he had almost made of Elijah Warriner's life. "But it makes me feel better to try."

Tanner must have realised that Milton's mind was made up. "All right," he said. "I'll give him a call and then I'll call you back."

22

M ilton parked the rental in the large parking lot behind the school. It was an officious-looking building, square and concrete, with evenly spaced windows and little adornment. Black wire lettering was mounted on the brick near the entrance. "North Kansas City Junior High School. Est. 1957." Smaller letters underneath read *"Et bene valet pugna vicisses."* Milton tried to remember the Latin that he had been taught at Fettes when he was a boy, but it had been far too long.

"'The good fight is worth winning.'"

The man's voice was deep and confident. He had come out to greet him in person, one of the main doors swinging shut behind him as he strolled over to where Milton was standing.

"Sorry?"

"You were looking at the sign. 'The good fight is worth winning'—that's the translation. Not a bad motto to live your life by."

"I can agree with that."

The man extended a hand and they shook. "Julio Fernández. Most folks here just call me Coach."

He looked younger than Milton, perhaps in his mid-thirties, and obviously fit. He was clean shaven and had a full head of thick black hair. His brow was furrowed in a permanent frown, and there were two vertical clefts between his eyebrows that pointed down to his nose.

"I'm John Smith," Milton said. "Thanks for agreeing to see me on such short notice."

"You know Tanner?"

"That's right," Milton said. "From back in England."

"He says you think a student might be in trouble."

"I do. I was at an auction yesterday. A teenage boy bought a vehicle, and then two guys tried to steal it from him."

Fernández shrugged. "And?"

"I know," Milton said. "You probably think I'm naïve."

"It happens every day around here."

"I think it was more than that," Milton said, choosing his words carefully. "The two men didn't look like the type who would steal a vehicle so that they could sell it for drugs. There was something about them—about *it*—that didn't sit right with me. I wouldn't be able to live with myself if something happened to the kid and I'd done nothing."

"And you think he's here?"

"I tracked him down to the store where he works—they said he comes here to help with the kids."

"There are a couple who fit that description." Fernández nodded towards the entrance. "You'd better come on inside."

The coach opened one of the outsized grey doors, holding its heavy steel bulk wide until Milton was inside. The main hallway tube lights glinted off the polished floor. The left wall was lined with grey steel lockers. A handful of students milled around, but the volume of their chatter dropped as soon as they saw a teacher.

Fernández turned left; the corridor darkened at the entrance to the old gymnasium. It had room for a full-sized basketball court, and two more rims had been set up on each side for practises. At the back was a raised wooden stage that Milton guessed was somewhere around five feet high.

The kid that Milton had seen at the drum display in the store had set up a pair of radio-controlled drones, four-prop whirlybirds with under-mounted cameras. He was demonstrating to five or six kids, some pre-teen, others older. The guitar player sat on a stool near the far wall. Four kids sat around him on plastic chairs, each balancing their own instrument on their thighs as he went through note patterns on his Stratocaster's neck.

Along the right wall, between the two sets of doors, a small booth had been set up. A banner across the top of the booth announced the No Violence Alliance. A middle-aged man with straw-blond hair and a pencil moustache was sitting behind it, his hands crossed as he waited patiently for any of the kids to ask him questions. No one seemed to be biting.

"What's that?"

"It's the police anti-gang program. That's Detective Nicol. We asked them to send someone down, and they gave us him on account of the fact that he used to live in the neighbourhood. Let me introduce you."

Milton bit down on his lip in irritation. He had no interest in involving the police if it could be helped, but he couldn't really say no. He followed Fernández to the booth.

"David," Fernández said, "got a new recruit for our little venture here. That right, John?"

Milton smiled. "I'm afraid I'm only in town for a few days."

Nicol rose and offered a handshake. "Your loss, Mr...?"

"Smith. John Smith."

"John's worried about a student," Fernández said.

"That right?"

"He was in a fight," Milton explained. "Nothing too serious. I just wanted to make sure he's okay."

"Hope so," Nicol said. "These kids already have enough to deal with."

Milton was relieved when Fernández changed the subject. "David used to own a little one-bedroom place just around the corner from here on Brighton Avenue."

Nicol took his seat once more. "My wife loved it until we had our first kid."

Milton gave him a smile and took his opportunity to end the conversation. "It was nice meeting you, Detective."

"Please—call me David. Detective is for bad guys."

Nicol put out his hand. Milton shook it again, said goodbye, and then followed Fernández across the gym.

"You see the one you're worried about?"

Milton gestured to the opposite wall. "The kid on the guitar."

"Really? He's kind of a special case."

"I know. I've heard him play."

"Not just that. Enzo has personal issues. I mean, technically, as part of the program, which is mine and not the school's—they just rent me the space. Anyway, technically, the mentors agree to speak with whoever I assign. But that's supposed to mean the kids they're mentoring. This is a bit different. I don't know how comfortable I'd be having a stranger—"

"What if you were involved?" Milton cut over him. "It

doesn't need to be in private. It probably *shouldn't* be in private. And it should only take a few minutes."

He still looked uncomfortable. "Enzo's on the spectrum. He's a great kid, but he comes off as rude to some folks, particularly when they're excited about something and he isn't. Or worse, he tells them why they shouldn't be."

"I understand," Milton said.

"Look, knowing him, it's just as likely that whatever dispute you saw, he probably started it without even realising what he was doing by saying something inappropriate. It's happened before."

Milton knew that had not been the case, but he didn't want to say anything more than was necessary. "I'd feel better if we could have a quick word. It'd only be a couple of minutes."

The coach let out a deep breath, perhaps signalling to himself that it was time to stop worrying. "I guess it's okay."

They both turned back to where the guitar player had been giving lessons, but the four young students sat alone. Milton caught motion from the corner of his eye and turned his head to the right, just in time to see the second set of doors, adjacent to stage right, swinging shut.

23

E nzo felt his stomach flip end over end. He had eaten a bad egg once as a child, and it felt just like that, the same way he'd felt just moments before he'd been sick at the church social, ruining Carmen Galaraga's best dress. It was like someone had dropped an iron weight into the pit of his gut.

He had recognised the man talking to Coach Fernández right away, as soon as he came into the gym.

"Enzo?"

It was the same man; Enzo was *sure* of it.

"Enzo?"

Enzo came out of his thoughts. One of the students—an eighth-grade boy named Daniel—was trying to get his attention.

"Sorry," he said. "Look, I'm sorry, guys—I just realised I have a scheduling problem. I got to get out of here a little bit early."

He moved slowly and cautiously, staying low as he raised himself off the stool and turned around, moving a few feet to the back wall. His guitar's hard-shell case was propped against it. He packed the Stratocaster away carefully, folding the strap overtop of its seafoam-green body before closing the lid and latching it. He unplugged his amplifier, coiled the power plug's wire, and stored it in the compartment on the back of it. He kept his head down, picked up both items, and calmly crossed the gym to the north exit.

Once he was past the doors, he sped up to a quick walk. He was encumbered by the nearly sixty-pound weight of the amp, but he had hauled it around before and knew that it was easiest if he let it swing in time with his strides. The hallway was empty. At its end was a set of stairs to the left; the north parking lot exit was to his right. He turned that way, using his elbow to put enough weight on the door handle that he could push it open without putting his gear down.

He stepped through and let the door slam behind him. The van was parked along the back wall. If he was lucky, he could get loaded up and out of there before...

"Enzo!"

He froze.

"Hold on there, bud."

It was Coach. Enzo put the guitar case and amplifier down next to the van. Fernández was twenty yards away, just ahead of the doors. The English guy was with him.

"Coach," he said, "I gotta go. I'm already late."

"Just give me a minute. I'd like you to meet someone."

Enzo wasn't sure what to say. He could have said that he had met the English guy before, but then it would look like he was fleeing and there would be questions. Enzo did not want Coach thinking that he was mixed up in anything. And the English man had defended him, after all. But maybe it was some sort of hustle. Enzo was confused. His condition made reading people's intentions difficult. It wasn't that he *couldn't* read them; it was just that he couldn't anticipate when someone was being serious or joking, when something was trivial or important.

Normal people *already* worried him, and the Englishman's behaviour at the auction house had been crazy, taking on those two guys like he had. It might have escalated. The men had been strapped—one of them had pulled back his jacket to show him the piece he was carrying—and what the English guy had done, tussling with them like that, could easily have ended up with him getting shot.

People got shot all the time in KC, and often for stupid reasons. Enzo watched the news and read the papers. He knew that half of the victims didn't know their shooter, and that the city had the highest rate of random homicide in the country. It was mostly quick flareups between young dudes with more bullets than IQ points. It made him anxious to think about it. The street had claimed his father's life a decade earlier, and Enzo wanted none of it. It was why he kept on at Francesco to stay away from his uncle Luca. It was why he told him to concentrate on playing his bass, on getting better, that a life in music was better than a lifestyle that might look glamorous but would probably end up being short. Enzo knew it: nothing good came from the streets. There was only one way out of that life.

"This is John Smith," Fernández said.

"Hello. Look, Mr. Smith—"

"Call me John."

He felt uncomfortable at the suggestion of informality. "Look," he said, "I don't wanna be rude or nothing, but I'm late for a meeting. My mom—"

Fernández put his hand on Enzo's shoulder. "Mr. Smith says some men gave you trouble at an auction? I think he'd just like to know that you're okay. Maybe see if you'd like to report it?"

Enzo shook his head firmly. *Hell no.* He didn't trust the police any more than Smith, whoever he was. "It's nothing, Coach, really. Man—you know how stuff goes down sometimes. It was a misunderstanding, that's all. It ain't nothing. Seriously."

Smith looked at him coolly. "Do you know how long it took me to find you?"

Enzo shrugged.

Smith handed him the orange guitar pick. "I went to the store and asked around. It took less than an hour. If it was that easy for me—and I've never even been to Kansas City before—can you imagine how easy it'll be for the men who wanted your van?"

Enzo shrugged again. "Why, though? Why would they go to the trouble of trying to find me? They were trying to steal the van. Big deal. It was a carjacking, that's all. It happens here all the time, right, Coach?"

Fernández nodded. "Sure. But—"

"They didn't get what they wanted, and now they've forgotten all about me and moved on to some other guy."

Smith shook his head. "I don't agree. Why would they want your van? How much was it? Five hundred?"

Enzo nodded.

"So two guys came after a young man like you just so that they could get a five-hundred-dollar van? At an auction where there were witnesses around? And they were armed. I saw."

"You didn't say that," Fernández said to Enzo.

"One of them was carrying a sidearm—the other one probably was, too," Milton went on. "That was not a carjacking. It was something else."

Enzo shot him an angry look. Talking about guns might give Coach a reason to call his mother, and the last thing Enzo wanted was to get her involved. She would worry, like she always did, and there was no need. Not this time. He was okay. It was nothing.

"I appreciate what you're trying to do, but nobody's coming after me. And I have to get home. My mom is expecting me, and I'm gonna be late."

He opened the side doors to the van and lifted his guitar in first. Coach helped by leaning down to pick up the heavy amplifier, straining a little as he hoisted it onto the van floor.

Smith hadn't given up. "You're wrong, Enzo. I think they were professionals."

"Not *very* professional," he scoffed. "You handled them pretty easily."

He didn't react to that. "Professionals don't give up quite so easily when you have something they want."

Enzo slammed the side doors closed. "Okay. Thanks and everything, but I got to go. Coach—I'll see you Monday."

"Keep this." The Englishman handed him a piece of paper with a phone number written on it. "If they come back, you'll need help. You can call me."

Enzo accepted the paper and shoved it into the pocket of his cargo pants. "Okay," he said, in the hope that it might give the man a reason to back off so that he could get away. He walked around to the driver's side and climbed in. The van's door creaked slightly from age as he slammed it shut. He slotted the key into the ignition and turned over the engine. It fired up immediately, rumbling and burbling, the chassis of the vehicle gently shuddering. He had to get home, away from any nonsense. Smith might have been trying to help, but he would just make things worse, and Enzo didn't need that.

He had goals to meet and no interest in getting waylaid by shit like this. His mom thought he worried too much. She said that he had grown up too quickly, that he was too serious for a boy his age.

Enzo knew better. Living in a neighbourhood like theirs was a reason for worry.

KC was Killa City, and he wasn't going down like his father.

24

F rancesco di Cello stomped his feet, trying to fight off the cold. He waited outside the front doors of the school, his bass guitar case propped up against the wall. He was short and looked younger than the other kids in his year. He used to attend school here, a year ago, but that was before he dropped out. School was for losers. What good were grades going to do for someone like him? Books and tests and shit? *No thanks.* It made more sense to hustle for cash and do odd jobs for his uncle Luca.

Luca was about the only cool adult that Francesco knew. He hung with mobbed-up guys and knew some of the dudes from the west coast outfits who came to KC. He had an insane sneaker collection, wore low-slung jeans that cost two hundred bucks a pair, and drove a 1977 Cadillac DeVille with lifters and an eighteen-speaker sound system in the back. Luca worked for Sal Provenzano, in charge of a handful of dealers who slung crystal meth and crack to local addicts, re-upping a few times a week at one of the places that Sal kept for that purpose. He helped shake down the owners of businesses in East KC, persuading them that it was worth paying him insurance to make sure bad things didn't happen to their property. He had boasted that he and some of the others had hit trucks that brought fancy goods to the department stores in town, stopping them on the interstate on their way in and ripping them off.

Luca was legit, but, more than that, he treated Francesco like an adult. He wasn't always friendly—he could be cold as ice sometimes—but he was there when Francesco needed a ride, or a few bucks for food, or a joint.

"Your uncle picking you up?"

Francesco turned his head. Aldo had his drums packed up in three special cases, each round and with a large cloth handle on one side. He was a big kid and made carrying them look easy. Francesco was jealous of Aldo because he was happy. He could make the best of almost any situation and, no matter what they faced in the course of the day, it was rare to find him in a bad mood. Francesco hated that sometimes, especially when he was in the kind of low funk that took hours to shift.

"He's been looking out for me for years now, man," he said defensively. "Don't start bad-mouthing him."

"I wasn't going to."

"No? You usually do."

"He's just got a rep... you know."

"Yeah? Well, nobody's giving him nothing, same as the rest of us. Some of the guys he knows, some of the business he gets done, the dollar bills..." He sucked his teeth. "Man, I'd be lucky if he lined me up some work slinging—you know?"

Aldo looked uncomfortable. "Don't say that kind of thing. You're better than that."

As if on cue, a dark-purple Caddy turned in to the school parking lot, circled the perimeter, and pulled up beside

them. The windows were tinted just slightly, and the driver
didn't even bother looking over.

"You want to tell *him* that?"

"I just worry about you. Enzo does, too."

"Whatever," Francesco said. "I'm good—it's all good. I
gotta split—we're headed down south."

"Why?"

"You know—business."

Aldo frowned with worry. "You sure?"

"Just chill. Luca's got my back."

"Just don't go making the mistake of looking up to him."

Francesco scowled. What the hell was *wrong* with him?
Aldo would never understand what it had been like for
Franny, coming up the way he did. Aldo had never had a
father who beat him, who took off his belt and whaled on
him with it. And Aldo's mother was sweet and kind. Franny's
mother sure wasn't; rather than make sure that he always
had new school clothes, shoes that didn't have holes in
them, and enough money in his pocket for a meal every day,
she stole his ADHD meds and partied all night with men
other than his father. His parents didn't give a shit about
him. He had learned, early on, that you had to look out for
yourself in this life because damn sure no one else was
going to.

He crossed the sidewalk and opened the passenger door.
The thump of a subwoofer punctuated Drake's latest track.
Francesco put his guitar in the back and got into the front
next to his uncle.

"You all right?" Luca said.

"Fine," he said. "Cold." He slammed the door behind
him and looked to the left as Luca pulled away from the
kerb. He saw Enzo talking with Coach and another guy next
to his new van. He sighed.

"What?"

"You know Enzo?"

"Your retard friend?"

"He's not a retard," Francesco protested.

"Kidding," Luca said. "Your *weird* friend. What about him?"

"He bought himself some wheels yesterday."

"What he get?"

"This beat-up old van. Says he'll be able to use it to get us to gigs—you know, all the gear we got to bring. Got to be thirty years old."

"How much did he pay?"

"Five hundred."

"So it's probably a piece of shit, Franny. You get what you pay for. Five hundred don't buy much."

"I know," he said.

"So why the long face?"

"At least he has wheels."

"You don't like riding in a car like this?"

"I didn't mean that. It's just that it's about time I got something for myself. For my—well, for my *independence*, right? I don't wanna feel like I'm putting you out."

"You ain't doing shit. And if you want money, then you know I can help with that. We can see about that right now, if you like. You want to give me a hand?"

Francesco knew what his uncle was suggesting. He knew that it wouldn't be legal, and that it had the potential to be dangerous, too. But, on the other hand, it wasn't as if he had any other options when it came to making paper. Enzo had his thing at the store and the side hustle with the amplifiers, but Francesco didn't have any of that. He'd been busted for buying weed twice in the last six months, and that kind of shit left a stain on your record. He didn't have anyone to give him a reference, either, and no business was going to be interested in employing a kid with those kinds of issues who didn't have anyone to vouch for him. What else was he going to do? You needed money to make a mark in the world, and the street was the only option he had. At least he had his uncle to make it easier for him to get his start.

"Little man?" Luca pressed.

"Okay," Francesco said. "Sounds good."

25

It started snowing again as they drove down Jackson Avenue, heading towards Swope Park in the southeast of the city. It was a regular first afternoon stop for Luca. Francesco knew the drill. Luca would pick up a half pound of crystal, stopping by one of the places Sal ran for Bobby Whitesox before heading to the main trap house down in Blue Ridge. Francesco watched his uncle drive. The Caddy had a big 7.0L engine, but Luca kept it right at the speed limit at all times. The last thing that he wanted to do was to give the police the chance to say that he was speeding. There was always something illegal in the car. Luca was so cautious that he sometimes seemed almost boring.

He reached over and turned the music down, then nodded in Francesco's direction. "You got something else eating at you today?"

"It's nothing. The guys—they think I was stupid for dropping out of school."

"Why'd you care what they think?"

"They're my friends."

"They don't like making money?"

He shrugged. "They don't get it. And they've got it easy compared to me."

Luca reached up and scratched his nose. "Some people, man, they don't get the streets. But what else are you gonna do? You don't want to get a job flipping burgers, right?"

Francesco shook his head.

"Exactly. I know, man—I been there. Besides, you got those attention problems. You ain't never gonna be one for books. Better off making green than hanging around with kids and teachers who don't respect you."

Luca was referring to his ADHD, and, like just about everyone else, he didn't get it. Most people thought that his symptoms—the forgetfulness, the restlessness, the carelessness and lack of attention to detail—were just signs of laziness and bad behaviour. Enzo was different. He got it. He knew what it was really like, probably better than anyone else. He had his own issues, and he had always been someone in whom Francesco could confide, at least until recently. Now it was starting to feel as if the two of them had started drifting away from each other. It didn't feel as if their friendship was there anymore, at least not like it had been when they were kids. Was it normal to go in different ways as you got older? Francesco didn't know, but the thought of it made him sad.

THEY TURNED off the avenue and onto a residential street. A series of low-rise apartments sat halfway up the block on the left. They were white stucco with tin roofs, built decades earlier, now mostly subsidised housing for those who didn't have the money for anything else. Luca pulled the Cadillac into a small lot that had just enough spaces for one car per dwelling. All but one of the spaces was empty. He parked on the opposite side of the lot, away from a newer-model Lexus sedan with an inch-deep coating of snow.

The two of them climbed out of the car and slammed the doors, keeping their eyes on the street and the lot. Luca had taught Francesco to be wary of trouble around trap houses. You had the police to think about; legitimate cops busted the houses for easy arrests to bump up their numbers, while crooked cops shook the cats down for bribes so that they would look the other way. And, police aside, the houses were favourite spots for desperate robbers who were looking to make a score.

They crossed the lot to the small flight of double-sided stairs that led up to the two front doors. No one worried about what the neighbours would think; Sal had the entire building, running dope out of one apartment while using another as a place to stash the gear and a third as a dummy for the police. A fake wall between the two units at the front of the building let junkies pick up their stash at one while it was prepared from the supplies in the other. Luca had explained it all to him: normal search warrants only covered one living space, and, on that basis, it made it much more difficult to be busted if the cops were following the rules.

Luca rapped his knuckles five times on the right-side door. A window slid open and then the door opened. A short man with a dark goatee-moustache combination held it open until they were both inside.

The door led to the living room. Francesco looked around: three men were lounging around on light-brown furniture, watching a horror movie. One was eating a bowl of cereal. Behind them, in the kitchen, Francesco noticed a long table that was covered with small baggies. Each was filled with crystal meth, the drug broken into jagged chunks like rock salt.

The man with the bowl of cereal looked up. Francesco recognised him at once: Salvatore Provenzano.

"It's Luca and his nephew," Sal said.

"Sal," Luca said, "didn't know you'd be here."

"Just passing through."

Francesco had heard that Sal had been imported from Italy, that the Mafia there had sent him to help Bobby Whitesox stay in control of his outfit as he got older. He spoke with a thick accent that stuck out against the Midwestern drawls of the others in the room.

Sal put his spoon into the empty bowl and sat up. He pointed to Francesco. "I forgot your name?"

"Franny."

"And what are you doing here? You want to make some money? Do some slinging?"

Luca answered before Francesco could speak. "He's gonna help me, Sal. Just along for the ride."

"Yeah?" Sal's eyes were tiny and jet black, and he seemed to stare right through Francesco like he wasn't there. "You know how it is. Anyone coming in here comes to pick up and sell. Anyone else comes in, perhaps I think we have a security problem."

"Come on," Luca said. "He's with me."

"You vouch for him?"

Luca spread his hands. "You know I do."

Sal turned to Francesco. "You want to make some money yourself?"

"Sure."

"Do you have a car?"

Francesco looked down at his shoes, nervous and embarrassed.

"He don't," Luca said. He gave him a playful punch on the shoulder. "If he had wheels, then I don't got to drive his dumb ass everywhere."

Sal put the bowl down on the floor. "You don't want to *earn* some money so you can buy yourself a ride?"

Francesco shrugged, still too cowed by the older man to look up and hold his eye.

"What is it?" Sal said. "Cat got your tongue?"

"He's pissed," Luca said. "His friend bought himself some wheels, so now he has to hear about how he's the only one doesn't have his own ride."

"That right? What'd he buy?"

Francesco cleared his throat. "A van," he said. "This dumbass piece of shit he bought for five hundred bucks at a cop auction."

Sal stood up abruptly. "What did you say?"

"He bought a van for five hundred bucks."

"At a cop auction?"

Francesco nodded.

"You seen it?"

"It's just an old piece of junk. I'm surprised it still runs."

"Describe it."

Francesco couldn't work out why someone like Sal would be so interested in Enzo's junk van, and, confused, he shrugged. "I don't know," he said. "It's just a van."

Sal closed the distance between them before Francesco could react. He grabbed the lapels of his coat and shoved him back against the wall. He reached into his waistband, pulled out a black pistol, and pressed the muzzle against Francesco's forehead.

"What the fuck, Sal?" Luca protested.

Sal ignored him. "Think," he said, his voice low and

loaded with menace. "Describe the van—don't make me ask you three times."

Francesco felt his breath shorten to spasms and his knees go weak. He always bragged about what it was like to live on the street, but, in all his years, no one had ever held a gun to his head before. His bladder felt weak, as if he was about to urinate all over himself. He knew Sal Provenzano. Everyone did. Sal killed people for Bobby, and they said he liked doing it.

"It was b-b-black," he stammered. "Old. Nothing special."

Francesco glimpsed Luca and saw his fear and knew that he wasn't going to do anything to help him.

"Think *really* carefully," Sal said. "This next question is important. Is it *all* black?"

"No," he said. "One of the panels at the front is white. Like someone replaced it to fix the damage from an accident."

Sal reached down with his left hand and cupped Francesco's chin. He turned his face around and then held it up so that he could look down at him with his cold, intense eyes. "*Molto bene*," he said. "Well done. Now—next question. What's your friend's name?"

Francesco tried to swallow, but his throat was dry.

"It's Enzo," Luca said.

Francesco looked over at his uncle. Luca's face was tense, and he gave a little dip of his head as if encouraging him to answer Sal's questions.

Sal's gaze was lifeless, like a lizard inspecting its prey. "Enzo, then," he said. "All right. Surname?"

"Pizzolato."

Provenzano nodded. "Last question. Where does he live?"

Francesco felt a rush of fear. *Shit.* What had he done? Sal was looking for the van. Enzo had told him and Aldo what had happened at the auction, about the men who had tried to steal the van from him. Maybe those men had been part of Bobby Whitesox's crew.

Maybe Sal had been one of them.

Shit, shit, shit.

"Let him go," Luca said. "I know where he lives."

Enzo was in trouble and Francesco had just made it worse.

Much worse.

26

Enzo pulled the van into the space ahead of the townhouse's one-car garage, backing it onto the downslope and yanking up on the handbrake. A level surface would have been ideal, he thought, but, either way, it meant he could load and unload directly from the bottom of the front steps.

He was climbing out when his phone rang. He grabbed it from his pocket; it was Francesco's number. He slammed the driver's side door and killed the call. Enzo was used to it by now: Franny calling to whine about how he hated band practise or how life wasn't fair or how Aldo had pissed him off... Enzo didn't have the time or inclination to humour him right now. It could wait.

He unloaded the guitar and amplifier and carried them up the stairs. He was fishing for the door key when it opened from the inside.

His mother was standing inside. "I thought you were practising until dinner time."

Enzo squeezed past her. "Coach needed us to help with the kids for a couple of hours."

"Haven't you got the Battle coming up?"

"We'll practise again tomorrow. It'll be okay."

He went up the carpeted stairs and turned left, into one of the two bedrooms. The room was small and, because of that, it had to be neatly arranged. He had a bed and a wardrobe and a small writing desk under the eaves, and that was all.

"I'm making cannoli for dessert," his mother yelled up to him.

Enzo's phone rang again. Francesco. He frowned and wished that he would just chill out. Enzo knew that Francesco's untreated ADHD caused him emotional problems and meant that he was still immature. Enzo was constantly talking him down off ledges, but he knew—from bitter experience—that it didn't help to enable him when he was having a tantrum. Enzo had sensed that another was brewing when they had been practising. He would let him settle down for half an hour and then call him after dinner to make sure he was okay.

He went downstairs and followed the narrow corridor. At the very end was the bathroom, with the kitchen to the left and the living room on the right. The home was modest, dating from the era when a single working adult could pay off a mortgage in a few years. It had seen better days, but his mother worked hard to keep the photographs and pictures dusted and the carpets clean. She was house proud and Enzo was, too. Their home was always tidy.

His mother was standing in front of the open fridge, looking for something, her hair haloed by the light from inside the unit. Enzo watched her for a moment and smiled. She was the finest person that he knew. Their life had never been easy, but she had worked her fingers to the bone to make hardship as unnoticeable to him as possible. She worked multiple jobs to make sure that they had enough money coming in. He had never had to go to school in dirty clothes like Francesco, and she had made sure that he got treatment for his condition. Amazingly, she had somehow found a little more so that he could indulge his passion for music, too. She had also helped him with the money for his wheels, and he frowned a little now at the nagging thought that he had done wrong by buying the van and not a car, like they had planned.

She noticed him from the corner of her eye and looked his way. "We're out of ricotta and mascarpone." She took a few steps towards the table and took off her apron. "I'm going down to the corner store."

He smiled as she put on her coat. In a world of real problems just outside their front door, the fact that she worried about something so small just to make his favourite dessert—just to make him happy—was profound to Enzo, like being wrapped in a security blanket. His good fortune made him think of Francesco again and the stark differences in their lives. Franny didn't have that, not really. His mother tried her best, but she was scatter-brained, badly affected by her own mental health, and lacked the money to resolve any of their family's many problems.

She collected her purse from the table and slung it over her shoulder. "You need anything, baby?"

"I'm good."

"All right. I won't be long."

She walked out of the kitchen. Enzo heard the screen door clink shut. He crossed to the fridge and took out a carton of orange juice. He collected a small glass from the plain lime-green cupboard and filled it, then put the carton back in the fridge. He took the glass to the living room, where his PlayStation was hooked up to the television. He sat down and reached for the remote.

His phone rang again.

Come on, dude...

He flicked on the television. An old episode of *Friends* was playing. The phone kept ringing. He took out the phone and dropped it onto the table.

It kept ringing.

He leaned forward and took a look at the screen.

Francesco wasn't giving up.

He moved his thumb over the ignore button, but, this time, he hesitated. Francesco might be frantic, and it was never a good idea to let him get really bad. His anxiety could be so profound that it just about disabled him; he'd never admit it, not even to Enzo, because he thought it made him look weak.

Enzo relented. Franny obviously needed somebody to talk to.

He took the call. "What's up, dude?"

"Why didn't you answer?"

"I'm sorry. I was—"

"It's Sal, man."

"What?"

"Sal Provenzano."

Enzo swallowed. Everyone knew Provenzano's name. "What's wrong? What's he done?"

"The van you bought."

"Right..."

"He wants it. He's coming over to your place right now."

Enzo frowned; that didn't make any sense. "I don't get it. He wants my van? Why?"

"I don't know, but he just put a fucking gun to my head until I told him what he wanted to know."

Enzo's mind began to race. "So... so... so I'll give it to him."

"No, that ain't gonna work. You got to get out of there. Right now, man. Bail. He's serious—I swear to God he was gonna kill me if I didn't answer his questions. You don't know him like I do. He won't wait to talk about things. He don't work like that. You need to get out of there—*right now*."

"Okay, okay," Enzo said, getting up from the sofa and walking as he talked. "We'll just grab..." He stopped. He realised he couldn't leave. "Shit."

"What?"

"My mom—she went out to the store. I mean, she'll be back any minute. Like—maybe twenty minutes, a half hour at most."

"Dude," Francesco pressed, "we're way south from you, but he already left, like, ten minutes ago. You're lucky if you've got twenty before he gets there. Just go, man. Get out. Phone your mom; tell her not to come back. Just—"

"Okay," Enzo said, cutting over him. He closed his eyes and thought about what they needed to do. He looked down the hallway to the front door. The van needed gas, but he thought that it had enough for now.

"Enzo?"

"I got to go."

Enzo hung up the call and immediately dialled his mom. He heard a buzz from the telephone table, three feet away.

Shit.

She had left her phone in the house.

He killed the call and paced the hallway. He didn't know what to do. He could leave, he supposed, just abandon the van so that they could take it. But would they do that? What if his mom came back before Enzo could get to her? She was proud, and he knew that there was no way that she would let someone steal the vehicle. But Salvatore Provenzano would kill her just as soon as say hello. Maybe not there and then, on the street, but he was the kind of guy who bore grudges. They didn't want him as an enemy.

He looked at the phone on the table and clenched his fists in frustration. Of *all* the times to forget your phone, why today? What was the point in having a cell if you left it behind? Old people exasperated him.

He closed his eyes and tried to think of another option. Maybe he could just talk to Sal? He'd explain that he bought the van by mistake and that he had no idea that someone as important as him wanted it. How could he have known? Maybe he could make him listen to reason.

He shook his head. Who was he kidding? Sal wasn't known for his understanding. He had got to where he was because he was ruthless and brutal. He would kill him the second he got here, take the van, find his mom and then kill her, too.

What had Coach suggested when he had mentioned the fight at the auction? Call the police? Speak to someone like Detective Nicol? No way. You didn't talk to the police around here. No one did. If word got around that he had snitched, he'd be dead in a week.

He had no option but to pray that his mother got home before Sal arrived.

He felt helpless.

And then he remembered.

The scrap of paper.

Coach's friend, the English guy. Smith. He had seemed heartfelt, like he really wanted to help. And Enzo remembered what had happened at the auction. He had taken out those two guys who had been after the van like they were nothing. He was tough. Enzo fished out the card and dialled the number.

It was answered on the second ring.

"John Smith."

"It's Enzo—Enzo Pizzolato. You met me at the school. I... um... I think—"

Smith cut over him. "How can I help?"

27

M ilton had taken a drive to give himself time to
think about whether there was any way that he
could help the kid when his help appeared to
be unwanted, and had concluded that there was little he
could do. He decided that he would wait in town until
Tanner had delivered whatever new intelligence on the
Group he could dig up, and then he would move on.

He was waiting at a red light when a Ford Mustang
Shelby GT500 rumbled by in the opposite direction. He had
been thinking about the Olds at the auction and had
decided that he was definitely going to continue his road
trip. He wondered whether he might be able to top up the
twenty-five grand that he had put aside for a set of wheels,
go back to Kelly's, and see whether there was anything else
that took his fancy. Maybe he would be able to pick up a
Chevy Corvette or Camaro. A Pontiac Firebird. A Dodge
Charger.

He could easily have drifted off into a daydream and
might have were it not for two distractions: the impatient

horn of the car behind him and the buzzing of his phone in the holder on the dashboard. He pressed to answer as he rolled the car across the junction.

"John Smith," he said, not recognising the number.

"It's Enzo—Enzo Pizzolato. You met me at the school. I... um... I think—"

"How can I help?"

The boy sounded distraught.

"You know what you said about calling if I needed help? I think I need help."

"Okay—where are you?"

"At home."

"Address?"

Enzo gave an address in Blue Hills. Milton was on the north side of the Missouri River, and knew from his phone's map that the neighbourhood was south, below Midtown. He swung the wheel and turned the car around, sliding the back wheels over the icy crust that covered the road. He picked a route that would take him over the Christopher S. Bond Bridge, pushed the car up to the legal limit and held it there, hoping against hope that he would avoid the worst of the rush hour traffic.

"All right," he said. "I'm on my way. Tell me what's happened."

Enzo recounted his situation, explaining how he had been warned by a friend that a man was on his way to his home to take the van from him.

"The guy," Milton said. "What's his name?"

"Salvatore Provenzano."

Milton rushed across the river and continued south along Bruce R. Watkins Drive. "Who is he?"

"He's part of Bobby Whitesox's outfit."

Milton recalled the name from Mollie Tanner's warning over dinner. "The Mafia?"

"Yes."

The highway had just crossed East Nineteenth when Milton saw a line of traffic ahead and the flash of an ambulance's lights. He suspected a crash and, gambling that he was right, he exited the highway and continued south on Troost. He immediately hit a red light and had no choice but to brake.

"Mr. Smith? Are you still there?"

"I am," Milton said. "I'm about ten minutes away."

"So what do I do?"

"Do you know how long you have before he arrives?"

"I don't know. Not long. I'm scared."

Scared didn't cut it; he sounded *terrified*.

"You need to leave the house."

"I can't," he protested, sounding as if he was close to tears. "My mom just went out to the store. She'll be home soon. If she's here when Sal arrives..."

"Okay," Milton said. "I'm coming. Stay inside. Keep it together for a little while longer."

The light went to green, and Milton stepped on the gas. The Mustang's big engine roared, the back wheels peeling out as he slung the loose, older transmission into second gear. The car roared through the intersection; a jaywalker paused in the crosswalk ahead, thought better of it and stepped back to the safety of the median to let him pass. Milton heel-toed the brake and gas, gunning it into third, redlining the engine as he reached the corner of Troost and East Thirty-Ninth. The back end slid out and sprayed slush as he downshifted and braked, the car drifting around the corner in a smooth arc. He flung the wheel back over, heel and toe working in unison, the engine on the slight down-rev as he flung it back into third, powering the Mustang ahead.

"Mr. Smith?"

"Still here." He swerved around a bus, racing by it in a blur. "Have you thought about calling the police?"

"No way."

"Why not?"

"You don't do that. Not around here. If I get a reputation as a snitch, it won't make any difference what happens with Sal."

Milton assessed. They had two options: he could either set up some sort of defence at the house or get Enzo out of there. The latter option was best, but only if the kid's mother was back by the time he arrived. He would get the two of them as far away as he could and then buy enough time to work out what to do about the van and whoever Provenzano was. If the mother wasn't there, things would be different. He couldn't take the kid and leave her. He would have to deal with Provenzano and whoever he brought along.

"Mr. Smith?"

"Think about somewhere you can hide if he gets there before me."

"The wardrobe upstairs—in my mom's bedroom."

"That's good. What about weapons? Do you have any in the house?"

"No. My mom hates guns."

"Something else?"

"I got a baseball bat."

"That'll do. Go and get it."

Milton heard the sound of footsteps and a cupboard door opening on hinges that needed oil.

"You got it?"

"Yeah," he said.

"Good. I'm at Swope Parkway—I'll be there soon. Leave this call open, and let me know straight away if anything changes."

"Okay."

Milton settled into a familiar stoicism, driven and yet icily calm. It had ceased to be about the fear of death, or Enzo's panic, or the boy's love for his mother.

He was going to work.

The car's V8 engine bellowed with a deep, glottal roar. There was an intersection a block ahead and, as Milton assessed the lights, they turned to yellow. Milton stood on the accelerator, then shifted into fourth. The car heaved forward. He snatched the wheel to the right, gunning the car around a red compact, then left again to pass a truck.

The house was just a couple of blocks ahead. He took a sharp left and saw the van from the auction parked facing the road on a downslope to a one-car garage under the townhouse. The aberrant white panel on the driver's side had caught the sun, a dim spark of late afternoon light glowing against it.

Milton pulled the car over to the kerb and grabbed his phone.

"Enzo?" he said as he opened the door and stepped out.

"Yes?"

"I'm here."

"Any sign of him?"

"No."

Milton checked both directions on the sidewalk, but saw no one. He walked past the first two homes on the street—both small and modest—and reached the van. He stopped behind it. He checked the home's front porch. It appeared clear. Fresh snow had settled there, and Milton saw two sets of prints, one going in and the other going out. The former had been left by a pair of sneakers; the latter by boots, smaller, likely feminine. He took the steps quickly and tapped on the door. The curtain covering the half window fluttered. Milton shoved his phone into his pocket as Enzo opened the door.

"She's not back yet," he said, his voice thick with panic.

"You should call the police."

"I told you," he hissed. "No police. We don't do that around here."

"We need to talk this over. Can I come in?"

Enzo stepped aside so that Milton could cross the threshold.

"Hey!"

Milton turned to see a middle-aged woman, dark brown hair, attractive in old-fashioned duffel coat and boots. She stood on the sidewalk with a reusable shopping bag in one hand and a frown on her face.

"Mom!"

"Excuse me," the woman said. She strode towards the steps. "Excuse me, sir, who are you, and why are you talking to my son? You just hold on right there."

Enzo stepped up to the door. "Mama," he said, "this is Coach's friend—John."

"And what's he doing in our house?"

"We don't have time," Enzo said. "I'm in trouble."

She peered at him as if he had gone crazy. "What? What are you talking about? I just left. I was gone for, like, fifteen, twenty minutes. How can you have got into trouble in twenty minutes?"

Milton knew that he was going to need to take over. There was no time to debate the situation on the stoop.

"Your son is mixed up in some trouble through no fault of his own."

"And you are who exactly?" She turned to Enzo. "Who is this gentleman lecturing me on my own porch?" She faced Milton again. "Sir, my son's a good boy—"

"Mrs. Pizzolato," he said patiently, "*please*. Enzo called me because he's worried some dangerous men are on their way here."

She turned to the boy. "What? Who? What does that mean, Enzo?"

Enzo did not have time to answer. A black Lexus sedan turned the corner onto the street. Milton recognised the pedigree immediately; an eighty-thousand-dollar ride was out of the price bracket of anyone who would live on a street like this.

"We're out of time. Mrs. Pizzolato, please come inside. You have to listen to me. If you both do as I say, then I'll keep you both safe."

"I'm not doing anything until someone has explained what this is all about."

"Mom, *please*."

Milton took her by the elbow and, with a firm grip, he impelled her into the house. She was distracted and did not resist.

"Enzo," Milton said, "is there any chance Provenzano will negotiate?"

"Provenzano?" his mother said in a quiet voice. "Sal Provenzano? What's going *on?*"

"We can talk about it later." Milton pushed them both down the corridor. "Enzo—will he negotiate?"

"I don't know," he said.

Milton would have to assume not. "Go to a room upstairs and close the door," he said. "Don't open it to anyone apart from me."

He turned back in time to see the Lexus pull over and park just ahead of his rental. All four doors opened and four men got out. He ducked inside before they could spot him, closed the door and bolted it.

28

Milton worked out the geography of the property: kitchen, sitting room and toilet on the ground floor, with stairs up to the first. He retreated down the hallway to the kitchen and opened all the drawers, finding the kitchen knives in the second drawer down next to the stove. He took out the chef's knife and hefted it; it was solid, made entirely of metal, with a heavy handle and a blade that had recently been whetted. Milton knew that he was going to be outgunned, but it would have to do.

The back door rattled. Milton could see the top of a man's head, an outline that was visible behind the cream-coloured half curtain that covered most of the glass. He leaned across the kitchen counter and turned the under-sized white plastic microwave's dial to thirty seconds, then hit start. It hummed and the interior lit up as its small glass rotisserie plate rotated.

The door rattled more violently as whoever was outside tried to force the lock.

Milton crouched down and moved over to the north

wall, putting his back to the space next to the door. The window on the door shattered. A gloved fist punched through the pane and then slid the bolt. Milton resisted the temptation to take the invader out quickly; he wasn't sure how many men were at each door, and he needed to pace himself. He had to understand the scope of the problem before he could begin to deal with it.

He heard a rattle from the front of the house; they were trying to open the door there, too. A fist banged on the door frame.

"Enzo! Open up. We won't hurt you."

Milton held his breath as a man crept through the back door. He was of average height and slender, with a big revolver in his right hand. The weapon was cocked and held up, the barrel pointed ahead. Milton counted to three to ensure that they had only sent this one man to the back, but no one else followed.

The microwave beeped as it completed its program. The gunman turned, paused, then took a couple of hesitant steps towards the unit. Milton encircled the man's throat with his left arm and nestled the man's larynx in the crook of his elbow. He grasped his left wrist with his right hand and pulled back, choking the flow of oxygen to the man's brain. He was unconscious in five seconds.

Milton lowered him to the floor and collected his gun. It was a Colt Single Action Army, a sidearm from the days of the West and most commonly known as the Peacemaker. He checked the cylinder; it was chambered for .357 Magnum and was fully loaded. It had a 5.5-inch blued barrel, a spurred trigger and a colourful case-hardened frame. It was heavy, too, maybe three pounds in the hand. It would do.

The man wouldn't be out for long. Milton crouched by his side and undid his belt, yanking hard to draw it from the loops. He secured the man's hands and then reached back to collect the dish towel from where it had been hung on the oven door and shoved it into the man's mouth.

Milton stood up. He went to the back door, closed it again, and bolted it, adding the safety chain. He leaned to look through the entryway, with just enough of an angle to see the front door. There was a heavy impact and the door buckled inwards. A second impact splintered the frame and forced it open. A man leaned halfway around the edge, a nine-millimetre in his right hand. Milton was working on the assumption that four men had come to the house, and knew that one of them was out of commission. Taking this second one out would cede the element of surprise that he currently enjoyed, but two on one was a lot better than three on one, so he decided to take the shot.

He lined the man up and fired. The big revolver kicked, and the bullet caught the man in the sternum, knocking him back onto the porch.

A pair of voices yelled out in a mixture of English and Italian. Milton extended his arm with the revolver aimed straight ahead. He brought his left hand up to balance a second shot, inhaling and then emptying his lungs. He was ready to fire, but, after seeing what had just happened to the colleague who had tried to breach the door, the men outside were being much more reticent. Neither man crossed the open doorway to check their associate, as Milton had hoped that they might.

The window to the side of the door shattered as a barrage was fired through it. Milton threw himself sideways, back into the kitchen and out of range. Another fusillade blasted through the remains of the window, bullets hammering the bathroom at the end of the hall, splinters of wall and door flying in all directions.

It was a random, wasteful volley, but it did force Milton back and removed the chance of picking them off as they came inside. There was a mirror on the wall of the hallway, and he watched in its reflection as they came in. Two men: one tall, the other short. They entered cautiously, pistols clasped in double-handed grips.

Milton leaned around the corner and got off a quick shot. The two men hit the floor, the taller man's pistol clattering out of his hand to the bottom of the steps. The smaller man fired back, more splinters bouncing off Milton's coat, keeping him pinned down. He heard the two speak, but couldn't make out what was said. He risked a quick glance around the door frame, and a bullet whizzed past his ear, so near he could feel the heat from it.

He heard footsteps.

One of them was slowly going up the stairs.

"You're outnumbered." The voice was even, with no excitement or anger.

"Just barely," Milton called. "The guy you sent around the back is down. The guy who came through the front door, too, but you saw that."

"Put the weapon down and maybe we don't kill you."

He spoke in a clipped and matter-of-fact fashion, his words coloured by a thick Italian accent of diphthongs, elongated vowels, and spongy *sh* sounds. Milton had been to the south of that country and recognised the slow drawl as Neapolitan.

"Salvatore?"

"Who are you?"

"The name doesn't matter."

"Not very polite."

"All you need to know is that you don't want me coming after you."

"That right?"

Milton could still hear the treads on the stair, nearing the top now. Enzo and his mother did not have long.

"I'm giving you a chance to walk out of here," Milton said. "You can even take the van. The kid doesn't want it."

"Yeah, well, like you said—you just took out two of my guys. We don't leave."

"Last chance."

"How many shots do you have left? I've got nine and two spare mags. Who do you think is going to run out first?"

29

Milton heard the sound of impact—something like wood on bone—and then the thud as something heavy fell to the floor above him. He waited, knowing that if the gangster called down, then the game was up for Enzo and his mother. But there was no call. The invader must have been caught by surprise and taken the baseball bat to the head.

Milton started to harbour the hope that they might have a chance.

"Just you now, Salvatore," Milton said. "Just you and me."

"Why you want to help these people? You're not from here."

"How do you know that?"

"Because you are English."

"Very observant."

"And because if you *did* come from here, then you would know who I am, and who I represent, and, if you knew *that*, you'd know how stupid it is to be doing what you are doing."

"No, I don't know you," Milton said. "But the kid does.

He says everyone thinks you're a hard case. But I'm not impressed, Sal. Not at all. There's just one of me, and I'm not as young as I used to be. This should've been a walk in the park for you."

"Keep talking."

"One of me and four of you. I choked out the man you sent to the back, and I put a bullet into the one who came in through the front. Two down. Your friend upstairs? The tall guy? I can't be sure, but if you asked me to bet, I'd say he just got his brains scrambled with a baseball bat. That's three. That just leaves me and you."

"Big talk when I can't see you. Put that piece down and come out here. We can talk about how tough I am."

"I don't like bullies, Sal, and that's what you are. A bully who needs four men to go after a kid and his mother. The thing is, your luck was out today. I don't like bullies and I'm not scared of you. Like I said, you've already lost three of the men you came in here with. You stick around another five minutes and I'm going to make it four out of four."

Milton heard sirens, but they were not near enough for him to know whether they were headed their way or somewhere else.

"Come on," Provenzano said. "Put the gun down and come out. We can talk this out."

"I'll tell you what—the *second* you step through that door, I'm going to decorate the wall with whatever rattles around in your head. How's that?"

The sirens were louder now.

Provenzano cursed in Italian. "You want to talk about luck? *You* got lucky today. But it is not going to last. I know who they are now—the kid and his mother. They cannot hide in this city, not from me. There's nowhere I could not find them. And when I do, I kill them both, and then I kill you, too."

Milton heard the footsteps and then the opening of the door. He waited a beat, aware that Provenzano might well be trying to dupe him, but, as he looked at the reflection in the remaining shards of the mirror, he could see the street outside and a blur of motion as the man hurried away towards the Lexus.

Milton ran to the stairs.

"Mrs. Pizzolato?"

There was no reply.

"Enzo?"

"We're here," the woman called back.

"They've gone."

He heard the sound of footsteps and then saw the woman and her son as they descended the stairs. She was holding a baseball bat in both hands, the heavy end up by her head. The wood was stained with blood.

Milton nodded in the direction of the first floor. "The guy who went up?"

"On the floor," she said.

"Well done." Milton kept them at the bottom of the stairs, out of sight of the open doorway. He didn't want to take the chance that Provenzano might still be nearby, waiting for them to put their heads outside. He knew, also, that there was a body just outside and that, while they were going to have to step over it to get away from the house, it would be better to keep it out of their view for the moment.

"We need to leave," he said.

"Can't we call the police?"

"I don't think that's the best idea."

"They just broke into my house."

"They did, but Enzo said that Provenzano is involved with the Mafia."

She nodded.

"In my experience, they'll have police officers working for them. It might not be safe."

"In your experience?" she said. "What does that mean?"

"We can talk about that on the way."

"How?" she said. "We take my car?"

"The van," Milton said.

Her eyes widened. "Why? If we leave it, maybe they come and take it, forget about us."

"I don't think they're going to forget," Milton said. "They were embarrassed today. They'll come back, and you'll need something to offer them. It's got to be the van—we know they want it. It's the only leverage you've got. Enzo—where are the keys?"

The boy reached into his pocket. "Here," he said, holding them up.

"Give them to me."

The boy did as he was told. Milton took them and hustled mother and son towards the door. He doubted that they would be able to return to their home until this mess had been sorted out.

Provenzano would not take a setback like this lying down.

He would be coming for them.

30

Milton found a truck stop on the outskirts of the city. US 400 was an ageing grey strip, a straight shot south past farmland and small towns and through miles and miles of snow-covered fields. Cows grazed on hay bales fifty yards back from the highway, and a snowplough worked the road heading back into the city. The surface was treacherous and Milton drove with care.

Connie and Enzo had visited the bathroom and were heading back across the lot. Milton was standing at a payphone and had just finished the second of two phone calls. He put the receiver back in the cradle and looked back to where the mother and son were getting back into the van. He had parked it behind a big eighteen-wheeler so that it would be hidden from anyone who might be passing on the road.

He went into the store, bought three bottles of water and three bags of chips, and made his way back.

"Are you two okay?" Milton asked them as he got back into the driver's seat.

They both nodded.

"Here," he said, handing them each a bottle of water and a bag of chips.

"Thank you," Connie said.

She cranked the cap off the bottle and took a long drink, then replaced the cap and screwed it back on. The atmosphere was tense. Milton could see that there was something on her mind and that she was looking for the right way to broach it.

"Just *ask* him, Mom," Enzo prompted.

She rested the bottle of water on the seat next to her. "I need to ask you a question."

"Why should you trust me?" Milton suggested.

She nodded. "Don't be offended. I'm grateful for what you've done for us, but I don't know you. Why would you put yourself in danger for us?"

Milton was not offended. He could guess how she might be feeling. She would be panicking and worrying about her son. She would be wondering why she would put their lives into the hands of a stranger.

"I don't blame you for being cautious," he said. "I would be, too."

"I just need to understand," she said. "When did you meet Enzo?"

"I was at the auction. I saw what happened when he bought the van."

"What?" She turned back to look at Enzo. "What happened?"

"Some men tried to jump me," the boy said sheepishly.

"The men who came to the house?"

"No," he said. "Not them. They were different. Pretty sure they were Irish."

"You didn't say!"

"I didn't want to worry you."

"You didn't want to..." Connie crossed herself. "*Díos mío,* Enzo."

"Mr. Smith helped me. They tried to take the van, he saw what was happening, and he stopped them. He didn't have to do that."

"'Stopped them'? What does that mean?"

"There was an altercation," Milton said. "I persuaded them that they should leave Enzo alone."

"He knocked both of them out," the boy clarified with obvious enthusiasm.

"*Hijo,*" Connie said, putting her hand to her forehead. "What about the house—why were you there?"

"Enzo called me and said that he was in trouble."

She frowned. "How did he know to call you?"

"He gave me his number, Mom."

"I didn't think what happened at the lot was finished," Milton said. "I thought they might come after him, and I wanted to help."

"You still haven't answered my question. This doesn't make sense." She waved her hand around the interior of the van. "None of it does. Why would you do something like that?"

"It was the right thing to do."

"People don't react that way."

"I do."

She was quiet for a moment as she looked out of the window. A truck rumbled into the parking lot and parked next to the fuel pumps.

"No," she said. "That's not a good enough answer."

"I've done some bad things in my life," he said. "The job I used to have—I had to do things that, looking back now, I wish that I hadn't."

"What job?"

"Government work," Milton said. "I'm afraid that's something I can't talk about. But I don't do that job anymore. I quit and, after I left, I decided that I would try to make up for some of those things that I did by helping others who might not otherwise have anyone to stand up for them. I've seen men like the ones at the auction house and the men who came to your house. I have experience in dealing with people like that. This might sound strange, Mrs. Pizzolato—and this is probably the wrong word to use—but, given the circumstances, you've been lucky."

"*Lucky?*"

"To have found someone who can help. And who *will* help, if you want it."

"There's no agenda? No other reason why you're doing this?"

"None," he said.

"Because, I mean, if it's money, you're wasting your time —we don't have any."

"I don't want money. I don't want anything. The chance to help is enough for me. I promise."

Connie dipped her head slightly to hide her flushed cheeks. "I'm sorry," she said. "This is a lot to deal with, Mr. Smith."

"Please... it's John."

"Thank you, John."

She took a drink. Milton gave her a moment.

"So, say I'm okay with this," she said. "What do we do now?"

"I just called a friend," Milton said. "He knows Coach Fernández. He gave me his number and I spoke to him. He—"

"No!" Enzo protested, cutting over him. "We can't speak to him about this. Coach works with the police department."

"He won't call the police," Milton said.

"He works with the gang unit," Enzo insisted, "and they work with ICE. My mom..." He caught himself before he finished the thought.

Milton looked over at Connie. ICE was the American Immigrations and Customs Enforcement agency. "Are you here illegally?"

She nodded. "I'm from El Salvador. I left when I was younger. It wasn't safe." She took a beat, then continued. "I tried to get my papers, of course, but then I met Enzo's father, Leonardo. He was second-generation Italian. But he had a difficult life and made many wrong choices. He was involved with the Mafia, and I knew that there was no way I could get my papers while I was married to a criminal."

Milton could feel her tense as she criticised Enzo's father in front of him. But the boy did not appear overly bothered. Milton guessed that he was more than bright enough to have accepted who his father had been.

"So you see?" Enzo said. "You see why we can't go to the police?"

"I do," Milton said. "But Fernández won't call the police if you don't want him to."

"How can you know that?"

"Because I asked him not to, and he said that he wouldn't."

Milton knew that they would probably have to get the police involved at some point or another, but that could wait. They needed an interval where they could be certain that they were safe, and that was what Fernández had offered. It was not permanent, but they didn't need it to be. They just needed a moment to breathe and to think. Milton would work out the options more carefully once he knew the family were safe.

"So where are we going?" Enzo asked.

Milton glanced across the cabin to the young man. Enzo was direct and his face was implacable and serious. Milton could see how other people might mistake his earnestness for annoyance or even anger. He suspected that it must have caused the boy no end of problems with others his own age.

"Fernández says his family owns a small quarry just outside Louisburg. It hasn't been used for years. He said they leased it to personnel from a local army munitions plant."

"I know it," Connie said.

"Really?"

She nodded. "The area, anyway. Leonardo—Enzo's father—had a job there for a couple of months. The plant closed a few years ago."

"Small world," Milton said. "Coach said his sister returned to take it over, but she's in California on vacation. It sounds like an ideal spot to lie low. We can use the time to work out what to do next."

That seemed to satisfy them. Milton was unsure how he was going to untangle the mess that had been created by the van's purchase. But he knew one thing: it had not been Enzo's fault, and he'd be damned if the boy and his mother would pay a price for it.

31

The pianist had almost finished the song. It was an old Jay McShann standard about being better to the woman he loved. The stand-up bass player kept perfect time while the drummer's brushes lightly swept the snare. Four feet from the stage, at a circular two-person table that was permanently reserved in his name, Kenny O'Connor watched the trio. The song was a favourite of his, and they did it better than most. But, like most things for Kenny, it was just an exercise in mechanics. The passion had been bleached out of the music in favour of a search for sophistication and a consideration of fine detail. It had no life.

The trio hit their mark in unison and brought the song to an end. The crowd of thirty or so rewarded them with polite applause. Kenny took a swallow of scotch, then noticed the tumbler was empty. A waiter appeared beside his table with a fresh drink. He took Kenny's glass, placed a new paper napkin on the tablecloth, and then replaced the drink. Kenny did not say anything or tip the man; he spent so much here that he felt no compunction to speak to the staff, save the chef or manager, and only then as necessary. He lifted the tumbler and sniffed at the thirty-six-year-old Laphroaig. The waiter knew how he liked the drink and had added a half-teaspoon of lukewarm water. It separated the multiple undertones into more complex flavours: chocolate, orange, and anise.

Kenny came to the Green Lady four or five times a week and, when he did, he had two or three glasses. The single malt cost a hundred bucks a glass. He had made the calculation during an idle moment and had worked out that he had spent nearly sixty grand in the last year alone.

"Mr. O'Connor."

He turned. It was Reynolds, the manager of the club. "Evening," he said.

"How are you?"

"I'm well," Kenny said.

Reynolds had served in the army and had been invalided out after an ambush outside Kabul. Kenny had allowed him to labour under the misapprehension that the military was something that they had in common. Reynolds thought that Kenny had served, too, and Kenny had allowed him to foster the idea that there might be mutual respect between them. Reynolds made no secret of the fact that he had hated his time in Afghanistan. He had explained, over a glass after the club had closed one night, that, even though he had escaped without any physical damage, he had seen everyone else in the vehicle die. There had been tearful talk of survivor guilt and PTSD.

Survivor guilt.

Jaysus. Kenny thought it was *pathetic*.

Kenny had been an active member of the Real IRA before it had become necessary for him to leave the country. He had loved his time fighting the Brits. He hadn't wanted to leave, but that was a consequence of the number of scalps that he had taken. He had received a tip that his exploits had accorded him a special MI5 file and that, if they couldn't arrest him, they would take him out instead. He had packed up and left before that could happen.

The whole experience might as well have been tailor-made for him. He knew himself well enough to realise that he was different, and always had been. He didn't feel things properly; or, at least, he felt them *differently*. His boyhood had almost been a cliché, with regular sessions torturing neighbourhood animals to assess their reactions. He knew what it meant: he was a psychopath. His brother was different. Patrick had always been the clever one—always into books and computers—but Kenny didn't share the same interests and aptitudes. He was self-aware enough to identify that he was remorseless and that, if properly deployed, that quality could be of advantage. The IRA had seemed like a natural outlet for someone of his proclivities and, by the time he had concluded his first three months, he had arrived at some additional conclusions about himself: first, that he was asexual, and that normal relationships didn't suit him; and, second, that the only thing he found truly exciting was gratifying himself in the hour after a killing.

Reynolds had just been a regular grunt. Kenny might not have been legitimate—at least in the eyes of polite society—but he had been elite. He and the other men in his service unit had been tasked with numerous missions, often clandestine. By the time he had left Armagh and joined his brother in Missouri, Kenny had murdered four British soldiers and eight civilians who were convicted of collaborating with the enemy. The faces of his victims had long since blended together. The more they begged, the more they screamed, the more they cried or offered him money to stop, the more he felt his excitement build.

Reynolds was going on and on about the bar and who he had booked for the next few weeks. Kenny nodded along, hardly listening.

"Evening."

Reynolds stopped. Kenny turned. It was his brother.

"About time," he said.

"Been a little busy." Patrick stared at Reynolds. "Go and get me a drink."

Reynolds looked as if he might take offence at Patrick's tone, but wisely bit his tongue. Kenny could see that his brother was in high dudgeon; Reynolds had probably saved himself a smack in the face. He went to the bar to fetch the drink.

"I've been trying to call you," Patrick said.

"Sorry. Been here all night."

"I guessed."

"Did Nicol and Bird get anything on the kid?"

"He registered with the DMV. They got his address."

"So?"

"So it turns out we were too late. I went to look and there were police outside. The place had been shot up, and there was a body being brought out on a gurney. I asked around. The woman who lives opposite said Sal Provenzano was there. Him and other guys from Bobby's crew. She said they broke into the house and then she heard shooting. One guy shot dead, two others put in the hospital. Sal left, and then the kid and his mother came out with a bloke she didn't recognise. She took a picture of him, though. Showed it to me. It was him. Blue eyes and a scar on his face. No question. The fucking guy from the lot."

"And the van?"

"Gone."

Kenny sipped his drink. He could see that Patrick was on edge, and he didn't particularly want to aggravate him.

"Where's my bloody drink?" Patrick said.

Kenny put his glass back down on the table and looked over to his brother.

"So what do we do now?"

"Not *we*," Patrick said. "*You*."

"Fine, Patrick. What do you need *me* to do?"

"I spoke to Bird, and he spoke to whoever it is he knows who works for Kelly. She said that the English guy was brought to the auction by another English guy—name of Tanner. Fills the water coolers, apparently."

"So the two of them know each other?"

"That would be the reasonable conclusion, Kenneth."

He ignored the jibe. "So you want me to go and see Kelly?"

"I do. Go have a word with him. Find out who the guy is. Find out where he is. If we get to him, we get to the van. And be quick. Bobby's after the van, too. We had a head start on him, but that's gone now. It's a race. And if he gets it first, we're done."

Kenny took out his money clip and stood. The band had launched into another number, the piano player thumping out a boogie-woogie beat, and he considered staying, seeing if the man could get through a single song without dragging the eleventh bar.

"I'd better get started, then," Kenny said. He laid a hundred on the table and grinned. "Jack's not gonna torture himself now, is he?"

32

The coach's place was a couple of miles north-northwest of Louisburg, one of a handful of ranches between the town and Neodesha along US 400. There was a faded sign at the side of the road, loaded down with snow: LOUISBURG AGGREGATES. Milton turned the wheel and headed down along a private gravel road. He saw ditches on either side, then fields, the frontage lined by uniformly spaced elm trees. A small copse of elm and Osage orange trees was to their right, partially concealing the way to a finger-shaped watering hole a few hundred yards away, a shaft of moonlight glinting off black water.

"Doesn't look like anything is happening out here," Connie said. "Looks like it went bust."

"Like most of the places around here," Enzo said. "We did a lab on it last year in Economics. Businesses around here are all struggling because commodity prices are so low."

"The ones that aren't cooking meth," Connie interjected.

"Aren't there other employers?" Milton asked. He had to

raise his voice to be heard over the rattling of the van; its firm suspension was doing little to cushion them from sharp jolts.

"Louisburg had munitions, but that's gone now. There's some meatpacking across the rest of the state. Call centres. But nothing much is going on in rural Kansas anymore. The population's dying; poverty and crime are growing. When I first got together with Enzo's father, we lived in Osawatomie for a while. It was already bad then. But now? Just look at the news. There's no reason for people to come here."

"Apart from the quiet," Milton said, nodding out to the wide-open and empty snow-covered fields. "There's a value in that. It'll suit us very well for now."

There were two buildings ahead: one was the shape of a large home, and the other was a barn of some sort, perhaps a garage. A figure stepped away from the home and was just visible under the porch light, waving his cap above his head as a signal.

"That's Coach," Enzo said.

"I just hope he has hot coffee," Connie said, and sighed.

33

Milton rolled the van to a stop, the lights picking out the burly figure of Julio Fernández. He watched as the coach made his way across to the van. He should have looked angry, or concerned, or just irritated that he had been inconvenienced like this. He didn't; when he opened the passenger door to greet them, he was smiling and his arms were spread wide.

He hugged Connie. "Mrs. Pizzolato."

"Coach," she said, "I'm sorry about—"

"No need," he said, cutting her off. "Glad to help."

"Thank you."

Enzo clambered down and Fernández offered him his hand. "Young man," he said.

"Hi, Coach," Enzo said, his cheeks flushed.

Milton got out and locked the van.

Fernández nodded at him. "Mr. Smith, heck of a way to have you out here for a visit."

"I would have preferred it to be under different circumstances."

"We can talk about that," he said. "Anyhow—we should go on inside. It's cold. There's more snow forecast."

He led them up the porch steps and opened the screen door for them. The oak front door, which looked to be of the same 1940s or 1950s vintage as the rest of the building, was propped open. "My sister's away in California," he said. "She hates the winters. Anyway, we've got the run of the place, not that there's much running to be done around here anymore."

They stepped into the foyer, and Milton started an informal assessment. A broad flight of curved wooden stairs led up to the next floor. There were doors to the left and right, opening into a living area and what looked like a den.

Fernández pointed left. "Kitchen and family room are through the living room. The study's on the right, and then you got the boiler room and two garages. Connie, you'll be taking the main bedroom—up the stairs and to the left. Enzo—you're opposite, across the hall. John and I can sleep on the couches in the living room."

"I can't take your bedroom," Connie protested.

Fernández waved her concern away. "It's fine. I've fallen asleep down here after a few too many beers so often, my sister thinks I should just move a bed down. Truth to tell, the sofa's a big old sectional and it's comfy as hell. That lumpy old mattress you're going to be on wasn't doing my back any favours. So don't you feel guilty about nothing. What about you, John? You're gonna be okay with the couch? I've got a fridge full of beer to take the edge off."

Milton held up a palm. "Not my thing anymore."

Fernández didn't comment. Instead, he nodded towards the living room. "You all take a load off, and I'll get us some coffee."

"A milk for Enzo?" Connie asked.

The boy looked irritated. "I like coffee."

"It's ten o'clock," she said. "If you have coffee now, I'll be peeling you off the ceiling at midnight."

"I'll help," Milton said, following the coach to the arch that led into the kitchen. "It'll give us a chance to go over a few things."

Coach nodded. He pushed open the swinging galley-style door, and Milton followed him. The kitchen was large and L-shaped, with old-fashioned stainless-steel chef's counters and a rectangular island. There was a family space and an open butler's pantry that led through to another room.

Fernández reached up into a cabinet and took out a container of coffee. "You want to tell me what's going on?"

"I'm sorry for dragging you into this mess."

He shook his head. "Forget it. If I didn't want to help, we wouldn't be out here. Nobody forced my hand."

"I appreciate that. But this could be dangerous. Enzo is in trouble. If the men who are chasing him find out where he is, we'll all be at risk—you, too."

The coach doled out scoops of coffee into the drip machine's paper filter. "I did two tours in Iraq and one in Afghanistan with the Rangers. I've been shot at more than once. Can't say I particularly appreciated it, but, if we go down that path again, it wouldn't be my first rodeo." He closed the coffee pot's lid. "KC is a tough town. I wouldn't be a teacher there if I wasn't ready to do what's needed for my kids. And Enzo's one of the good ones."

"If they find out where he is, they'll come in numbers."

"I understand," the coach said, flicking on the machine. "And I'm still here. How do you want to play it?"

"Sleep first," Milton said. "They're tired. I am, too. I'll take stock in the morning."

"Figure out the best ways to defend the place?"

"Just to be on the safe side."

"And then? I doubt this is something that can just be waited out."

"No," he said. "I don't think it is. I'll head back into the city and see if I can find a resolution that doesn't involve everyone shooting at one another."

Fernández poured out a mug of black coffee and handed it to Milton. "And if that doesn't work?"

Milton put the mug to his lips and sipped the hot brew. If that didn't work, then there might not be anything other than a violent denouement to this unfortunate incident. But the coach did not need to hear that.

"Some of my best ideas come to me when I improvise."

PART III

34

Milton woke at six. He looked around, taking a second to remember where he was. Fernández was asleep on the sofa opposite him, pushed down into the cushions, his limbs at odd angles from moving in his sleep. He was snoring. Milton rose quietly and went to the window, parting the curtains enough to look outside. Snow was falling, a thick curtain that mopped up the light and carpeted the ground in a smooth white mantle.

Milton went through the dining room and the butler's pantry and into the kitchen. He found the carafe of coffee from the previous night and reheated a mug of it in the steel-tone microwave. It beeped and he pressed the button to open the door.

"You got another one left in that pot?"

Milton turned. Connie was standing in the doorway.

"Up early, too?"

"Not the best night of sleep I ever had."

"Worrying?"

She nodded. "Couldn't stop thinking about it."

"I'm not surprised."

Milton filled a second cup, then put it into the microwave.

"This is actually late for me," she said. "Enzo had to be ready for school by seven forty-five for years, so I was always up by five thirty. I had to get his clothes ready, make sure he had a packed lunch, get him up and out..." The machine bleeped and Milton collected the mug and gave it to her. "Thanks. Would you like to sit down and talk? I still have a few things to ask, if you don't mind."

Milton had hoped to make a tactical assessment of the property. "Why don't we go for a stroll?"

She pointed to the window. "You've seen the weather, right?"

"I know. But I really need to get a look at the place. We can talk afterwards if you like?"

Her coat had been left over the back of one of the dining room chairs. She grabbed it. "Come on, then. Let's go."

THERE WAS a door to the outside between the kitchen and family room. They went out and emerged into the rear yard, where a family-sized swimming pool sat covered by a tarpaulin. Its pump was almost completely submerged beneath the snow. To the left of the pool was another small outbuilding, perhaps a workshop or a garage for family vehicles; a gravel driveway to its wide double doors snaked around the house and merged with the track that they had driven along last night. To their right, thirty yards or more away, a wide space that Milton assumed was a lawn ended and the watering hole—more a small lake, really—took over. The backyard stopped twenty yards past the pool, where more fields stretched to a tree line that was a mile or more away.

The property was well positioned: it was remote and would be difficult to approach across the open ground without revealing yourself. The snow would be helpful, too. It was a smooth blanket that was marked only by the prints of a deer out late to forage for food.

Milton led the way, following the perimeter of the lawn. They waded through the snow, their boots crunching as they pressed through the icy crust.

"It's cold," Connie said. "And quiet."

"Peaceful," Milton agreed.

"In better circumstances, maybe."

They walked on. Milton was silent, letting his thoughts settle. Their breath steamed in front of their faces, and Milton could feel the freezing air in his lungs.

Connie sighed. "I don't know what we're going to do. I mean, how does this work out for us? I don't know how you get someone like Sal Provenzano to leave us alone."

"There'll be a way out. We just have to find it."

"You know anything about the Kansas City Mafia?"

"Not much."

"My husband was involved."

"You said."

"He was obsessed with the history of it. It's something about being Italian in America, the camaraderie of it. 'This thing of ours,' the omerta, all that." She exhaled sharply, derisively. "Boys who need to grow up, if you ask me."

"How big was it here?"

"In the sixties and seventies, it was as big as it was anywhere. They controlled places like River Quay, and they had connections with the casinos in Vegas. The feds went after them in the eighties and nineties, and they pulled back. They never disappeared, though. You ever heard of Bobby Romano?"

"That's Bobby Whitesox, right?"

She nodded. "I remember him from when Leonardo was involved. I never met him, but Leo talked, especially when he'd been drinking. Jesus, did he talk—Bobby this, Bobby that." She chuckled dryly, and Milton doubted that it was a happy memory. "The mob was all about gambling and prostitution and extortion back in the day. There was tradition there—the things they'd always done. I doubt they do that so much now. Times change, right? It'll be drugs now, probably, just like everyone else."

"And Sal is connected to Romano?"

"The story is that Sal came over from Naples. I don't know how much of it is true, but they say Bobby met him when he went out there, liked him, and asked the Italians if he could borrow him. That was almost twenty years ago, and he's still here, still doing Bobby's dirty work."

She paused.

"Did your husband know him well?"

"Leo was never officially part of the crew. He grew up with Vito Luciano, and when Vito got made, he brought Leo along as an associate. They got involved in protection, shaking down the businesses in Brookside and giving a cut to Bobby. Leo said you had to do that—he said Bobby always got to 'dip his beak.' Leo said it was stupid, and I guess he got greedy. He started a side business—he started robbing the trucks that delivered goods to the stores at Oak Park Mall. He had a guy on the inside at the trucking company, and he'd tell him when the deliveries were going to be made. He started coming home with clothes from Macy's, big TVs from Walmart, Disney toys for Enzo."

"Did you ever tell him to stop?"

"Of course I did," she said. "I hated it. I never wanted shit like that—we were happy, once, before he got dragged into it all. He said he was doing it for us, but that was bullshit. He got addicted to the glamour of it. He thought he was going to be a made man, really be part of the crew. But he wasn't pure Italian. His mother was Mexican. The others looked down on him because of that, and it was only when he realised that he was never going to be completely accepted that he went off the rails."

"What happened?"

"He hit a truck that was under Bobby's protection. I doubt he knew—he was a dumbass, but not even he would be *that* stupid. Bobby found out and he sent someone to deal with it. I was at the mall with Enzo when it happened. Leo had been out all night and was sleeping it off. I came back and the door was open. I found his body—they'd put a bag over his head and then shot him."

She exhaled and was quiet, gazing out over the property.

"I'm sorry," Milton said.

"We were through by then," she said, "but still—finding your husband like that isn't something I'd wish on anyone. The only saving grace is that Enzo was asleep in his stroller. He didn't see anything."

"Does he remember his dad?"

"No. I know that bothers him."

They trudged on. "And you think Sal was responsible for what happened?"

"That's what I heard. It would be the kind of thing he did. The word is that he's killed dozens of people for Bobby. That's the thing I couldn't get out of my head last night. Someone like him, coming to our house for Enzo. The thought of it... it's terrifying. How are we going to get around it?"

Milton knew there were always options, but many of them that he might consider would be unpalatable to normal people like Connie. They would be frightening. He knew that he would have to be tactful.

"I've seen situations that were worse than this."

"Really?"

"Much worse. And I've seen them get resolved, too. There's always a way. We just have to work out what it is. Or *I* do, anyway—I don't want either of you getting any more involved with these people than you already are."

She stopped walking and turned to face him. "I know how the world works, John. Maybe you can't see it, but I had a hard life before Enzo was born. My family..." She shook her head. "Some of my family make Sal look like a Boy Scout. You ever heard of MS-13?"

"The cartel," he said.

"I got two brothers. Both of them were police officers in San Salvador. They both got bought by the gang. My older brother, Francisco, he got killed by Barrio 18. They hung his body from the bridge out of the city as a warning. So I understand what's at stake. I'm just not sure that you do. I'm still confused why you'd take a risk this big for two people you don't know. Be honest. I need to know."

Milton chewed the inside of his lip.

"Please," she pressed. "If you can't say, I don't know how I can trust you."

"I told you," he said. "There are some things about me that I can't tell you."

"Can't or won't?"

"Both."

"So start with what you can. You said you used to work for the government. Doing what?"

"I was what you might call a fixer."

"Fixing what?"

"Let's say there's a problem that can't be solved by normal means—a man like me would be sent to try to fix it in another way."

"With violence?"

"Sometimes," he admitted. "I've done some bad things in my life. Things I regret—like I said."

Milton set off again, brushing off the snow that had settled on his shoulders. Connie followed alongside.

"Have you killed people?"

"Yes."

There was no point in lying, and she considered his answer in silence. He wondered how her view of him would change. He knew that it would—how could it not?—and mourned the death of innocence in their nascent friendship. He had seen what the truth could do, but he had decided to be candid with her; it was her choice what that meant for what happened next.

"How many?" she said.

"Does it matter?"

"One? Two? More?"

"I told you—I've done some bad things. But I have the sort of experience that I think you and your son are going to need. You won't be able to talk to Sal and Bobby about this. We'll need to send them a message that they'll understand."

She stopped walking again and stared back at the house. "Enzo said the coach was in the Rangers."

"He told me he did three tours overseas."

"Then he would be like you, too?"

"How do you mean?"

"He's killed people."

"Maybe," Milton said. "And now he spends every waking moment working to stop kids joining gangs and dying on the streets." Fernández had done what Milton had struggled to do: reintegrated into society and given up the martial life. "He's twice the man I am."

"You helped Enzo."

"I did."

"You didn't have to do that."

Milton nodded. "There was a time when I thought the best thing I could do was just to disappear. I could have— made myself anonymous and let it all wash over me. But I don't want to do that. It's cowardly. I want to help. I *can* help."

She glanced away, the intimacy of the moment making them both a little uncomfortable.

"So what do you think?" she said after a moment, gesturing around them.

"Do I think we're safe here?" he said. He knew that he would need to take a look in the sheds, to take an inventory, and then do his best to seal all points of ingress to the house. But, even on a cursory inspection, he could see that this was going to be a lot easier to defend than Connie and Enzo's place in Blue Hills. "I think this will be fine."

He said it with as much assuredness as he could muster, and she seemed happy. It was what she needed to hear, but, in truth, Milton had no idea what odds they might face. Probably quite long. Sal would not come out here on his own, or with just a couple of guns. There would be more of them. And then Milton thought of Patrick and Kenneth O'Connor, the two Irish men he had fought at the auction. They weren't Mafiosi, so how did they fit in?

Everyone wanted the van. They were going to have to work out why.

Milton felt a sense of foreboding. He looked around the

property and knew that this could only be a temporary respite.

He nodded towards the house. "Come on," he said. "The others will be up soon. Let's go make them some breakfast."

"You cook?"

He smiled. "You might be surprised."

They began walking back, the mood lighter for the talk that they had shared. That was how it needed to be right now. But they couldn't stay there forever. They couldn't wait until whatever it was that had caused Enzo so much trouble had blown over. Milton would need to find out what it was and then take steps to deal with it.

35

Bobby Romano's irritation grew more pronounced by the moment. He was sitting up in bed, his back against the padded headboard, watching as his mistress dressed. His wife was due back just after lunch from visiting her family, and he hadn't arranged the limousine to pick her up from the airport. He had no time for that, nor for this stupid *puttana* as she tried on yet another of the revealing dresses that she had bought on his credit. Bobby was trying to keep his mind off Sal's failure to bring him the van that the kid had bought from under their noses at the auction. He wasn't sure which irritated him more: spending thousands of dollars on satisfying the woman's vanity or the prospect of dealing with the consequences of Sal's fuck-up and yet another day without his money.

"Get a move on," he said.

"Bobby..."

"What?"

"I wanna look good."

Bobby was in his seventies, and Jessica was in her late twenties. He found it droll that he could buy a piece like her, that she would sell herself just to be around his money and power. It wasn't as if she was the only one, either. He had met her at Showgirls, the nude club Bobby part-owned on Main Street. He'd met plenty of others there, too, over the years.

"You look good," he said. "You always look good. It's the only reason I put up with you."

"Fuck *you*, Bobby."

As if on cue, Bobby's phone rang on the table next to the bed. He reached over for it. "What?"

"Bobby—it's me."

It was Giuseppe Maldini, Bobby's *consigliere*. "What's up?"

"Sal's at the club. He wants to speak to you."

"He's shown his face?"

"Yes. He says he was worried about being out last night. The police—you know."

Giuseppe was being deliberately vague; no business was discussed on the phone. "Tell him I'll be there in an hour."

"Yes, boss."

Bobby killed the call and turned back to Jessica. "Out, now. I've got business."

"Bobby..." she whined.

He picked up her clutch and tossed it at her. "Go!"

He waved her towards the door. Jessica grabbed her jacket from the chair and made her way quickly out of the bedroom. Bobby heard her heels clack as she made her way downstairs. He swung his legs off the bed and padded across the room to the en suite bathroom. He stripped naked and stepped into the marble-lined shower, twisting the brass faucet and letting the hot water rain down onto him. He took a breath, trying to still the irritation that was just beneath the surface. Sal was one of his most loyal capos, and he was usually ruthlessly effective.

But he had fucked up. He had fucked up *badly*.

Retrieving the van should have been a simple task, yet, as it had been explained to him by Giuseppe last night— and he was going to understand *everything* about it before the morning was out—a single man had killed one of Sal's soldiers, put two in the hospital, and then driven away with Bobby's property. The man who had been killed was a *cugine* called Michael, an up-and-comer who was striving to get made. Bobby knew his mother, and now he was going to have to deal with her grief, too.

The whole mess was unacceptable. Bobby knew that he had to set an example. If word got around that someone had taken advantage of him like that, the others in his crew or the guys on the street might perceive weakness. Not to mention the beaner gangs that would look at that and think it was time to make a move. They might recognise this failure as an opportunity, and Bobby could not tolerate that.

No. He was going to find the man who had done this and make an example of him.

He turned off the faucet and stepped out of the shower, grabbing a towel from the hook and drying himself with it. He went into the walk-in wardrobe and dressed, then checked his image in the mirror. His beard was neatly trimmed; the cut of his steel-grey suit was immaculate; his black silk shirt was impeccable. He opened the drawer where he kept the white tube socks that had become his trademark. He never wore the same pair twice, his maid refreshing the drawer every week. He pulled them on and slipped his feet into a pair of five-hundred-dollar patent leather shoes.

He opened his safe and took out the .40-calibre Beretta.

He checked the magazine and the barrel before ensuring the decocker lever was in place; then he pushed it into the waistband of his trousers. The Beretta wasn't the prettiest piece in the world, but it had smooth lines that let him draw it cleanly. It never jammed and, since he was getting older and not as strong as he used to be, the gentle recoil was easy to handle. It was a nice piece for his daily carry.

He had learned when he was a boy, growing up in the streets of the city sixty years ago, that the man who showed weakness would always suffer for it. Weak men could never be fully in control. One instance stood out in his memory even now. Joseph DeLuna had been the local bully, and he had made it his duty to make Bobby as miserable as he could. He stole from him and, when that wasn't enough, he beat him up. Bobby could have gone to his father, but he knew that would only have earned him another beating for bringing dishonour on the family name. He had dealt with DeLuna himself. He'd stolen his mother's kitchen knife and plunged it into the bigger boy's thigh the next time he'd raised his fists to him.

DeLuna never bothered him again.

No one did.

Power was all about image and perception. Bobby had learned that lesson that day, and he had also learned how power was repelled by weakness. Those who abided frailty were as bad as the frail themselves. Pity, mercy and compassion were the hallmarks of the weak, and Bobby had vowed that he would never be weak again.

He wasn't about to start now.

36

B obby made his way to Showgirls. He was a silent partner in the club and had used it to launder his dirty money before he had employed Patrick O'Connor to take care of that for him. He had wrestled with the decision to offload that function to someone outside his crew, but O'Connor was a straight-up genius and had promised that he would be able to clean the proceeds of Bobby's illicit businesses on a much greater scale than he could manage himself. The feds had been sniffing around him at the time, too, and Bobby had concluded that handing it off to someone not connected to him made sense.

The results during the first six months of their relationship had been so spectacular that Bobby had taken steps to ensure that O'Connor would never be able to break away or work for anyone else ever again. The hit on the arcade where the Irishman kept the dirty money had been a pretty smart move, even if he did say so himself. Bobby thought of it now and smirked: he had robbed O'Connor of the money that he himself had given him, thereby putting the Irishman in his debt. It had been an easy job, and Sal had pulled it off without a hitch.

But thinking of Sal's success then reminded him of his most recent failure—the missing van and its contents—and darkened his mood.

He opened the door and went inside. The cleaner was making his way around the room with a mop and bucket, working soapy water into the sticky floor. The barstools had been upturned and rested on the tables. The place always looked different in the daytime, without staff or customers and with the old jukebox quiet and the TVs off. It would be very different when it opened in the late afternoon.

Giuseppe Maldini was waiting by the bar. The two of them had grown up together, and Bobby trusted him as much as he trusted anyone. Maldini had hung on to Bobby's coattails as he became more and more senior within the family. He was a good man, loyal and smart, but he did not have the drive with which Bobby had been blessed. Giuseppe was a follower, not a leader, and, to his credit, he recognised that. His lack of ambition and satisfaction with the life that Bobby had given him—the house, the car, the women—were the reasons he had been allowed to draw so close. His clear thinking and the familiarity that gave him the confidence to question Bobby's decisions were the benefits that he offered.

"Where is he?" Bobby asked.

Giuseppe nodded to the back room.

"Alone?"

Giuseppe shook his head. "With Luca Monteverde. They know you won't be pleased."

"No shit. Come in with me."

The door to the office was ajar, and Bobby did not slow

down or pause to announce himself as he went in. It was a plain space with a wooden desk and a battered old chesterfield sofa pushed up against the wall. There was a filing cabinet with a bottle of whisky atop it. Sal was sitting on the chesterfield, one leg crossed over the other. Luca Monteverde was standing, picking at the skin on his left hand. He looked tense.

Bobby went around the desk and sat down. Giuseppe stood by the door.

"Well?"

Luca looked down. Sal stared ahead, his face as emotionless as ever. His eyes were cold and hard, and his nose was pointed and slender. He was the only one of his small crew with whom Bobby had always been confident. He was a cold-blooded killer and he rarely made mistakes. That was what was bothering him so much about the last few days; it wasn't auspicious when his best man started fucking up.

"Sal?"

He shrugged. "I am sorry, boss."

"I'm disappointed. It's your fault we lost the van in the first place."

"I know."

"And then you fuck up buying it back at the auction." He turned to Giuseppe. "Did we ever find out what happened?"

Giuseppe shrugged. "They moved the auction. We should've been told, but we weren't. I'm finding out why."

Bobby sucked his teeth. He turned back to Sal and Luca. "Go on, then—tell me. What happened yesterday? How'd you find the van?"

Sal looked at Luca.

"Go on," Bobby said.

"My nephew," Luca said. "His friend just bought a van at a police auction. He described it—it's obviously the same one."

"Who's the kid?"

"Enzo Pizzolato."

"Seriously? Leonardo's kid?"

"He lives with his mother in Blue Hills," Giuseppe added. "I got guys asking around."

"And the van was there?"

Sal nodded. "It was parked on the driveway."

"So why don't we have it now?"

Sal's lip curled up just a little as he recalled it. "It was locked, so I knocked on the door to the house. We get keys, we get van—it is all good."

"But?"

"But there is this guy there. Waiting for us." He turned to Luca. "Tell him."

The younger man cleared his throat. "I went in through the back door," he said. "He jumped me from behind. Choked me out."

"You didn't see him?"

"I'm sorry, boss. Like I said—he jumped me."

"He shot Michael as he went in," Sal said, "and the kid's Mom hit Matteo with a baseball bat."

Bobby sighed. "Unbelievable. What a fuck-up."

Sal spread his hands. "I am sorry, boss."

Bobby stared into the Italian's dark eyes. "Sorry don't get me shit. What are you going to do about it?"

Sal looked away; he knew better than to provoke him. "I ask around now. The kid has friends. He plays in a band with Luca's nephew. We told him what he needs to do—as soon as the Pizzolato kid gets in touch, we know about it.

And, when we do, we go and take care of it. You got my word."

"I don't want that," Bobby said. "I want my money."

"I got it, boss. I'm on it."

"Make sure you are, Sal. No more mistakes."

Sal uncrossed his legs and got up. "No more mistakes."

37

It was just before lunch when Tanner drove the truck into the lot and backed it into his usual space. It was a Saturday, and the place was shut for the weekend. He took a breath, drumming his fingers on the leatherette cover that sheathed the wheel. He had been worried about Milton. He was concerned about what the Group would do with his tip-off and, more to the point, what Milton would do if he found out that he had been betrayed. Tanner knew Milton well enough to know that he was ruthless. He had to be; it had been how he had survived for nearly a decade. Milton could talk about how he was a changed man, about how he had given up that way of life, but a leopard couldn't change its spots. A killer would always be a killer; it was in his nature. It was what he was.

And Milton *was* a killer.

He was the most dangerous man Tanner had ever met.

That meant being prepared. Tanner was planning on visiting the military arms store a few blocks away to pick up some extra rounds for the shotgun he kept in a case under the office counter. If anyone intended to visit grief upon him

—either the criminals that Milton was tied up with or Milton himself—Tanner would offer a gutful of buckshot as a reason why they should think again.

He locked up the truck and hobbled over to the door to the office. He unlocked the glass-and-steel front door and opened it.

His phone rang. He took it out and looked at the screen. It was Milton.

He answered. "David Tanner."

"It's John."

"Are you okay?"

"Yes."

"So what's happening?"

"You know the kid I mentioned?"

"From the auction."

"Yeah. I was right—he's in trouble. He blew me off when I spoke to him, but I gave him my number and said that he could call if he needed me. It's a good thing I did. Four guys came after him yesterday afternoon."

"The O'Connors?"

"No," Milton said. "Bobby Romano."

"Shit."

Tanner had known the name even before Mollie had brought him up at dinner on Thursday night. She had spoken about him at length on any number of occasions, usually when she was half-cut and regaling him with the tales she was going to include in the book she was writing about the golden age of crime in KC.

"What happened?" Tanner asked.

"I was able to help," Milton said. "I was inside the house before they got there, and I managed to fight them off."

"What does that mean?"

"I shot one of them. Choked another out. Enzo's mum clocked a third with a baseball bat."

"You *shot* one?"

"With one of their guns."

"Dead?"

"That's what it looked like."

Tanner shook his head. "From Irish money launderers to the mob," he said. "Shit, John. You've only been here three days."

Milton replied with a bitter chuckle. "Trouble tends to follow me around."

Tanner's stump hurt, and he sat down to take the weight off. "I don't get it. Why would Bobby Romano want the kid?"

"It's something to do with the van he bought. As far as I can make out, both the O'Connors and the Mafia want it—I just haven't worked out why."

"Where is it now?"

"With us."

"Have you searched it?"

"It's not obvious," Milton said. "I went over it, just in case the police missed something, and I couldn't find a thing. I was thinking hollow bumpers."

"Like in *The French Connection*."

"Exactly. But there's nothing—nothing I could see, anyway."

"Where are you?"

"We had to find somewhere to lie low."

Tanner reached for the pad of paper that he kept behind the till and found a pen in his pocket. "Where's that?"

"I'll tell you later."

Tanner gritted his teeth. He knew that Milton's location would be the first thing that anyone dispatched from London would want to know.

"Anything I can do to help?" he asked.

"Not now," Milton said. "I was calling to check in. And to make sure you were okay."

"We're fine," Tanner said. He felt a little frisson of concern. "Why wouldn't we be?"

"No particular reason—I was just concerned that this might blow back on you."

"No one knows you came to me."

"No," he said. "But I've made a career out of paranoia. Prepare for everything. Do you have a firearm?"

"A double-barrelled ten-gauge."

"And Mollie?"

"She has a little snub-nosed."

"Good. I don't think there's anything in particular to concern yourself with, but—well, you know. Just be careful."

Tanner bit his lip. "Have you spoken to the police?"

"Not yet. Men like Romano have police on the payroll. The word gets around and, all of a sudden, the family isn't safe, even hidden out here. I'd prefer to avoid that for as long as possible." Milton paused. "There was one thing I was going to ask—do you think Mollie might have heard of a local gang detective named Nicol?"

"I can ask."

"He volunteers with the coach's program. Something to do with outreach for the local kids."

"What do you want to know?"

"Whether he can be trusted. Working with the coach makes Nicol as good a person as any to start with if we decide to go that way."

"I'll ask," he said.

"Call me if you get anything."

38

Aldo, Enzo and Franny had agreed to meet at Sonny's at ten. Aldo had arrived five minutes early, as was his habit, but neither of his friends were there. He waited until ten fifteen, then tried to call them. He called Enzo first and had no luck. He called Francesco next.

"Yeah?"

"Where are you?"

"Shit. Sorry, man. I forgot."

"You heard anything from Enzo this morning?"

Francesco paused.

"Dude?"

"Nah," he said. "Nothing. Why?"

"He's never late if it's to do with the band. He wants to buy a new capo for his Strat. He's been going on about it all week. I was going to get some new skins."

"So maybe he forgot?"

"Seriously? When's the last time he forgot something like that? We got the contest next week, too. It's all he's been talking about."

"I guess."

Aldo waved goodbye to the guys on the counter and went back outside. "You still there?"

Franny said that he was.

"I'm going to drive over to his place. Maybe he slept in. I'll pick you up on the way through."

ALDO DIVERTED to Francesco's place and tapped the horn. Francesco came outside, zipping up his coat and stepping through a drift of snow that had blown up against the door.

"I tried calling again," Aldo told him as he dropped into the passenger seat. "Still nothing."

Franny shrugged. "Probably lost his phone or something."

"Seriously? You know what he's like. He never loses his phone. He never loses anything."

"I don't know, then," Francesco said irritably.

Aldo looked over at his friend. It was not unusual for him to be irascible, especially in the mornings, but there was an edge to his attitude today that was different. He put it to one side; there was not much point in trying to interpret the vicissitudes of Francesco's moods.

Aldo put the car into drive and pulled away.

Franny put his feet on the dash.

"Come on, man," Aldo said. "I asked you not to do that."

"Whatever." He lowered his legs. There was a moment of uncomfortable silence before Francesco spoke again. "What did you think of that van Enzo bought?"

"Pretty good for five hundred bucks."

"You think? I thought it was a piece of shit."

Aldo found his patience sorely depleted. "What's eating you this morning?"

Franny looked away, gazing out of the window. Aldo noticed that his hands were trembling, and that he had bitten the nails down to the quick. Francesco had his own problems with his mental health, and his home life was difficult, but he seemed worse today than usual. He reminded himself that, compared to his friend, he had it pretty good; he would try to bear that in mind and cut him some slack.

ALDO TURNED onto Enzo's street and hit the brakes. There was a marked police car outside the house and an unmarked Crown Vic of the sort used by detectives was parked next to it.

"What the fuck?"

He pulled over and parked at the side of the road.

He switched off the engine and turned to Francesco. "What's going on?"

The colour had drained out of Francesco's face. "I have no idea."

Aldo opened the door and stepped out, his feet sliding over the icy sidewalk. He waited for Franny to join him and then led the way along the street until they were next to the sloped drive. The door to the house was open, and Aldo could see activity inside. He saw a flash of light, perhaps from a camera, and a man crouching down inside the door as he looked at something on the floor. Aldo was still staring when the door of the Crown Vic opened and a man stepped out. Aldo recognised him: it was Detective Nicol, the officer who came to Coach Fernández's after-school club.

Nicol saw the two of them and came over. "You're from the school, right? You play in the band with Enzo?"

"That's right," Aldo said. "Can I ask what's happened here?"

"There's been a shooting."

Aldo's mouth fell open. "Seriously?"

The detective nodded. "Yesterday afternoon. A man was killed just outside the front door."

"Shit," Aldo said. "Our friend lives here—Enzo Pizzolato."

"That's right. Do you know where Enzo and his mom are now?"

"No," Aldo said. "I haven't seen him since school yesterday."

The detective turned to Francesco. "What about you, son? What's your name again?"

"Francesco di Cello."

"That's right," Nicol said. "Franny. You seen Enzo?"

"No. Same as him—last time I saw him was yesterday."

"You sure about that?"

Anger flickered across Francesco's face. Aldo knew that Franny did not like to be doubted, and he always made it very clear how much he hated the police. Aldo got ready to step in and defuse an argument.

"I'm sure," Francesco said.

"So where have they gone?"

"Isn't that your job to find out?" Franny said.

Nicol looked as if he was going to chide him for his attitude, but he gave a shallow nod of his head and reached into his breast pocket. He took out two business cards. "We're worried about Mrs. Pizzolato and Enzo. If you happen to find out where they are, you need to give me a call, okay?"

He gave one card each to Aldo and Francesco. "Will you do that for me?"

"Sure," Aldo said.

"Franny?"

"Yeah," he said, turning and walking away.

The detective patted Aldo on the shoulder. "Good man."

ALDO GOT BACK into the car and waited for Franny to join him. He slammed the door and glared in the mirror as Nicol made his way into the house.

"What was *that*, man?" Aldo said.

"What?"

"The way you spoke to him."

Franny snorted. "Like he gives a shit about Enzo."

"He's not so bad. Not one of the worst, anyway."

"Whoa," Franny said sneeringly. "'Not one of the worst'? Like that's high praise."

Aldo started the engine. "You sure you're okay?"

"It's nothing."

"You're not worried about Enzo?"

"Of course I am. I just got other shit on my mind, too. Family shit."

There was no point in trying to help; Franny rarely spoke about the trouble he had at home, and Aldo had long since decided that he would be ready to listen if his friend wanted to talk, but that he wouldn't pry. He looked back in the mirror as they pulled away. Nicol was leaning against the side of his car with his phone to his ear. Aldo tried to think about where Enzo might have gone, and how he could reach him. It was out of character for his friend to go off the grid like this, and he was worried.

39

Tanner hung up the phone and stared at it; then he reached under the counter and took out the double-barrelled shotgun. He checked both chambers to satisfy himself they contained shells, then set it across his lap as he rested on the tall stool and stared at the door. What was he doing? Should he have just kept Milton's visit to himself? He swallowed on a dry throat. He knew that he had been caught in an impossible situation: Milton might come after him if he found out that he had been betrayed, but Control would do the same if she discovered that Tanner had been holding back on her. It was impossible, but it didn't make the situation easier to deal with.

He looked at the clock over the counter. It was half eleven. Mollie had said that she would come by at four. He would have liked to talk the whole situation through with her, but he knew that wasn't something that he could do. She had no idea of the kind of work that he had facilitated while he had worked for the Group, and it wasn't something that he wanted to discuss now—or, he realised with a grim shake of his head, ever. Some things were best left consigned to the past.

The thought of his daughter prompted him to glance across the office to the opposite wall and the cream-coloured bathroom door. He groaned. She had reinstalled the pneumatic hinge. She had fixed it a while back after the door had slammed closed on a disabled customer, adjusting it so that the rate of closure was slowed over the last inch or so. But that had also meant that Tanner had to give it a slight extra tug to open it, which, with his prosthetic leg, had made it a little more awkward. He had taken the hinge off completely last week, but now she had put it back up again.

He took the phone again and dialled Mollie's number.

"Hey, Dad."

"You put the spring back on the bathroom door."

"You know why—"

"For one customer. And he never came back."

"He might. Or someone else might come in who might appreciate it."

"I told you—I don't like it."

"I know you did, Dad. And I told you we have to think about our customers who are less able."

"*I'm* less able!" he protested. "Fine—it doesn't slam on people with walkers. Great. But now it's harder to open for people like me with only one good leg."

She sighed in a manner that suggested that she wasn't entirely convinced. "I'll take a look at it. Maybe there's an adjustment we can make. I'll be over later."

"It won't be on the door when you get here."

"Dad!"

"Kidding."

"Sure you are. Look—I'm at work."

"It's Saturday."

"I'm working on my book. Did you call just to tell me about the hinge?"

"No. I need a favour."

"Sure."

"It's for John, actually. He wanted to know if you could ask around about a police officer."

"Why?"

"He didn't say. Can you?"

"I guess. What's his name?"

"Nicol—works on outreach with kids who might end up in the gangs."

"What does John want to know about him?"

"Whether he's a good guy or not. Whether he's trustworthy."

"Why would he want to know that?"

He paused for just long enough to unnerve her.

"What?" she asked. "What happened? He's not getting involved with those two clowns, is he?"

"He called me a moment ago. The kid he was trying to help seems like he's in pretty deep. John's looking after him —he's trying to find a policeman he can be sure is above board."

"Patrick O'Connor's bad news, Dad."

"I know that—you said. And the whole thing's beginning to make me nervous. Do me a favour, sweetheart; make sure you've got that snub-nosed in your purse, okay?"

Now it was Mollie's turn to pause, unsure whether her father was telling her the entire story. "Is there anything else I need to know?"

"No," he said. "There's nothing, I promise. I just want you to be careful. Can you check Nicol out?"

"I'll see what I can find."

"And can you stop by the store on the way? Grab me a pack of Slim Jims and a carton of Camels?"

"You should quit those damn things," she said.

"I know. But you ever try having a black coffee without a cigarette? Sacrilege."

She laughed. "You're awful."

"I know. See you later."

TANNER WORKED his way through a backlog of paperwork for the rest of the day. It was four o'clock when he decided that he needed a break. He looked over at the hinge on the bathroom door and berated himself for forgetting to take care of it. Damned if it was staying up there. He fished through his jacket pocket for his multitool.

The doorbell rang.

Tanner looked at the door as it swung open. He had forgotten to lock it. He looked back at the counter, five feet away, where he had left the shotgun. It was out of reach.

The man who stepped through the door was wearing jeans and a black leather jacket. He was also wearing thin nitrile gloves, the sort that paramedics or crime scene investigators wore, together with overshoes made of the same material and a plastic hairnet. He reached into his jacket pocket and withdrew a suppressed Glock pistol.

Tanner's first thought was that he was from the Group, but that didn't make sense. Why would an agent pull a weapon on him? Who was he? A crook? He was too well dressed to be a junkie.

"Hey," Tanner said. "Relax. There's no need for that." He took a step toward the counter.

The man waved the pistol to hold him in place. "Don't be daft."

"You want what's in the till? There's not much, but you can take it."

"I don't want money," the man said.

"All right. What do you want?"

The man spoke with a thick Irish brogue. "A chat. I got some questions about a friend of yours. You and I need to have a little talk."

40

Mollie had been writing about the golden age of crime in Kansas City. It had been known as the Paris of the Plains during the years of Prohibition; the rules had largely been ignored, with well-stocked saloons and jazz joints on Eighteenth and Vine that welcomed musicians, who would go on to be famous, including Count Basie, Julia Lee, Charlie "Bird" Parker and Bennie Moten. The city had been ruled by Tom Pendergast back then, his control exerted by bribes, election fraud and corrupt law enforcement. She had been digging into the relationship between Boss Tom and Harry S. Truman, the future president who had launched his career in KC. She had found enough material for a whole chapter and had just about finished it.

Remembering her conversation with her father from earlier, she pushed away from her desk and went to Sarah Toyoshiba's office. Sarah worked the crime desk and had done so for over twenty years. She had an encyclopaedic knowledge of the city's criminals and the police who tried to catch them. Toyoshiba was working at her PC, a pencil shoved through her bun of thick dark hair. She was in her fifties now and had always been generous with her experience. Mollie had sent her an email when she was looking for a job, and Sarah had invited her into the newsroom for a tour; a week later, she had arranged a position for her as an intern, and her career had followed.

Sarah had the usual classical music playing quietly from a small Bluetooth speaker that sat on the desk, and there was a mug of peppermint tea next to the mouse. She had decorated the office with pictures of her kids and framed certificates and citations from her long career. There was a row of framed front pages showing some of the numerous stories that she had broken. Mollie had always found Sarah's stature within the local community to be a little daunting, but she wore it lightly and had never been anything other than completely accommodating when junior members of staff needed help.

Mollie rapped her knuckles against the frame of the door.

Sarah looked up and smiled. "Afternoon."

"Can I have a word?"

"Sure—come in."

Mollie did, and sat down in the seat that faced the desk.

"What are you doing in on a Saturday?"

"Writing my book," Mollie said.

"And?"

"It's going well."

Sarah had offered to provide a foreword, and, to that end, she had already read through the first half dozen chapters. Her praise had been the motivation that Mollie needed to press on when she was struggling through a sticky patch.

"You want to talk to me about it?"

"Actually, no," Mollie said. "I'm looking for information

on a couple of people. One's a police officer and another's a criminal."

"Intriguing. Who's first?"

"Patrick O'Connor."

"The money launderer—allegedly, of course. What do you want to know?"

"I just wondered if you could give me a little background."

"Can I ask what for?"

"My dad's asking. A friend of his got into an altercation with O'Connor and his brother. He was at Jack Kelly's auction house, and there was an argument about a vehicle that was sold. O'Connor was pushing around the kid who bought it, and the friend got involved."

"That might not have been the smartest move," Sarah said. "O'Connor's connected. Last I heard, he was laundering money for Bobby Whitesox. I spoke to him once outside court. His brother, Kenny, was arrested for punching an off-duty cop in the mall, and Patrick was there as a witness. He might not be as nasty as his brother, but he's clever."

"What's the brother like?"

"He's the muscle. The rumour is that he was in the Irish independence movement before he came to KC."

"The IRA?"

"He's not that old. One of the offshoots that the diehards set up. He's not someone I'd want to piss off, let's put it that way—neither of them are."

"That's pretty much what I thought," Mollie said.

Sarah sipped her tea. "And the cop?"

"Detective Nicol. He works with the kids in the anti-gang unit."

She smiled. "David Nicol. I've known him since he was a

rookie. He's good people. Why'd you want to know about him?"

"It concerns the kid who got into the argument with O'Connor. They're worried that they'll have to go to the cops, and they want to find one they can trust. I think Nicol volunteers at the kid's school. They figured he might be a good option."

"I would say so," she said. "I haven't seen him for a couple of years, but he was always a straight shooter. There are plenty of bad apples, but I wouldn't have said he was one of them."

Mollie stood.

"Anything else?" Sarah asked her.

"That's all," she said. "Thanks."

"Tell your dad and his friend to be careful with the O'Connors. Guys like that? They don't mess around."

MOLLIE WENT BACK to her desk and took her phone out of her bag. She called her father's cell.

It rang.

She checked her watch. Just before five. No reason why he wouldn't answer.

It kept ringing.

She frowned. He sometimes left the cellphone somewhere where he couldn't get to it. It was irritating, but not unusual.

She ended the call and tried the office landline. She knew how her father's mind worked: anyone calling that number was calling about business, and he *hated* the prospect of missing out on the chance of new work.

The call rang and rang.

He wouldn't have gone out. It was a Saturday.

He was probably just in the bathroom.

But… no. She knew it, with a daughter's intuition: something was wrong.

She had been concerned about what John Smith had been asking, and Sarah had just confirmed it: getting mixed up with a lowlife like O'Connor was a bad, bad idea. She wondered if Smith and her father had told her everything. What if they were holding something back? What if they were planning something together? Her father knew that she worried about him, and he wouldn't have wanted that. He wouldn't have told her if they were planning something dangerous.

She remembered: her father had asked her about her little .38. Why had he done that? What was he concerned about?

She was frightened.

She ended the call, dropped the phone into her bag, and grabbed her jacket. It was ten miles from McGee Street to the business. Her car was in the shop after the fender bender last week, but she would grab a taxi outside and head across town now.

41

The man took Tanner down to the office basement and used a roll of duct tape to secure him to an old wooden chair that was kept down there.

"What do you want?"

"Just a little chat," the man said.

"Fine. You don't have to tie me up." He nodded at the man's gun. "And you don't need that."

The man smiled, but didn't reply. He tilted his head slightly as if assessing Tanner. There was a second chair against the bare brick wall. The man pulled it over and sat down, one leg crossed over the other. He withdrew what looked to Tanner like a stick, the size of a pencil, and began to chew on it.

"Liquorice root," he said. "I used to smoke these little Cuban cigars. They were lovely—great taste, not too heavy —but you can't get them anymore. I thought that was a sign. Time to quit. Then I found these. I mean, it's not the same, couldn't be, but they're not too shabby as a substitute. I'd offer you one, but I wouldn't want to encourage bad habits."

The man spoke with a thick Irish accent. Was this Patrick O'Connor? He tried to recall the photograph that Milton had shown him. Patrick was bald and this man was not. His brother, then? It had to be one of them.

"You'll be wondering what I want with you," he said. "Coming in here like this, putting a shooter in your face."

Tanner was sweating. He felt a drop roll into his eye and blinked it away. Another rolled down past his nose and fell into his mouth.

"Don't you think it's weird?" He sucked on the stick. "Don't answer that—it's rhetorical. But it *is* weird, right? You English and me Irish, each finding ourselves in a place like this. Kansas City. Not the sort of place you'd expect to find two blokes like us. My name's Kenny, by the way. You're Tanner—right?"

"I know who you are."

"Is that right?"

"What do you want?"

Kenny ignored the question. "You know what's weirder? There's this bloke—six feet tall, scar on his face, blue eyes. I met him at the auction, and he went and put his nose in my business. The crazy thing, though, given all this context, is that *he's* English, too. Two English blokes and two Irish lads, if you count my brother. What are the odds? Four blokes like us in a place like this, our business all getting tangled up together. That's why I'm here. That's what I want to chat with you about. Your pal. I want you to tell me who he is and where I can find him."

"I don't know who you're talking about."

"Really?"

"I don't know anyone from England here."

"Bollocks."

"I don't."

"It's not what Jack said."

"What?"

"Jack Kelly. I spoke to him earlier. He took a little warming up, but he told me everything in the end. Told me that you know the bloke. You took him to the auction."

"Jack's wrong. I don't know who you mean."

Kenny got up and shook his head. "Nah," he said. "Don't believe you. Like I said, Jack was reluctant to speak at first, but I got to work on him, and he spilled everything. I didn't mind him messing me around. I didn't really give a shit. I was going to have fun with him either way. Same goes for you. Shall we try again?"

The man reached into his pocket and took out a slim leather package. It was around twenty centimetres long and ten centimetres wide and held together by two leather laces. Kenny put the package on the table, untied the laces and opened it. He moved in front of it before Tanner could see what was inside.

"What's his name, Tanner?"

"I don't know anyone from England here."

He sucked on his teeth. "Shame. I thought you might say that, but it's still a shame. Jack told me you were in the military back home. That right?"

"Yes."

"Do any tours in Ireland?"

"Yes."

"I was in the Irish Republican Army. Younger than you, though, else maybe our paths would've crossed. I made something of a reputation for myself. The lads would bring people who they thought might be working for the other side—for *your* side. They'd deny it, of course; they all knew what happened to collaborators. But I'd always get through to them in the end. They'd be singing like canaries. Anyway, it got a little hot for me over there, so I came to join my brother. I work for him—Patrick."

"I've heard the name."

"Course you have. He's going places. I do little bits and pieces for him now and again. He'll get some toe-rag taking liberties, thinking they can take advantage of his good nature, and he'll ask me to pay them a visit and set them straight. Kind of what this is about. It's your friend, see—*he's* taking liberties, all right. Big bleeding liberties, big fucking liberties like you wouldn't believe."

"I told you—"

"Yeah, you don't know him. Course. But Jack Kelly says different. And, the thing is, the state he was in when he told me, there's no way it was a lie. That's how it usually is. You can fib about things all you like when there's nothing on the line, but when you see how dangerous that is, when you're left in no doubt that telling porkies is going to get you killed, when the bloke you're talking to has your nuts in a vice, so to speak, that's when the truth comes out. Jack was like that. Very accommodating in the end. Very forthright."

"I don't know what you're—"

Kenny turned around quickly, backhanding Tanner without warning. The blow caught him flush in the nose, snapping the bone. Streams of blood and mucus ran from his nostrils.

"I'm what you'd call a man of uncommon interests. Some people go in for art or music. Others like to work with their hands. Others like sport. We all have one thing, right? That one special thing that makes us complete. And if we really love it, if we stick with it, maybe we become good at it, and then it's that much more rewarding. That's what life is really all about, isn't it? The journey, not the destination." He snorted. "Sorry. That sounded a little bit *X Factor*, didn't it?"

"So what?" Tanner said, his voice rendered nasal by his damaged nose.

Kenny leaned in a little closer. "I've never really found a traditional hobby. I tried things that I was supposed to do—like behaving myself, minding my Ps and Qs—and it turns out they weren't really for me. So I tried things I *wasn't* supposed to do—like setting fire to cars and drowning bags of puppies—and it turns out that's more the kind of thing I'm cut out for. This, too—" He took Tanner's broken nose and waggled it left and right. "Turns out I'm *mustard* at this."

Tanner yelled out from the sudden spark of pain.

"Come on," Kenny said. "That was nothing. We're just getting started. Let me give you a little something to loosen that tongue."

He went back to the table. Tanner could see inside the package now. He saw a syringe and two glass ampoules. He took one of the ampoules between his thumb and forefinger and held it up. "Pentobarbital. You know what it is?"

Tanner looked away, ducking his head so that the blood from his nose didn't run into his mouth.

"It's a barbiturate," Kenneth said. "Lowers inhibitions when you use it in small doses. It'll kill you in bigger doses, though. Vets use it to euthanise pets. Some states use it to off prisoners. They use it for that here, in Missouri."

"Maybe you'll get some of it yourself," Tanner mumbled through the pain.

"Maybe." Kenny switched the ampoule to his left hand and picked up the syringe in his right. He slid the needle through the rubber top and pulled back on the plunger, filling the barrel with liquid. "You're lucky. I could take my time with Jack. Probably took too long. Patrick called me before I came in here. Wants to find your friend pronto, so I'm going to have to cut to the chase. You could tell me something now, but there's no way I would be able to be sure if it was the truth or some flannel to try to get yourself off the hook. I shoot you up with this, though? You won't be able to lie. That's the thing with it—I won't be able to shut you up."

Tanner struggled, but his wrists and ankles were secured tightly to the arms and legs of the chair. Kenny held him down with his left hand and jabbed the needle into his neck. He felt a sensation of iciness as the liquid passed into his blood. He felt it in his shoulder, in his arm, then down his back. There was nothing that he could do.

He thought of Mollie and prayed that she wouldn't come in while the man was still here. She was everything to him since his wife had died. He didn't care about himself. He didn't matter. He had lived his life. He had hoped for another twenty or thirty years, time that he could spend with her, but he had done things during his career that meant that perhaps this was deserved. Not *done* them, as such, but enabled men like John Milton to do them. The assets might have pulled the trigger, but he had blood on his hands, just the same.

He would have to live with that. He had no choice.

But if anything happened to Mollie...

He felt an urge to chuckle. He knew it was the drug, but, even as he recognised that fact, the last wisps of his resolve were dispersed. It felt as if he had been drinking for hours. He chuckled again and then laughed harder. He giggled. He felt the urge to speak.

The man leaned over him. Tanner had forgotten his

name.

"Let's try again," the man said. "Your friend—who is he, and where can I find him?"

42

J ulio Fernández beamed from ear to ear while Milton smiled back politely. He had spent long enough in America to know how much gun owners loved their weapons. It was a peculiar facet of the national character, and one that was particularly jarring to a European, although Milton had an understanding of it given his own history. But it still surprised him to see Fernández express pride at the contents of a locker.

Fernández had explained that the large garage had once been used to repair the vehicles that were used at the quarry. Now the majority of the space was taken up by storage shelves, each constructed from metal framing and about five feet tall, each equipped with four or five shelves. The shelves bore identical white plastic tubs.

"What's in the boxes?" Milton asked.

"My sister uses them," Fernández said. "She runs a second-hand book business. She keeps her stock here."

Fernández turned his attention back to the locker. He had opened the electronic lock with a five-digit code and then opened the doors wide. "I bought this right after I got out of the Rangers," he said. "Figured I'd fill it then get another. Then I started spending all of my time working with the kids, and I didn't get many opportunities for hunting or target shooting. So it's just the six weapons in there, for now at least. But they're all beautiful pieces of engineering. Go on—help yourself. Take them out and have a look."

Milton reached into the rack and withdrew the first of two shotguns.

"Twenty-gauge Beretta Orvis Uplander," Fernández said proudly. "English grip, ejectors, custom-carved walnut stock. With most shotguns, there's an element of crossing your fingers and hoping for the best. Not with this. She's accurate out to a hundred feet and weighs six pounds, which is completely nuts. I got a ring-necked pheasant with her last year. She was coming out of the tree line and I picked her off from seventy-five feet away."

Milton's eye was drawn to one of the rifles. "Is that what I think it is?"

Fernández grinned. "What do you think it is?"

"A Mark II?"

Fernández nodded.

"May I?"

Fernández took it down and Milton swapped the shotgun for it. The rifle was semi-automatic and, with a twenty-inch match-grade barrel, was engineered to be accurate on targets that were a decent distance downrange.

"Not official issue, of course," Fernández said, "so technically she's an SR-25, but she's modded the right way. She's got the Picatinny rail, and the pouch on the shelf underneath her is for the QD sound suppressor. Good out to a thousand metres. Picked her up a few months after I rostered out. Nostalgia, I guess."

Milton shouldered the pristine rifle and squinted down to the iron sight. "You were a sniper?"

"I did lots of things. Now, though?" He patted his rotund belly. "Now I just look like I ate several things." He chuckled. "What about you?"

"What *about* me?"

"I see the way you move, the way you read a room. You know your firearms. And Tanner told me what happened at the auction house. He said you put down the two guys who were bothering Enzo. I'm guessing your time in the service wasn't spent riding a desk."

"No," Milton said. "That wasn't me."

"Action?"

"A lot of it."

"You gonna tell me where?"

Milton sighed. This wasn't really a conversation that he wanted to have, yet he already liked Fernández and didn't want to lie to him. "All the usual places," he conceded. "I worked out in Afghanistan and Iraq, and before that I did tours of Northern Ireland before that all calmed down. There were other jobs in between."

"You clocked up the miles, then?"

"I did." Milton ran his fingertips over the rifle's breech and changed the subject. "I haven't used one of these in a long time."

"And hopefully we won't have to. I don't take her out much. I don't think my sister likes me recalling the bad old days. But the shotguns get used whenever I get the chance."

Milton turned his attention back to the locker. Hanging from the last peg was a crossbow pistol. It was all black, with a handgrip that reminded Milton of a target shooter's gun. There was a small lever-arm on the top that cranked the bow back and slotted a new bolt from a side cartridge.

Milton pointed to it. "Could I take a look at that?"

Fernández reached up, took it down for him, and passed it over. "The bolts are on the shelf. I try not to fool around with it too much—they have a tendency to snap down the middle if they hit anything too solid, like a brick wall. But it's no toy—you fire one of those bolts at a man and it'll go clean through him up to about twenty yards. After that, it'll just kill him stone dead."

Milton examined the small ammunition box that was fitted to the top of the bow. It had a rotating chamber that was preloaded with five bolts. "Clever," he said. He put it back on the rack.

The shelf beneath the crossbow bore a long, thin lockbox that had been printed with *EXPLOSIVES: CAUTION*. Fernández saw that it had snagged Milton's attention.

"Sticks of dynamite and some C-4. Some souvenirs from when the family worked the quarry. We use them as tree-stump removers now."

Milton's phone rang. He checked the number and saw that it was Tanner. He indicated to Fernández that he needed to take the call, then answered.

"Tanner?"

"Hello, John."

It wasn't Tanner. "Who's this?"

"My name's Kenny. We met at the auction." The man had a strong Irish accent. "You remember me, don't you?"

"Where's Tanner?"

"He can't speak right now."

Milton took a quarter turn away from Fernández and lowered his voice. "What do you want?"

"You have something that doesn't belong to you."

"And what's that?"

"A black van with a single white panel on the driver's side. The piece of shit that the kid bought at the auction."

"What about it?"

"I need you to bring it to me."

Fernández was watching Milton with concern on his face.

"Why would I do that?"

"Because if you don't, I'm going to murder your friend. And when I've done that, I'm going to find where you're hiding, and then it'll be the same for you, the kid, his mother, Uncle Tom Cobley and anyone else I think might have been stupid enough to help him."

"How do I know you're not bluffing?"

"Check your messages."

The phone buzzed. Milton took it away from his ear and looked at the screen. He had been sent a message from Tanner's phone. He opened it and found that a picture was included. Tanner was sitting down and staring into the lens of the camera. His nose was bloodied and at an unnatural angle. His eyes had a glazed, unfocused aspect. It looked as if he had been drugged.

"I'm not bluffing."

"Okay," Milton said. "Fine. Where are you?"

"There's an old apartment block on Lister and East Twenty-Fourth. No one lives there now. Bring the van. Park it outside and come up to the third floor. You give me the keys, and I'll let you have your friend. And no cops. Don't give me any reason to think that you're fucking with me— this goes arseways and your mate gets a bullet between the eyes."

"When?"

"Tonight. I'll be there at nine and you'd better be, too. Don't be a gimp, John. Don't mess me about."

The line went dead.

"What is it?" Fernández said.

Milton realised that he had been clutching the phone. He put it in his pocket and opened his fingers, stretching them out.

"Tanner?"

"He's in trouble," Milton said. "Someone's got to him."

"Shit," Fernández said.

"They want me to take them the van."

"Where?"

"Lister and East Twenty-Fourth—you know it?"

Fernández nodded. "Over by Ingleside? That's a bad part of town. Strange place to want to meet."

"It'll be a trap," he said, "but I don't really have a choice."

The coach reached for the shotgun. "So we do it together."

Milton reached up and nudged Fernández's hand back from the shelf. "No, we don't. One of us has to stay here and keep an eye on Connie and Enzo. And we have no idea what I'm walking into. I'll be able to get in and out alone more easily than if there are two of us. They might have numbers there—two of us wouldn't make much of a difference. It's not worth it."

"Then we should call the police." He nodded back to the house. "I know she's worried about ICE getting involved, but this is different."

Milton shook his head. "They see police coming and they'll kill him."

Fernández cursed and leaned against the wall. "There's no other way?"

"I can't see one where Tanner doesn't get killed. They have leverage, but so do we. They want the van, but they can't have it yet—they'll just kill me, then him, and take it.

But I can meet, and we can set up an exchange that we can control. Somewhere public."

Fernández clucked his tongue against his teeth. "I don't know. That doesn't sound like a great idea."

"Got a better one?"

He shrugged. "I'm fresh out." He stood straight and gestured to the locker. "At least take some protection."

"The guns are all registered to you?"

"Registered and insured."

"So, no—I can't. We don't want anything tied back to you in case something goes wrong and I have to use them." He took out the Peacemaker that he had taken from the man at the Pizzolato house. "You got any ammunition for this?"

"What do you need—.357s? I got a Desert Eagle that uses them. Pretty sure I got a box of fifty."

He took out a white and blue cardboard box and withdrew a plastic tray. Fifty bright brass shells were arranged on the tray in ten neat rows that were each five deep. Milton picked out one of the rounds and held it up for an examination.

"One-hundred-and-fifty-eight-grain semi-jacketed soft points," the coach said. "Okay?"

Milton took a handful of them and dropped them into his pocket.

"Anything else?" Fernández said.

"Binoculars?"

"Sure," he said.

"Anything with a night filter?"

Fernández went over to a workbench and returned with a Boblov night-vision binocular. Milton picked it up. It was more like a monocular device, with the feed displayed on a digital screen. It allowed surroundings to be viewed in low light and even complete darkness by way of an infrared sensor.

"We had a problem with kids coming onto the property to race bikes at night," he explained.

"Perfect," Milton said. "And I'm going to need a vehicle to get into town."

Fernández walked over to a wooden board that had been fixed to the wall. A series of hooks had been screwed into the board, and each hook—neatly labelled—held a key on a key ring. Fernández found the key that he wanted, unhooked it and tossed it over.

"Take the old Chevy out the front of the house. Stick shift. Second gear sticks a little, but otherwise she's in good working order for a twenty-eight-year-old truck."

"Thank you."

"When are you going?"

"Now. I'd prefer to get there early and scout it out."

"What should I tell Connie?"

"Say I've gone into town. No sense in worrying her yet. If I don't come back, you'll have to be honest with her. At that point, they'll have to go to the police. But hopefully it doesn't come to that."

43

Kenny O'Connor ended the call. He felt as if he had made excellent progress. He looked down at the barely conscious man taped to the chair. The pentobarbital had loosened his tongue enough for him to spill the information that Patrick needed. He reached down and cupped Tanner's chin in his hand. His head lolled, his face slack and his eyes glassy and lifeless. "You're banjaxed, mate," he said. "It'll be over soon. And then I'll put you and your mate out of your misery."

He swiped through his phone's contacts for his brother's number and placed the call.

"It's me."

"Where are you?" Patrick said.

"Still with the guy."

"And?"

"And I've made good progress, thank you very much. The man we're after is called Milton. John Milton. Used to be in the military, and then he worked for the government."

"Where is he?"

"Somewhere near Louisburg."

"'Somewhere'?"

"It doesn't matter. I called him and had a chat, like you said. He's going to come out to Ingleside."

"When?"

"I told him to be there at nine."

"What about Kelly?"

"I took him over there before I came here. It's all ready."

"Well done, Kenny," Patrick said. "Very good work."

Kenny smiled; his brother's praise was as rare as hen's teeth.

"I'll finish off here and then head over," Kenny said.

"I'll call Bird and Nicol—they can help."

"Should be easy enough."

"Is he going to bring the van?"

"I told him to. Won't matter if he doesn't. I'll find out where it is, and then I'll go and get it."

"Be careful, Kenny."

"Don't be soft. There'll be three of us."

"Maybe," he said, "but he knows how to handle himself."

Kenny reached into his pocket and took out a second ampoule. "It'll be like falling off a log."

He ended the call and put the phone down on the table. The ampoule contained Pavulon, and Kenny used it to fill the syringe for a second time, loading the barrel with five millilitres of the liquid.

Kenny crouched down next to Tanner. "I'm going to have to put you to sleep now."

Tanner let out a low moan, but was too weak to resist. Kenny used his left hand to anchor Tanner's head and jabbed him in the neck. He depressed the plunger. He let go and Tanner's head slumped down, his chin resting against his sternum.

"Night-night."

Kenny glanced around the basement until he was confident that he had not left any evidence that he had been here. He had been wearing the gloves, overshoes and hair net for the entirety of the time that he had been inside the premises, and, even then, he had been careful with what he had touched. He had done this before and knew that the precautions he had taken would be enough. The police department in the city was underfunded. They might get someone from the regional crime lab to come and have a look, but it wouldn't make much difference. They wouldn't find anything that would tie him to what had happened to the unfortunate Tanner.

He heard the tread on the stair, but by the time he turned around, it was already too late. The man who was watching from the doorway was huge; Kenny guessed that he must have been six four and two hundred and fifty pounds. He was tanned, as if he had only recently arrived in the city from abroad, but the blond hair and blue eyes looked Scandinavian. The man was holding a suppressed pistol in his right hand. The weapon was aimed at his chest.

"Hands," the man said. "Nice and easy, please."

Kenny raised his hands. The man's voice was sonorous, with a heavy accent. Kenny tried to place it. Danish? Norwegian? It was hard to say. The confident way in which he handled the pistol suggested he had used it before.

"Who the fuck are you?"

The big man considered the situation for a moment. Kenny felt the bump of the Glock against his back where he had pressed it into the waistband of his trousers.

"What's your name?"

"Susan," Kenny said. "What's yours?"

The man didn't respond as Kenny had expected. There

was no reaction to his insolence and no further questions. Kenny saw the flash from the muzzle but was dead before he could hear the sound of the shot.

Björn Thorsson looked down at the dead man. The bullet had struck him just above his right eye, drilling a neat little hole through his skull through which a mixture of blood and ichor was now leaking. There would be a bigger exit wound at the back of his head; the wall behind where he had been standing was marked with a crimson spray.

Björn did not recognise him. It wasn't Milton; he was familiar with his predecessor as Number One after meeting him in Colombia and then studying his details on the flight. There had been nothing in the file that Control had delivered to suggest that Tanner was under any threat, either. What had happened here was a mystery, at least for now. Björn suspected that he was going to have to unravel it before he was able to achieve what he had been sent here to do.

He took out a phone-sized device from his inside pocket. It had been developed by Group Six and supplied to him by the quartermaster in Missouri. It was made of black plastic and had a three-inch opaque panel on the front and a camera on the back. Björn took a photograph of the dead man's face, then took his right hand and removed the glove that he had been wearing. He held the man's index finger against the front panel. The device was equipped with a capacitive fingerprint sensor, and it captured the whorls and loops of the print. Björn worked through all four fingers and then the man's thumb, checking that the prints and photographs had been safely recorded. He replaced the device in his pocket.

He collected the brass cartridge case from the single bullet that he had fired, put it in his pocket, and then frisked the man quickly and efficiently. He found a wallet inside his jacket pocket and flipped it open: there was a Missouri driver's licence in the name of Kenneth O'Connor with the man's photograph. There were credit cards in the same name and several hundred dollars in notes. Björn continued to search the body. There was a Beretta pushed into his waistband and a magazine with additional 9mm rounds. He found a set of car keys in the right trouser pocket. He found a phone, too, but, when he touched the screen, it was locked. It had a scanner on the back, and Björn took the dead man's hand and held his index finger against it; the phone blinked to life. He didn't have time to investigate the contents now, so he quickly tapped through to the settings and disabled the automatic lock.

Björn replaced the glove on the man's hand and went to check on Tanner. He was breathing, but each inhalation and exhalation was weak. He gave him a gentle shake. "Tanner," he said. Nothing. He took out his flick knife and used the tip to slice the duct tape away from his wrists and ankles. He shook him again, a little harder this time. "Tanner, wake up."

Still nothing.

There was a syringe on the table and, next to it, two

small bottles. Björn picked up the first bottle. It was empty. He turned it so that he could read the label: Trapanal. He replaced the first bottle and picked up the second: Pavulon. He had an idea what the first bottle might have been used for, but he needed to be sure.

He took out his phone and called a London number.

"Global Logistics. How can I direct your call?"

"I'd like to speak to a chemist on the ninth floor, please."

"Who shall I say is calling?"

"It's Eiður Guðjohnsen from the fifteenth floor."

"Please hold."

Global Logistics was the legend under which Group Fifteen did its business. It was a real, operational concern, offering planning, management, implementation and monitoring of the physical flow of goods for client corporations all around the world. It sent out real representatives who secured real contracts and then performed those contracts. It also dispatched operators who travelled under the cloak of legitimacy in order to carry out the real purpose of the organisation: conducting the business of the state where diplomacy had failed.

There was a pause as the call was rerouted and encrypted.

"This is Group Nine," a woman's voice said.

Group Nine was responsible for scientific support. A series of subject matter experts—physicists, chemists, biologists, computer scientists—were on hand to answer questions posed during operational planning and in-field execution.

"I need a check on two chemicals," he said.

"Go ahead."

"Trapanal and Pavulon."

"Trapanal is sodium thiopental. It's a rapid-onset short-acting barbiturate."

"And it does what?"

"It's an anaesthetic. What's your context?"

"An interrogation."

"Makes sense. It lowers inhibitions."

Björn picked up the second bottle. "And the Pavulon?"

"Pancuronium bromide. It's a muscle relaxant. Used during euthanasia procedures—it's one of the three drugs used during lethal injections in the United States."

Björn could deduce what had happened easily enough. Kenneth O'Connor had jumped Tanner and secured him to the chair. He had interrogated him—the bloody nose was suggestive—and Tanner had resisted. O'Connor had shot him full of barbiturates in an attempt to loosen his tongue. The muscle relaxant would have been used to murder him. Björn wondered if he had arrived in time to prevent that from happening.

The analyst spoke again. "Do you need anything else, Agent?"

"I'm with a man. He's unresponsive. It looks like both drugs have been administered."

"How much has your subject been given?"

He picked up the bottles and read off the labels. "Ten cc of each."

"That's a high dose."

"What do I do?"

"Is he breathing?"

"Shallow."

"The Pavulon will depress his respiratory function. He'll need medical treatment. Might need positive-pressure oxygen, maybe even ventilation."

"Thank you."

Björn ended the call and put the phone back into his pocket. He checked the room one final time. He was confident that he had not left any forensic evidence that might betray his presence, but, even if he had, it would be unlikely that anything would be tied back to him. The hackers who worked in Group Two had expunged his personnel records from the military and had sanitised all other references that could be found online. He had never been fingerprinted, and his DNA had never been taken. He was as near to a ghost as it was possible to be, but a little added caution went a long way.

He collected the empty bottles and went back to Tanner. He had two choices: leave him or get help. He knew that the first choice probably meant that Tanner would die. It was a Saturday and the business was closed; there was a good chance that he would be left down here, unnoticed, until it was too late. The file did not require him to assist; quite the contrary, the main requirement of his orders was to eliminate Milton without leaving evidence that might be traced back to London. Assisting Tanner now—even if that help was limited to the bare minimum—would inevitably lead to scrutiny that could otherwise be avoided. On the other hand, Tanner was the only source who might be able to lead him to Milton. He needed to question him and, for that to be possible, Tanner needed treatment for his overdose.

Björn reached down and grabbed him, then levered him out of the chair. He stooped down and put him over his shoulder, carrying him out of the basement, up the stairs and into the office. He laid him on the floor next to the counter and went to the door, peeking between the poster that had been stuck there and the CLOSED sign until he was confident that the street was quiet and he wouldn't be seen. He opened the door, picked Tanner up again and carried him outside, where he rested him on the ground and then put him into the recovery position. He locked the door, took the empty Trapanal bottle, and put it into Tanner's pocket. He took out his phone and dialled.

"Nine-one-one," the operator said. "What's your emergency?"

"I found a man in the street," he said. "He's unconscious. I need an ambulance."

45

Mollie gripped the door handle of the taxi so tightly that her knuckles showed white.

"Faster," she said.

"I can't go no faster than this," the driver complained. "I get caught over the limit and I'll lose my medallion. That's my livelihood right there. Ain't no tip you can offer me that'd be worth that."

The more she worried about why her father was not answering his phone, the more frightened she became. He had mentioned that there had been a shooting outside the office a month ago. What if something like that had happened? What if a thief had broken into the office in search of cash and jumped her father? Why had he asked about her .38? She thought about the pistol in her handbag and tried to remember the last time she had practised on the range.

The cab raced around the final corner. She saw the ambulance parked at the side of the road outside the office.

Oh shit.

"Here," she said, leaning forward and slapping her hand

against the scratched Perspex screen that separated her from the driver. "Park here."

"Okay, okay," the man said, flicking the indicator and pulling over.

She paid him with a twenty and didn't wait for the change, his confused thanks echoing in her ear as she opened the door and hurried across the sidewalk to the ambulance. The doors were open and she could see into the patient compartment. A man was strapped to a gurney with an oxygen mask on his face. A female paramedic was in the back, too. She reached out and closed the door.

"Hey," Mollie called out. "Wait."

She sprinted, but it was no good. The ambulance pulled away from the kerb, its lights flashing on and then, a moment later, the siren sounding out. Mollie reached the entrance to the parking lot and bent double, sobbing as she gasped for breath.

"Excuse me? Miss?"

She looked up. The speaker was a big man, a clear head and shoulders taller than she was. He had blond hair and bright blue eyes.

"Yes?"

"Do you know the man in the ambulance?"

"I think so. Can you describe him?"

"Late middle age. Dark hair."

"That's my father. Do you know what happened to him?"

The man gave a little dip of his head. "I found him. I was just going to the gym when I saw him." He pointed to the parking lot. "He was on the ground, wasn't moving. I went over to see if I could help, and I saw that he was unconscious. I called 911 and waited here until they arrived." He shrugged. "I'm sorry—that's all I know. I hope he's okay."

"Did the paramedics say anything?"

"They said it looked like a drug overdose."

"What? He doesn't do drugs. That's not possible."

"I overheard them when they were examining him. I'm sorry. Is there anything I can do to help?"

She frowned, finding it difficult to order the competing thoughts that were racing through her head. "I don't know. I mean... sorry... what's your name?"

"Eidur," the man said.

"What?"

"Eidur. I'm from Iceland."

"Right," she said, still confused. "I guess I need to get to the hospital." She remembered that her car was in the shop. "Shit."

"What is it?"

"I don't have a car. I'll have to get another taxi."

She turned and looked up and down the street. Her cab had already left, so she took out her phone, fumbled it awake, and tapped the Uber app.

"My car's just there," Eidur said, pointing to the parking lot for Flex Fitness. "I could drive you if you like?"

"I can't—"

"It's no bother," he said, interrupting her. He smiled. "And I'd like to know that he's okay."

"That's really kind of you."

"It's the least I can do. Please. I'm happy I can help."

46

Björn took a seat in the emergency waiting room while Mollie was taken through to speak to a doctor about her father. There were six other people waiting: a mother and father who had delivered their asthmatic daughter; the boyfriend of an alcoholic who was having her stomach pumped; a man who looked to have broken his arm; a young single mother who was concerned about her baby's fever. Tanner had been taken into a bay where he was being assessed. Björn saw a nurse emerge from behind the curtains with a concerned expression on her face, and overheard her telling a colleague that they were going to need to improve the oxygen levels in his blood as quickly as possible.

Björn got up and found a quiet spot just outside the entrance. He placed another call to London, and this time he asked to speak to someone from the second floor. He recognised the voice of the technician who answered. It was a man with whom he had worked before.

"I need you to check whether there are any IP-CCTV cameras at an address."

"Go ahead."

He recited the address of Kansas City Fresh.

"Got it. What am I looking for?"

"Any footage with me going inside the property."

"If I find any?"

"Scrub it."

"Anything else?"

"I've got a cellphone that I need analysing. I'll upload it when I get back to the hotel. Full report, please."

"You need anything in particular?"

"I don't know," Björn said. He thought of the man he had shot in Tanner's basement and realised just how little he knew about him: he had his name, but, beyond that, he was blind. "A profile of the owner, frequent contacts, recent call history and text messaging—a full workup."

"Won't be a problem."

HE WENT BACK INSIDE and saw that Tanner's daughter was sitting next to the seat he had just vacated. There was a vending machine in the lobby, and he slotted in the change for a couple of cups of coffee. He looked back to where the young woman was sitting. A doctor was standing next to her, and she was remonstrating with him. Björn was a little too far away to hear what was being said, but her demeanour and the occasional word that he caught—'impossible' was repeated more than once—suggested that she was protesting against something that the doctor had told her.

The first cup dispensed. Björn took it and waited for the second. He was confident that he had a little extra time to investigate what had happened before the body in the basement was discovered. He had locked the door to the

premises, and the sign had already been flipped over to indicate that it was closed. It was late, too. No one was going in
at this hour.

Björn wondered whether it might make sense for him to
go back and dispose of the body, but dismissed it. There was
nothing that tied him to what had happened, save that the
police would be told that he had discovered Tanner. The
footage recorded by the security cameras would soon be
wiped, if it hadn't been already. It seemed unlikely that he
could be connected to Tanner's misfortune, but even if it was
possible, it would take time. Björn did not intend to remain
in Missouri for long. Once he had found and dealt with
Milton, he would be on the first flight back to London.

The machine beeped as it finished pouring the second
cup. Björn took them over to the waiting area. The doctor
had just finished his conversation with Tanner's daughter
and had moved away.

"Here," Björn said, handing her one of the cups.

"Got anything stronger?"

"Actually, I do." He reached into his pocket and took out
a small silver hip flask and unscrewed the top. "It's called
Flóki," he said. "It's a single malt from Iceland."

"Seriously?"

He smiled and shrugged.

She held out her cup and Björn poured in a finger's
worth, then poured a similar measure into his own cup.

"Is Iceland known for its whisky?"

"No," he said, "although they are saying that might
change. The weather is good for distilling. And we have a lot
of sheep dung."

"I'm sorry?"

"Dung—we smoke the whisky with it. The first settlers
to Iceland had little wood for fuel, but plenty of dung. That's

where one of our traditional festive dishes comes from. Hangikjöt—lamb smoked over dung."

"Well," she said, "I'll be honest—that's not something I thought I'd be doing today. Drinking sheep-dung whisky. Thank you."

"My pleasure," he said. He sat down on the seat next to her. "You didn't tell me your name."

"Mollie," she said. "Mollie Tanner. Sorry—I forgot yours."

"Eidur."

"That's right—Eidur from Iceland."

"That's me."

They sipped their coffees, both of them watching the doctor engaged in a hushed conversation with the nurse who was outside Tanner's bay. The curtain was open and Björn could see through it into the cubicle. Tanner had been put into a bed, and a full-face oxygen mask had been fitted. He could hear the mechanical exhalations as a pump pushed oxygen into his lungs.

"You were right," Mollie said. "Drug overdose. They found a bottle. Some sort of barbiturate."

"And you didn't know?"

"No," she protested. "And I still don't believe it. I suppose it might be something to do with pain relief. He lost his leg when he was in the army."

"What are they going to do?"

"They're giving him a lot of oxygen. The stuff—the Trapanal—they think he's taken enough to affect the muscles he needs to breathe. His oxygen saturation levels are low."

"But he'll recover?"

"Don't know. They said it's mostly a case of supporting his body until the drugs have been flushed out."

"Did they say how long that might take?"

"No, but it's obviously not going to be quick. They're going to sedate him."

Björn hid his frustration behind another sip of his coffee. Tanner had been in contact with Milton, but, beyond the rudiments of the conversation with him that Tanner had reported when he had called London with his tip, he had given Björn nothing to go on. The plan had been to use Tanner to arrange another meeting where he could take Milton out; that wasn't going to be possible if Tanner was unconscious.

Björn wondered whether Mollie might have met Milton, or whether Tanner might have mentioned him to her, but, try as he might, he couldn't think of a way of asking without drawing attention to himself. Björn had introduced himself as a stranger. She would be suspicious if he started asking questions that he had no obvious right to ask. She would question his motives in helping her, and the chances of a future angle that he might be able to work with her would be lost. It was irritating, but there was nothing else for it; he would have to be patient.

He thought of the man in the basement. What had happened surely had to be connected with Milton's arrival in Kansas City. He had the dead man's cellphone. That, at least, was one avenue of investigation that he could still pursue. He just needed to find a decent internet connection so that he could upload the data to the Group Two servers.

"I'd better be going," he said.

"Thank you," she said. "For everything—you've been amazing."

He smiled at her. "I'm just happy I could help. Would you let me know how he is?"

"Of course," she said, smiling. "Give me your number."

There was a magazine on the table next to him. He tore out a page and noted down the number of the phone that he had purchased upon his arrival. He would use it while he was here and then dispose of it. He gave her the page and she folded it and put it in her purse.

"Thanks again," she said, laying her hand on his forearm.

"Goodbye, Mollie. Please do let me know how he is."

"I will," she said.

Björn stood, took one last look at the unconscious Tanner, and left his daughter to watch over him.

The drive from Louisburg to Kansas City took forty minutes, and darkness had fallen by the time Milton reached the city limits. Snow was falling heavily again, and Milton passed two minor fender benders where cars had slid across the icy surface into vehicles stopped ahead of them.

He reached Mount Saint Mary's Cemetery and stopped for a red light. His attention had been distracted during the drive north. How had O'Connor found Tanner? Connie and Enzo hadn't called anyone, at least not as far as he was aware. Fernández knew where they were, but, if he was going to betray them, this was a strange way of doing it. If he had wanted to sell them out, or if he had some ulterior motive, he could have done that back at the quarry.

He had no idea what he would find at the meeting, but he had prepared himself as well as he could. He had loaded the revolver and had the night-vision monocular on the passenger seat. He had no illusions that he would be able to walk into unfamiliar territory, retrieve Tanner, and get out again without conflict. He was heading into a trap, and that made him itchy with nerves. But he knew that he had no choice. If he did nothing, Tanner would be killed. He had already looked pretty beaten up in the picture that O'Connor had sent.

He knew the only place he would get the answers he needed was at the rendezvous. The light changed, and he stood on the gas, throwing the truck's gears through their paces and ignoring the scraping of the clutch whenever he released it too quickly.

MILTON DABBED the brakes and brought the truck's speed down to thirty. The building he was looking for was in the city's eastern community, just a few blocks off US 70. Milton followed the map on his phone, trying to keep his eyes on it and the road. He knew he was close when the tall buildings were replaced by older homes, turn-of-the-century colonials with big porches and smaller A-frames on narrow lots. The houses became increasingly distressed and decrepit the further east he went; he saw windows that looked as if they had been boarded up for decades and doors sealed shut with planks. Garbage was piled up on street corners and in otherwise empty front yards. Many of the homes were made of brick; some featured grand double chimneys, stately arches and pillars. It was a jarring contradiction. These were homes that, in any other place, might be worth hundreds of thousands of dollars. Here, though? No one wanted them, so now they were rotting and slowly falling in on themselves.

He turned onto East Twenty-Fourth Street and passed old brick shops and department stores, long since shuttered. He stopped at a four-way sign. On the opposite corner, a group of young men stood and stared over at him. Milton pulled ahead, keeping his eye on the rear-view mirror as he approached the speed limit. He glanced at the phone. He was a block before the address he had been given. He saw a side street on his right and turned the truck into it.

It was dark now and the streetlights were nearly all faulty. Milton could still hear the background rush of the city: car horns, a bus wheezing to a stop, a police siren. Mollie Tanner had told him over dinner about the city's history of segregation, of how black and Latino homeowners had been kept east of Troost Avenue for decades. Milton guessed that this neighbourhood was one of the oldest; it certainly looked like it had been neglected for years. It bore the hallmarks of people who had been abandoned. With no money, and no prospects or future, what point was there in maintaining the bricks and mortar of their community?

Milton drove on. He kept to the south side of East Twenty-Fourth, then turned right onto the next block. Lister Avenue. The homes here were fronted by trees and fences. Televisions flickered in the front windows.

Milton saw the block that he wanted. The building was brick, three storeys tall, and perhaps fifty feet from front to back. It looked as if there would once have been a fair number of apartments within it; Milton guessed at six on each floor. There was a red commercial-sized dumpster at the base of the building, nearly overflowing with what looked like rolls of old cellulose and fibreglass insulation. The building was derelict, with smashed windows on the upper floors and boards over those at ground level. A sign at the front of the building warned that trespassers would be prosecuted. The words 'The Mabele' had been carved out of the granite relief that separated the brick between the second and third floors.

Milton watched for five minutes, looking for motion.

There were no cars parked anywhere nearby and no pedestrians out this late. He took out the binoculars, switched on the night vision, and checked each window. He looked for fluttering curtains or any lights that had been left on. He looked for the white and grey blurs that would betray a heat source. Nothing.

He scanned the entire street ahead of him. Nothing.

He was going to have to go inside.

Milton checked both directions for anyone paying attention. A young kid on a BMX scooted past over compacted snow, a loose spoke rattling in one of the wheels. Milton opened the door of the truck and checked that the .357 was still safely stowed against his back, held in place by his belt. He left his hand there, his fingers wrapped around the weapon's grip, and walked toward the building.

<h1>48</h1>

Björn drove back to his hotel, left his rental in the lot, and made his way to his room on the fifth floor. He went to the safe and unlocked it, taking out the iPad that he had deposited there. The device looked standard—the kind of tablet that one could purchase in a store —but it had been given some modifications by the R&D experts in Group Six. It used a virtual private network to encrypt all internet traffic between field devices and the central server, together with whole-disk encryption to keep local files safe, too. Björn was no expert, but knew enough about tech to know that the device was secure and that it was safe to use it to send and receive sensitive data.

He put the tablet on the table and collected a beer from the minibar. He popped the lid and went back to the table. He took out O'Connor's phone and used a cable to connect it to the tablet. He opened an uploader that would copy the files from the phone to the iPad, and then from that to the Group Two server. The software indicated that the process would take five minutes.

That done, he took out his own phone and transferred

the photographs that he had taken of Kenneth O'Connor onto the iPad. He then uploaded these to the server as well, asking for an urgent search of all relevant databases and social media services.

BJÖRN HAD JUST FINISHED his beer when his phone buzzed.

"Yes?"

"Call from Global Logistics for you. Second floor."

"Put them through."

The operator thanked him and there was a moment's pause as the call was rerouted.

"Hello?"

"We've analysed the data that you uploaded," the analyst reported.

"Go ahead."

"Your subject is Kenneth O'Connor. He was born in Dublin in 1985. MI5 believes that he served in the Real IRA between 2010 and 2015. He has an extensive criminal record —multiple assaults, armed robbery and arson. MI5 suspects that he was responsible for the murder of four British soldiers and several civilians suspected of collaboration with the RUC. He was considered significant enough that his file was passed to Group Fifteen for actioning in September 2015. There was a concerted effort to find him, and it appears that he decided that it was getting too hot for him. He was never found."

"Until now," Björn said. "What else?"

"He has a brother—Patrick O'Connor—who moved to Kansas City ten years ago. I ran his details through the US National Crime Information Center. The police suspect Patrick of money laundering for various local criminals.

There is some suggestion that he might have a connection to the Kansas City Mafia and local drug dealers."

"Send me his file."

"It's already on its way."

Björn thanked him and ended the call. He woke his tablet and navigated to the encrypted folder where information could be shared safely between field agents and London. He entered his credentials, decrypted the new content and opened it. There was a packet of information on Kenneth O'Connor. Björn opened his police record; his mugshot was the first document, and Björn could see that it was the same man as the one he had met in the basement.

He scrolled through the information until he found the details that had been gathered on Patrick O'Connor. It appeared that he was something of an entrepreneur. He was the sole director of Dublin Investments, Inc, a company which was itself the majority shareholder in a number of businesses: a strip club, a golf driving range, and several nail salons and massage parlours. The registered office for Dublin Investments was 1020 Petticoat Lane, Kansas City. Björn opened Google Maps and typed in the address. It was in the middle of downtown. He dragged the Street View icon to Petticoat Lane and scouted the area: office blocks on either side of the road, most of them housing professional firms. Number 1020 looked like a block that housed several smaller businesses. Björn zoomed in on the building: the name of O'Connor's business was proudly engraved on a brass plate next to the double doors.

He decided that he would pay it a visit.

49

Bird and Nicol were parked around the corner next to a two-storey building that, like its neighbour across the street, had also been abandoned. Its siding sagged, shingles were missing from the roof, and the windows and front door were boarded up. The wooden panels had been spray-painted with graffiti. A bracket protruded from the first floor; it looked like the kind of structure that might support a real estate agent's hoarding, but the advertisement that the property was available for purchase—if indeed it had ever been there at all—was now missing. Its absence summed up the area. No one was interested in it. Everyone had moved on.

Bird looked out of the window with disgust. He had worked these streets for years, and nothing had changed. If anything, it had got worse. He reached around to the back seat for the six-pack of Pabst Blue Ribbon that they had picked up from the 7-Eleven back on Van Brunt Boulevard. He tore a can out of the cardboard carrier, popped the lid, and handed it to Nicol.

"Thanks."

Bird took a second can. "This fucking place," he said. "I won't miss it when I'm done."

They had driven past the apartment block fifteen minutes earlier. The place was a dump, just like the rest of the neighbourhood. Patrick O'Connor had said that the preparations had already been made, that they just had to be on hand to close the trap when the moment came. The whole setup had been the Irishman's idea.

"What do you make of O'Connor?" Bird asked.

"Patrick?"

"Kenny."

Nicol tapped a finger against his forehead. "I think he's missing something inside."

"How'd you mean?"

"Have you looked in his eyes?"

"Not really my type."

Nicol raised his middle finger. "There's something not there. They're just kinda... dead. No light in them. Blank."

Bird nodded. Kenny creeped him out, too, even though he had plenty of experience dealing with his type. He was different to the others. Bird had met him on two previous occasions and had left with the firm impression that Kenny was a man who enjoyed his calling, and that he would kill for pleasure and without the promise of payment.

"When are you gonna call him?" Nicol said.

"When we know the dude is inside."

Patrick O'Connor had promised that his brother would be keeping watch across the street in the abandoned building on the corner. Bird had seen a truck pull up and, although he could only see the back of the building from where he was, he assumed that O'Connor had gone inside to take up his position.

Bird took a swig from the can. "What'd he say the English guy's name was?"

"Milton."

"So maybe he's not coming. I mean, dude would have to be pretty dumb to just walk in here."

"Then we stay here and drink beer," Nicol said. "I'm easy either way."

Nicol was right. They just had to be patient. Patrick had told them that the guy was a pro, and that he had military experience. But Bird had yet to meet the man who didn't bleed when you shot him. Milton would be no different.

"Hey," Nicol said, gesturing through the windshield to the junction ahead of them.

A kid on a BMX turned the corner and wheeled up to the car. He came to a stop. Bird wound down the window.

"Dude's just gone inside," the kid said.

"Describe him."

"White." The kid shrugged. "I don't know."

"'White,'" Bird repeated. "That all you got?"

The kid shrugged. "White dude, medium height. What else do you want?"

"Jesus."

"You didn't ask me to write an essay about him. You said look for a guy hanging around outside, so that's what I did. There's a guy hanging around outside." He put out his right hand, palm up, and tapped the fingers of his left hand against it. "Pay me."

Bird grumbled as he reached for his wallet, opening it and taking out a twenty. He held it out of the open window and waited for the kid to take it. He tried, but Bird moved it away at the last moment. "That's the problem with kids these days," he said to Nicol. "Just do the bare minimum. No pride in the job."

"Come on, man. Gimme."

Bird held the note out again and allowed the kid to take it. "Get the fuck out of here."

The kid pocketed the note and wheeled away.

Nicol had his phone to his ear. Bird was about to make a comment about attitude and how the prospects of the kids who lived here would never rise beyond being corner boys, but he saw the look of irritation on his partner's face and paused.

"What is it?"

"It's Kenny," he said. "He's not answering."

"Patrick said he'd be here."

Nicol took the phone away and tapped the screen to try the call again. "You heard the same as I did. Said he'd be in the building keeping watch." He put the phone on speaker so that Bird could hear the call. "But he's not picking up."

"Shit," Bird said. "What do you want to do?"

"Milton's inside," Nicol said. "Kelly's there, too. Patrick made it pretty clear. We go in, confirm he's there; then we take care of him. We don't need O'Connor for that."

"Guess not."

"And twenty grand is a nice little bonus. I'm up for it if you are."

"Let's get it over with."

Bird turned the key in the ignition, put the car into drive, and rolled away from the side of the street. Patrick had offered them ten grand apiece to sort out the poor sap who had had the misfortune to piss him off. Bird didn't know why the guy was in O'Connor's shithouse, and he didn't care. This wasn't fixing to be a difficult job, and the money was good. His old lady had been on at him for weeks about going down to Lauderdale for a month in winter, and the money would go a long way towards paying for the trip. Bird didn't give two shits about the man they were about to take out. He wasn't the first and he probably wouldn't be the last.

He reached down and popped the retaining strap on his holster.

50

Milton didn't know whether Tanner was inside. Probably not. He doubted that the man to whom he had spoken was honourable. That might mean that Tanner was already dead—Milton thought that the odds favoured it—but he had to check. And, if he was right and this was a trap, what he would do now would later be seen as vengeance.

He walked by the front of the building, looking for any sign of activity. It looked as if there might have been footprints leading to the front door, but the heavy snow had erased them almost to the point of invisibility. He followed the weed-entangled fence to the north and turned left until he was parallel to the middle of the building. He slipped over the four-foot barrier, dropping to the other side halfway along. There were five windows that served the basement. They were flush with the ground and reached up to where the first floor proper started. All of them were covered with cheap pine boards that had been slapped with the same paint as the base of the building.

The board that covered the second window from the

east entrance, to the building's rear, had already been yanked on by someone. They had managed to draw a nail away from the window frame. Milton slid his fingers behind the bent corner and tugged it as gently as he could. The board came away a little more. The wood around each nail was rotten and, by focussing his attention on the nails one at a time, he was able to prise each of them out. It was impossible to remove the board without any noise, however, and he paused to see whether the soft creaks had been heard. He waited and listened. A dog was barking a few blocks away, and the night traffic on the nearby US 70 pulsed with a constant dull roar.

Milton set the board against the wall and removed his jacket. There were jagged edges of glass still attached to the frame, and he used the coat to cover them. He leaned inside and scoped the basement room. It was dark, and visibility was limited to what the outside light could illuminate, but he could see that there was debris scattered on the floor and a darker oblong in the far wall that suggested a door. He turned around and lowered himself inside, feet first. He held onto the jacket and dropped down to the floor.

He put on his coat again and drew the Peacemaker. He held it in a comfortable grip with both hands and stepped away from the wall. His boots splashed through puddles of rainwater that had seeped in from outside. The room smelled of urine and wet dirt. He could make out the doorway, just ahead; beyond it was a corridor that was lit by the dim light that leaked around a board that covered the tall window above the back door. Milton cocked the .357 and moved slowly and deliberately, using half steps to ensure that he did not turn an ankle. The ground was littered with bricks, wood and other debris, and a rat the size of a small dog scurried across the floor ahead of him, disappearing into the shadows.

He climbed the stairs from the basement, pausing near the top to listen for breathing or movement.

He still couldn't hear anything.

He climbed the last step, paused again, and then turned around the corner with the gun out and ready to fire. There was a lobby that stretched across the width of the building. He was nearest to the rear door. The front door was opposite. Both were unattended. There was a staircase leading up from the middle of the lobby.

He took the stairs to the second floor and reached a landing with six doors off it, three on each side. Five of them were sealed with solid steel security doors to deter squatters. The middle door on the north side of the building was open, though, the steel door removed and resting against the wall. Milton peeked carefully inside.

The room was pitch black. Milton checked his six again and walked in slowly, his gun in both hands.

There was someone near the back of the room, slumped against the wall.

Tanner?

Milton kept one eye on the door as he shuffled over to the prone figure. It was a man. He was on his side, facing the wall. Milton rolled him over.

Not Tanner.

Jack Kelly.

He had been badly beaten, and there was a gunshot wound in the middle of his forehead.

Shit.

Milton heard movement outside and then the sound of a vehicle. He moved over to the window and looked through a dime-sized hole in the board that covered it. A police sedan was idling at the kerb. The doors opened and two officers hurried out, their weapons drawn as they crossed to the front door.

Milton recognised one of the men. It was Nicol, the officer who helped Fernández with the kids.

He heard the front door open and then footsteps.

"Police," a voice called out from below. "We know you're in here."

51

Milton backed away from Jack Kelly's body and retreated to the door.

"We saw you come inside," Nicol called up to him. "Get down here now—hands where we can see them."

"I don't particularly want to get shot."

"We're not going to shoot you."

"Really? You'll excuse me if I don't take your word for that."

"We got a report of gunshots fired."

"No, you didn't," Milton said. "You've been waiting outside for me to show up."

"What are we going to find up there?"

"You know, Detective. You're going to find Jack Kelly. Shot through the head."

"Is that right? And you up there with him... How'd you think that's going to look?"

"It's going to look like I've been fitted up."

Milton heard the squelch of a radio and muttered words. The second officer was calling for backup. Milton looked around for an exit. The steel security panels on the other five doors were substantial, and Milton knew that he wouldn't be able to open them without tools. The way he saw it, he had three options: surrender, try to shoot his way out, or climb up to the next floor and look for another option for getting clear.

Surrendering would probably get him shot; they'd say he was resisting arrest.

Shooting his way out was possible, but the cops would have the advantage on him.

Going up was his best option for now. He made his way to the staircase.

"It's Milton, isn't it?" Nicol called up. "John Milton. We know all about you."

"Good for you."

"We know what happened, too. You and Jack got into it over a car. You lost the auction and you took it personally. You murdered him."

"Nice try."

Moving quietly, Milton climbed the stairs and reached the third floor. It was the mirror image of the floor below, except that only three of the apartments had been secured. Milton moved to the nearest of the open doors as he heard the sound of sirens in the distance.

"You hear that?" Nicol called up, his voice a little fainter now that there was another floor between them. "My partner just called for backup. This place is gonna be swarming with police in five minutes. Do you really want to go out like that? Cornered like a rat? Better to come down here now and give yourself up."

His options were running out. He knew that there was no percentage in staying put. He was already outnumbered and, very soon, those odds were going to get even worse.

They would either outwait him or outgun him. He couldn't flee the building the way he'd come in. They would shoot him dead before he got halfway down the stairs. He couldn't go up any farther, either. There might be a door onto the roof, but the building wasn't close to any of its neighbours, and he would be trapped there.

"You're running out of time," Nicol called up. "What's it gonna be?"

The sirens were much louder now, and, as Milton glanced back to the front of the building, he saw blue light strobing between the cracks in the boards. He heard one car, and then another, pulling to sudden stops. He heard doors opening and then excited voices. Milton went to the window and looked out between the gaps in the boards. He saw the three cars and watched as the last officer disappeared into the building. They had left one man out the front, but Milton knew that he would be able to get around him without too much difficulty. He just had to get down there without getting shot.

He had one option. He had registered it earlier, but had dismissed it as too dangerous. The circumstances had changed now, and he didn't have any other choices. He left the room, crossed the landing and made his way to the apartment on the opposite side of the corridor. The windows there were boarded up, but, like most of the others that he had seen, the plywood was rotten and weak.

"Police!"

He heard the clatter of feet coming up the stairs.

It was now or never. Milton backed up to the edge of the room and then sprinted at the window. He leapt at it shoulder first and threw himself into the boards. They splintered and tore free of the frame, and Milton fell into space, plunging towards the ground forty feet below.

52

The dumpster beneath the window was more than half-full with insulation. Milton came down fast, and, despite the soft material to break his fall, he still felt his right shoulder pop out of joint. The pain was excruciating, and he knew at once that he had dislocated it.

He had to move. He reached out with his left hand and grabbed the lip of the dumpster. He righted himself and found his footing, then tried to raise his leg over the edge. The pain in his shoulder was almost unbearable. Flashes sparked across his vision and he felt as if he might pass out, but he managed to ignore it. He hooked his right leg over the lip and then pushed up with his left, managing to straddle the dumpster until he was able to put enough weight over the side to unbalance himself. He rolled over it and dropped to the ground, landing on his back with a thud that sent another blast of pain out from his shoulder.

Milton heard the yell from above. "Stop!"

He had to fix his shoulder.

"He's outside," the voice from above yelled. "He went through the window."

He had some mobility in the joint, and his rudimentary battlefield medicine suggested a subluxation rather than a full dislocation: the ball of his arm bone had popped a little way out of the socket. He turned to face the dumpster and, gritting his teeth, he swivelled at the hips and drove himself at it. He gasped with the pain and his knees buckled, but the shoulder popped back into the joint. The pain flared and then—miraculously—dissipated to a continuous, nauseating throb. He knew that his therapy was medieval and that he faced the prospect of surgery if he had damaged the tissue around the joint, but that would have to wait.

He heard voices from the building and ran, his legs pumping as he sprinted west. Shots rang out like distant firecrackers, but he put them out of his mind. It would need an outrageously lucky marksman to pick him off at range in the dark. Milton sprinted across Lister Avenue and between a pair of houses. He reached the next block over and slowed as he tried to orient himself.

Sirens rang out from behind him. He couldn't get back to Fernández's truck; he was going to have to abandon it. He recalled the map that he had studied before coming here. If he could get up to Twenty-Third Street, he would be near to a used-car dealership. Maybe he would find older cars there, models that would be simple to hot-wire.

He kept his head down and ran hard, not worrying about being seen. This was the kind of neighbourhood that would be accustomed to sirens and chases. This spectacle would not be unusual. He could take advantage of that, but it could only be temporary. He knew that he was going to need a new appearance, and quickly. Nicol had seen him, and he knew that it wouldn't be long before his description was circulated.

Milton reached the corner of Lawn Avenue and Twenty-

Third. He avoided the sidewalk, climbing up a shallow incline and running west behind the stands of old-growth elm and poplar. A pair of squad cars rolled by, lights on, then squealed to a halt. They had spotted him. They would have blocks set up on all the main intersections, the roads obstructed by pairs of cruisers with no way in or out. He needed to be clear of the area before they could do that, and he doubted that he would be able to manage that on foot. His shoulder ached and it was slowing him down.

A gunshot cracked the night air, the round missing him. He heard the snap and crunch of broken branches behind him. They weren't just shutting down the street, they were in active pursuit through the trees and backyards. There was a fence blocking the way ahead, and he accelerated toward it, planting the hand of his good arm and vaulting over it.

He crossed Elmwood, Cypress, Kensington and Spruce Avenues, popping out of the trees at the corner of Jackson. There was a city bus stop ahead of him, and the Number 21 Northbound was just slowing down. Milton waved his good arm, and the bus indicated to stop. The doors opened and he climbed aboard.

The elderly African American driver had a look of concern on his face. "You okay, buddy?" Milton could guess why he might ask that: he was a middle-aged white guy, stumbling out of the toughest neighbourhood in the city, clasping his shoulder and dripping with sweat. "You need me to call a police officer or something?"

"I'm fine. Thanks."

He reached into his back pocket and took out his money clip, peeling off a five.

"Sorry—exact change only."

"Keep it."

The man took the bill and pocketed it in his uniform

jacket. He clicked six quarters from a change holder on his belt and dropped them into the fare caddy. "Watch your step, sir, and please stay behind the line. We're on our way."

Milton went to the back of the bus and dropped into the seat. He took a moment to catch his breath as the bus pulled away, and checked their direction. They were heading north on Jackson. They were on the next block by the time that he gazed through the back window and saw two men emerge from the bushes that had covered his escape from the street. He knew that they would have seen the bus and that they would be calling ahead to have it stopped. How long did he have? A minute? Two minutes if he was lucky.

The bus pulled up to the corner of East Twentieth Street. Milton disembarked via the side door as two new passengers climbed aboard. His shoulder was throbbing, and he knew that the swelling that would follow would restrict his range of motion, but at least he could still use his hand. He followed the barely lit sidewalk east, past a few homes, then cut between them. He took out his phone and checked the map: it put a service station on the next corner, and that would mean vehicles.

It was a Conoco. A parking lot wrapped around the pumps and the store, and Milton checked it cautiously from the tree line. A pair of bikers were sitting on their Harleys, drinking convenience store coffee and smoking cigarettes, oblivious to or uncaring of the fact that there were gas pumps nearby. On the back of the shorter man's leather vest was a swooping insignia that said "Satan's Crew," and then in smaller print underneath, "Ride Hard, Ride Free."

Milton didn't have time to fool around. He was five feet from them before they noticed he was there, and the .357 was extended before either man could react.

They both reached inside their denim jackets.

"Don't," Milton said.

The guy with the insignia squared up to him. "Brother, you're messing with the wrong dudes."

"Get off the bike," Milton said. "It'll come back to you. Check with the city tomorrow. It'll be in the pound."

Milton heard the sound of sirens. They were a few blocks away, but it sounded as if they were drawing closer. He flicked the .357 to encourage the two men to step away from the bikes. They did, and Milton mounted the nearest one: a softail frame with LED lights and big saddlebags on either side. He started the Milwaukee-Eight twin engine and used the toe shifter to click it into first gear. The sirens were even closer now, but Milton doubted that the two bikers would resort to speaking to the police. That was one of the upsides to relieving an outlaw of his wheels.

Milton popped the clutch and pulled out onto the road. His shoulder throbbed, but he was able to turn the handlebars. He needed to get downtown, back to the hotel, and to contact Mollie. Tanner was still out there somewhere— maybe alive and wounded, maybe dead—and now Milton had the entire Kansas City police department after him.

53

Milton had been careful during the ride and had plotted a course that avoided the major roads. He left the bike in an alley near his hotel. The effort of riding it had done his shoulder no favours. He probed it with his fingers and felt the swelling around the cuff of the joint where he had forced it back into place. He was reluctant to use stronger painkillers given his predilection for addictive substances, but he doubted that he was going to have an option this time. He knew that any denouement to the mess that he had stumbled into was likely to be physical, and he wouldn't last long if pain left him with just one working arm.

He kept his hands in his pockets and his head down and found a convenience store that was open late. He bought a pair of reading glasses with dark green frames, a preloaded disposable cellphone, a Kansas City Chiefs ball cap, a matching jersey with MAHOMES across the back, a packet of Kools and a lighter.

He went to the counter and paid, then used the store's bathroom to change. He pushed the corrective lenses out of the reading glasses and slipped on the frames and the cap. He checked the mirror. It was a pretty average disguise, but it was the best that he would be able to do on short notice. He took out the phone that he had been using and transferred the numbers that he would need: Tanner's, Enzo's and Fernández's. His own number was compromised; Tanner's assailant had called him on it, and Milton was not prepared to run the risk that he—or, more likely, the corrupt police officers—might have access to someone at the phone company who could triangulate his location. He took out the phone's SIM and flushed that down the toilet. He dropped the body of the phone into the trash.

There was a Walgreens pharmacy next door. Milton went up to the counter.

The clerk looked up with a warm smile. "Can I help you, sir?"

"What are the strongest painkillers I can get without prescription?"

"We got Haltran over there," the clerk said, pointing to the aisle over to the left. "Nuprin. Q-Profen."

"Anything stronger?"

The woman shook her head. "No, sir. Not without a prescription."

Milton bought two packets of Nuprin and a packet of Aleve. He went out to the front of the store and opened the Nuprin. Each tablet contained 400mg of ibuprofen, and the maximum daily dose was 1200mg. Milton popped four tablets out of the blister pack and dry-swallowed them. He popped out three Aleve and swallowed those, too. He would have preferred something stronger—codeine would have been much better—but he would not be able to get that without seeing a doctor. This would have to do for now.

MILTON WALKED BACK to the hotel. He saw a police patrol car waiting for the lights at the junction with a side street that he was going to have to cross. He could have turned back or crossed the road so that he could walk by with a little more distance between them, but he didn't want to draw attention to himself. The snow was still falling, and the car had its wipers on, the blades squeaking over the glass.

Milton got to the junction and stopped. He risked a quick glimpse into the car; there were two officers riding up front, and they both looked bored. If he was recognised here, downtown, it was going to be much more difficult to get away. There were no yards to run through here, no trees to shield him. The officer in the passenger seat glanced his way, then held his gaze, looking him up and down.

The light changed and the car pulled out. Milton stayed where he was. He waited for the car to stop or for the blip of the siren.

Nothing.

He exhaled, saw that the light had changed to green, and continued on his way. He reached the hotel and went inside. The lobby was empty save for the night manager on the front desk. Milton knew that the police might contact local hotels on account of his accent, but he doubted that that was something that could be arranged so soon. He would assume that he had time to get in, get his stuff, and then get out again. He had no wheels: the Mustang was still at the Pizzolato house, and Fernández's truck was at Lister Avenue. He would have to use the stolen bike and hope that the bikers had not reported the theft.

Milton rode the elevator up to the third floor and followed the ancient yellow-and-rust-patterned rug back to his room. He took out the burner phone, opened the box, and plugged it in to charge. He packed his bag as he waited for it to boot up, and then sat down with his back to the wall and opened his mail on the new phone. He found the email that Mollie had sent him with the list of local music venues that she had recommended. Her email had her contact details in the footer, and he pressed her number and waited for the phone to dial it.

"Hello?"

"It's John."

"John? Ohmigod... where are you?"

"I'm in the city," he said. Her voice was tight with tension, and he feared the worst. "Is everything okay?"

"No," she said. "It's not. My dad... He's in the ER at Truman. I'm with him now—been here for hours. They're saying it's an overdose."

"What? Drugs?"

"I know. They think it might have been for pain relief. I don't know, though. It's not him. He never said anything to me."

Milton told her that he was on his way and ended the call. He opened a map and saw that the hospital was close. He put his things into his rucksack and made sure that he hadn't left anything behind. He zipped up the bag, slung it over his good shoulder, and made his way down to the lobby again.

PART IV

54

The city was muffled beneath the mantle of snow as one o'clock approached. Milton made it across to the hospital without incident and left the bike in the lot at the back of the building. He paused outside for a moment, considering the good sense of being here. He couldn't go inside. Kenny O'Connor had extracted Milton's details from Tanner. They had his cellphone number and name at a minimum and, if Tanner had given those up, Milton had to assume that he had given up more besides. Tanner knew that Milton had been in contact with Fernández. He had to assume that they would be able to find out that he was connected with the quarry.

He called Fernández's number, and the coach picked up on the second ring. "Hey," he said. "What happened?"

Milton gave him a quick summary of what had taken place over the course of the last five hours. He told him about the ambush at the apartment building and about the involvement of the crooked detectives.

"Tanner?"

"He was found outside the business. He's in the hospital."

"Is he going to be okay?"

"I don't know. I haven't seen him. His daughter says that he's had a drug overdose."

"Drugs? That's not him."

"That's what she said."

Milton waited for a couple to exit the building and crunch over the compacted snow to the parking lot.

"You still there?" Fernández said.

"Yes," Milton said. "Have you told anyone that the Pizzolatos are with you?"

"Of course not."

"Good. And you said that the quarry is in your sister's name?"

"That's right. Why?"

"Tanner was interrogated, and I don't know what he might have said. He knows that I wanted to speak to you—they might start looking that way."

"The quarry's registered under her married name, not Fernández. It'll be a huge stretch to go from you asking Tanner to introduce us to them being out here—and that's assuming they can find out that I'm connected to the quarry, which won't be easy. I wouldn't worry about it. I think we're okay."

"Do you have any other family?"

"Not really."

"Are you married?"

"No. They go to my place and all they'll find is a hungry goldfish."

"I just wanted to check."

"It's all good."

Milton didn't share his optimism. "Keep your eyes

open," he said. "I'm going to see Tanner's daughter now. I'll be back there as soon as I can. In the meantime, tell Enzo and his mother not to leave and not to contact anyone. We have to be very careful."

"You got it," Fernández said.

MILTON WAITED in the parking lot and watched the entrance to the hospital. They had baited a trap for Milton with Tanner once before, and it stood to reason that they would try to repeat the trick now. Milton would have to assume that the room was being watched and act accordingly. He took out his phone, called Mollie again, and asked her to meet him outside in the parking lot.

She came down quickly, and Milton signalled for her to come over, away from the entrance.

"What's going on?" she asked.

"I can't come in," he said.

"Why?"

"I think people might be looking for me."

"What? Why?"

Milton dodged the question, although he knew that he would have to answer it eventually. "How is he?"

She looked bereft, the sadness weighing down her shoulders. "Not great."

"Tell me what happened."

"He was found outside the office. On the ground—unconscious. He'd called me earlier to ask me about a police officer you wanted to know about."

"Nicol," Milton said.

She nodded. "I wanted to talk to him about it, but he wasn't picking up my calls. That was weird for him, so I came to check he was okay. I got there just as they were loading him into the ambulance."

"Have you spoken to the doctors?"

"They say he OD'd on Trapanal. I'd never even heard of it."

Milton knew what Trapanal was; he had administered it before. He guessed that it had been used during Tanner's questioning.

"The doctors are testing his blood to be sure, but they say the symptoms are what they'd expect if he'd overdosed. They asked me if I thought he was depressed, if it was something that he might have done to himself."

"There are easier ways to go than to inject something like that," he said.

"And that assumes that he was suicidal, which he was not. He's happy—you saw him at dinner. Killing yourself with something like that would need planning. He would've had to get hold of the stuff and a syringe somehow. Did he strike you as someone who might have been thinking about killing himself?"

"Not at all."

"How could anyone do something like that to him? He didn't have any enemies—no one had a bad word to say about him."

Milton wondered how much of his professional history Tanner had shared with his daughter. He guessed that it wouldn't have been very much.

"Who found him?"

"A guy," she said.

"Did you see him?"

"Yes."

"Can you describe him?"

"Big. Tall—six four, maybe six five. He said he was going

into the gym next door and he saw Dad on the ground. Blond hair. Blue eyes. Tanned—he'd obviously just got here from somewhere else."

Milton started to feel a little sick. "Anything else?"

"He was foreign. Icelandic."

Milton bit down on the inside of his lip. He knew exactly who that was. Björn Thorsson was in Missouri. The last Milton had seen him was when he had been led away by the Colombian police in Medellín. The conclusions were easy to draw: first, the Group had extricated their best agent from Colombian custody; second, Tanner had sold him out.

"He said his name was Eidur," she said. "He gave me his card."

Milton felt vulnerable. He had come to Kansas City to ask Tanner whether he knew anything about Group Fifteen's attitude toward him following his interference in their operation in Medellín. Tanner had said that he would ask, but that was all moot now. Tanner had contacted London, and Control had sent Thorsson. That told Milton everything that he needed to know. There was a third conclusion to draw: Control wanted him dead, and she was prepared to send Number One to see that it was done. It felt as if he were being sucked into a vortex.

It had been difficult before, but now he had three antagonists to consider: the Kansas City Mafia, the O'Connor brothers *and* the Group.

He glanced around the lot, looking for any sign that they were being watched. He couldn't see anything that gave him cause for concern, but that didn't mean that he was ready to relax.

"What is it?" Mollie asked.

"Nothing," Milton muttered.

"Bullshit. Why do I get the feeling you're not telling me everything? Why can't you go inside?"

Milton didn't particularly want to answer her questions, but he knew that he couldn't avoid them. Mollie had a right to know what had happened, or at least as much of it as he could safely tell her.

"John?" she pressed. "Please."

"I'll tell you what I know," he said, "but not here. Have you been back to the warehouse?"

"Just outside," she said. "Eidur brought me here. We followed the ambulance."

"Could you take me there now?"

She looked back to the hospital. "I don't know. I need to stay with him."

"Is he in immediate danger?"

"No," she said. "They've sedated him."

"It won't take long. I don't think your father tried to kill himself. I think someone did that to him."

"That doesn't make any sense. Why?"

"I need to go to the warehouse, Mollie. You could give me the key if you prefer, but it would be better if you came with me."

She swallowed. "All right," she said. "An hour, maximum."

"We won't need any more than that," Milton said.

55

T hey got a taxi to the premises of Kansas City Fresh. Milton told the driver to park a block away, paid him and—ignoring the look of confusion on Mollie's face—got out, motioning for her to follow.

She joined him on the sidewalk. "What are we doing?"

"Is there a back entrance?"

"Why?"

"Please, Mollie. Just tell me."

"Yes," she said. "But you need to tell me what's going on. Why did we get out here?"

"I want to make sure that the place isn't being watched."

"Why would it be?"

He fixed her with an unblinking stare. "Until I know exactly what happened to your father, we need to be very careful. All right?"

She nodded and, after a pause to gather her breath, she indicated that she was ready to move. Milton went first, leading the way along North Oak Trafficway. Mollie indicated that they should take a right onto NE Seventieth and then a left, bringing them to an alley that skirted the back of the building that accommodated Kansas City Fresh. There was a fire door behind a row of industrial dumpsters, and, after fumbling in her purse for a moment, Mollie took out a key and unlocked it.

She was about to step in, but Milton motioned her to stop, and took out the Peacemaker.

She looked at the big gun with dismay. "Jesus."

Milton stepped inside and indicated that she should follow him. "Tell me if anything looks out of place."

He followed Mollie's directions through the stockroom and through a door that led into the main area of the building. Milton paused and listened for any indication that they were not alone. He heard nothing. The lights were off, and Mollie reached around his shoulder for the switch. The strip lights flickered and then came on.

"That shouldn't be there," she said.

"What?"

She pointed to the counter. "The shotgun. It belongs on the shelf down there, not on top."

Milton saw the Benelli on the counter. Tanner would not have left a weapon out in full view.

He pointed to the second door behind the counter. "What's through there?"

"Stairs down to the basement."

Milton made his way to the door and, with his sleeve covering his fingertips, he reached down and opened it. There was a flight of stairs leading down into darkness. There was a drawstring to the right, and Milton yanked on it. Two bulbs were lit: one at the top of the stairs and one in the room below. He made his way down, slowly and carefully, holding the Peacemaker in both hands.

He reached the bottom and stopped.

Mollie was behind him. "Shit."

There was a body sprawled out on the floor.

A man.

Milton looked down at him. Blood had sprayed out across the whitewashed blocks of the wall behind him. A bullet had been fired into the man's face at close range.

56

Milton sent Mollie back upstairs while he searched the body. Milton recognised him: it was one of the two Irishmen who had accosted Enzo at the auction. He was wearing forensic gloves and overshoes, and a hairnet was still fastened around his head, the front of the elasticated band singed from the passage of the bullet. There was a leather pouch on the table to the side and a syringe and empty bottle on the floor. He frisked the body and found a wallet with a driver's licence and bank cards in the name of Kenneth O'Connor. The man had no cellphone, but Milton was not surprised by that at all. He was sure that O'Connor had been killed by Björn Thorsson and equally sure that the phone would have been confiscated for the data that it held.

Milton took the empty bottle and reconvened with Mollie upstairs. She was pacing the space in front of the counter. Her face was deathly pale. "What the fuck?" she said, pointing a finger in the direction of the basement. "I mean, John—what the *fuck?*"

"I know it's a shock."

"A shock? A *shock*? Are you *kidding*? My dad and now this." She looked as if she was about to be sick. "What do I do? There's a dead body in the basement. Do you know who it is?"

"It's Kenneth O'Connor," Milton said.

"My God," she said. "So this *is* about you—about the fight at the car lot?"

"It looks like it."

"Fuck you, John. This is your fault."

She wheeled around and paced away to the other side of the office. She had her cellphone in her hand, the screen lighting up the gloom where a flickering bulb failed to illuminate the space properly. She looked as if she was about to place a call, put the phone to her ear, then relented.

"What do I do?" she asked him.

"Call the police."

"And?"

"Tell them about O'Connor. Tell them you found him."

"But he's dead. He's been *shot*."

"He came here to see your father. The O'Connors are trying to find the kid I helped at the auction."

She put her hand to her face and covered her eyes.

"My best guess would be that O'Connor was disturbed while he was with your father."

"Right, okay—but by *whom*?"

Milton was tempted to tell her what he suspected—that Thorsson, pretending to be Eidur, had found and shot O'Connor, and that it was Milton's presence in Kansas City that had summoned him—but he feared taking her down a rabbit hole from which there would be no easy way out. He was increasingly sure that Tanner had kept his daughter ignorant to his professional history, and the decision as to whether she should be told was one for him, not Milton.

Tanner might have betrayed him, but Milton did not feel the need to bring further confusion down upon Mollie's head. The sins of the father did not extend to the daughter. She had already been given a heavy enough burden to bear.

"John—by whom? *Who* disturbed him?"

"I don't know. But whoever it was, he or she probably saved your father's life. They came in and shot O'Connor, and then they took your father up to the street and left him there to be discovered."

She frowned. "You think it might have been Eidur?"

Milton kept a straight face. "I don't know."

"Because he found him and called the paramedics. I mean..." The sentence drifted off and, for a moment, she looked lost. It didn't last long; her anger flared quickly, like fire consuming a piece of tinder. "This is *ridiculous*. None of it makes any sense. Why would O'Connor want to hurt Dad?"

"It's because of the kid." He decided that he had to give her more. "I got a call from your father's phone tonight. It was O'Connor. He said that he had your dad, that he was alive and, if I wanted it to stay that way, I should meet him at an address in East Kansas City."

"What?" Her voice was barely a whisper.

"I went there," he said. "Jack Kelly's body was inside. He'd been murdered."

Mollie reached a hand out for the counter and braced herself. Milton took a step forward, but she held up a hand to stop him.

"It was an ambush," Milton said. "The detective I asked your father to ask you about—"

"Nicol," she cut in.

Milton nodded. "Detective Nicol and his partner were waiting for me. They trapped me in the building. I think they were planning to frame me for the murder and then shoot me for resisting arrest. But I was able to get away."

"What does Kelly have to do with this?"

"O'Connor probably knew that Kelly and your father were friends. The Trapanal that they gave your father is often used in interrogations. Hollywood would call it truth serum—it relaxes inhibitions. Makes it harder to keep secrets. I think O'Connor got your father's details from Kelly and then tried to get your father to tell him about me." Milton held up the empty bottle. "This is Pavulon. It's used during executions. It's a muscle relaxant. I think O'Connor planned to use this to murder your father. You need to give this to the hospital and tell them you found it down here."

She looked at him suspiciously. "How would you know all that?"

"It doesn't matter."

Mollie looked pale and weak. She leaned against the counter and exhaled. "I need a fucking smoke."

Milton reached into his pocket and took out his pack of Kools. He took out two, handed one to Mollie, and then lit both.

"We need to think carefully about what to do next," he said. "I saw a couple of cameras in here. Do they work?"

"Yes," she said. "He's always been careful about security." She swallowed, realising what she had just said. "I always thought it was paranoia. Turns out I was only half-right."

"Could you have a look and see if they've recorded anything?"

"For evidence—right?"

"Yes," he said. "And, in my case, exoneration. Nicol and his partner are going to try to pin Kelly's murder on me. They might try the same trick with your father—try to argue that that was me, too. Neither holds up if we can show what really happened here."

"I will," she said. "What about you?"

"I'm going to find whoever was responsible for what happened."

"Patrick O'Connor?"

"Yes."

Milton heard steel in her voice. "And then?"

"There'll be justice for what he's done."

57

P atrick O'Connor had told them to drive to Mount Saint Mary's Cemetery on Cleveland Avenue. Bird parked the car on the street next to the open stone gate.

"What are we gonna tell him?" Nicol said.

"There's no point not saying. He's gonna find out eventually."

"And what about what happened with Milton? At the block?"

"The truth," Bird said.

"The truth makes us look bad. We had him caught on the top floor of the building, multiple cops waiting for him, and he still gets away?"

"What about Patrick's pissant brother? He was supposed to be there, too, and he wasn't. You heard the radio—he got himself killed. Patrick wants to talk to us about mistakes? Fine. I can do that. It's not all on us."

Nicol sighed. "Take it easy. Maybe he doesn't know. Either way, he's not going to take it well, is he?"

"Not my problem."

Bird opened the door of the car and got out. Nicol killed the engine and followed him.

"I fucking hate this," he muttered.

"But you like his money well enough."

"Let's just get it over with."

THEY HAD MET in the cemetery before. O'Connor was waiting for them behind the small stone building where the municipal workers stored the lawnmowers, the snowblowers, and the rest of their gear. It was quiet here, with little chance of being observed save by the crackheads and junkies who drifted along the pitted asphalt trails.

Nicol saw the red glow of O'Connor's cigarette first. He was pacing, a sign that he was unnerved. Nicol didn't know the Irishman all that well, but they had done enough favours for him recently that he had an understanding of his tells. He had seen him like this before; a jangle of tension, ready to lash out without warning.

"Hey," Nicol said.

O'Connor stopped pacing. "You're late."

"Just running a few checks to see if anything came up."

The red tip of the cigarette flared as O'Connor drew down on it. "And has it?"

"Look, Patrick. There's something we need to—"

"Don't you 'look, Patrick' me. You want to tell me what happened?"

"There's something you need—"

"Just tell me what fucking happened!"

Nicol exchanged a glance with Bird, then shrugged. "Milton turned up. He went inside the building."

"And Kelly's body was there?"

"Your brother left him there."

"And then?"

"We called for backup."

"And *then?*"

"And then Milton got away," Nicol said. "He jumped out of the top-floor window and landed in a dumpster full of trash."

"We'll find him," Bird added. "I mean, where's he gonna go? We put the word out, and now the whole department's looking for him. He's not local. He won't know where to go. Fish out of water. Don't worry about it."

"Shut it," O'Connor said. "You got some neck, coming out here and telling me I don't need to worry. You mess up something as simple as taking care of one man my brother practically serves up to you on a platter, and then you come down here, giving it large, telling me that you're going to fix it."

Bird squared up to him. "You want to talk about messing up?"

"Easy," Nicol warned, aware of his partner's temper. "Patrick—please, just listen for a minute. There's something that you need to hear."

"No. I've heard enough."

"It's about your brother."

O'Connor stopped. "What?"

"We had a plan," Nicol said. "Kenny was supposed to be there, outside the building. He was watching for Milton and, when he turned up, we were all going to go in and take him out. He didn't. He wasn't there. We thought he'd bailed on us; then we got a call. A one-forty—you know what that is?"

"No."

"A murder," Bird said.

Patrick stared at him.

"There's no easy way to say this," Nicol said. "Kenneth was found in the basement of Kansas City Fresh—the business owned by Jack Kelly's friend. The guy's name is Tanner, and his daughter called it in. I've seen a picture. It's definitely him. I'm sorry, Patrick."

"No," O'Connor said. "No way. No fucking way." He took out his phone and woke it, the screen bathing his face in white light. He tapped to place a call and then put the phone to his ear. He waited fifteen seconds and then killed the call. He bit his lip.

"Did he tell anyone what he was going to do?" Bird asked.

"Of course he didn't! He's not an amateur. This isn't the first time he's done something like this."

"No one's saying it is," Nicol said.

O'Connor sucked down on the cigarette until the red tip touched his fingers. "When was the last time you heard from him?"

"He called us from Tanner's. He said that the guy's name was Milton, that he'd set up the meet, and that he'd be there. That was that. He must've been killed just after."

"Where's Tanner?"

"In the hospital," Bird said. "He's being treated for an overdose. Looks like Kenny gave it to him, but someone interrupted him before he could leave."

"Who?"

"We don't know."

"Can't be Milton."

"I don't know," Nicol said. "Could he have taken the call from your brother and then gone to Tanner's place?"

"I don't see it," Bird said. "Kenny said he was going to the apartment. Why wait?"

"So?" O'Connor snapped. "Who did it? Someone connected to him? It has to be, right?"

"An investigation's been opened," Nicol said. "We'll make sure we stay on top of it."

O'Connor dipped his head. His breathing grew a little ragged. "What is it with people?" he muttered. "You ask for something simple, something a monkey could do, and it doesn't get done. I should've done it myself."

Nicol could see the payday that they had been promised fading away into the distance. "Look," he said. "Patrick, we'll find Milton. Bird's right. Where's he gonna go? He's not local. And you didn't see the drop from the window to the dumpster. What was that, Frank? Thirty feet?"

"At least."

"Two of the boys who saw him said he was walking awkwardly, holding his arm. Maybe he broke it. We check the hospitals and there's got to be a chance he turns up."

"And my brother? Where is he?"

"The medical examiner picked him up. They'll be getting ready to autopsy him."

O'Connor flicked the dog end against a nearby gravestone and took out another cigarette. He lit it; the flame jerked left and right as his fingers shook.

"What about the kid and the van?"

"We find Milton, we find them."

"And what if Bobby finds them first? We already know he's got Sal and his boys looking. What happens then?"

"They won't," Nicol said. "We will."

58

There was a parking lot three blocks from Tanner's business, with a few cars dotted around the space; Milton stole a Honda Civic and headed south toward downtown. He'd reached Oakwood Park when he saw that the tank was almost empty. He pulled over into the forecourt of a gas station that had a twenty-four-hour diner attached to it. He was aware of the CCTV cameras overhead, but pulled down his cap and kept his head down as he filled up. He moved the car to the lot and then went into the diner to get something to eat. It hit all the clichés of 1950s Americana, with red vinyl benches faded to sunset orange, glass-domed serving dishes displaying banana and coconut cream pie behind the counter, brown plastic industrial coffee machines and glass coffee pots that sat until they were almost empty, the contents as black as pitch.

Milton took a seat at a table next to the window.

The waitress ambled over. "What can I get you?"

"The ham and cheese omelette, please," Milton said.

"They come with all-you-can-eat hash browns," the waitress said.

"Perfect."

"You want coffee?"

"Yes, please."

The woman found a mug for him and filled it to the brim with coffee. "You want more, you just let me know. I'll be back with your food in a moment."

There were only four other patrons inside the diner: an ageing rummy sought to mitigate his hangover, a mug of coffee clutched between worn fingers; three teens who must have been out all night were in the last booth on the other side of the restaurant, the girl asleep against the shoulder of one of the guys.

Milton took another couple of Tylenol from the packet and swallowed them with a mouthful of coffee. His shoulder was sore, but not unbearably so. He thought, perhaps, he might have been fortunate. He had a decent range of move-ment and, the pain masked by the drugs, he didn't feel as if it would impede him too much.

He checked his watch. It was three. There was no great risk to being here; as far as he knew, the two corrupt cops did not have a picture of him, which meant that any descrip-tion circulated to other police would rely upon Nicol's memory. Milton had changed his appearance enough that the morning news—if it even covered Kelly's murder—would likely present a different likeness to its viewers.

The waitress brought his eggs with a side of hash browns and a plate of toast. Milton picked at the eggs. He thought about what he had learned over the course of the last few hours. Tanner had sold him out; that much was certain. Milton tried not to condemn him, especially given the price that he had paid for being drawn into Milton's malign slip-stream. He brought pain and suffering wherever he went, and this was a reminder—if one was needed—that there was nothing that he could do to change that fact. He had felt optimistic upon his arrival. He had done good in Medellín; Beau Baxter's death had been avenged, and the leadership of the El Centro cartel had been gutted. But even that had not been enough to provide redress for the wrongs that he had done, and now he had been punished for his presumption. It would never stop. He would forever be making amends.

The waitress came over with the coffee. "Want a refill?"

"Thank you."

"Lemme guess," she said. "Shift change?" She had a face that appeared young from a distance, but was weathered and pale at closer range.

"That's right," Milton said.

"What do you do?"

"Security guard," he lied, easily and fluently.

"You know the gravel pits they used to have down near Swope Park? My old man used to do security there. You want to talk about a cushy gig? Eight hours of peace and quiet to read, watch the game, whatever. Had the nerve to come home and complain that he was tired."

Milton smiled politely, not really wanting to continue the conversation but not wanting to appear rude. He was always surprised by the American propensity to break into personal conversations with perfect strangers. That kind of familiarity was anathema at home. He had been flummoxed by it when he had first visited the country, but his frequent returns had worn that down to a combination of discomfort —typically at the lack of commonality—and appreciation of the effort.

"Coffee okay?" the waitress said.

"Just what the doctor ordered."

She smiled at that. "It's just the crap that Dino buys in bulk. But if you make it strong enough to stand up and salute a person's stomach, it still works fine. You want some more hash browns? I'm just about to clean the grill."

"I'm good, thanks," Milton said.

He took a moment to consider what to do next. The way he saw it, he had two choices: he could go back to the quarry and help Fernández keep the Pizzolatos safe; or he could be proactive and take the fight to those who were in pursuit of the van. The latter held more appeal. Milton had always preferred to control events rather than have them come to him. He had no reason to fear that the location of Enzo and his mother had been compromised, and, although he feared that might not last forever, he was confident that he had a window when he did not need to be there. He took out his phone and opened the email that Mollie had sent him with details of Patrick O'Connor's business. The registered office of Dublin Investments was on Petticoat Lane.

He downed the last of his coffee and winced slightly at the bitterness. He drew his money clip and left a ten on the table.

Time to pay the Irishman a visit.

etticoat Lane was dedicated to office space and, at three in the morning, it was deserted. Milton saw the sign on the wall that announced Dublin Investments, and got out to take a closer look. He glanced in through the glass doors to the lobby beyond and saw a waiting area and a receptionist's desk. The door looked reasonably substantial and was exposed to the street; there might not have been any passing traffic, but Milton had no doubt that the area would be flooded with CCTV coverage. It was not going to be easy to get inside.

He went back to the car and reversed it until he was next to the only other car that had been left there. He had just decided that he would stay here and watch the building when his phone rang. It was Mollie. He took the call.

"You okay?"

"I'm all right."

"And your dad?"

"Still sedated," she said. "They say it's just to give his body time to recover."

"You told them about the Pavulon?"

"I did. They think he'll make it. But they said that another ten minutes and it might have been different."

"What about the cops?"

"They're at the office now. They wanted me to go to the station with them so that they could take a statement, but I said I needed to be here with Dad. They're sending someone to speak to me."

"You're at the ER?"

"Outside his room," she said.

"Have you seen anyone else?"

"Just the hospital staff—why?"

"Eidur?"

"No. There's been no one. Do I need to be careful with him?"

"I wouldn't be trusting anyone at the moment."

"What about you?"

"You can trust me, Mollie, although I can understand why you'd be hesitant."

She was quiet. Milton swapped the phone from his left hand to his right, watching as a garbage truck rumbled along the street.

"Where are you?" she asked him.

"Downtown."

"Why?"

"I want to know a little more about Patrick O'Connor."

"All right," she said. "Will you tell me if you find out anything?"

"Of course."

Milton was about to end the call when Mollie interrupted him.

"I almost forgot. I checked the CCTV footage like you asked. It was weird, though. The last twelve hours' worth of files were corrupted. The system uploads to the cloud, but I couldn't find anything to play. That's never happened before. You think that's strange?"

"It's certainly unfortunate."

"Just seems like too much of a coincidence," she said. "There's nothing about what happened to Dad."

"Maybe O'Connor did something," Milton offered, knowing that wasn't what had happened.

"Maybe," she said.

Milton ended the call and put the phone on the dash. He knew, from experience, who had erased the footage. Björn Thorsson would have put in a request with Group Two to scrub all evidence that Number One had ever been at Tanner's place. Milton had enjoyed that kind of assistance before. It was a sobering reminder of what he was facing: a dangerous operative, supported by a lavishly funded organisation with no qualms about breaking the law in the furtherance of its objective.

And its objective now?

They wanted him dead.

60

I t was ten minutes to ten and Milton was on his second cup of coffee from the stand on the corner of Petticoat Lane and Main Street when he saw Björn Thorsson. He turned the corner and stopped at the stand to order a drink. Milton was twenty-five metres away and his car was facing away from him, enough for him to be confident that the Icelander would not notice him. Nevertheless, Milton opened the glovebox, took out the Peacemaker, and slid it beneath his belt so that the butt pressed up against the bottom of his back. He had no interest in a confrontation with Thorsson, but he was not going to make the mistake of unpreparedness.

He watched Thorsson in the mirror. He had a paper cup in his hand, and he was using it as a prop while he reconnoitred the street. He said something to the man who ran the stand and then set off along the sidewalk in the direction of O'Connor's office.

Milton could guess why Thorsson was here: he would have told London what had happened at Tanner's business, and one of the analysts in Group One would have provided him with a dossier on the O'Connors. Thorsson was following the breadcrumbs from Tanner to Kenneth O'Connor and now to his brother. In some ways, it was reassuring. If Thorsson had known where Milton was, he would have come straight for him. He evidently did not know and was investigating the remaining Irishman in the hope that he might be able to extract the information that would lead him to his prey.

Milton wondered whether this might be the moment to remove the threat against him. Thorsson did not know that he was here, and it would be a simple enough matter to take him out. He quickly dismissed the idea: there were witnesses here, and a killing in broad daylight would bring down heat on him that would make it very difficult for him to continue to protect Enzo and his mother. And, more than that, Milton reminded himself that he was not in the business of cold-blooded murder any longer, that he had given that up the moment he told Control that he was not interested in killing for him any longer. He would defend himself if it came to that, but he wouldn't act pre-emptively.

Milton kept his eye on the rear-view mirror as Thorsson continued along the street. He was clearly engaged in a recce, making his way slowly while he sipped at the contents of the cup. He paused when he reached the offices of Dublin Investments, looking through the door before continuing toward Milton. He stopped just before Milton's car and crossed over, continuing the same careful scrutiny from the other side of the street. He continued back to the junction with Main Street, crossed back onto Milton's side of the road, and then headed back to O'Connor's office. He paused again, crouching down to tie a shoelace that did not need to be tied, and, his mind seemingly made up, he reached for the heavy metal handle, pushed the door open and went inside.

61

A ldo Maniscalco and Francesco di Cello were standing in the lobby of the Cheesecake Factory at the Country Club Plaza. Aldo had been unable to sleep, thinking about Enzo. He had looked through all the online news reports in the hope of finding something that might give him a clue about what had happened at the Pizzolato house, and where his friend might be. All he had found was a report of a shooting, that a man had been murdered there, and that the police had opened an investigation. Beyond that, there was nothing. He had tried calling, too, and had left half a dozen voicemail messages until Enzo's mailbox was full. There had been no return call. No text. Nothing. He had called Francesco and arranged to meet him here so that they could compare notes. But Franny, too, was all out of ideas. Aldo still thought that he was holding something back, just like yesterday, but he had no idea what it was or how he could broach the subject without causing an argument.

His attention had drifted up to the big-screen TV that

was tuned to *Good Morning America*. A man was being interviewed by Amy Robach and George Stephanopoulos.

He pointed at the screen. "That's the guy I was telling you about," he told Francesco. "Sebastian Maniscalco."

Francesco's eyes narrowed. "And you're saying you're related?"

Aldo shrugged.

"You *ain't* related," Francesco scoffed. "You're full of it. Man, you knew someone famous, your fat ass wouldn't be hanging around KC. You'd be up around him like a fly around shit, trying to make a buck."

"No, man, it's true. We're, like, fourth cousins on my mother's side."

Francesco laughed. "Come on, bitch. You think I was born yesterday?"

"I'm telling you, it's true. He made it. That show he's talking about, that's his Netflix special. Man…" Aldo looked up at the TV again, his eyes wide. "Someday I'm going to have something like that."

"Stick to drums, man. You're good at that. But you ain't funny." He noticed his friend's frown and realised that he had been unfair. Aldo could be pretty hilarious. "Sorry. I mean, you're funny and all, but not like *professional* funny. But you never miss a beat on that kick drum. That's what you need to concentrate on."

Aldo rubbed his expansive stomach. "I'm gonna concentrate on getting breakfast. I got paid yesterday—you want something?"

"I don't need your charity, Aldo. And I don't want to hear about your lame-ass job."

He turned and made his way to the exit. Aldo could guess what was eating him. Mention of the fact that he had got paid had made Francesco feel bad. He had said before how he hated to hear his friends jawing about their jobs like they were something special, or like having a job somehow made them better than him. Aldo knew he was sensitive about it, and tried to remember not to mention it around him. He knew that Francesco's parents had shown him how to steal from stores when he was a kid, when he was too young to get in trouble. Francesco rarely spoke about it, especially now that they were all older, but he had told Aldo once that his folks believed that hustling for a buck was the only way to ever get ahead in a world where no one would ever give someone like them a break. Franny had taken a beating from his father the first time that he had questioned it. He had never questioned it again, and he said that in time he had grown to believe they were right.

Francesco went outside and Aldo followed him.

"I'm sorry," he said. "I wasn't making a point. Just wanted to see if you were hungry, that's all."

"Well, I'm not. Just leave it."

Franny walked on down the street. Aldo followed and, as he caught up, his phone rang. He fished it out and looked at the screen: the number was unfamiliar. He held the screen up for Francesco to see; the other boy shook his head. Aldo shrugged again and hit answer.

"Yeah? Who's this?"

"It's me."

"Enzo! You okay, man?"

Francesco stopped walking.

"I'm fine," Enzo said.

"Where have you been, man? You haven't been answering your calls."

"I'm sorry."

"And then we went to your place yesterday. The police were there. They're saying someone was shot."

"Are you on your own?"

"I'm with Franny. We're at the mall."

"Can anyone else hear you?"

"We're outside. It's just us."

"Put me on speaker. You both need to hear this."

Aldo did as he was asked.

"Franny—have you told Aldo what happened?"

Aldo looked at Francesco, who looked away, his face flushed.

"No," Aldo said. "He hasn't said anything."

"Franny—listen to me. I don't blame you for what happened. It's not your fault, okay? I'm not mad."

"What happened?" Aldo said.

"We had to leave town. Me and my mom. You know that van I bought? I don't know why, but it turns out that Sal Provenzano wants it. Franny called me on Saturday afternoon and said that Sal was on his way."

"*What?*"

"Sal and three guys. They were all strapped."

"How does Sal know where you live?"

"Franny told him."

Aldo turned to Francesco. "Why would you *do* that?"

Francesco's face clouded with anger. "Fuck off, Aldo. You have no idea."

"I'm not mad," Enzo repeated. "It's not your fault, Franny. No arguing, guys. *Please.* I need to tell you something, and you got to listen and do what I tell you to do. All right?"

Aldo glared at Francesco. "I'm listening."

"I got into trouble at the auction. Two guys tried to take the van from me. This guy got rid of them for me, and he said I was probably going to have more trouble. He said I could call him if that happened, and I did. He got to my place before Sal. There was a shoot-out, and one of Sal's guys got capped. That's why we had to hide. We had to get out of town quick."

"Shit."

"I'm just calling because you need to be careful—both of you. Sal's still going to be looking for me. He probably wants me even more now, after what happened."

"You're shitting me."

"I'm *telling* you."

"So give the van to him."

"I don't think that's gonna play now, not after what happened. I'm good, for now, anyway, but I'm worried about you guys. If they can't find me, they'll go after people who know me. Sal already knows we're friends, Franny. He'll be back. And it won't be hard to figure out we're tight, Aldo—it's not like I got many friends."

"I'm not going anywhere," Francesco said, standing up straighter now. "Sal ain't gonna hurt me. My uncle's part of his crew."

"*Listen* to me, man. I ain't fooling here. You need to get your ass out of town and come hide out with us."

Francesco glanced over at Aldo. He looked conflicted, and Francesco could guess why: Enzo was the most level-headed of all of them, probably because of his autism. Everything was usually logic with him. But this time? He sounded scared.

"You guys still there?" Enzo said. "You gotta come. It ain't safe. Come out here—just for a few days until it gets fixed."

"No," Francesco said. "This is your mess, not mine. I didn't buy the stinking van. I ain't going nowhere. I ain't done nothing. Besides, cowards run and hide. You got to be a man about things. Show you got a set."

"Fuck." Aldo swallowed. "I'm scared."

"Well, I ain't." Francesco lifted his shirt to show the pistol that he had stuck inside his belt. "Got myself strapped."

"What is it?" Enzo said over the phone.

Aldo was stunned. "You bought a piece?" He leaned closer to the phone. "Francesco has lost his shit, man. He got a nine."

"My uncle gave it to me," Francesco explained proudly. "He says I can start running for him pretty soon." He dropped his shirt to conceal the gun in his waistband once more. "Man, you little bitches can work two, three lousy jobs and you're never going to make the kind of money you need to protect yourself. You never gonna have the things you want in life. I ain't going out like that. You get me? My father... before he got all messed up, he said we got one thing to protect in this life, one thing no one else will ever have. And that's the family name. I'm Francesco di Cello, and nobody ever takes what I want from me, and I'm damn sure I ain't running because of something you've gone and done."

Aldo hung his head. He and Enzo had been listening to Franny's angry pronouncements since they were little kids. But they were all just about to be adults now, ready to move away from their families and make their own marks in the world. Aldo knew there was only one outcome for Franny if he was determined to be like his uncle.

A car pulled up to the kerb, a gold-brown sedan with police-style speed hubs. Aldo recognised it from somewhere. The passenger window rolled down. It was the cop from Coach's after-school program: Detective Nicol.

"Hey there, boys," Nicol said pleasantly, waving a hand.

"Hold on," Aldo said into the phone. "It's Five-O."

Nicol smiled at them. "You're Aldo, right? And you're

Francesco. You remember me? I see you at the club after school."

Aldo had not known the detective for long. Having a gang cop at the school made him nervous, just like all the others. But, more than that, Nicol had always creeped him out. He was way too friendly. The joke was that he was into kids or something. Aldo didn't buy that; his guess was that he was trying to cultivate snitches, and that was almost as bad.

"We were just going," Aldo said, giving Francesco a nod down the street.

They began to walk away from the storefront. The driver's side door opened, and another man climbed out of the police car. He came around the car and stood on the sidewalk ahead of them, blocking the way. Aldo thought that he recognised him.

"Guys," Nicol said, "wait a minute. That's my partner, Detective Bird. We just want to have a little chat."

Aldo remembered where he'd seen Bird before: he was the dude who kept rolling LeKwon Green and the other corner boys in East KC. He had heard stories about how Bird used to beat on the kids he pulled, and there was a rumour —at least he *hoped* it was a rumour—that Bird had kneecapped a kid who had given him lip. That might or might not have been true, but one thing was certain: Bird was bad news.

"Run!" Francesco yelled.

Aldo did not need any encouragement. They turned and ran into the road, darting through the slow-moving traffic and putting as much distance between themselves and the two cops as they could. The unmarked car's siren bipped. Its tyres squealed as it pulled a hard U-turn to give chase.

62

Patrick O'Connor parked the car outside the office, killed the engine, and scrubbed his eyes. They felt red and raw. That wasn't surprising: he had hardly slept. The police had called him soon after he had finished with Bird and Nicol last night, and asked him to come to the station. He'd asked why, and they'd told him that they had news about his brother that really had to be delivered in person; when he'd made to complain about the hour, the officer had said that it couldn't wait. He had driven to the station and had hit all the right notes when they told him that his brother had been shot dead in the basement of a business in Gladstone. It was a bravura performance that had run the gamut of what might have been expected: hostility at being hauled into the station at four in the morning, disbelief when he was told what had happened, confusion as to who would do such a thing, and then fury. He hadn't felt any of those emotions; instead, he'd felt as if a live wire were buzzing just behind his eyes, buzzing and popping and fizzing, an itch that he couldn't scratch.

They wanted him to identify his brother's body, and he

did, waiting as a mortuary technician pulled back the sheet to reveal Kenny's face; there was a neat little hole above his right eyebrow. The woman had asked if it was his brother, and Patrick had given a curt nod in the affirmative, asked if there was anything else that they needed from him, then taken his leave. He had gone back to his apartment and had tried to sleep, failed, and then given up. He had poured himself a drink and sat with it at the kitchen table, staring into the dark liquid and the ice cubes that clunked against the side of the glass as they slowly rotated.

He was going to find out what had happened to his brother. He was going to kill whoever was responsible. He would do it himself, and he would enjoy it, but he would wait until he had found the van and made himself whole with Bobby Whitesox. And then, when he had done that, and when he had put himself into a position where he didn't need Bobby's patronage any longer, he would kill the thieving wop and anyone else who was stupid enough to stand in his way.

Patrick got out of the car, locked it, and made his way across the sidewalk to the front door of the building. He went inside. His secretary, Sonya, was behind her desk, and a man whom Patrick had never seen before was standing in front of her. The man was big—he must have been six feet four—and he was deeply tanned, with hair so blond that it was almost white.

"Good morning," Patrick said.

Sonya looked up and smiled. "Morning, Mr. O'Connor. This is Mr. Stef... Mr. Stef..."

"Stefansson," the man finished for her. "Stefan Karl Stefansson."

She smiled apologetically. "Thank you. Mr. Stefansson

said he called last week, but I'm afraid I don't have a record of it."

"It was Tuesday or Wednesday," Stefansson said. "Toward the end of the day."

"There's nothing on the system," she said.

"Oh," Stefansson said. He turned to Patrick. "I've come from River Market. I don't suppose there's a chance I could see you now, is there? I'd rather not have to come back."

Patrick forced himself to relax. "What can I do for you?"

"I'm looking for investment in my business."

"What kind of business do you have?"

"I have six launderettes." He smiled a little goofily. "We're doing well and we're looking to expand—we just don't have the cash for it."

"How did you find out about me?"

"A friend of mine hits balls at the range out in Northland. You own it, right? He said he'd heard you were always looking for opportunities to invest in good businesses that just need an injection of cash to get to the next level. I think that's us."

Patrick smelled an opportunity, but the timing couldn't have been worse. He was tempted to take the meeting, but decided against it. He knew that he was at his best when he was prepared, and he didn't have the information that he would need to push Stefansson's buttons. What was more, he didn't have the energy for the performance.

"Look, I'm really sorry if there's been a misunderstanding. My diary is full this morning, and there's nothing I can do."

Stefansson looked disappointed.

Patrick let the moment hang for a moment and then added, "Look, I'll tell you what—give your address to Sonya, tell her about your business, and email me your company's financial papers: the P&L, bank statements, business plan, projections—anything that you think might be helpful. I'll drive over to see you next week. Can't have you driving over here twice."

Stefansson brightened up. "Thank you," he said. "I appreciate that."

"My pleasure. I'll see you next week."

Patrick shook Stefansson's hand and then waited until he had left the office.

"I'm sorry," Sonya said. "I didn't—"

"Clear my diary," Patrick cut over her. "No calls, no walk-ins, nothing. I'm going to be busy all day."

63

Enzo stared at the phone. The line had gone dead. He was sitting in the kitchen, alone, after leaving his mother to read an old magazine as she sat on the end of the living room sofa. He was usually stoic, but his chronic anxiety could sometimes lead him to panic or freeze. Aldo had said the police had shown up, and he had heard a name he recognised over the open line: Nicol. Then Franny had yelled that they should run. They were obviously in trouble.

Enzo felt fear and guilt. It didn't feel like he had persuaded either Aldo or Franny to leave the city. He thought that he might still be able to persuade Aldo, but Franny was different. There seemed to be nothing he could do to get through the bravado that his friend wore like a shell to protect against his insecurity.

And he was carrying a piece now?

He thought about talking to his mother, but decided not to worry her. Coach was a better bet. He went outside, crossed the yard to the side door of the corrugated tin building, and knocked.

"Yeah?" a voice yelled from inside.

He opened the door and stepped in. "Down here," Coach yelled from the other end of the room, past the shelving units.

Fernández was in the middle of the large building, pacing around the van.

"Hey," Enzo said. "What you doing?"

Fernández stroked his chin. "Trying to figure out why this van is so valuable. You okay?"

Enzo bit his lip. "I'm worried about my friends."

"Aldo and Franny? Why?"

"I was speaking to them just now—"

Coach interrupted him. "You spoke to them? How?"

"I called them."

The coach's face darkened. "I told you, Enzo. You can't do that."

"It's my friends, man. They're worried about me. They don't know where I am."

"You didn't tell them, did you?"

"No," he said. "I tried to get them to come out here, too. I thought maybe John could go and get them."

"And?"

"I didn't get to ask them. It sounded like they were running from someone. Like someone tried to grab them."

"You sure?" Enzo nodded. "You know who?"

"Detective Nicol."

"He's not a bad guy."

"He was with another cop—Bird."

Coach closed his eyes and sighed. "Shit. That's different."

"You know him?"

"He's a piece of..." He paused, then chose different words. "He's bad news. Do you have any idea where they were?"

"Country Club Plaza."

"All right. Hold on."

He took out his phone and placed a call, putting it on speaker.

John Smith answered on the second ring. "Hello, Coach."

Enzo found that he was relieved to hear Smith's voice.

"We got a problem," Fernández said. "Enzo's friends may be in trouble. Aldo Maniscalco and Francesco di Cello. They were talking on the phone—"

"What?"

"I've told him not to do that again," Fernández said.

"*Please*, Enzo. That's important."

"I know," Enzo said. "I'm sorry."

"Okay. What happened?"

"Two cops are chasing them."

"Who?"

"Detective Nicol and Detective Bird."

Enzo heard Smith's long sigh.

"You met Nicol," Fernández said.

"I know," Milton replied. "And Bird, too."

"Bird is a bad dude," Fernández said. "He's beaten on kids from school before."

"So is Nicol."

The coach frowned. "What? Nicol's okay—he comes to the school."

"We had a run-in last night. Me and both of them. I'll explain later—but Nicol is not a good guy. Enzo—when was this?"

"Just now."

"Where?"

"Country Club Plaza."

"That's on West Forty-Seventh," Fernández said.

"I'm close. I'll head that way now and see if I can find them."

64

A ldo and Francesco sprinted down the sidewalk, trying to avoid the other pedestrians, bumping shoulders with some and pushing others aside. They blew past the red-brick low-rise boutiques and restaurants of the Country Club Plaza, their sneakers thudding off the snow-covered concrete, surprised breakfasters watching them through plate-glass windows. The siren was a block away. Nicol and Bird had lost them for a few moments when they cut between buildings, but they were back on them again now.

Aldo was five inches taller and more than a hundred pounds heavier than Francesco, but he was a natural athlete who had played football for years before giving it up to concentrate on the drums. He was a good five yards ahead of his friend and intended to stay there. He was aiming for Brush Creek, less than a block away. If they could cross over on the footbridge, then they might be able to get ahead of Nicol and Bird and stay there.

The siren was getting louder. Aldo wondered whether they would call for backup. He looked over his shoulder and saw that Francesco was still there, gaining a few feet as Aldo slowed. But so was the detectives' car, the flashing lights just half a block away now. Aldo turned left onto Nichols Road, crashing into a woman in front of the Rolex watch store, knocking her onto her backside as the two of them sprinted by. He heard the brakes of the car as it flew by the turn. They neared the end of the block. The siren screeched, nearer still. Aldo cut left, crossing the snowy median, with Franny right behind him as he turned left onto Central Street, past more upscale eateries and shops.

"Come on," he gasped. "We need to get over the bridge."

The broad, dark waters of Brush Creek were right ahead, the footbridge sitting amidst the strip of park parallel to the riverbank and the four-laned Ward Parkway. Aldo looked both ways as he ran across the road, Franny hot on his heels; cars veered crazily, honking and slamming on their brakes as drivers tried to avoid the two kids.

Aldo hoped they might get lucky. The cops might choose to head a block west to the two-lane road bridge and, if they did, the two of them would have a chance. They could lose them amidst the taller buildings in the plaza area, the hotels and condos around West Forty-Ninth. Aldo's breath was heavy now, his pace beginning to slow. Francesco had caught up to him and was looking backwards, his eyes wide at the sight of the flashing lights closing in on them now.

65

"D amn it!" Bird yelled, smacking the dash with his free right hand. The kids had reached the green-belt across Ward Parkway, heading for the Sister City footbridge. He began to pull the car over.

"No," Nicol said. "Take a right and take Wornall. We can double back."

He did not trust his own footspeed to keep up with a pair of eighteen-year-olds. Even if he had been able to match them, he was damn sure that Bird—nearer sixty than forty—would not. They needed to stay in the car.

He did not want to have to call for backup, but he knew that they might have to resort to that if they couldn't corral the kids themselves. It would be a last resort. Explaining away what had happened with John Milton at the Lister Avenue apartment block had been easy enough, given Milton's prior contact with Jack Kelly and the fact that he had been seen brawling with the O'Connors at the auction. He would also be able to find a reason to explain why they were in pursuit of the teens, but that meant other officers would be there when they caught them. Questioning them privately would be impossible, and threatening them to get the answers that Patrick O'Connor wanted would be out of the question.

It would be so much better if they could get to them alone.

Bird threw the wheel over and stamped on the gas, the back end fishtailing as they corrected their heading onto Ward Parkway. The cars around them did not have time to pull aside, and Bird swerved between them. The siren wailed, and Nicol braced himself as his partner spun the wheel left and then right, tyres sliding out on the ice again as they roared through the two-lane traffic on Wornall Road. The car flew across the bridge over the creek and past the eight-storey, double-winged Raphael Hotel.

"Take West Forty-Ninth. They're headed there. They'll try to lose us between the buildings. Get a block ahead of them and we can come back."

Bird braked hard, swinging the car left towards the trio of grand, eighteen-storey condominiums. Nicol scanned the sidewalks and the buildings on both sides. He stared into the miniature park at Central and West Forty-Ninth as the car headed east, downhill.

"There."

A block ahead, two figures had emerged from behind the Sulgrave Apartment towers. They were still jogging, but just a little slower now. They were glancing around nervously. Nicol guessed that they thought they had escaped them.

Bird flattened the accelerator, and the Crown Vic's engine howled as the car lurched forward.

The boys turned in panic at the sudden roar, then gained the opposite sidewalk. They sprinted down the ramp of a multi-storey parking lot.

"Pull over," Nicol said.

Bird did. "You been inside before?" he said. "It's on tiers. If they cut out on one of the higher levels to the street above, we'll be three blocks out of our way."

"Go around with the car and cut them off on West Fiftieth," Nicol said. "I'll follow on foot and shepherd them your way."

Nicol undid his belt and opened the door, climbed out onto the sidewalk, and jogged towards the coral-coloured parking building.

66

Milton saw the Crown Vic as it raced across the bridge, and settled in behind it, slowing down as the driver idled along West Forty-Ninth. It was obvious that he was looking for someone. Milton scouted ahead, too, and saw the two boys at the same time the detectives did. The car leapt ahead and pursued them to a large multi-storey car park. The boys sprinted down the ramp. The car stopped and Nicol got out and followed. The Crown Vic raced away, headed south. Milton knew what they were doing: Nicol would play sweeper and usher the two boys out at a location where Bird could grab them.

He would have to get to them before that could happen.

The parking lot was automated, with ticket machines at the three front gates. Milton drove the stolen Civic to the gate farthest from the one that Nicol had dodged around to get inside, pressed the button to collect a ticket, and pulled it out of the slot. The gate rose and Milton edged ahead. He found an empty spot and parked the car. He drew the Peacemaker and stepped out of the car.

The lot was dimly lit. It had been built around a central

core of ramps, and Milton jogged up the nearest one to reach the second level. Nothing. He kept ascending and, on the third floor, spotted Nicol. The officer was moving slowly, checking between cars. He craned his neck to look west of the open-sided parking levels, making sure that the boys had not jumped out into the adjacent street-level parking lot, which emptied onto the next street over.

"Boys," Nicol called out, "I just want to talk. I'm a police officer. You don't have anything to worry about. I work at your school. Come on—you *know* me."

Milton stayed low, hugging the central wall and staying out of Nicol's line of sight. A car rounded the corner, looking for a spot. It crawled past, the driver ignoring him. Nicol tucked his hand behind his suit jacket's left breast, most likely concealing a pistol.

The detective waited until the car had passed, its running lights playing across his stern face, barely visible in the dim half-light. "Come on, boys. This is nuts. You can't hide in here forever. You want me to call for backup? You'll have to run eventually, but, by then, this entire neighbourhood will be crawling with uniformed officers and dogs. *Dogs.* You don't want that. *I* don't want that. All we got to do is sit down and have a little chat."

Nicol rounded the corner to the next tier. Milton stayed right behind him, just twenty yards back. The detective evidently did not feel the need to be careful; his Oxford dress shoes sounded loudly on the asphalt.

Milton reached the fourth floor. The parking slots along the interior wall were all occupied, and, seeking cover, he crouched low and manoeuvred through the small gap in front of them. He stayed down, out of sight, drawing close enough that he would be able to reach Nicol by sprinting.

He saw a flash of yellow as a large teenage boy popped

out from behind a car ten yards ahead. Milton recognised him: it was the drummer from the band. Just behind him came the smaller bass guitarist. Enzo's friends: Aldo and Francesco. The kids ran for the slope to the roof deck level. Nicol took off after them, surprising Milton with his quickness. Milton pushed hard, making up the ground before they were caught out in the open air.

Nicol ran up the last slope to the double-sized walk-out doors that led to the roof. They were propped open, and he slid on a patch of black ice as he bolted around the corner. He regained his footing, then kept on moving. Milton was just ten feet behind now, still unobserved. Nicol raised his gun as he hurried outside. Milton dropped his head and sprinted, the ache in his damaged shoulder numbed by adrenaline.

"Stop!" Nicol yelled.

The boys were halfway across the roof. The yellow-lined bays were all empty. They were streaking towards the edge, where the drop to the next lot was only ten feet.

The detective aimed into the air and fired.

Milton slammed into him, his shoulder catching Nicol flush in the lower back. The detective was pitched off balance, both of them crashing to the concrete. Milton scrambled to his feet just as Nicol rolled onto his back and aimed the pistol, bracing it against his knee.

Milton lashed out, his heel catching Nicol on the side of the jaw. The detective's head shot back and cracked against the hard ground, and Nicol lay still. His eyes rolled back into his head.

Milton kicked the detective's pistol across the roof. The two teens were at the edge of the building and, as he watched, they jumped down to the next lot. Milton gave chase, reached the edge and dropped down. He landed on the balls of his feet and rolled forward. He got up and ran, just twenty yards back.

"Aldo!"

The boy kept running.

"Francesco! Enzo sent me to get you."

The two of them looked back, kept running for a few more feet, and then—perhaps realising that it wasn't Nicol —stopped and looked back again.

Milton reached them.

"I remember you," Aldo said between gasps for air. "You were at the school."

Milton stopped next to them, looking for any sign of Bird and the unmarked squad car. Nothing.

"My car is downstairs," he said. "If we take the fire exit, we should be able to get down there without being seen."

The other kid—Francesco—was staring wide-eyed at him.

"Are you coming?" Milton said.

Francesco took a step back. "No way, man. Fuck that. Aldo—you going to trust him? You don't know him."

"He says Enzo sent him. That's good enough for me. I ain't hanging around to get shot by the cops. You want proof that we're in trouble? That was it." He pointed up to the level they'd just jumped from. "We need to get somewhere safe until we can figure out what's going on."

"And I told you," Francesco said, backing away, "I ain't leaving, especially with someone I don't know."

He withdrew a pistol from his belt.

Milton tightened his grip on the Peacemaker, but he kept it pointed down.

"Put it away," he said.

"Why should I? I'm tired of running like a coward.

Anyone comes after me, this is how I'm gonna take care of myself."

"Francesco," Milton began carefully.

"Don't talk to me like you know me!"

Aldo looked at Milton and shook his head. "Forget it, he ain't gonna listen. Where's your car?"

"Lower floor," he said. He fixed Francesco with his icy stare. "I'm not the enemy here. I can't make you come with me if you don't want to, but at least take some advice. Keep your head down. Stay out of sight."

Francesco shrugged. "Whatever. I got this."

He held up the pistol, grinned, then turned and ran.

Milton shook his head.

"He'll be okay," Aldo said, but there was no conviction in his voice.

Milton nodded to the fire escape. "This way."

67

Enzo sat in the corner of the workshop on a tall stool. He had his phone in both hands, and his thumbs flew across the screen. Fernández watched him for a few seconds as he took a break from inspecting the van. He had chastised the kid for calling his friends earlier that morning. Smith had made it clear, and Fernández had underlined it: no outbound calls or texts or any attempt to speak with anyone in the city. They had no idea what resources might be ranged against them, but Fernández had learned enough from the true crime podcasts that he enjoyed to know that it was not beyond the realm of possibility that Bobby Romano or the O'Connors or the police—especially the police—would be able to trace any calls back to the quarry.

"Enzo," he said.

The boy looked up. "Huh?"

"What are you doing?"

"Playing a game. Why?"

"You're not texting anyone?"

The boy turned the screen so that Fernández could see it. It was some sort of puzzle.

"Remember—" Fernández began.

"No calls or texts," he said with a heavy sigh. "I know."

Fernández was not a fan of phones. He had seen the school go from a place where voices filled the halls and where the kids had little choice in class but to pay attention, to a place where they sat with their heads bent over glowing screens rather than engaging in conversation, or just... being kids. He knew he sounded like a curmudgeon, but he wouldn't be persuaded that this was better than the rambunctious childhood that he had enjoyed.

"I wish I could call them," Enzo said.

"Who?"

"Aldo and Franny. Franny wouldn't listen to me. Why does he have to be so stubborn? I don't understand."

The boy's scowl gave way to a forlorn look, an expression that said he had felt that same confusion many times. Fernández had had students with autism spectrum disorder before, but none quite as bright as Enzo. Most of them were too busy just trying to avoid being picked on. Enzo ordinarily lacked their extreme levels of anxiety; he was savant-like, and his mother protected him, and that just left him level-headed and unemotional. It was not that he was uncaring, just that he seemed immune to emotional swings and was never carried away by sentiment. He only seemed to care about things when he had taken the chance to think about whether he really should.

Fernández had always thought Enzo was missing so much—so many of the peaks and valleys of human existence—because he was never swept away by his feelings like a neurotypical person. But he wondered now, right then in that moment, if there wasn't something healthier about the way Enzo saw things. Perhaps most people were too easy to please and too quick to anger based on what others were doing, without giving any real consideration to their own reactions. Perhaps there was something to a more dispassionate and analytical approach to life.

"Don't be too hard on Francesco," Fernández said. "He's had a hard life."

"I know."

"Don't tell him I said this," he said, "but his parents haven't done the best job. His uncle's mobbed up, and no one really looks out for him other than you and Aldo. And he doesn't have your gifts, so everything's harder for him. That means that he's angry a lot of the time. We're all born a little different, but some of us have more challenges than others."

"*I* have challenges," Enzo said defensively. "You don't understand what it's like when everyone thinks you're either rude or bored." He smiled. "Still, I wouldn't want to be a normal person. Man..." He shook his head. "Y'all are *crazy*." He slipped the phone into his pocket and nodded towards the pile of paper on the floor. "What's that?"

Fernández nodded towards the old Ford. "It's the operating guide and schematic for this beast. I downloaded it. I figured they might have the really detailed drawings they used to use. I was hoping that I might spot a hiding place or something that might explain why they want this thing so badly. A solid gold fuel pump or something." He smiled wryly. "No luck so far. Everything's where it's supposed to be."

He heard steps in the doorway and turned to see Connie watching them.

"Hey," he said.

"Let Enzo have a look at it. He has a knack for spotting patterns."

Fernández gestured to the papers on the floor. "Go for it."

Enzo collected the papers and began flicking through them as he walked over to the engine block. He found the engine schematic and went through everything methodically. Then he squatted down low, in front of the grille, turned around and lay down on his back. The vinyl-painted floor was smooth enough for him to slide under the vehicle, leaving only his feet sticking out.

He called out, "Do you have a flashlight?"

Fernández walked over to one of the storage shelves and opened a red tin toolbox. He took out a yellow flashlight, walked back to Enzo, and crouched down so that he could pass it to him. They waited another minute. But instead of sliding back out, Enzo shuffled his way further underneath.

"Careful, son," Fernández said. "The clearance isn't the best."

"I got room. Screwdriver?"

Had he found something? Fernández scooted back over to the toolbox and found a flathead. He handed it to him. "What you got?"

"Might be nothing."

They heard scraping, the sound of metal chiming against metal, and then a series of grunts.

"Enzo?" Connie said.

He wriggled his way out again and then got to his feet in front of the van. He brushed the rust flakes off his shirt and grinned.

"What?"

"I was wrong," he said. "It's definitely something."

68

Nicol sat in the car with the bag of frozen peas that he had just picked up from a 7-Eleven pressed against the side of his head. It throbbed and, when he pulled the bag away and looked in the mirror, he saw the start of a spectacular bruise that began above his eyebrow and disappeared into his scalp.

"I'm beginning to think Milton doesn't like us," Bird said.

"That's right," Nicol said, pressing the bag back against his head again. "Laugh it up."

The kids had both disappeared by the time Nicol had picked himself up. He had made his way down to the entrance, and Bird had picked him up. The whole thing had been a mess.

"We're here," Bird said.

Nicol looked up. They were at the range in Northland. O'Connor owned it and, in happier times, they had held meetings up here after firing a hundred balls down the range. This wasn't one of those times. O'Connor had asked to see them for an update, and there was no point in trying to delay it. There would also be no point in trying to sugar-coat what had happened. They had messed up again, and now they were going to have to face the music.

"Let's get this over with," Nicol said.

THE RANGE DIDN'T OPEN until later, but, as they approached the line of covered cabins, each open at one end, they heard a series of thwacks and watched as balls flew down-range. Nicol entered the range and followed the bays all the way to the end, where Patrick O'Connor was practising. He had a trolley of clubs and a plastic bucket filled with dozens of balls. He had poured a good number of balls into a low tray next to his tee and used his club to fish one out, positioning it in front of him and then swinging hard. There was a monitor on the wall ahead of him, and the trajectory of each shot was tracked and measured. There was a bottle of vodka on the ledge that divided O'Connor's bay from its neighbour.

Nicol cleared his throat. "Afternoon."

O'Connor turned around. He was about to speak but paused, frowning. He raised his club and used it to point to Nicol's head. "What happened?"

"Our friend Milton," Nicol said.

"Again?"

"'Again'?" Bird said. "What does that mean?"

"I mean he's already made the two of you look stupid once."

"I had no idea he was there," Nicol said. "He took me out from behind."

O'Connor picked up the vodka bottle by the neck and put it to his lips, taking a long draw and then putting it back.

"Please tell me this was *after* you got the kids?" he said, slurring a little. "After you found out where the fucking van has been hidden?"

Nicol shook his head. "No," he said. "He took me out and the kids bailed."

O'Connor turned his back to them both, scooped a ball out of the tray and rolled it to the centre of the mat. "You want to know what I think?" he said. He addressed the ball, brought the club up behind his head, and then swung, the contact clean and the ball streaking away. "I think you two useless pieces of shit are a disgrace. My brother's dead, you can't find a teenage kid and, because of that, I'm no nearer to getting the van back."

"Take it easy," Nicol said. "Your brother had nothing to do with us."

O'Connor scooped out another ball and used his foot to position it. "I think it had everything to do with you."

"You're drunk," Bird said.

O'Connor shrugged. "And?"

"You wanna lay the blame?" Bird said angrily. "How's this? If your brother hadn't fucked up when he did, if he'd been at the apartment like he said he was gonna be, we'd have Milton and chances are this would've all been wrapped up yesterday."

"You're blaming the dead?"

"I'm blaming your feckless brother."

O'Connor straightened up and swung the club at the screen. The driver tore the unit off its bracket, and it fell to the floor with a crash. He swung around to face them, his face engorged with blood, the club drawn back and ready to be swung at them.

"Say that again."

"Patrick," Nicol said, his palms raised, "come on. Put that down."

"Give me one good reason why I shouldn't top the both of you."

"Because we're cops, you idiot," Bird said.

Nicol saw his partner's hand move to the holster where he held his pistol. He held up his palm in warning, and Bird's hand stopped.

"You're *my* cops," O'Connor slurred. "I bought you. I *own* you."

Nicol ignored that. "If you think you've got heat on you now, it'll be a hundred times worse if you attack two on-duty detectives."

"What difference does it make? If I don't get Bobby his money—the money that he stole from me—if I don't make him whole by this time tomorrow, he's gonna shoot me and toss me in the Missouri."

"Not necessarily—"

"So, given that it's your incompetence that's got me in this hole, and since I don't have a future because of it, I'm struggling to see why I shouldn't take you two hopeless tools out with me. I mean, come on, lads—you deserve it."

O'Connor blinked and, for a moment, Nicol thought he was going to swing at them. He didn't. Instead, he changed the angle at which he was standing and, rather than bringing the driver around at them, he aimed at the bottle of vodka. The glass shattered as the club smashed through it, liquid and shards of crystal spraying out in its wake. He drew the club back once more and swung it into the trolley, then swung it so hard at the wooden strut that supported the roof that the shaft shattered in the middle. He raised the half he was holding above his head and slammed it down against the ground, again and again, his eyes bulging and spittle running down from his mouth.

"Come on," Nicol said to Bird.

The two cops backed away from O'Connor and made their exit.

BIRD STALKED across the parking lot to the Crown Vic. Nicol could see that he was furious. His clenched jaw jutted forward, and he had balled his fists so tight that Nicol could see the whites of his knuckles. Nicol knew that Bird had beaten kids on the street who had given him that kind of lip before, arrested them and tossed them in the back of the car and then taken them somewhere quiet where he could educate them about the benefits of respect and good manners. Nicol had seen him do it.

"No one talks to me like that," Bird said. "*No one*, especially not some lousy Mick who thinks his shit don't stink."

"Let it go."

"What? Seriously? He spoke to us like we were the shit on his shoe. Did you hear what he said? He *owns* us? What the fuck, man?"

"I heard," Nicol said. "And I agree. He's gone too far."

"You think? Give me one good reason why I don't go back in there right now and cap him."

"Because that would be stupid," Nicol said. "There's another way. We got options."

"Such as?"

"He's not thinking straight. It's not smart to stay with him. He's going to go down, and I'd rather not be nearby when that happens."

"So? What do we do?"

Nicol leaned against the side of the car and closed his eyes.

"Dave? Come on—we got to do something."

"I got an idea," he said. "Get in."

69

M ilton arrived back at the quarry and parked up next to the house. Aldo had been quiet during the ride south. Milton had given him the time to compose himself after what had happened to him that morning. He didn't look like the kind of kid who would have been in trouble with the police, and the experience had clearly unsettled him.

Milton unclipped his belt and killed the engine. "This is it."

"Where's Enzo?"

"He'll be around somewhere. We'll find him. But there's one thing we need to talk about first."

"What?"

"Don't call anyone," Milton said.

"What about my folks?"

"Not yet," Milton said "I'll think of a way we can let them know. Give me a couple of hours."

Aldo shook his head. "This is weird."

"I know. But it'll be fixed soon. You won't need to be out here for long." He opened the door. "Let's go and find Enzo."

MILTON FOLLOWED the sound of banging to the barn where they had hidden the Econoline. They were all there: Fernández, Connie and Enzo. The three of them were gathered next to the van.

"Afternoon," Milton called out.

The others turned; Enzo's face broke into a wide smile when he saw his friend.

"Dude," Aldo said, "you okay?"

Enzo was about to speak, but paused. He frowned. "Where's Franny?"

"Wouldn't come," Aldo said. "Mr. Smith tried to persuade him, but he said he wasn't going to run. You know what he's like."

"He's an idiot," Enzo said.

Aldo and Enzo bumped fists and moved away from the adults so that they could talk in private. Fernández came over to Milton and guided him off to the side.

"That's not good," Fernández said.

"I can't make him come," Milton said.

"He's headstrong."

"I could see that. He's going to get himself in trouble, too. He pulled a pistol."

Fernández sighed. "Jesus."

"There wasn't much that I could do," Milton said. "The best way to keep them all safe is to bring this to a head as quickly as we can."

"And you got any ideas about how you can do that?"

"Not yet," Milton said. "I'm working on it." Milton saw that Fernández had rusty powder on his left hand. "What is it?"

"We've been busy," he said. "Come over here—we think

we might have found something."

Enzo overheard them. "Who found something?"

"You did," the coach said with a grin.

Milton looked at the van and didn't see anything. "Show me."

"The axle and undercarriage," the boy said. "I think they've been replaced."

"I was just saying maybe the police repaired it," Fernández suggested. "The vehicle probably got taken in an arrest. It might have been damaged   "

"No, that's not it," Enzo interrupted. "You can tell from the scratch marks around the bolts that it's been taken apart and put back together."

"That was probably them searching it," Milton said.

"Sure," Enzo said impatiently. "But that misses the point —the undercarriage itself is new. It looks like it's been sprayed with something to make it look older, and then it's been covered in dirt and muck." He held up his own filthy hands. "Someone has tried to make it look like those parts are as old as the rest of the van. But they're not."

"I don't get it," Connie said. "Why would they do that?"

Enzo paced around the vehicle, weighing the options, trying to put himself in the position of whoever it was who had undertaken that not inconsiderable job. "It's got to be smuggling, right? Something from over the border."

"Seems most likely," Milton said.

"They're not going to try hollow parts," Fernández said. "Too dangerous to drive it all the way here like that. And they're not stashing anything underneath it, inside it or in the engine block. What about the tank? You're certain the police would check?"

"First thing they'd do," Milton said. "But it would be nice if we could be sure. We could take it apart."

Enzo waved the idea away. "No, you're right. That's not it. I read about this, and ICE…" He looked at his mother, and Milton knew that he had been researching on her behalf. "They've got fibre-optic cameras on flex lines that they shove inside. They'll have looked in every chamber and in every pipe. Won't be that."

Fernández shrugged. "Beats me, then."

Enzo frowned and suddenly retreated a quarter step, as if taken aback. "Wait… I think I've got something." His face was a model of intense concentration as he walked around to the front of the van and stared at it for several seconds. Milton walked over to join him, and watched as the boy flicked through the manual to an overhead shot showing the sunroof. Then Enzo flicked forward a few more pages until he found a greyscale picture showing the front of the vehicle; numbered arrows pointed to the grille, to the lights and to the front bumper. He walked around the van, the fingertips of his left hand tracing the body. When he had completed a circuit, he stopped right next to his mother.

"What?" she said. "What have you found?"

"Coach…" he said.

"What's up?"

"Do you have something that could cut it open?"

"I have an angle grinder."

"*You* won't be using *that*," Connie interceded.

"Why?" Fernández said. "You're thinking the headlights? You want me to take them off?"

Enzo shook his head. "It's not the headlights or the block or the undercarriage or the fuel tanks. And it's not inside, either."

"Then what?" Connie asked. "I don't get it."

Enzo gestured to the vehicle. "It's the van itself. The body panels."

Milton frowned. "The interior panels? They would have been the first things the police took off if they searched it."

"Not the interior panels. The body itself is a shell. It's made of steel—yes—but it's too wide to be the original body of the van. Look—look at the distance between the lights, the grille and the wheel hub. You compare it to this schematic and it's obvious. It's three inches wider all the way across the front. The reason we didn't see it is that the axle track has been widened. The wheels aren't recessed into the hubs all the way, like they should be —see? They disguised the work with paint and dirt. I bet if we measured the dimensions inside, we'd find that they're the regular size. But that doesn't make sense, right? Where did the extra space go?"

Fernández's mouth dropped open. "Holy shit," he said; then, realising that he had cursed in front of the boy, he turned to Connie and mouthed an apology. She didn't seem to have heard; she was beaming with pride as her son explained his theory.

"It's a false shell," Enzo said. "Whatever has been hidden is inside the gap that they've made. That's why nothing has been found. The police would never have found it. I mean, look—visually, the whole thing looks completely proportional. They could look in all the usual places, take off the interior panels and check the tank, but they wouldn't find anything. The only way they could've found it was by cutting the van in two, and they wouldn't have had any reason to go to all that trouble. They would've had to be certain that there was something inside, and they probably weren't."

Fernández headed towards the far wall and his workbench. "Your son is an amazing kid," he called back to Connie.

She blushed. "I know." She put a hand on the back of Enzo's head and ran her fingers through his hair. "He makes me very proud."

Fernández collected the angle grinder and brought it over to the van. He pointed to the vehicle. "Okay, Enzo, it's your ball game. Where do we start?"

Enzo thought about it, his eyes taking in the length of the frame. "The joints are probably fixed at the points where the frame is reinforced. Cut right behind the passenger window—where the crumple zone would be."

"Right you are." Fernández nodded as he pulled on a pair of safety goggles.

"Go top to bottom and stay as close to the window frame as you can," Enzo instructed. "If they left any space in there, that's going to be where it's at."

Fernández lined up the edge of the angle grinder's wheel. "Okay, then," he said. "Give me some room. Maybe get over to the other side of the van while I'm cutting."

Milton led Enzo and his mother a safe distance from the van. Fernández held the grinder so that the wheel was up at the join between the roof and the frame. Sparks flew as he sliced through the metal, yellow-orange particles falling down like blossoms. It wasn't long—just a few minutes, as Fernández crouched lower and lower—until he reached the bottom and shut the grinder off. He stood up and lifted the goggles; sweat was beading on his forehead from the effort. Connie and Enzo rounded the van to join him as, using his gloved hand, he pulled away the loose piece of steel and let it clatter onto the floor.

They stood and gaped as thick plastic-wrapped packages begun to tumble out of the enclosure. Each was around six inches by six inches by two inches. Milton felt an ache in the pit of his gut as he crouched down to pick one up. The plastic covering was thin and opaque. He used the nails of his thumb and index finger and peeled the corner back, then tugged the top of the plastic away.

Aldo whistled.

There was a stack of banknotes inside. Milton removed the rest of the plastic. The bundle was secured at both ends with rubber bands, and there were paper bands around the middle that subdivided the stack into smaller bundles. Each paper band was labelled "$10K" in scrawled blue ink. There were five paper bands.

"How much?" Enzo said.

"Fifty thousand," Milton said.

He turned the bundle so that it was right-side up and ran his finger down the notes. They were used, and the smell of them was strong.

Six of these packages had fallen out. Three hundred thousand. Milton left them on the floor and changed position so that he could look along the body of the Econoline, into the gap that remained behind the opening that Fernández had just cut. "Enzo," he said, "there's a flashlight over there. Pass it over."

The boy did as he was told. Milton turned it on, but he did not have to look far. The frame was stuffed with more packages. He stepped back and turned off the flashlight. "I'm guessing a hundred bundles per side, with the same under the roof. That's three hundred bundles, each holding ten thousand dollars. That's..."

"Three million dollars," Connie finished for him.

"Holy fucking shit," Enzo said.

His mother didn't scold him.

Fernández crossed his arms and stared down his nose at the van. "I think we're in a whole lot of trouble."

70

The room behind the counter at the pork store was small and dimly lit, and Nicol was nervous. It wasn't hard to imagine the sorts of things that might have happened here over the years. His mind jumped from one macabre thought to the next. He knew the files and knew that there had been a lot of missing bodies during the heyday of the mob's run in Kansas City. How many of them might have ended up here to be dismembered and then thrown in the river, or buried, or burned?

He had made the suggestion to Bird that they come down here right after they had left the range. Neither officer was comfortable with the arrangement with the Irishman anymore, and they both knew it was time to make a change. Nicol had suggested that offering their services elsewhere might afford them both a new revenue stream *and* protection. Bird had agreed.

Bobby Romano came inside, wiping the corner of his mouth with a paper napkin.

"You boys do me a favour when we're done and try the special," he said. "He does the best Italian speck I ever tasted

—ages it for thirty weeks rather than eighteen. Tell him I said you should take some to go and thank me later." He lowered himself into his chair and looked at them both through narrowed lids. "It's Nicol and Bird, right?"

"That's right," Nicol said. "Thanks for seeing us."

Bobby waved his gratitude away. Nicol was nervous. Bobby Romano might have been old, and perhaps his influence had waned since its apogee in the seventies and eighties, but a guy like him didn't get to where he was without a ruthlessness that made his rivals fear him. Nicol knew the stories about what Bobby had done. The murders everyone knew he was guilty of, but no one could prove. He had seen a recent example: giving millions to Patrick O'Connor to launder and then stealing it back from him just so he could cement an exclusive relationship.

"What can I do for you, Detectives?"

"Maybe you know," Nicol said, "and maybe you don't. We've had a business relationship with Patrick O'Connor for the last few months. We do little bits and pieces of work for him when he needs something."

"Do you?" He feigned ignorance, but Nicol could tell from the way that he said it that Bobby knew *all* about it.

"We did," Bird corrected.

"Past tense?"

"We quit."

"Really?"

"Between us, Bobby, O'Connor's lost his mind."

Nicol gritted his teeth. He had specifically told Bird that he would do the talking. His partner had many talents— mostly malign—but diplomacy was not one of them. He was worried that he would open his mouth now and say something stupid.

"I know Patrick," Bobby said. "Maybe you know that? He does work for me."

Nicol didn't speak, and willed Bird to keep his mouth shut, too.

"He's been under a lot of stress," Bobby said. "You should give him a break."

Nicol kept his face carefully neutral. Bobby was dropping a pretty big hint about the lost money; was he suggesting that he knew the two of them had been involved in the Irishman's attempt to relocate it? Their interview might head in a very uncomfortable direction *very* quickly if he did.

"We're grateful you've agreed to see us," Nicol said. "We'd like to make you a proposal."

He spread his arms. "I'm all ears, boys."

"We can offer you exactly the same services as we offered O'Connor. If you need details on someone, you give us a call and we'll tell you where they are. Maybe someone gets arrested and starts talking—we can tell you what they're saying."

"We'd give you warning if we hear that one of your businesses is about to get hit," Bird added.

"Exactly," Nicol said, his bland smile disguising his irritation that Frank was still flapping his gums.

"And in exchange?"

"Fair compensation," Nicol said.

"Your idea of fair might be different from mine." Bobby chuckled. "What was the Irishman paying?"

There was no point in lying; Nicol suspected Bobby already knew. "Ten grand a month," he said. "Five for him, five for me."

Bobby leaned back and steepled his fingers in front of his chest. It was tense. Bird gripped his knee with a clawlike left hand, while Nicol clenched and unclenched the muscles in his behind. The room could not have been more than fourteen feet across, and part of that was taken up by a slab where the butchery took place. It felt claustrophobic.

"You got a deal," Bobby said, standing up. "Ten grand a month, starting today. Just so happens there's something that I need a little help with right now. There's this van—couple of my boys got stopped driving it into the city. I want it back. You two help me do that, I'll give you another twenty on top as a thank-you. You know my man Sal?"

"Sure," Nicol said.

"Go speak to him. He'll get you started. Then go get my van."

71

Milton stood next to Fernández and stared at the pile of money. He shook his head in disbelief. The past few days suddenly made quite a bit more sense. They had underestimated; there was five million in used banknotes hidden in the van. That was a compelling reason to try to recover it.

"What do you think all this cash was doing in there?" Fernández said.

"It's meant to be laundered. They'll have someone who can run it through the books of a legitimate business and then bank it offshore."

"But something happened to it before it was delivered."

"We know the police impounded it. The two men who went after Enzo at the auction were after it. Patrick and Kenneth O'Connor."

"And who do you think they are? The launderers?"

"I think so," he said.

"And Sal Provenzano?" Connie said. "What about him?"

Milton shrugged. "Either it's his money and he's trying to get it back, or he's trying to steal it for someone else."

"So—what now?" she said. "The police are chasing you."

"I'm not concerned about that," Milton said. "I can just move on. It's you I'm worried about. They'll find out that you're here illegally."

"Could we give it back?" Enzo asked.

"To who?"

"The Irish guys?"

"Or to Sal?" Connie suggested.

Milton shook his head "It's too late for that, and giving it to one group will just upset the other. We can't do that."

"But we can't stay here forever," Connie protested.

"No," Milton said. "You can't. I think there are two options." He didn't want to overwhelm them any more than was necessary, but he couldn't postpone a decision about what to do next any longer. They had to choose. "One involves violence," he said, "but none of you will be at risk. The other involves no violence, but it will put us all at considerable risk."

Enzo spoke up first. "It's obvious, then. It has to be the second."

"Enzo..." Milton began to explain.

"He's right," Connie said. "No violence."

Milton had hoped that they would shy away from that choice. It depended upon them helping him, and being patient while he moved the necessary pieces into place. It would take a few days and, despite the level of danger being reduced, that didn't mean that there was no risk at all. There was. The two crooked cops had certainly been after Aldo and Francesco, and there was a good chance that they had caught up with the truculent kid by now. Would they force him to help them locate the group at the quarry?

"The first option is safer," Milton said. "You should think about it."

"But it involves violence?"

He nodded.

"Would it put you at risk?"

"Yes," he said. "It probably would. I'd go back to the city and get things straightened out."

Connie shook her head. "It's unacceptable on both counts—I don't want anything violent done in our names, and I don't want to put you in harm's way. What's the second choice?"

Milton exhaled; he wasn't going to push them, and, anyway, perhaps this was the better call.

"I have a friend," he said. "Her name is Ellie. She's an FBI agent. There must be a federal crime in this mess somewhere. I should be able to get her to open a federal racketeering investigation, and she'll be able to send agents to protect you."

"No, no, no," Enzo said. "You know Mom's illegal. They'll send her away."

"Not if she agrees to be a witness. They won't deport her then. You'll have to move away from the city to be safe, but they'll protect you both."

"I don't know," Connie said. Milton could detect a natural—and probably understandable—fear of the authorities.

"Enzo was born here," Fernández said. "That's got to mean something—right? He's an American citizen and she's his mother."

"Doesn't mean so much these days," Connie said.

Enzo shook his head. "And if she goes, I go."

Connie wagged a finger in his direction. "Don't you say that. You are going to MIT. We're *not* going to let this get in the way of that. You... you..." Her anger flagged and her arm fell to her side. She sighed helplessly.

"You have to trust me, Connie," Milton said. "Both of you."

"I haven't been given much reason to trust anyone recently," she said. "I know that's not fair, but it's just how it is. I know you're doing what you think is right."

"If you're not sure about the FBI, then we still have the other option. You all wait here while I go back to the city."

"No," she said firmly. "You helped Enzo; you helped Aldo; you helped me. You didn't have to, and you've asked for nothing. I'd be ashamed if we treated you like anything less than family. And I will not send a member of my family into harm's way. I just won't."

Milton felt a moment of embarrassment, acutely aware that he did not deserve her kindness. He avoided looking her directly in the eyes for fear of seeing his skeletons reflected back at him.

"So it's the second option," he said. "The FBI. You're sure that's what you want?"

"It is." She walked over to her son and put her arm around his shoulders, then looked over at Milton, her face full of resolve now. "Call your friend and see what she can do."

"I will," he said. "There's something else we all need to do if we're going to be staying here while this gets sorted. There's no reason to say we'll need it, but I want to be sure that this place is as safe as we can make it."

"Need what?" Fernández said.

"I'd like to make the house a little easier to defend," Milton said. "I'm afraid it's going to mean we make a bit of a mess of the place."

72

Francesco was feeling brash again by lunch. The run-in with the cops was done, and he had put it behind him. They must have wanted to speak to him and Aldo about what had happened at Enzo's house, but he had no interest in helping them out. Even being seen talking to the police was a guarantee of trouble. The last thing he wanted was any of the guys in the neighbourhood thinking he was dropping a dime.

He knew that Aldo or Enzo would call him to try to persuade him to change his mind and, not wishing to deal with them, he switched off his phone. He went back to the mall and looked around for something to do. He saw a couple of corner boys he recognised. It looked like they were slinging dope for one of the crews who worked there, but Francesco knew there was no angle for him. It was low rent, anyway; he was destined for better than that. He bought a doughnut and a coffee and sat down in the food court to eat it.

He thought of the English guy who had stepped up to Nicol and what he had said afterwards. What was it? Enzo had sent him to get them? What were they going to do? Hide? Francesco wasn't going to do that, run off and leave the city at the slightest sniff of danger. What would that say about him? What would Luca think if he did that? The whole idea was crazy.

He spent his last twenty dollars to buy two grams of weed from one of the corner boys, found a quiet spot, and took out his last Swisher cigar. He opened it up to empty out the tobacco and replaced it with crushed pot. He lit the blunt with his Bic and thought about how pathetic it was, a guy like him, a guy with entrepreneurial spirit, having no money. It was ridiculous. He needed to earn some paper, and he only really had one way to do that.

He finished the coffee, tossed it and the paper that had been wrapped around the doughnut, and set off home. He had the new NBA game for his PS4, and maybe he'd waste a couple of hours on that.

But then he thought about the humiliation of his empty wallet and the need to make some money. He took out his phone, stared at it for a long moment, then switched it on. He saw a series of missed calls, but, to his surprise, they weren't from his friends; they were from his uncle. There was a voicemail, too; Francesco stared at the display, his finger hovering over it, and wondered what was so important that Luca had gone to such effort to reach him. It had to be serendipity. He had been just about to call his uncle to see if he could hook him up with work, and here he was, trying to reach him.

He found that his throat was a little dry as he tapped the screen to call Luca back.

73

Björn parked his rental in the hospital parking lot and killed the engine. He had exhausted all of the angles that were available to him to help track down Milton. It was still unclear what business Patrick and Kenneth O'Connor had with Tanner; at this point, it wasn't even obvious to Björn that there was a connection between them and Milton at all. He thought it was likely, but, in the absence of any new information that might enable him to cast light on a possible relationship, he had decided that he needed to change tack. Tanner certainly had information on Milton, and Björn had reached the point where he was going to have to take a few chances in order to get it.

He glanced up at the sky as he got out of the car. The clouds, the black and purple of a bruise, were promising more snow. The forecaster on the radio had confirmed as much, suggesting that there could be another four or five inches between now and the morning. Björn had no problem with inclement weather—he was from Iceland—but the grim relentlessness of the Missouri winter was depressing. It was different back home. The winters offered a lot of snow, and the temperature was usually much colder than this, but at least Icelanders had the bounties of their landscape: the otherworldly glaciers, the geysers where you could bathe in warm natural water, moss-covered volcanic ranges that extended for miles, the fjord-cut coastline. This city, and the landscape that surrounded it, was deathly dull in comparison.

He locked up and stomped through the snow to the entrance.

BJÖRN REACHED the room where Tanner was being treated, and saw, to his annoyance, that his daughter was sitting next to the bed. He needed to speak to Tanner alone, and, as far as she was concerned, the two of them had no connection other than that Björn was the man who'd found him on the street. She would quite rightly be suspicious if he tried to speak to Tanner in private. He was going to have to be creative.

He waited at the door until she saw him, and then, with an uncertain smile, she got up and came outside.

"Hello," he said.

She looked puzzled to see him. "Hi."

He smiled warmly, then turned his head and nodded to the hospital room. "I was driving by, and I thought I'd come and see how he was."

"They say he's out of the woods," she said.

"That's wonderful. You must be relieved."

"Very. There were moments after they brought him in when I think it could've gone either way."

"That's such good news. I'm pleased I came by."

He was about to make his excuses when she stood up

and put her arm on his elbow, guiding him to a quieter spot along the corridor.

"What is it?"

She looked pensive. "Can I ask you a question?"

"Of course."

"When you found him, did you see anyone else?"

"Like who?"

"I don't know—someone who might have been involved with what happened to him."

"No," he said. "He was on the ground, like I said. There wasn't anyone else there. Why?"

"I still can't get it in my head that he would have taken drugs. It's just not him."

"You think someone might have given them to him?"

She shrugged. "Maybe. I think it's possible. Have the police spoken to you?"

"They haven't," he said. "But I'm happy to help if they think it would be useful. Do you still have my number?"

"I think so," she said.

"Please—let them have it if they ask."

She smiled. "Thank you. And thank you for coming to see him. You're very thoughtful."

"Not really. I'm just happy that he's on the mend." He put out his hand and shook hers. "It was nice to see you again. Goodbye, Mollie."

She said goodbye and made her way back to her father. Björn watched her go, then went to the elevators. Tanner was his only lead. He wasn't sure if he would be able to locate Milton unless he was able to speak to him. He took out his phone and tapped a finger against the screen as he weighed up his options. There was nothing else for it; he was going to need help.

He waited until he was in the parking lot and then placed a call to London.

"Global Logistics—how can I direct your call?"

"It's Eiður Guðjohnsen from the fifteenth floor," he said. "I need to speak to a researcher on the first floor, please."

Milton and Fernández made their way into the barn.

"So," the coach said, "what do you need?"

Milton reeled off the items he wanted. "Some empty tin cans," he said as they stepped inside.

"Got plenty out back—use them for target practise."

"Perfect. Fishing line and paracord?"

"Sure," Fernández said. "Got fishing line in the shed near the lake, and I got several lines of cord over there in the toolbox."

"Spare bootlaces?"

"In the house, cupboard under the stairs. Help yourself."

"Fuel?"

"Got a tank of red diesel for the tractor."

Milton pointed to the shelves and the plastic tubs that held some of the items that were stored there. "Three or four of those."

"Anything else?"

"You said you had dynamite?"

"A few sticks."

He went over to a rack of tools and picked out two shovels. "I'm going to need those boys to chip in, too," he said. "I need them to clear some of the snow."

Fernández gave him a quizzical look. "What is this—some kind of MacGyver-type shit?"

Milton ran his finger across the blade of the shovel. "Something like that."

MILTON WALKED out of the house and followed the track until he was two hundred feet away. There was a line of trees here, marking the boundary of the land that had been given over to the house itself and then the much larger expanse that formed the rest of the ranch. He had studied a map of the property and knew that the track was the obvious way to reach the property. The quarry was to the south, and there was no easy or safe way to traverse it, especially not at night and in these conditions. He was confident that Sal would come from the north. That said, laxity in his planning was not something Milton had ever tolerated, and he wanted to make sure that he had all bases covered. He would start with the track and then work outwards, taking into account the most likely alternative means of ingress.

There was an old oak tree with a split trunk at the side of the road. Milton opened the trash bag that he had taken from the kitchen and tipped out the empty cans. He took a knife and used the tip to pierce the cans and then threaded a bootlace through them, knotting the lace so that it held the cans together. He took a length of paracord and fed it through the loop of the lace, then tied the ends of the cord to the sides of the tree trunk so that the cans were suspended in the cleft, four feet off the ground. He took another piece of cord and fed it around the trunk below the cans, ensuring that there was plenty of slack in the middle. He took one of the wooden stakes that he had found in the barn and twisted the cord around it, turning it over and over until the cord had enough tautness in it for what he had in mind. The stake was centred and arranged so that it would spin through the cans if the tension was suddenly released. He twisted some more, pleased with the noise that the cluster of cans made when the stick clattered against them. When he was happy with the tension on the line, Milton took a stick from the ground and used it to brace the stake so that it pushed up against it, but was unable to spin. He added a smaller trigger stick, placing it between the brace and the stake so that it was held in place.

He went back to his bag of supplies and took out the fishing line that Fernández had given him. He carefully tied one end to the trigger stick and then fed it out until it reached across the track. The line was translucent and difficult to see against the snow; it would be invisible at night. Milton used stakes to position the line, leaving it an inch above the snow, and then tied it off against a trunk on the opposite side of the track. He went back to the trigger stick and tied on a second piece of line, extending this out in the other direction so that it ran between the trees.

He stepped back and assessed his work. The line, when tripped, would yank the trigger stick away, and the torque on the paracord would send the stake through the cans a dozen times, generating a noise that he would easily be able to hear back at the house. The tripwires stretched twenty feet in either direction, covering the track and the scrubby ground on either side of it.

It was a good start. This part of the approach was covered, but that wasn't enough. Milton looked left and right and saw terrain that would invite a stealthy advance: a depression between two shallow mounds, two copses of trees with animal tracks picking routes between the trunks.

He stood up and stretched his shoulders. He looked back to the house and saw that Enzo and Aldo were busy with the shovels. Milton had told them to dig three holes in the snow at fifteen-foot intervals along the tree line. Once they had been excavated, the boys would move across to the other side of the open field and dig three more holes. They didn't have to be particularly deep—knee height—and the snow was soft and easy to dig. Fernández had emptied six of the storage tubs and was filling them with fuel from the property's main reservoir. Milton would get to work once the coach and the boys had finished.

He checked his watch. It was the middle of the afternoon, and they probably had another hour or two of light. He really wanted to be finished before sundown; he would be able to work with a flashlight, but it would be easier now. He also had additional preparation to do inside the house and guessed he'd need another couple of hours for that.

He collected his things and made his way toward the copse. He had plenty of work to do.

75

Connie sat on the swinging porch bench and watched Enzo and Aldo digging, shovels turning over the snow and building a mound behind them. Milton had told them what to do, and had helped with the first of the holes. Once he was satisfied that they knew what they were doing, he had disappeared off up the track with a bag slung over his shoulder. She had watched as, in the distance, he had worked on something near the track that led to the house. After an hour he had walked back, and he and Coach Fernández had gone into the barn. She had heard the sounds of a hammer against nails and power tools cutting through wood. She had no idea what they were doing, and was not of the mind to ask.

He came out again now, and, after stopping for a moment to check the boys' work, he climbed the steps to the porch to take a sip from the flask of hot coffee that he had left on the rail.

"They're hard workers," Milton said, nodding back down to the snowy field.

"I don't get it," she said. "How are a bunch of holes going to stop anybody?"

"It's not the holes," he said. "It's what we're going to put in them that they'll have to worry about."

"Which is…?"

"A surprise," he said. "Something to make them wonder what they'll find if they keep coming."

If she didn't know better, Connie might have suspected that Milton was enjoying himself.

"Have you spoken to your friend yet?" she asked him.

"I left a message. Don't worry—she'll come through for us. She's reliable."

He seemed utterly assured, and, strangely, that worried her even more. He could say whatever he wanted, but she knew the odds against them had to be daunting. That meant he was a good actor, and *that* meant she couldn't help but doubt almost anything he said.

"And when this is all done?" she said. "If we can hold out until your friends come?"

"If they think you can give them anything valuable, they'll offer you witness protection and relocation."

"And if they don't?"

"They will."

"You can't be sure of that."

Milton cocked an eyebrow. "If they don't? Then we'll have to look at the first option. I'll have a free hand to go back into the city and deal with your issues."

He had a way about him, a confidence that—even when inappropriate—made her feel stronger. "I'm scared. I'm scared for my son. And for myself."

"I'm not surprised," he said. "That's natural. It's fine to be scared—but I *will* get you through this."

76

L uca sat behind the wheel of his Caddy in slow-moving traffic. He called Sal's phone the moment after he hung up on Francesco.

"What?"

"My nephew just called."

"About time."

"I've been looking for him all day, Sal."

"He's a kid. How hard can he be to find?"

"I called a dozen times. He wasn't picking up."

"So where is he?"

"At the mall. I'm going to pick him up. What do you want me to do?"

"Bring him here. The house off Jackson, near the cemetery."

Sal ended the call. Luca looked at his phone again and, for a moment, felt a flicker of the concern that he guessed someone who cared for his family might feel. Luca didn't care, though, and hadn't ever since he had been thrown out of the house by his father ten years earlier. He had another family now, one with bonds that were deep and permanent, sealed by an oath of silence and governed by a code. You never betrayed secrets. You never violated the wife or children of another member. You never used drugs. The Mafia gave Luca the structure that he had never had before, and he owed Bobby his life because of it. He had been running wild when Bobby had taken him in, and he knew he would have been dead without him. *That* was family. His kid nephew? Who cared? He was collateral.

Luca touched the gas and the car rolled forward slowly. Francesco's night was about to get a lot more dangerous than it would have been if he hadn't called him. He fished a cigarette out of his jacket and lit it, then blew a plume of smoke out of the side window. Francesco's problems were just that: *his* problems. Nobody ever said living the life would be easy. Francesco had never understood that. He always needed someone's help.

Luca flicked cigarette ash out of the window and took another drag as traffic slowed to a stop once more. Sal would do what he had to do. He would scare the kid a little, put some fear into him so that he did what they needed him to do. He'd shit his pants, but that was it. He'd walk away at the end of it, and they would have what they needed.

It was just business.

He turned the car onto East Thirty-First Street. The mall was just a couple of blocks ahead. The parking lot was two-thirds empty, and Luca could see the small figure under the central streetlamp, waiting near the cart return. He flicked the indicator as he reached the entrance, waited for the traffic to ease, then turned across the road and pulled up to his cousin.

He powered down the side window. "You okay?" he said with a smile.

"Hey, Luca."

"Where've you been?"

"Lying low," he said. "The cops came after me this morning."

"That right?"

He nodded. "I think it's to do with Enzo. The shit that went down at his house."

Luca reached over and opened the passenger door. Francesco got inside.

"You still want to earn?"

"Yeah, man."

Luca nodded. "All right, then. We've just got to make one little stop first. Won't take five minutes."

77

Milton's shoulder was aching by the time that he had finished the work outside and made his way back through the snow to the house. The exterior preparation was done, and he was satisfied that it was about as good as he could make it in the limited time that he had available.

He came inside, glad for the warmth, and hung his coat on the bannister. He reached into his pocket for his phone and dialled Ellie Flowers again. The call rang for ten seconds and then went to voicemail. Milton left another message, calmly explaining that he needed her to contact him as soon as possible, and ended the call. He stared at the screen as the light faded and it switched off. She really was his best hope. He still felt uncomfortable with the prospect of calling the KCPD, especially given that at least two of its detectives were corrupt. He wondered whether he should call the FBI's Kansas City field office, and concluded that he would in the event that Ellie didn't return his call by the time they had finished dinner.

He was worried, but in the meantime, there was more

that he could do to increase their safety. He put the phone in his pocket and went to the box of items that he had assembled in the barn. He had more fishing line, a selection of nails and other ironmongery, a power drill, a soldering iron, a roll of aluminium tape and a length of magnet wire.

Milton heard footsteps on the porch and the door opened. Fernández came inside with the crossbow from his gun cabinet.

"What are you going to do with this?" he said, handing it to Milton.

"I'm going to leave them a little surprise," Milton said. "Just in case."

He took the crossbow and set to work.

78

L uca pulled the car up to the house. The neighbourhood around here was challenged, just like it was around all of Bobby's places, but the house itself was clean and inviting, the better to avoid attention from police. Francesco looked out of the car's windows as he tried to work out where they were and why, exactly, his uncle had brought him here. The fact that he was with Luca eased his concern, but that didn't mean that he didn't have a little knot of nerves in the pit of his stomach.

"How come we're stopping here?"

Luca removed the keys from the ignition. "I just have a couple of things to take care of. It won't take long."

Francesco looked out at the dark street again; two of the streetlights had burned out and had not been replaced. The place was foreboding. The house was the nicest on the block, but that didn't mean it was nice. It looked like the kind of place where things just went down whether you wanted them to or not.

"Come on," Luca said.

"Who's inside?"

"Just the guys. Don't worry. You know I've got your back, right? We're family."

Luca gave his nephew a big reassuring smile and Francesco nodded. He wanted to deny his nerves, but he knew that his uncle would see right through it. Luca climbed out of the car and Francesco followed. He checked up and down the street again as they each slammed their doors and walked towards the front stoop. The street was quiet.

"Relax," Luca said.

"I'm good."

"You look scared. No need for that. Nothing bad's gonna happen."

He stopped walking. "Luca?"

His uncle looked annoyed. "What?"

"You love me, right?"

"What do you mean?"

"Not like sissy or nothing, but... like family. Right?"

Luca rolled his eyes. "What's eating you tonight? You can trust me—you know that."

Francesco felt like he *should* trust Luca, but there was something about his manner that gave him pause. His uncle had looked away for a second as he said it, just for a fraction of a second, enough for Franny to know that he was holding something back.

Luca clapped him on the shoulder. "You smoke a joint today?"

"Yeah," he said.

"It's making you paranoid."

Luca walked up the steps. He knocked twice on the steel reinforced door, then twice again, then once more. A peephole slid open and a pair of eyes studied him. The door swung open. A tall, bald white guy was on the other side, and he stepped to the left so that they could go through. The room beyond was smoky. Francesco tasted the choking haze of pot in the back of his throat. The room was littered with pizza boxes, empty fast-food containers and soda bottles. Three stoners sat on a threadbare brown sofa, playing video games on a widescreen. At the back of the room, between the stairs to the second floor and the kitchen door, three more men were playing cards. A naked light bulb over the living room swayed ever so gently, buffeted by the slowly rotating ceiling fan.

They crossed the room, and Luca bumped fists with the men at the table. They were playing for cash, with piles of dollar bills on the table.

A shorter man with a goatee and an earring nodded towards Francesco, then turned back to Luca. "Sal's in back. Take him through."

Luca nodded and led Francesco across the room to a closed door. Francesco felt his nerves flare, and he knew now, for certain, that coming inside was a mistake. He should have listened to the sense of foreboding that he had felt. He wanted to turn and run, but his legs were numb.

Luca rapped a fist on the door. Francesco heard footsteps from inside. The door opened: it looked like the room beyond was a bedroom, with a bed and a couple of wooden chairs. Sal stood in the doorway and, behind him, a man sat on the far side of the bed with his back turned.

Sal smiled at Francesco. "Francesco," he said, "you okay?"

Franny swallowed. "I'm good."

"Sorry about the other day. I was impatient. I should not have threatened you—please, my apologies."

Francesco felt the quiver in his heartbeat, and hot blood filled his cheeks. "Sure."

"We need your help. We are having trouble finding your friend Enzo, and it is very important that we know where he is. Do you know?"

"No," he said. "He disappeared after..." He paused. "After what happened at his house."

"Are you sure?"

His hands began to tremble, so he shoved them in his pockets. "I'm sure. I don't know where he's gone."

Sal smiled again. "I believe you. But we *do* need to find him, and you can help us. Will you do that for me?"

Francesco felt weak. How could he say no?

Sal stepped aside and indicated that Francesco should come all the way inside. He wanted to back away, but, even as he dawdled, he felt Luca's hands on his shoulders, firmly pushing him through the door.

The man on the bed stood up and turned around.

It was Detective Nicol.

"Hello, Franny," he said.

Franny tried to reverse, but his uncle was right up against him. "What's going on?"

"I need you to call Enzo," Nicol said. "You need to call him, you need to sound completely normal, and you need to keep him on the line for as long as you can. You got it?"

79

Björn drove back to the hospital and parked in a spot where he could watch the entrance without making his presence obvious. He took out his phone, messaged London, and then sat back to wait.

He didn't have to wait long.

Less than five minutes had passed before he saw Mollie Tanner hurrying outside. She walked quickly into the lot, located her car, and drove away. A member of Operational Support from Group One had faked a call from the KCPD to suggest that there had been a break-in at the offices of Kansas City Fresh. It would take Mollie fifteen minutes to drive there, fifteen minutes to find out that the call was mistaken, and another fifteen to drive back. That would be plenty of time for Björn to do what he needed to do.

He arranged his shoulder holster so that his pistol was comfortable, zipped up his jacket so that it was hidden, and then stepped out of the car. He looked up into the night sky; the heavy blanket of clouds didn't look as if it was about to go anywhere, and, as he watched, the first flakes of a fresh fall drifted down through the amber glow that spilled out of the hospital windows.

BJÖRN MADE his way to the room where Tanner was being treated. The corridor was quiet, with a doctor tapping something into a tablet and a couple reading magazines in the waiting area. Björn walked down the corridor with the confidence of a relative who was supposed to be there, ready with fake ID and a cover story should he be stopped. No one paid him any heed, and he was able to reach the closed door to Tanner's room without incident. He took a moment to look up and down the corridor and, happy that he was not attracting undue attention, he opened the door and went inside.

Tanner was lying in bed, his head angled to the door. His eyes were closed and he was breathing deeply; he was fast asleep. There was a bank of medical equipment on a trolley next to him with wires that ran to probes attached to his arm; a cannula in his wrist was connected to a bag of saline that hung from a stand behind him; a screen overhead reported his vital signs.

Björn closed the door behind him, pulled up a chair so that it was next to the bed, and sat down.

"Tanner," he said, "wake up."

His eyelids fluttered; Björn took an inch of flesh on the underside of his arm and squeezed it.

Tanner winced.

"Wake up."

His eyelids opened a crack, enough for Björn to see the whites of his eyes. Björn was about to give him a second pinch when Tanner grunted, inhaled and exhaled deeply, and shifted a little in the bed. Björn watched as his eyelids climbed up the rest of the way.

He tried to speak, but his throat was evidently dry, and all that he managed was a rasping growl. There was a glass of water on the table next to the bed, and Björn took it and held it to Tanner's lips. He drank, sighed deeply, and slumped back into the mattress.

"Listen to me, Tanner," Björn said. "I work for the Group. You called with a message for Control—she sent me."

"How..." he croaked. "What happened?"

"You were being interrogated by Kenneth O'Connor. He gave you an overdose—I brought you here."

"What happened to him?"

"I shot him."

Tanner's eyes opened wide now. Panicked, he gripped the handles on the bed with both hands; he would have tried to raise himself if Björn hadn't held him in place.

"Your daughter is safe," he said. "I've spoken to her. You don't need to worry."

"Where is she?"

"She was here earlier. I needed to get her out of the way—she's been told there's been a break-in at your business."

The rigidity in Tanner's body disappeared and he fell back again.

"I need you to tell me how I can find Milton."

Björn watched Tanner's face; there was reluctance there, and regret, and, beneath it all, there was fear.

"It will be handled discreetly," Björn said. "There's no risk to you or to your daughter."

Tanner closed his eyes and, for a moment, Björn thought that he had fallen asleep again.

"What will you do?" he rasped, his eyes still closed.

"It will be quick and then I'll be gone. And you will have Control's gratitude for service to the Group."

There was no need to underline that he would earn her displeasure if he did not cooperate; Björn could see that Tanner's fear of what Milton might do was balanced by his fear of Control's anger if he denied her now. The conflict between those battling trepidations lasted for another moment until, perhaps, Tanner came to the conclusion that Björn was here right now, and Milton was not.

"There's a quarry outside Louisburg," he said. "South of the city. It's owned by Julio Fernández. Milton went there."

"Thank you, Tanner," Björn said. He got up and replaced his chair so that it rested neatly beneath the table. "Get well soon."

He left the room. The doctor with the tablet watched him leave, giving him a puzzled smile. Björn nodded his farewell, returned the smile with a confident one of his own, and made his way to the corridor and the exit beyond.

He checked his watch. It was getting late. He had a little preparation to do, but nothing to delay him unduly. He had a rough location now, and that ought to be enough for Groups One and Three to research where Milton could be found. Björn wanted to make his way there as soon as he could so that he could carry out his orders. The file that he had been given was clear. There was to be no negotiation, no invitation to come back in from the cold. Control had made it very plain: John Milton could not be allowed to live. It would be down to Björn to bring Milton's flight from justice to an end.

80

E nzo was in the upstairs bathroom of the house and, as he looked out of the window and onto the expansive grounds that surrounded the property, he could see Smith working by flashlight. He had carried six large plastic storage tubs out to the holes in the snow that Enzo and Aldo had excavated, and had almost completely buried them. Smith was too far away for Enzo to see what he was doing, but it looked as if he had attached something to the top of each tub and then strung wires that stretched from one to the other and then disappeared into the tree line. Enzo had no idea what he was doing.

Smith had told everyone that he had spoken to his friend at the FBI and that she was going to try to liaise with the KC field office so that local agents could be dispatched. Enzo's mother had asked him how long that might take, and he had replied that he didn't know. He had told his contact that it was urgent, but, beyond that, there was nothing that he could do to speed the process along. He had told them that, in all likelihood, they would need to stay at the property overnight and, all being well, they would be taken into protective custody in the morning.

That was the best that anyone could hope for and, although he was impatient and scared, Enzo had accepted it.

He pulled back the shower curtain that was draped across the tub and turned on the faucet. He was cold from working out in the snow, and his mother had suggested a shower to warm up. He took off his shirt and, as he did so, he felt his phone vibrating in the pocket of his jeans. He thought he had turned it off, like Smith had suggested, then remembered that he had switched it back on again so that he could see whether Franny had been in contact. He must have forgotten to switch it off again.

He took it out and saw that Franny was calling now.

Shit.

He didn't know what to do. Smith had told him that he should not have contact with anyone back in the city, but Enzo knew that Francesco needed to be out here with them, too. He was just as vulnerable as Aldo and, even if he had initially sneered at Smith's suggestion that he come away until the situation had been resolved, Enzo knew that he would think about it and, eventually, his hot blood would subside and he would see reason.

He couldn't just abandon him.

The phone kept ringing. Enzo swallowed. He couldn't ignore him. Franny was his friend; he and Aldo were Franny's *only* friends. He had disabled the phone's location services, and it wasn't as if he was calling Franny. It was the other way around. That had to be safe, right? And this was Franny. What risk could there be in speaking to his friend?

He accepted the call.

"Hey," Franny said.

"You okay?"

"Yeah," he said. "I'm good."

"Aldo said you didn't want to come out here."

"Yeah," he said. "I know. I been thinking about it, though. Maybe I was wrong."

"Where are you now?"

There was a pause. "Home," he said.

"And you're okay?"

"Yeah."

"You haven't seen Sal or any of his guys?"

"No," he said. "Nothing like that. But I been thinking about it, and I think you and Aldo are right. There's something they want in that van—they *really* want it, or else they wouldn't have done what they did at your house. Right?"

"Exactly. Come out here—it'll only be for the night. Mr. Smith's got someone he knows in the FBI. He thinks they'll be sending agents tomorrow to get us away. We hold out until then and this'll all get fixed."

Francesco paused again and, across the line, Enzo thought that he heard a second voice.

"Who are you with?" he asked.

"No one," he said.

There was another pause, and Enzo closed his eyes and concentrated hard on whether he could hear anything—or anyone—in the background.

"Franny? You still there?"

Enzo frowned as he strained to listen and was rewarded with the faintest sound of two words, whispered so quietly that they were almost inaudible.

"Ask him."

Enzo felt icy fear running up and down his spine. "Franny? Who's with you?"

His answer, when it came, was full of panic and fear; the

words tumbled out in a jumble. "Sal's coming for you. Switch off your phone. Don't answer it. Don't—"

Enzo heard the sound of a slap, and Franny was cut off mid-sentence.

"Franny? *Franny?*"

"Enzo," came a new voice, "you need to tell me where you are. You have something that doesn't belong to you. If you give it to me, we can forget this whole thing ever happened, and you and your friends can go about your business."

The voice was deep and accented. Italian. He recognised it. It was Sal.

"Enzo? Are you there?"

"I don't trust you," he said.

Enzo heard the sound of footsteps climbing the stairs that led up to the bathroom, and then there was a tapping on the door.

"Enzo," Smith said, his voice muffled, "who are you talking to?"

He still had the phone pressed to his ear. "I only ask you once," Sal said. "If I have to come and find you, it will not be good for you. You, your mother, your friend—and anyone who is helping you. Please, Enzo. It is better you tell me where you are."

"No."

"Enzo," Smith said, "open the door."

"Look at your screen," Sal told him. "I show you something."

Enzo took the phone away from his ear and looked at the display. There was a notification: Francesco—Sal—was requesting a video call.

Smith tried the handle, but the door rattled up against the bolt. "Enzo! Kill the call. Don't talk to them."

Enzo ignored him. Instead, almost without knowing what he was doing, he tapped the screen. He saw Francesco's face. His friend had been crying; light glistened in the tears that slicked the skin around his eyes. He was pale and his lip was quivering. Enzo glimpsed the room behind Francesco and saw a man he recognised: Detective Nicol.

"Last chance, Enzo," Sal said from off-camera. "Tell me where you are, and we come and fix this whole mess. You say no? I shoot your friend in the knee."

Francesco's eyes bulged. He looked right into the lens and shook his head. Enzo knew what it meant: *Don't tell him.*

There was a loud crash as Smith kicked in the door.

"Where are you, Enzo?" Sal asked.

Enzo couldn't move. Smith grabbed his wrist with his right hand and prised the phone away with his left. Enzo heard the gunshot and Francesco's scream of pain. As he looked up into Smith's face, he saw him wince.

Enzo lurched up and stumbled the two steps to the toilet. He bent over it and, dizzied and feverish, he vomited into the bowl.

MILTON TOOK the phone out to the landing and went into the bedroom where Enzo wouldn't be able to hear him.

"That was a mistake, Sal," he said.

"He'll be okay. He might walk with a limp, but that is it. But you don't tell me where you are, though, where the van is, and maybe I put a bullet through the other knee. Then maybe he is in a wheelchair the rest of his life."

"Detective Nicol," Milton said, "I see you."

"Tell him where to find the van," Nicol said. "This doesn't need to get any worse than it already is."

"You're tracing this call? Let me save you the effort. We're at a quarry just north of Louisburg. Why don't you all come out? Bring Francesco with you. You give me the boy, and I'll give you the money that we took out of the van."

"When?" Sal asked.

"Tonight."

Sal turned Francesco's phone so that he was looking directly into the camera. "Don't get smart. Don't try to play me. You can't run. I'll always find—"

"I'm not running. I just told you where I am. The money is here. Bring the kid and you can have it."

Sal started to reply, but Milton cut the call.

81

E nzo was pale and he looked sickly; Milton didn't think that the boy had been able to see the phone when the shot was fired into Francesco's knee, but he had certainly heard it. Milton knew that violence was not an abstract concept where Enzo had grown up, but this might have been the first time that it had struck so close since the death of his father. Shock was possible. They would have to watch for that.

Milton gave him five minutes to void his guts into the toilet before telling him to clean himself up and get downstairs. Milton's first response was to be irritated, but then he remembered: the boy was young, and it was unfair to impose his own standards on someone so naïve. Enzo hadn't called Francesco; Francesco had called him, and, as Enzo had explained with his head over the toilet bowl, he had been worried about his friend.

Milton gathered everyone in the kitchen, waited for Enzo to join them, and then explained what had just happened. Enzo looked out of the window, his bottom lip quivering and his eyes wet. His mother went to him and wrapped an arm over his shoulders.

"Enzo," Fernández said, "we *told* you not to use your phone."

"I didn't think," he said quietly. "Franny's still in the city, and his family won't help him."

"It's all right," Connie said. "I don't blame you."

"Nor do I," Milton said, with a stern look in Fernández's direction. "There's no point in recriminations: what's done is done."

"I'm sorry," Fernández said. "John's right. It's not your fault."

Enzo's shoulders shook, and he buried his head against his mother's neck.

Milton stood. "But we do need to think about what we're going to do."

He went to the window and looked outside; darkness had fallen, and visibility had decreased to the extent that he could no longer see the trenches that they had dug in the lawn.

"You think they know where we are?" Aldo asked.

"They do."

"And they'll come here?"

"They will. I told them to. They've got Francesco. I'm worried that something even worse will happen to him unless we give them the money. I'll stay here to make the exchange."

"And what do we do? Leave?"

"That's going to be the safest thing for you all," Milton said. "Get as far away from here as possible. I'll give you the number of my friend at the FBI, and you can call her once you're safe. She'll tell you where to go."

Enzo shook his head. "But if you give the money to them, why wouldn't they just kill you and Franny?"

"There might be a way to make sure that doesn't happen if Coach is prepared to stay and help."

Fernández didn't hesitate. "Whatever you need."

"Then that's settled," Milton said. "You might want to fill a couple of bottles with water and grab blankets for the ride. We'll see you down by the truck."

MILTON TOOK a moment to compose himself and wondered if he could have played that a little differently. He knew that Sal would have learned where they were without his tip—it was obvious that the call had been staged in order to allow the crooked detectives to triangulate Enzo's phone, most likely through a similarly corrupt contact at the cellphone provider —but perhaps he could have avoided goading Sal. But Milton's anger had flashed after what Sal had done to Francesco, and, perhaps, he had allowed that to colour his judgement. Milton *wanted* Sal to come. He would have chosen the first option that he had put to Connie and the others— that he would go back to the city and conclude the matter in his own way—but he had given them the choice, expecting that they would choose the more pacific alternative.

Milton knew himself well enough by now to know that he had—unconsciously or not—subverted their decision by what he had just done. Handing the Pizzolatos over to the FBI without taking care of the situation in the city was not a guarantee of safety: Ellie might not be able to arrange protection for them and, for as long as Bobby Whitesox and Sal were out there, there was always the possibility that

Enzo would make the same kind of mistake as he had just made by accepting Francesco's call. They would be consigned to a lifetime of looking over their shoulders, and it would take only a momentary lapse to guarantee an unpleasant conclusion to their stories.

Milton's way was better. He was confident that he could keep everyone safe with the work that he had done to the grounds and the additional work he would now do to the interior of the house. He would have the benefit of familiarity here and preparation. Sal might have the advantage of numbers, but he had no idea what Milton was capable of.

82

Nicol's head throbbed as he made his way through the house, opened the door and went out into the snowy night. He took out his phone and called Bird. His partner had been busy with a contact at AT&T who had always done them a solid whenever they had needed phone data and didn't have time—or the cause—to get a warrant. They had Enzo's phone number, but, when the contact had tried to locate his phone through recent connection to a base tower, they'd struck out. That had required a tweak in the plan. They had needed someone to call him—someone the boy trusted—and Francesco had been chosen for the task.

"Hey," Bird said.

"He shot him in the knee," Nicol said.

"Who shot who?"

"Sal. The kid—Francesco. Put the gun to his knee, told Enzo to tell him where they were hiding, and, when he didn't... he fucking shot him, man."

Bird didn't immediately respond.

Nicol felt sweat on his palms despite the cold. "You got nothing to say?"

"The way I see it?" Bird said. "So what? So what if Sal caps him? It's no great loss. You know how it goes for mall-rats like him—if the street hasn't killed him already, it will soon enough. Sal would probably be doing him a favour."

Nicol clutched the phone in trembling fingers. He wasn't surprised at his partner's lack of empathy. He'd been like that for as long as they had worked together and, if anything, his callousness was getting worse the nearer he got to his retirement. Nicol had felt for a while that he was at the start of a slope that would end in the same place, and had already admitted to himself that he was looking forward to Bird's final day so that he could get a new partner. He knew that he was equally culpable for everything that they had done together, but he hadn't been as venal and cold before they had been partnered up. Bird's heartlessness and amorality were contagious, and Nicol knew that the only way he would be able to prevent his own irreversible slide into turpitude was with a clean slate.

"Forget the little guinea," Bird said. "You want the good news? We got the location. The little wop's in the middle of nowhere—looks like a property just outside Louisburg."

"I know," Nicol said. "Milton told us."

"What?"

"He told us where he is and that he'd wait there for Sal."

"What is he?" Bird said. "Nuts?"

"I don't know. But it's making me nervous."

"Relax. Just focus on the payday we just got."

"No, we didn't," Nicol said sharply. "We only get paid when Bobby gets the van." Nicol heard heavy footsteps from inside. The door opened and Sal stepped outside. "Hold on," he said to Bird, and muted the call.

Sal pointed to the phone. "That your partner?"

"Yes."

"Tell him he needs to meet us at the place. We leave now."

Sal went back into the house and started calling out orders.

"You still there?" Bird said.

Nicol unmuted the call. "I'm here."

"You got to stop worrying about Milton," Bird said. "He's shit out of luck."

"Yeah, well, we'll be able to see that for ourselves."

"What does that mean?"

"Sal's headed down there now, and he wants us to be there."

83

L uca Monteverde gripped the steering wheel of the SUV, nerves buzzing in his gut. Sal might not be concerned about Milton, but he was. The Englishman was capable enough to have escaped four of them at the kid's home, shooting one of them in the bargain and choking Luca out and leaving him on the kitchen floor. Plus, Milton had had no time to prepare for their arrival at Enzo's place, but he had taunted Sal to come and get him this time. He knew they were coming, and he'd had time to get ready. What if he had others with him? What if they were walking into a trap?

He rubbed his forehead and tried to relax.

Sal was in the passenger seat, staring at a satellite map of the property on his phone. Luca had glanced over and saw him zooming in and out, switching between different views, his brow creased in concentration. Luca wasn't sure how he felt about that; Sal was a brutal man, and he had a base animal cunning, but the Italian had never struck Luca as much of a planner. He operated on gut, working on the credo that the guy who hit first—and hardest—would usually be the one who walked away at the end of the day. Planning, though? Luca didn't think that was really Sal's style.

At least they had more men this time. Sal had rounded up a small posse: at the head of the line of vehicles was an unmarked sedan with Nicol and Bird, and behind that was a second SUV. Luca did the math again: three men in each SUV and the two detectives.

Eight.

Sal was Sal; he might be a psychopath, but there weren't many other men whom Luca would have wanted on his side if something like this went south. Two of the others—Nick Antonelli and Mario Longo—were veterans of Bobby Whitesox's crew, older guys with notches on their guns who ought to know what they were doing. Nicol and Bird were tough to assess; it was hard to know how they would respond if things got heated. Luis Scanga and Severo Addario were wannabes, street muscle that Sal brought in when he needed numbers on a job. They weren't skilled or experienced.

Still, they were all packing, and if eight armed men weren't enough to handle one troublemaker... well, they might as well fold up the tents and go home.

Luca turned and looked back at Francesco. His nephew was pale. They had bandaged his knee to staunch the blood, but the pain had to be unbearable. Every bump and jolt as the SUV ran over a pothole brought a little whimper of pain. Luca felt bad about what had happened. Sal had said that he would frighten Franny, would put the gun against his head until he had done what they wanted him to do, and, at least at the start, that was what he had done. The rest of it... shooting him through the knee? There had been no suggestion that the kid would be hurt.

Luca felt bad about what had happened and knew that it was his fault that he had come to harm, but he wasn't an idiot. Francesco was a stupid kid who was too big for his britches, and stupid kids who didn't know their place always got into trouble in the end. And what was Luca going to do? Go against Sal? No fucking way. Luca had made his way through life by looking at the choices with which he was presented and choosing the safest bets. Opposing Sal was a sure way to a bullet in the back of the head. Before they'd set off, Sal had said that Franny was just his leverage and, when he had recovered the van, he would let him go. That assurance was the best that Luca could hope for.

The unmarked police sedan ahead slowed to a crawl, its brake lights bright, as midnight approached. The car turned right, onto what looked like a small private road with a slight upslope. Luca flicked the indicator instinctively, even as he realised he was supposed to be turning off his headlights.

He shut off both, feeling Sal's stare burning a hole into his temple. "I know. Okay?"

There was a car off the road to the left. It was empty and looked as if it had been parked there. The two detectives drove along the road a little farther and then pulled over. The other vehicles slotted in behind the sedan. The doors opened and the cars all emptied out. Luca stared out at the terrain ahead. There was a crest in the road that would shield them from anyone who might be looking in their direction from the south, where the house lay, a bit further along. Sal had chosen to stop here for a reason. This was their muster point.

Sal checked the slide on his pistol. He turned back to Francesco and shone a vulpine grin down at his wounded knee. "Don't go anywhere."

84

Fernández met Milton down by the truck. Connie, Enzo and Aldo were upstairs, grabbing the things that they would need for the drive. Milton had told them they had twenty minutes to get ready, and then they would need to be on their way.

"You sure you don't want to go, too?" Fernández said.

"I can't," he said. "They'll keep coming. And they'll kill Francesco."

"So you just let him have the money?"

"I don't see any other way," he said.

"And once you leave town? What happens to Connie and the kids then?"

"They give evidence against Sal and Bobby, and they're put into witness protection."

Milton didn't add that a successful federal case against Bobby and Sal was going to be important for Fernández, too. The coach was involved now, and the Mafia would know that. There was a chance that retribution would be visited upon him, especially if the others were put out of reach. Milton knew that Fernández would have realised that, but he still didn't flinch. He was brave and selfless, an example that Milton felt unable to live up to.

If Fernández was contemplating the danger he was in, he didn't let it show. He clapped Milton on the shoulder. "What do you need?"

"You and that sniper rifle to cover me when I make the exchange," he said.

"You trust them?"

"Of course not. I'll feel a lot better about my prospects if you're watching."

Fernández nodded. "You got it. And then?"

Milton shrugged. "They take the money. We leave it to the feds."

Milton did not elaborate on what he had decided to do next, and Fernández didn't press it. "They'd better take my Ford," he said, indicating the pickup parked next to the house.

"Sorry about that," Milton said. "I left the other one in Ingleside."

"And it'll already be on blocks," Fernández said with a sigh. "That old tape deck still worked, too."

Connie, Enzo and Aldo made their way out of the door and joined them in the yard. Milton reached around to his back and withdrew the Peacemaker. He offered it to Connie.

"No," she said. "I don't want that."

"It's a last resort," Milton said. "If they find you and you have to use it, just remember you have to cock it first by pulling back the hammer with your thumb until it clicks into place. Just point at whoever is threatening you and squeeze the trigger hard without thinking about it. And be careful—it's heavy and it has a big kick."

"Okay." Relenting, she took the revolver and gripped it in both hands.

Fernández reached into his pocket and took out a set of keys. "It's that truck," he said, pointing to the Ford.

Connie turned to Milton. "Can't you come with us? Both of you?"

"That wouldn't be good for Francesco. And if Sal is sensible, it won't come to violence."

"But he's not, is he? I mean, he's not known for being reasonable."

"Coach will be in the house with a rifle. He can help focus Sal's mind on the good sense of playing straight."

Milton knew that there would be no peaceful resolution tonight. There would be blood. Either the exchange went south, and there would be a shoot-out at the quarry; or the exchange was made, and Milton followed Sal and his cronies back to the city and disposed of them there. Bobby Whitesox, too, and Patrick O'Connor. He was beyond the point where he might have considered a compromise. An FBI investigation involved a lot of variables, and the resolution was impossible to predict.

Milton could deliver certainty.

He looked at his watch. Sal would have set off as soon as he had the location; Milton guessed that they would be with them in twenty minutes, a half hour at the outside. "You'd better get going. You don't—"

He was interrupted by the sound of cans rattling against each other from the direction of the track that led to the house.

"What's that?" Connie said.

Fernández saw the expression on Milton's face.

"John?"

"I set tripwires on the perimeter of the house. That was one of them. Change of plan—you need to get inside and go down to the cellar. They're already here."

PART V

85

Björn flinched at the sudden noise and then, acting on instinct, he dropped to the ground. He rolled into the ditch at the side of the road, pulled his sidearm, and stayed there, listening intently for the sound of anyone approaching. He had parked his car a mile away from the property and was making his final approach on foot. He was furious with himself. The fishing line had been strung across the margin to the side of the track, and he hadn't seen it in the darkness.

What was Milton afraid of? It had to be something that had gone down with the man in Tanner's basement, but what? He knew that if he had gone to the trouble of setting up a perimeter alarm, he would certainly back that up with a rifle at the house and, duly alerted by the sounding of his perimeter alarm, he might be scouring the terrain for him now.

He took out his night-vision binoculars and wriggled as far up the lip of the ditch as he dared. He brought the glasses to his eyes and scanned the terrain from left to right.

He saw the barn, lit from the inside, and the yard that separated it from the main house. He had seen Milton and another man in the yard as he had approached; the two of them were deep in conversation, and Björn had decided to get just a little bit closer before he unslung his rifle and took his shot. He was good on the range out to five hundred metres, but Milton was not the sort of target you would want to wound. Taking him out from a distance wasn't sporting, but Björn did not allow that to concern him. Milton was a target, just like all the others he had liquidated as he had made his ascent through the Group. He was a combatant, too. He knew the rules of the game; if the shoe had been on the other foot, Björn knew that Milton would behave in exactly the same way. He would do him one favour, though, and draw in close enough to assure a headshot and an instant kill. Björn had no idea what had promoted Milton's breakdown, but, until then, he had served with a dedication that had become legendary, his reputation breaching even the secrecy that cloaked the Group and its operatives. He would do him the good grace of a quick, painless death.

He was considering what to do with the man to whom Milton was talking when the two of them were joined in the yard by a woman and two teenage boys. Perhaps it was the effort of trying to discern what was going on that distracted him; whatever it was, he had blundered into the tripwire, and now his clean kill looked anything but.

The five of them had hurried back into the house, and now there was no sign of movement. Björn was surer than ever that Milton and perhaps the other man he had seen were looking for him through rifle scopes. They had to know where he was, and there was open ground between here and the house. The snow would slow him down, too. He would be a sitting duck if he advanced.

Fokk.

He was going to have to retreat.

86

Sal got out of the car. Luca did the same, shutting the door behind him. Sal waited for the others to gather around.

"This is what we gonna do," he said. "The house is a mile south from here, down the road." He used a stick to draw a square in the snow. "This man—Milton—he has had time to prepare. Maybe he has a gun. He probably does."

"So what are we gonna do?" Severo Addario said.

"We split into two teams." Sal drew an arrow to the house. "Me, Luca, you and Luis will drive down the road to the house. We'll offer the exchange—the kid for the van. In the meantime, Nick and Mario go through the woods to the west." He drew a curved arrow that went around the left-hand side of the house. "Take the rifles and get in the trees. Get up close, but don't let him see you. Cover us if we need it."

The two men nodded their understanding.

"What about us?" Nicol said.

"You think I forget about you?" Sal said with a humourless smile. "You think you could just wait here and Bobby was gonna pay you?"

"Just tell us what you want us to do," Bird said.

"Bobby says you gotta be involved. You wanna work for him—you wanna take his money—you gotta have skin... how you say?"

"Skin in the game," Nicol finished for him.

"*Si.* Skin in the game."

"He doesn't think we already do? We found where Milton's been hiding out. That wasn't legal, Sal."

"*More* skin."

"What, then? What does he want?"

Sal pointed the stick at Bird and then Nicol. "You both go with Nick and Mario. We gonna make sure you pull your weight."

"I'm nearly sixty years old," Bird complained. "You think I'm tramping through a forest at night?"

"That's exactly what you're gonna do, or the deal is off. You don't do what Bobby wants, you don't get paid. It is simple."

Bird and Nicol exchanged a sour glance, then a nod.

"Fine," Nicol said.

"But if we find that money," Bird said, "we're gonna want more than he's promised us so far. This wasn't what we agreed."

"I don't care," Sal said, waving off their objections. "Talk to Bobby."

"That's the plan?" Bird said. "Just like that?"

"What?" Sal asked, irritated.

"Milton is dangerous. We've underestimated him before. So have you. This isn't going to be easy."

Sal didn't try to hide his disgust. "You want to run and hide?"

"Didn't say that."

"He's one man."

"But well trained."

"So? I don't care. Shoot him and he'll bleed just the same."

"And the kid? Pizzolato?"

"No witnesses. Him, his mother, anyone. As soon as we've got the van, you force your way inside that house. No one gets out alive. Are we done with questions?" Sal's tone suggested that further conversation would be unwise. "What are you waiting for? Go."

87

L uca got back into the driver's seat and pulled the SUV away from the side of the track. He drove them up and over the hill and then followed the track down to the edge of the snowy field that fronted the house. There was about four hundred yards of open space to cross before they reached the property. The house was large, with outbuildings spread out around it. One of the buildings —a barn, perhaps?—was lit, and the glow spread out across the landscape like a beacon. Enough light spilled out of its open doors to cast a pale wash over the house.

It also cast light on the vehicle that had been parked just outside.

"Shit," he said. "Look."

Sal squinted into the night.

"Is that the van?" Luca said.

"Looks like it."

There was no sign of anyone in the barn or near the van, and the main house was dark.

"Stop there," Sal said, pointing to a kink in the track fifty yards from the house.

Luca did as he was told.

"Switch on the lights. I want him to know we're here."

Luca flicked the switch, and the high beams shone out, twin shafts that reached across the darkened field until they bloomed against the wall of the house.

"Get out," Sal said. "Bring the kid out, too. I want Milton to see him."

They disembarked, Luis and Severo dragging Francesco out with them. They brought him to the front of the Escalade and dropped him into the snow.

BJÖRN WAS GETTING ready to pull back when he heard the sound of an approaching vehicle. He flattened himself in the ditch and waited as a Cadillac Escalade rumbled along the track just a few feet from where he was hiding. He was down too low to see into it and, besides, the windows were tinted. It drove slowly, rolling over the tripwire that had been set across the track but, since the trigger had already been pulled, the empty tin cans did not repeat their alarm. The Cadillac continued down the track to the edge of the field that faced this side of the house.

Björn brought his binoculars up and focused on the SUV. It came to a stop fifty yards away from the house. The new arrivals had to be the reason for the jury-rigged security measures that Milton had installed. Björn had no idea who was inside the car, nor what they wanted that had caused Milton to take precautions, but he wondered whether they might provide the distraction that would enable him to stay and complete his objective.

He was considering that when he heard the sound of footsteps crunching through the snow behind him. He swivelled in the ditch, making sure that he was hidden from the Cadillac and the house beyond it, and then scanned the darkness with the night-vision binoculars. He saw four men moving to the west, just cresting the hill behind which he had left his car. The trees were a little sparser on the plateau atop the hill and, although they were moving quickly and with what passed for stealth, they were still visible. The men took a wide route that would bring them around the house by way of the denser wood that had been planted on that side of the building.

Now Björn was sure: Milton was in trouble and, if he was still here, there would be an opportunity for Björn to do what he had come here to do. He picked up his rifle and shifted into a firing position. He put his eye to the scope and settled in to wait.

BIRD FOLLOWED at the back of the line as Nick Antonelli and Mario Longo followed an animal trail through the wood that clung to the top of the hill and then turned due south. They were jogging and he was quickly out of breath. The two men were toting automatic rifles; Antonelli had opened up his vehicle to reveal a small armoury of weapons. He had taken a Bushmaster ACR, and Longo a Daniels Defense M-4. Bird had reluctantly taken a Springfield with a sixteen-inch barrel, and Nicol had removed an AR-10. Bird would be pleased if he didn't have to use the rifle.

The terrain was interrupted by roots and depressions that were hidden in the snow, and he had stumbled on several occasions, almost falling twice. It was cold, but despite the temperature, his skin was quickly slicked with a frigid sweat. He reached up and wiped a bead of moisture out of his eye and, as he did, he missed the knuckle of an oak's roots. His foot caught it and he fell, landing flat on his stomach. The impact winded him and he was unable to prevent an involuntary grunt of pain.

Bird was tempted to stay there—to wait on the ground, plead a twisted ankle, or get up and go back to the car. He was too old for this shit. O'Connor's money had been easy; a little information here and there, a tip-off when it was warranted, and they got a nice pay-off every month. Bobby Whitesox was offering a different kind of deal, asking for more in return, and Bird couldn't help but wonder whether it was going to be worth the aggravation. He gathered his breath. The money *was* good, though, and he had meant what he said. They would demand more if they helped Bobby get his money back again.

Nicol slowed and looked back. "You okay?" he hissed.

"This is fucking ridiculous," he muttered as he hauled himself back to his feet.

"Come on," Nicol said.

Bird started to jog again, following Nicol and the other two as they picked a route through the darkened wood toward the outbuildings on the western side of the house.

88

M ilton had been up in the bedroom at the front of the house for ten minutes, looking for anything that might explain why the alarm had been tripped. His first thought was that it must have been Sal, but he had been unable to see anything even with the night-vision binoculars. He was starting to wonder whether an animal might have been responsible when he saw the vehicle heading south along the track.

He pushed the earbuds that were connected to his phone into his ears and spoke into the in-line microphone that was draped just below his chin. "They're coming. Single vehicle, lights off."

"I see it."

Milton followed the vehicle as it descended the shallow hill and started across the field that adjoined the house. "What about Connie and the kids?"

"They're in the cellar."

Milton nodded in satisfaction. He was conscious that the three of them were unguarded, but, on the other hand, he was sure that it would be safer for them away from the action. Connie had the Peacemaker, too, and, after what she had done with the baseball bat at the house, he was in no doubt that she would use it if she had to.

The vehicle was a big boxy SUV. It came to a stop fifty yards away from the house. Sal was being careful. The lights flicked on.

"Are you ready?"

"I am."

"Stay sharp."

Milton slipped the big Desert Eagle he had taken from Fernández's locker into the back of his jeans, cinched his belt to make sure it stayed there, and descended the stairs. There were two main ways to exit the house: the door in the kitchen that faced the SUV, and the door at the back. Milton went into the kitchen, making sure that the modification to the brass handle that he had rigged earlier was inactive before turning it and stepping outside.

It was cold, and his breath steamed in front of his face. The SUV's lights were pointed directly at him, and Milton made sure not to look into them so as to preserve his night vision. The doors of the vehicle opened, and the occupants disembarked. There were four of them, although he could make out no details with the lights shining out at the house. Two of the men hauled a much smaller figure outside. It had to be Francesco.

"Milton," Sal called out.

"You must be frightened, Sal."

"Why would you say that?"

"You've brought friends."

"It takes a lot to scare me."

Milton hissed into the microphone. "Hit the lights."

The house was equipped with three two-hundred-watt floodlights that had enough brightness to shine out across the field. Fernández hit the power, and they blazed to life, the sudden glare enough to force Sal to bring up his arm to shield his eyes.

"Turn them off," he yelled.

"I need to see you, Sal. Let's just get this over with, shall we?"

"Give me the keys for the van."

Milton took the keys from his pocket and held them up. "I'm going to come out halfway," he said. "One of you is going to help Francesco walk out to meet me. I'll throw them over to you after that."

"You think you're in control here? You're not. *I* am. Give me the keys, and maybe you all get to walk away."

"We do it like that, or we don't do it at all," Milton said. "And one other thing—don't do anything stupid. I've got a friend with a rifle up on the first floor. If anyone does anything that makes him think that you're not playing straight, he'll put a bullet in them. Just so we're clear."

Sal didn't answer, still shielding his eyes with his upraised arm. The lights were making him and the others uncomfortable—that was good—and it would be difficult for any of them to use their weapons with any degree of accuracy if they couldn't look at their targets.

"Start walking," Sal called out.

"I'm going," Milton said quietly into the microphone.

"I got your back," Fernández said. "Be careful."

89

Nicol followed the three men to the west, traversing the flank of the densely wooded slope to the flatter terrain that ran down to the house. The trees thinned out as the ground levelled off, but there was still enough cover to stay out of sight of the house. Nicol was glad of that. He did not want to be there, but, on the other hand, he recognised that a relationship with Bobby could be lucrative. Bird would be retiring soon, and he wanted to make as much money as he could before deciding whether he would be able to continue once he was paired up with a new partner. His thoughts drifted back to when he had been partnered with Bird for the first time, and he realised that Bird must have shared the same reservations about him. Bird had handled it with the skill of a veteran who had been on the take for years—a few minor infractions, corners cut and insignificant bribes accepted—before he had slowly increased Nicol's exposure to the full depth of his corruption. Bird had probably been indoctrinated in just the same way, and Nicol would have to follow that template now.

There was a symmetry there, a pattern of graft that reached back decades.

Being out here tonight might have been necessary, but it didn't mean that he had to like it. Sal could be as blithe as he wanted, but Nicol knew that Milton was dangerous.

He followed Antonelli and Longo into a deeper copse of trees—twenty or thirty yards wide and fifty yards deep—that was clustered around the north-western side of the property. There was a body of water beyond them that covered the remaining area to the neighbouring fence line. They pressed on into the pitch-black thicket, its highest tree-tops nearly twenty feet above. The trunks were so close together that it seemed impenetrable. There was a trail that led through the trees, most likely made by animals, and Antonelli crouched low and followed it. Nicol tried to make as little sound as he could, but the snow had an icy crust that crunched as he struggled through it.

Antonelli crept up to the edge of the tree line and held up his hand, telling the others to stop. Nicol parted the branches and gazed out onto the field beyond. The Escalade was parked fifty yards from the house, its lights blazing out. Sal was in front of the car, with the other three men—and the kid—behind him. Floodlights on the house had been lit, and they cast the lone figure standing in front of them in silhouette. It was Milton. A shouted conversation was taking place between him and Sal.

Antonelli held a finger to his lips and then indicated that he was going to set up here and the others should find their own firing positions. Nicol edged through the vegetation until he was ten feet away and found a dogwood with enough space beneath its lowest branches for him to slide underneath. He wriggled through the snow on his belly and rested the rifle on an exposed root, bracing it with his free hand. He looked down the barrel to the iron sight, edging it left from the Escalade until he had a rough bead on Milton.

90

L uca watched as Milton started to cross the space between them.

"Take the kid out to him," Sal said to Severo Addario.

Francesco was helped to his feet. He was half-carried, half-dragged between Sal and Luca, ignoring both of them, his face twisted with pain and fear. Addario kept him moving.

Milton reached the halfway point between the SUV and the house and stopped.

Luca found that he was clenching his fists. It was tense. He knew that the others would be in the woods somewhere, all of them armed with automatic weapons and ready to lay down a fusillade that would cut Milton in half. On the other hand, he had heard what Milton had said about a man with a rifle inside the house, and didn't doubt that for a moment. A decent shooter would have no difficulty in slotting at least one of them before they could get into cover; he wondered who had been targeted. Sal, probably, but what if it was him?

Addario and the kid walked on and reached Milton.

"The keys," Sal yelled. "Give him the keys."

Milton spoke to Francesco and looped an arm around his waist to help him to stand without putting weight on the damaged knee.

Sal drew his pistol and aimed it at Milton. "Give him the fucking keys!"

"We found the money," he said. "We cut the van open and took it out. It's stacked in the back now—every last cent of it."

"Really? You didn't help yourself to any?"

"Check it," Milton said. "The door's open."

Sal glanced to the side at Luca. "There's a flashlight in the car," Sal said. "Go make sure it's all there."

91

L ongo signalled to Antonelli and started to move through the wood, continuing to the south. He stayed inside the tree line, his attention split between the shouted conversation in the field to his left and the uncertain footing as he followed the animal trail through the vegetation.

Bird could see what he was doing: moving around a little so that he had a better angle to scope out anyone in the property. He wasn't surprised; Sal had never intended to go through with the exchange. He was going to take the money and then shoot Milton and, most likely, anyone else inside the house. Longo had a night scope on his rifle, and all he needed was the right angle; anyone observing from the house would be vulnerable.

Bird looked up and exchanged a glance with Nicol; his partner had seen Longo, too, and—at least judging by the pinched expression on his face—had reached the same conclusion. That was the difference between the two of them: Bird had been doing this long enough to have inured himself to the unpleasant necessities that were sometimes occasioned by the life that he had chosen. Nicol was greener, less cynical about it, less jaded. That would all come with time. Bird had been like that himself, once, although it was a struggle to reach back and remember it now.

He tightened his grip around the Springfield. He was a decent shot with his sidearm, but he couldn't remember the last time he'd been to the range with a long gun. He figured he'd soon find out how rusty he was.

Luca took the flashlight and walked across the field to the van. He went to the driver's side door and opened it. The cabin was just as he remembered it. He went around to the back. He looked through the tinted windows set halfway up the cargo doors. It was dark inside; the light from the house and the Escalade were at the wrong angles to illuminate it. He opened the doors, flicked on the flashlight and shone the beam inside, sweeping it from side to side.

Dozens of plastic-wrapped packages had been stacked in the load space. He took a brick from the top and hefted it: it was around six inches by six inches by two inches and had been wrapped tight. He peeled the plastic back to reveal the corner of a hundred-dollar bill. He put the brick to his nostrils and inhaled; it was redolent with the smell of money.

He backed away from the door and held up the brick so that Sal could see it. "There's a ton of money in the back."

"Happy?" Milton called out.

"Give me the keys," Sal called back.

Bᴊöʀɴ ᴄᴜʀsᴇᴅ ᴜɴᴅᴇʀ ʜɪs ʙʀᴇᴀᴛʜ. He had a reasonable shooting position and was confident that he would have been able to hit a target at Milton's range, but the newcomers were standing between him and his prey. The man who was doing all the talking, the one who spoke with an Italian accent, could not have been more unhelpful if he had tried, and the man who had taken the boy out to be exchanged was blocking the shot, too. And then there was the kid; he was standing next to Milton and, if Björn's aim was just a fraction off, then there was a chance that he might get hit.

Björn was going to have to be patient. He took a breath, ignored the cold of the snow, and took aim once more.

Bɪʀᴅ ᴡᴀᴛᴄʜᴇᴅ. Milton had stayed where he was, standing between the kid and Sal's gun. He reached into his pocket and took something out. It had to be the keys for the van.

Longo cut around Antonelli and continued to the south, looking for a position that would offer him a more advantageous angle from where he would be able to open fire on Milton without putting Sal or the others into a crossfire. He crouched low, his attention on the events in the field, his weapon held in both hands and pointed down.

Whatever Sal was planning, it would have to be soon.

Bird watched Longo as he came to a sudden stop.

He cursed and looked down at the ground.

There was a bright flash, then a feeling of intense heat that washed over him and a deafening roar. Bird was buffeted by something strong enough to shove him backwards through the snow. There was another explosion, ten feet away from the seat of the first, and then another and another. The field erupted each time, sending fountains of snow and dirt and grass high into the air.

Bird wiped snow from his eyes and looked back to where Longo had been standing. It took a moment to find him: he had been thrown through the air and had been smeared against the side of a large dogwood. He was on the ground, motionless, flames running across his body. His jacket caught quickly and melted onto his skin. The ground next to where he had been standing was smouldering; Bird smelled gasoline and saw fragments of smoking plastic on the field.

Milton had left booby traps in the wood. A tripwire, close to the house, rigged to detonate a series of explosions if anyone got too close.

There came the crack of a gunshot from the house, and then another. Severo Addario was caught between Sal and Milton, and he went down, his weapon firing off into the air as he collapsed.

Milton ran, dragging the injured kid after him.

Antonelli opened fire from the tree line, sending an automatic burst into the top-right window of the house.

Milton was very nearly knocked off his feet. The improvised fuel bombs were a distance away and, even from there, it was so loud that a ringing filled his head as if a gong had been struck between his ears. There was smoke everywhere.

He had been very aware that Sal was not to be trusted, and had taken steps to protect Connie, the boys, Fernández and himself in the event that he didn't play straight. He had left a number of precautions in and around the house, the most significant being the series of linked bombs that had just been triggered. He had taken four large single-skin tanks that he had found in the barn and filled them with red diesel—fuel marked only for off-road use—that he had found in a larger tank at the back of the house. Each tank stored thirty litres, and Milton had filled them all to the brim. He added soap flakes as a thickening agent and doled out a pot of oil-based paint for the aluminium powder that was contained within. Once his preparations were complete, he had dragged the tanks to the series of snow holes that the boys had excavated. He had taken the sticks of dynamite

from the quarry's supplies and taped one to the underside of
each container, attaching a detonator to each and then
wiring each package to its neighbour; he had wired the lot
of them to a spare car battery. He had used fishing line to
string out a series of tripwires through the trees. It took only
one of the tripwires to fire the detonators, which, in turn,
exploded the dynamite. The fuel vapour was ignited by the
burning aluminium powder in the paint and amplified the
destructive force of the explosion, effectively creating a
series of napalm bombs.

Milton grabbed Franny and hustled him toward the
house.

He looked up and saw Fernández in the open bedroom
window, saw the long barrel of the SR-25 catch the orange
glow of the trees that had caught fire. Franny flinched at the
loud boom as the rifle discharged. Fernández had taken a
shot at the man who was closest to Milton—the one who
had brought Franny over to him—and would be looking for
another target.

They were still twenty feet from the house when Milton
heard the unmistakable clatter of automatic gunfire. He
launched himself at Francesco, tackling him to the ground
and holding him there, presenting as narrow a profile as
possible.

"Cover us!" Milton yelled into the mic.

"They're in the woods," Fernández shouted back.

Milton put his arm over the boy's shoulders and kept
him down as low as he could. Rounds zipped overhead,
slamming into the brick wall of the house and puffing out
little plumes of powder. Milton heard the sound of glass
shattering, both from the direction of the house and
through the earbuds.

The rifle boomed from the window above: once, twice,

and then a third time. Milton knew that Fernández could only deter the shooters, that he was aiming at their muzzle flashes and that a hit under that much return fire would be a miracle. There was also the fact that the coach did not have an unlimited supply of ammunition, and, more pertinently, that Sal and the two other men from the Escalade would soon be on their feet again. Fernández couldn't deal with the men in the wood *and* Sal.

Milton had to get the boy inside.

He got to his feet, hauled the kid up by the scruff of his neck, and half-carried him, half-dragged him to the kitchen door. He tossed him inside and followed, kicking the door closed just as a round cracked against it.

"Fernández," he yelled, "get down here."

The coach clattered down the stairs.

"How many did you get?"

"The guy who came out to you," he said. "That's it, though. Sorry—the incoming was pretty hot."

"How many do you think were in the wood?"

"At least three. Might be more."

Milton ran the numbers: four in Sal's car, and Fernández had accounted for one of them; assume an additional four in the wood. A minimum of seven still standing, maybe more; they would all be armed, and some of them had automatics.

Seven against two.

Not good, and Milton was about to make the odds against him even longer still.

"Take the kid into the cellar with the others," he said. "Stay there with them and lock the door. Shoot anyone who comes in."

"No way, man. What about you?"

"Please," Milton said. "This isn't a discussion."

Milton heard shouted voices from outside. They would approach carefully, he knew, suspecting that the sniper was still upstairs, but, when they realised there was no more outbound fire, they would find the confidence to advance a little more quickly.

"Go!"

Fernández took Francesco by the shoulder and led him out of the kitchen and into the hall. Milton checked that his modification to the door handle was in place and, happy that it was, reached over and flicked the power socket into the on position.

93

The blasts had picked Nicol off his feet and tossed him five feet back into a bush. It was too dark to see what it was, but it was full of sharp thorns that had scraped bloody tracks across the exposed skin of his face, neck and throat. He disentangled himself, wincing as the thorns scratched and tore at his skin, and scrambled through the undergrowth for his Springfield. The firing from the house stopped.

"Tripwire," Antonelli called out. "I saw it. Watch where you put your feet."

The canopy ahead of them was on fire, orange and yellow flames feasting on the branches. Snow was melting and steam was mixing with the smoke.

"We need to pull back," Bird said.

"No," Antonelli snapped. "We need to get into the house."

"Fuck that," Bird said. "Did you see what just happened? The place is rigged. I'm not going anywhere."

"You want me to tell Sal you're bailing?"

"You can tell him what you want. I'm too old for this."

"I'll go," Nicol said. "He can cover us."

Nicol took a breath. He didn't want to be here, doing this —especially after what he had just seen, and what that might portend—but if Bird really was on the way out, then maybe this was a chance to demonstrate to Sal and Bobby that he was someone who could be counted upon. He parted the branches and used the light from the burning pit to see whether there was any evidence of additional traps. Tripwires would be difficult to set out in the open, but Milton had already demonstrated that he had had the time to excavate a shallow pit. What was to say that there were no others between here and the house?

"I got your six," Bird said, dropping down to his belly and taking up a prone shooting position.

"Ready?" Nicol said.

Antonelli held his rifle in both hands, bracing it diagonally across his chest. He nodded.

Nicol looked down at Bird. His partner gave a little shrug and then a nod, and lowered himself to the ground so that he could look along the barrel of the rifle.

"*Now.*"

They cut out of the trees and sprinted across the open ground, their feet sinking into the snow. Nicol was covered in sweat despite the cold. He kept his eyes on the windows ahead of them, ready to throw himself to the ground if he saw any sign that the sniper was changing his firing position. The windows were dark, though, and he saw nothing. They had fired a barrage at him from the trees and, although he knew that it would have been a fluke if any of the rounds had found their mark, the glass in the windows had been shattered and the sniper had seen fit to pull back.

Nicol ran hard, his legs pounding through the ankle-high snow until his thighs burned.

94

Enzo and Aldo sat side by side, leaning against the basement wall. Connie sat across from them. The room was small and fashioned with cinderblock walls, and Fernández had told them that it had once been used to store chopped firewood. The lights were out throughout the home, and the room was dark save for the illumination from Connie's phone as she tried to get a signal.

"I'm scared, man," Aldo whispered.

"Me too," Enzo replied. "But it won't help to focus on it. Try to think about something else."

"It's not as easy for me as it is for you."

"What do you mean?"

"The autism. You're always calm."

"Not always."

"I can't help thinking that we're going to die."

"We're not," Enzo said, but he didn't feel it.

Aldo nodded, but it was obvious that he wasn't convinced.

They both heard a deep boom from outside.

"Shit," Aldo said. "You think that was the dynamite?"

They had both seen what Milton had arranged in the pits that they had helped to excavate. Four separate traps, each activated by a tripwire that snaked between the trees. They had seen the tanks of fuel with the dynamite strapped to them, and the wires that ran to the car battery that provided the electrical charge for the detonators. Enzo braced for a second explosion, but, instead, they heard the sound of a gunshot and then the unmistakable clamour of automatic gunfire.

Connie reached over and grabbed Enzo by the hand. She squeezed and he squeezed back.

They heard the sound of a fist pounding against the door. "It's Fernández. Let me in."

Connie switched on her phone's flashlight so that she could see the way to the door. She unlocked it and pulled it aside; the coach was standing there, and, as he stepped to the left, Enzo saw that Francesco was behind him.

"Franny!" Enzo called up.

Fernández flicked on the light and helped the boy inside. The coach shut the door and stepped down, closing and locking it behind him.

"You okay?" Enzo asked as Francesco reached the bottom of the stairs.

"They shot me," he said. "My knee."

Connie looked down and saw the bloodstained bandage that had been wrapped around his leg. "Have they given you anything to help?"

He shook his head. Enzo could see that his face was bloodless with pain and fear.

Connie went to Fernández. "You got anything down here?"

"For a gunshot wound?" He shook his head. "Got a first-aid kit in the kitchen, but we can't go up there and get it now."

Connie turned to Francesco and laid her hand against his cheek. It was clammy. "He's in shock."

"He needs to get to the hospital," Enzo said.

There came another crack of gunfire from somewhere outside.

"We can't leave," Fernández said. "Help me get Franny stabilised for now."

He helped the boy to lie down on the floor and gently elevated his feet, being mindful of the injured leg. He found a coat and covered him.

Connie sat down beside him and took his hand. "What's happening outside?" she asked Fernández.

"They're here," Fernández said. "Sal and his men."

"Where's John?"

"He says he's going to deal with them. He told me to come down here and help you guard the kids."

"So he's on his own?"

"I said I'd help, but he said he didn't need me. I don't know if you've noticed, but, sometimes, when he says something, there's something about the way he says it that says you'd be wasting your time arguing."

Enzo had seen the way Smith gave instructions; he was open-minded, at least for the most part, but there were times—when he locked in with those icy blue eyes—when it was obvious that Smith wasn't interested in a debate, that this was how it was going to be.

"I've seen that," Connie said.

"Didn't feel like I had a choice," Fernández said.

95

Nicol and Antonelli reached the house without further incident; the sniper looked to have abandoned his post, and there were no other unpleasant surprises that Milton had left for them on the grounds of the property.

Sal, Luca Monteverde and Luis Scanga were waiting for them.

Antonelli reached them first.

"What the fuck happened?" Sal said.

"There was a tripwire," Antonelli said. "Mario didn't see it."

"He planted bombs?"

Antonelli nodded.

"*Andare a puttane*," Sal spat.

"What about Severo?" Antonelli asked.

Sal shook his head. "Guy in the window shot him."

"Shit."

Sal turned to Nicol. "Where's your partner?"

"Pussied out," Antonelli answered for him. "Stayed back in the trees."

"*Stare sui coglioni!* I said you *both* needed to be in this."

Nicol knew he had no choice but to be an enthusiastic participant. He was on his own now and, if he wanted to make a good impression—good enough to ensure he was given work in the future—he was going to have to step up to the plate now and deliver.

"*I'm* here, Sal," he said.

"He can forget working with Bobby," Sal said, as if he hadn't heard Nicol. "He's done."

"Like I said—I'm here. You wanna stand out here losing your temper, or do you wanna maybe break in and do whatever it is you want to do?"

Sal paused and, for a moment, Nicol did not know how he would react. His temper was well known, and Nicol realised that there was a chance that he might take his frustrations out on him. He found that he was sweating, even in the cold, the moisture slicking his palm where it pressed up against the stock of the AR-10.

After a beat, Sal gave a nod, as if a decision had been made. "We go inside and we kill every last one of them."

"I'm good with that," Nicol said.

Sal inclined his head towards the door and then gestured to Antonelli. "Open it carefully—he might be inside."

Antonelli examined the wooden door. It looked old, with a weighty brass handle that might have been the original. The snow on the porch had been disturbed by the passage of several sets of boots, most recently—Nicol assumed—those belonging to Milton. There were no windows nearby, nor anything that suggested that they would be in any danger; at least not until they got inside.

Sal shouldered his rifle and stepped back so that he could aim through the door. Nicol did the same.

Antonelli reached for the door handle and grasped it.

His body immediately went rigid and he gasped in pain.

"What is it?" Sal said.

Antonelli tried to speak, but all he could manage was a series of glottal grunts between jaws that appeared to be clenched tightly together. The muscles in his neck started to bunch and unbunch, and his arms and legs quivered with severe and evidently uncontrollable contractions.

"He's rigged the door," Luca exclaimed.

Antonelli was being electrocuted. A fine smoke started to rise from his body, and Nicol could smell the unmistakable odour of cooked meat. Nicol didn't know what to do. He had a pair of gloves in his pockets, but didn't know if that would protect him if he were to grasp Antonelli while he was still touching the door handle.

Sal did not take the time to think; he stepped around Antonelli and nodded that Luca should be ready to fire. He drew back his foot and then booted the door. It flew open; the handle was wrenched out of Antonelli's hand and he collapsed onto the porch.

Luca held his finger against the trigger and aimed left. He swivelled and aimed right. The hallway beyond was empty.

"Clear."

Luca stepped back, his heel nudging against Antonelli's arm so that his hand turned over and his palm fell open. The skin had been badly burned, his flesh a shocking black against the white of the snow and ice. He was seizing, his legs and arms twitching; he wasn't dead, at least not yet, but he wasn't going to be much help.

Sal hefted his rifle and nodded to the open doorway and the hall beyond. "Ready?"

Luca and Scanga nodded.

"Ready?" Sal said again, staring at Nicol.

"Ready."

"Kill them all."

96

Bird watched as Nicol and Antonelli crossed the field to the house. He tracked them with the rifle, his finger around the trigger and ready to take a shot at anyone who popped his or her head out of cover. The house was quiet, though, the windows empty and dark. He saw nothing and, after a quick scamper across the snow, both men reached the relative cover of the house's wall. Sal, Gianluca Monteverde and Luis Scanga were already there, and the five men huddled up and then made their way to the door that Milton had used to get into the house.

Five of them against Milton and whoever was sniping from the top floor; the numbers were in their favour, but this was unfamiliar terrain, and Bird knew that the odds would be evened out a little because of it. He would still have taken Sal over Milton, but he much preferred to be out here than inside.

He thought about Nicol. He had suspected that his partner might decide that he had to follow this through to the end. He was ambitious, not like Bird. Those days were long gone for him. Nicol wasn't jaded by years of looking over his shoulder; he was unscarred by the sleepless nights when all Bird could think about was the Internal Affairs investigation that he knew must surely come for him at some point. He knew the anxiety had contributed to the angina that was getting worse the older he got, and he was looking forward to putting it all behind him. He had already known that he was out, and coming out here and being bombed and shot at... that was all the confirmation that he needed.

Money, though. He had his pension, but it wasn't much. If he was going to call it quits, it wouldn't hurt to get a little extra coin to help him on his way.

He looked over at the van. He had guessed that there would come a point when it would be unguarded. He had heard Luca call out to Sal that there was money in the back. He knew, from the work that they had done for Patrick O'Connor, that Sal was in the business of moving a ton of money from Vegas to Kansas City so that the Irishman could wash it. That must have been what was in the back. How much? Enough to make Bobby send his men out to this godforsaken shithole in an attempt to get it back.

Six figures? Would that be enough?

He doubted it.

It had to be seven.

Had to be.

He knew that he was likely going to have a problem with Bobby and Sal when this whole sorry mess was resolved. He knew that he would—at the very least—be cut out of any future work, and that there would be no finder's fee for the work that he had already done in locating the kid and the van.

He could do a lot with a million bucks. It would be enough to move away from KC, take his wife somewhere warm, somewhere they would never be found. She had come home with a brochure from a retirement development in Cabo. Somewhere like that could work. He had no doubt that Bobby would have a long reach, but the old man was a dinosaur now. Bird doubted that he would have any reliable contacts in law enforcement who would be able to help him track down someone who had gone on the run; if he *did* have a contact, then surely he would not have needed their help in tracing the kid's phone?

He sucked on his teeth, staring out across the open field to where the van stood all alone and undefended.

I mean, he thought, *it's at least worth a look.*

Right?

Right.

He took a breath, pushed himself up on creaking, arthritic knees, and checked once more that the sniper was not still in the window. He couldn't see anything, but elected to wait another minute until Sal and the others made their move to get inside. There would be too much going on for someone to notice him then; and, he reminded himself, who was to say that Milton wouldn't take them all out? He had proven to be more than dangerous enough to do something like that.

He set off, moving as quickly as he could through drifts that reached up beyond his calves.

97

Nicol went inside and, once he was satisfied that the foyer was clear, he glanced back at the door. The handle had been wired to the mains by way of two strips of aluminium tape that were stuck on the brass doorknob, each equipped with a wire that created a circuit out of the knob. The handle had been live, and, once Antonelli touched it, the one hundred and ten volt mains had sent enough current through him to cause paralysis, his muscles involuntarily clenching and his jaw clamping shut.

The tripwire that triggered the fuel bombs outside.

The live doorknob.

Milton was ingenious, and he had been busy.

Nicol crept deeper into the house, the AR-10 cradled in both hands with the muzzle pointed ahead and his finger tight against the trigger. The man they called Luis was behind him. Sal and Luca had gone right, into a room that looked as if it had been turned into a den. The main feature of the foyer was a spiral staircase that swept up to the top floor, from where the sniper had been operating. Nicol paused at the foot of the stairs and aimed the rifle up into the darkness; he listened, biting his lip as he strained for any sound that might suggest there was someone above them. He couldn't hear anything, but that was no reassurance; they would have to clear the entire house, room to room, top to bottom. Milton, the sniper and the kids they were protecting were in here somewhere.

Luis moved ahead of him, crossing the foyer to the closed door on the left. Nicol followed. Luis crept forward and prepared to put his boot through the door. Nicol braced his rifle against his shoulder with his finger on the trigger as Luis drew back his foot and kicked.

The door swung back. Nicol saw what was waiting for them at the exact same time as Luis: two straight-backed chairs had been arranged behind the door, one of them positioned so that its back was around eight feet from the door and the second placed behind it. A crossbow had been balanced across the back rails of the chairs and then secured in place with duct tape. An eye screw had been inserted into the wood of the door's frame, next to the doorknob; fishing line had been looped around the doorknob and fed through the hook and then through a second eye screw that had been twisted into the shoulder stock of the crossbow. The action of opening the door tightened the line and pulled the trigger. The crossbow discharged, a bolt punching into Luis's chest from less than eight feet away, fired with such force that it passed through him from front to back and narrowly missed Nicol before thudding into the opposite wall of the foyer.

Luis fell forward onto his knees and then toppled over onto his side.

Nicol pulled the trigger and sprayed half a dozen rounds

through the doorway. It was an instinctive reaction, with no target in sight, and the crashing rattle of the weapon echoed around the foyer as it discharged. He took his finger off the trigger. The room beyond looked like a living space, with a sofa and armchairs. At least one round from his wild volley had struck the sofa, and a little puff of dusty upholstery had spilled out onto the cushions. Nicol stepped forward, making sure that he came through the door side-on so that any other crossbow bolts would miss him if it fired again.

He got a better look at the room—two large picture windows ahead and, to the left, a bulky old cathode ray TV set on a stand, a bookcase full of hardbacks—and, as he took another step inside, he saw, too late, the blur of movement as the man who had been standing behind the door reached out, grabbed him with one arm, and yanked him to the side. Nicol struggled, but his finger was caught in the trigger guard of the rifle, and, by the time he had freed it, he had felt the sting of something cold and sharp as it was drawn across his throat. His skin, still frigid from the temperatures outside, suddenly felt warm and wet as blood ran out of the freshly opened gash that stretched almost from ear to ear.

The man removed his arm and, without the support, Nicol found that his legs were no longer strong enough to bear his weight. His knees buckled and he fell forward, crashing into the two chairs that held up the crossbow, over-turning them and spilling the weapon onto the floor. He looked up and saw the black lens of a security camera, a green light shining atop the casing, and realised—much, much too late—that Milton was several steps ahead of them.

There came the roar of an automatic and the *thud-thud-thud* as rounds crashed into the wall on the other side of the room.

The firing stopped. A chunk of plaster was dislodged onto the sofa. Glass from the shattered TV tinkled as it broke into smaller shards upon hitting the floor. Nicol barely heard any of it. The room was already going dim.

"Sal," he heard from somewhere above and behind him, "just you and your friend now."

ird's legs were numb from the cold by the time he got to the van. He had moved as quickly as he could, crouching down a little to present as small a target as possible in the event that the sniper was still watching. He doubted that he was, and he felt more confident of his guess when he heard the sound of a door being kicked in on the other side of the house. Anyone still in the house was about to find their focus was on staying alive instead of taking potshots from out of the windows.

He sheltered behind the van and then stomped through the snow until he was at the open rear doors. He pulled them all the way back and looked inside; it was dark, but he could still see the wrapped bricks of money, all of them stacked up in neat piles.

He gave a moment's thought to how he could move as much of the cash as possible. He could stuff a few of the bundles into his pockets and carry more in his arms; it wasn't far to the car. It was an option but, he decided, not the best. If he was going to steal any of it, he might as well steal all of it; Bobby's penalty would be the same for five bucks or five hundred thousand. He didn't have time to go and get his car and bring it back, to unload the money from the van and dump it into the trunk. And a car arriving in the yard would be heard and spotted instantly. No— that wasn't going to work. He was going to have to hot-wire the van and drive it away. At least it was an older model, which meant there would be no modern technology to overcome. It ought to be as simple as using his penknife to open the steering column cover and then finding the wires to the ignition and battery, stripping off the insulation and twisting them together.

He was backing away from the doors when he heard a voice.

"Don't move."

His hand went reflexively toward his pistol.

He felt something against the back of his skull. "I wouldn't do that," the voice said. "Put both hands up, please, and come around to the side of the van."

The man's voice was unusual. Accented. Bird wasn't sure if he could place it. European, he thought. Russian?

The man stayed behind him as he backed up and walked around the van until it shielded him from the house.

"Turn around."

Bird did as he was told. He looked at his interlocutor and his mind ran straight to Viking. The man was holding a suppressed pistol in a relaxed two-handed grip, the barrel aimed at Bird's head, and had a rifle on a strap that he wore across his shoulder.

"I'm a cop," Bird said. "Put it down."

The man ignored the order. "The men you were with," he said. "Who are they?"

"Didn't you hear me? I'm a cop. Put the gun down."

The man switched his aim with a smooth and fluid downward motion and fired a single shot. The suppressor barked as the gun was discharged, the bullet punching into the bone and cartilage of Bird's right knee. The pain was sudden and excruciating, and he cried out as the joint gave way and he toppled over onto his side.

The man aimed down at his head. "Don't make me ask you again. Who are you with?"

"Sal Provenzano," he said. "He works for Bobby..." The pain increased and he had to grit his teeth. "For Bobby Whitesox."

"Why are you here?"

"The money," Bird said. "The money... in there. Take it. There's hundreds of thousands of dollars. Millions. You can take it."

"What does it have to do with John Milton?"

"What?"

The man switched his aim again and fired a second shot, this one into Bird's shoulder.

"What does all of this have to do with John Milton?"

Bird was nauseated by the pain. "He had the money," he grunted, each word an effort. "Bobby wants it back."

"What does this have to do with Patrick and Kenneth O'Connor?"

Bird swallowed. "They wanted the money, too. Everyone wants it. It's a shitload of cash, man. It's yours."

"I don't want it," the man said. He crouched down on his haunches and extended his arm so that the suppressor was pressed up against Bird's temple. "How many men are with Sal?"

"Five," he said.

"Sure?"

Bird nodded.

"And what about inside the house. How many?"

"I don't know," Bird said. "Milton and a guy with a rifle. The kid and his buddy. The kid's mom."

The man raised himself to his full height again and stepped back. "Thank you."

"Who the fuck are you?"

The man aimed down and fired.

99

S al was with Luca in the den when he heard the clatter of automatic gunfire from behind him in the foyer. He clutched the AR-15 a little tighter and pressed himself up against the wall, then put his head out to peer through the open doorway. He saw a body on the floor of the room on the other side of the foyer and a man—he thought it was Nicol—passing through the doorway, with smoke rising from the barrel of his weapon. He watched as Nicol stood to the side of a crossbow that had been arranged across two chairs, and caught the glimmer of a line that must have been used to trigger it. Another trap. Luis must have activated it the moment he opened the door.

Sal shouldered the rifle and was about to follow when he saw a quick smear of motion, a man stepping out from behind the open door, looping one arm around Nicol's chest. The blade of a knife shone dully in the moonlight as it was swiped from left to right, opening Nicol's throat. Milton dropped Nicol and stepped back as Sal raised the rifle and fired, a barrage that streaked from the den and across the foyer and into the room beyond.

"Sal," Milton called out from across the foyer, "just you and your friend now."

"You think I'm frightened of you?"

"You should be. I'm just getting started."

Sal clutched the rifle in both hands and waited until his heart had settled into a steadier beat. He tried to work out what he should do next. Running was a choice, but not one he would ever be able to take. He had worked his way from nothing, from the slums of Naples through the ranks of the 'Ndrangheta and then to America and his place at the right hand of Bobby Whitesox. He had done that through the power of his reputation. Sal Provenzano did *not* run. Luca would be witness to his cowardice if he chose to flee now; *he* would know, too, and that knowledge—and the effect that it would have on his own sense of worth—was not something that he could tolerate.

There would be no running.

They would stay and fight.

Sal gestured to Luca. "Keep that doorway covered," he whispered, pointing to where the crossbow had been set up. "Maybe I can flush him back to you."

Luca nodded, raised his AR-15 and aimed across the foyer.

Sal crossed the den to the door that exited to the north. Milton had put himself in harm's way to protect Luca's cousin. Sal could work with that: he now knew one of Milton's weaknesses. He was doing all this because of his conscience. He wanted to help the Pizzolatos and the kids that hung out with the boy. That was the pressure point; Sal just needed to find them, and the balance of power would shift.

But where were they? Upstairs? That was possible. The sniper had been up there, though; would they put the kids in the same place, knowing that finding the shooter would be one of the first things that Sal would want to do? He doubted it. There was probably a basement here, too, and that would have been a good place to hide, especially if there was a door that could be locked. But Sal didn't have the time or the opportunity to search the house from top to bottom, not with Milton looking to take him out. If he couldn't go to them, he would just have to see that they came to him.

He would smoke them out.

onnie and the others were sitting with their backs against the wall, and Fernández—as much as she could make out his dim shape after he'd turned on the light once more—was standing up with the rifle that he had brought with him aimed at the door.

Connie had never been so scared. She was frightened for herself, of course, but mostly for her son. She had not been blessed with the best life, but she had worked herself to the bone so that Enzo could have the advantages that she had not. He was smart, he worked hard, and—although she knew that she had a mother's bias—she knew that he was destined to be special. And now, after all the hours that she had worked, the sacrifices that she had made, it was all going to be taken away from Enzo because of a van that he had bought to help him earn the money to pursue his dreams?

No.

That was *not* going to happen.

Enzo was sitting to her right, and she reached out and took his hand in hers. She squeezed it, remembering the way that she had been able to wrap her fingers all the way around it when he had been tiny. His hand was bigger than hers now, and, when he squeezed back, she felt the grip of fingers that had grown strong from playing the guitar for hours on end.

They heard the racket of gunfire from somewhere above them.

"What was that?" Francesco whispered.

"Relax," Connie whispered back at him.

"It was a gun," he said. "It was a gun, wasn't it? They've got inside."

She could feel his panic.

Fernández came closer and crouched down in front of Francesco. "You've got to be quiet," he whispered.

"My knee," the boy hissed back, much too loud. "He shot me in the knee, Coach."

"We're safe here," Fernández whispered back.

"We're not!" Franny exclaimed, louder still. "It's killing me, Coach. I need something to stop it."

"We'll get you to the hospital," Fernández whispered back. "But we can't move until it's safe. We have to be quiet until then."

"I can't, Coach," he said. "It hurts too much. It really, really hurts."

Francesco's shoulder rubbed against Connie's as he started to rock back and forward. His breathing grew faster and louder. It sounded as if he was beginning to hyperventilate. She reached out with her left hand until she found his wrist, and gave it what she hoped would be a reassuring squeeze.

101

Milton checked his phone. The four security cameras that were placed around the property had been helpful. He had been able to watch Sal, Nicol and two other men as they broke into the foyer, and had been able to make the strategic decision that he would be able to take down two of the four by waiting behind the door in the living room. The crossbow had fired as he had planned, and he had been able to take advantage of the confusion to add Nicol to his list of victims.

That just left Sal and the fourth man.

Milton could see that he was in the den and was working out the best way to approach him. Sal said something to the fourth man and crossed the den to the door that led to the hall where the basement could be accessed. The fourth man stayed where he was, crouching down and aiming his rifle across the foyer. Milton would not be able to go that way without being fired upon.

Sal was going to try to flank him.

Sal took the second door out of the den and saw that it opened into a hallway. There were steps up to the floor above and steps down to a door that must open onto the cellar. He paused at the top of the stairs and listened; as he did, he heard the unmistakable sound of a whispered conversation.

He paused, holding his breath, and heard a little whimper of pain.

There you are.

He opened the door to his right and crept into a garage. There was a line of shelves neatly arranged along the nearest wall and, as he glanced across them, he saw a bottle of lighter fluid that would have been used to light the briquettes in a barbecue. He took the bottle down, felt the weight of it to confirm that it was full, and made his way carefully back to the hallway. Luca had the other half of the house covered. Sal stayed close to the wall, ready to empty the rifle if he saw Milton approaching from the kitchen.

He went back to the top of the stairs and unscrewed the cap on the bottle. The fluid was dispensed through a nozzle, and Sal aimed it down the stairs and then squeezed the bottle. The liquid sloshed across the wooden treads and dripped down the whitewashed walls. Sal emptied the bottle, struck a match and flicked it down the stairs.

The fuel ignited. The flames spread quickly, climbing the walls and rushing across the floor. Orange and red fire swam up and down the staircase, the desiccated old wooden treads catching as quickly as if they were dry tinder.

"Hey, Milton," Sal yelled over the hungry crackle of the fire. "How you like that? I burn this place to the ground."

There was no reply, or at least not one that he could hear.

He shouldered the rifle and followed the hallway to the right, toward an arch that looked as if it might open out into the kitchen. Milton would have to come this way if he wanted to save the kids, and, when he did, he would be waiting for him.

102

Fernández heard Sal Provenzano's voice. "How you like that? I burn this place to the ground."

He had heard the sound of liquid splashing on the stairs, and now he smelled burning. He looked over to the door and saw a yellow glow in the gap beneath it. He shuffled closer. The smell was stronger here. He removed the key from the lock and peered through the open keyhole. He saw the fire, right outside, the stairs alight. Sal was going to burn the place down in an effort to force them out. There was no point in hiding anymore and, with that, he reached up and switched on the light.

He could see the smoke much more clearly now. It was pouring in beneath the door, silvery-grey tendrils that rose up to the ceiling and started to spread out.

"We're gonna die," Francesco said. "We're all gonna burn to death."

Fernández put the key back into the lock and then stopped. What if Sal was waiting at the top of the stairs, aiming down, ready to shoot the first person who opened the door? The idea of standing behind it was suddenly not such a good one; the wood wasn't particularly thick, and he had little doubt that a barrage of nine-millimetre rounds would be able to punch through it.

Connie grabbed his arm. "What are we going to do?"

"I have an idea," Fernández said.

The single bulb wasn't strong enough to light all the way to the back of the basement. He took out his phone, switched on the flashlight, and aimed it toward the far wall. A lot of junk had collected down here over the years, but he remembered seeing something on the wall the last time he had helped his sister organise the boxes that had not yet been transferred over to the barn. He moved an old armchair out of the way, then a course of boxes, and then he saw it: a small iron door just underneath the line of the ceiling. It was six feet up and hadn't been opened for years.

"What's that?" Connie said.

"They used to drop the coal through there."

"You think we can get out that way?"

"I don't know."

Francesco started to cough. Fernández tried to blink the acrid smoke from his eyes. It was getting worse.

"We can't stay here," Connie said.

The smoke was gathering more and more quickly. Fernández covered his mouth with the sleeve of his shirt. "Try to block the gap under the door."

"The boxes," Aldo said. "Come on—help me."

Enzo and Aldo went to the nearest box and hauled it to the door, pushing it tight against it. The smoke continued to seep in, but the amount coming through was perhaps a little less.

Fernández looked up at the coal door. He was going to have to climb up to it and then pray that it still opened.

103

The house was made of old, dry wood and it was quickly well aflame. Milton had stayed in the butler's pantry that divided the dining room from the kitchen, choosing a spot that allowed him to see through the dining room and living space to his right and the kitchen and family room to his left. He was down low, the rifle pressed up against his shoulder with his cheek against the receiver. He swivelled at the hip, checking to the left and then to the right. There was no sign of Sal or the other guy and, with the smoke becoming thicker every minute, visibility was quickly becoming an issue.

He couldn't just stay and wait. The blaze looked like it had the potential to take hold of the entire house and, if it did, he doubted that the structure would stay standing for long. Connie, Fernández and the boys were locked in the basement and would be burned alive unless he was able to get them out.

He couldn't do that while Sal and his friend were waiting for him.

The smoke grew denser and, as it began to drift down

from the ceiling, Milton began to find it harder to breathe. He took off his shirt and wrapped it around his mouth and then crept ahead, staying low as he darted from the pantry to the cover afforded by the kitchen island. He had a better angle to look through the arch that opened onto the hallway, and he could see from the roaring flames that the fire must have been set there.

The stairs to the basement descended from the hallway; Sal must have realised that the others were hiding down there. Thick black smoke gushed out of the arch and billowed into the family room. Milton thought he saw movement amid the sooty fumes and aimed the rifle, his finger tightening on the trigger. The smoke stung his eyes, and he tried to blink them clear, questioning whether he had seen anything. He wanted to wait, recognised that that was the correct tactical call, but knew that if he didn't move now, then the two adults and three boys in the basement were all going to die. They would burn to death, and it would be his fault.

There came the groan of something heavy shifting position and then the crash of impact as the ceiling of the hallway collapsed. Plasterboard thumped down on the floor and then a large timber was dislodged from above and crashed into an occasional table.

Milton took out his phone and opened the app that displayed the feeds from the security cameras. The camera in the den, which had shown Sal and his friend, now just displayed an empty room. The man who had been there had moved. Milton guessed that the two of them would try to pin him down and, as he flicked to the second camera— positioned in the kitchen and pointing into the butler's pantry—he saw that he was right. The man was approaching, down low, moving through the dining room. The feed from the camera in the hallway above the basement was obscured by smoke, with no sign of Sal. Milton knew that he had to be there. His plan was obvious; they would clear the ground floor until they had located him, and then they would squeeze his space until there was nowhere for him to go.

He checked the feed from the kitchen camera again; the man he had seen had passed beneath it and had to be in the kitchen now. Sal had to be advancing, too. Milton knew that if he put his head up, he was liable to have it shot off.

"We know where you are," Sal called out.

Milton pressed himself up against the island, trying to work out which man would step out of cover first. His only chance was if one moved before the other; he had no hope if they advanced on him simultaneously.

The sound of falling masonry continued, masking—until it was too late—the sound of footsteps approaching Milton from behind. He spun around and saw that Sal had come around the side of the island. His rifle was aimed down, and he had his finger on the trigger.

"Put it down," Sal said, indicating Milton's rifle with a downward jerk of his head.

Milton did as he was told. He heard movement from the other side of the island, and, as he looked into the darkened glass of the floor-to-ceiling windows opposite him, he saw the second man. He, too, was aiming down at him.

Sal coughed for breath. "Give me the keys."

"They're in my pocket."

"So take them out—slowly."

Milton reached into his pocket, felt the sharp edge of the keys and, moving slowly, withdrew them. He knew that Sal would shoot him as soon as he had what he wanted, but Milton could not think of any way that he could delay him in the event that circumstances might intervene in his favour. He was out of ideas.

There came another crash from the direction of the hallway. Milton thought of the others and knew, with sickening certainty, that he had failed them.

"Slide them over to me," Sal said.

"You should leave the van and go," Milton said.

"I don't think so. Five million is a lot of money."

Milton coughed. "Can't use it when you're in jail, Sal."

"I'm not going to jail."

"The FBI is on its way. I called them."

"Sure you did." Sal coughed again. "Slide the keys here now or I'm gonna shoot you and take them."

Sal took a step forward, aiming the rifle down.

Milton knew that there was nothing more that he could do.

He set the keys on the floor and was about to slide them over to Sal when he heard the unmistakable exhalation of a single suppressed gunshot and, as he looked up at the reflection in the window, he saw a squib of blood splash out from the other guy's chest. The man jerked forward, reaching out for the stove to prevent himself from falling. Milton looked back up at Sal, and, as he did, he heard a second deadened report, and Sal put his free hand to his throat, just below his chin. He clutched it with his left hand, blood spraying out from between his fingers. His eyes bulged in almost comically exaggerated surprise. There came a third suppressed shot. Sal's rifle slipped out of his grasp, and he slapped his hand onto the countertop, leaving a trail of blood as it slid off. He collapsed onto the floor, leaving just his head and shoulders visible from Milton's vantage point.

Milton raised both hands and rose to a standing position.

He guessed who it was and, as he turned to the open door, he saw that he was right.

Björn Thorsson was standing there, a suppressed SIG Sauer P226 held in both hands, aimed calmly at Milton's head.

104

Thorsson was a professional. He had dispatched Sal and the other guy with cool efficiency: a shot to take down the farthest target first, the initial surprise giving him the opportunity for a second shot in the event that the first one missed, then two to the man who was closer and easier to hit. Milton had been trained the same way when he had joined the Group.

"Hands where I can see them, please," Thorsson said.

Milton glanced down at Sal's body. "He would have done your job for you."

"I have some respect for your career. You don't deserve to go out on your knees."

Milton kept his hands above his head. The fire continued to burn, a wall of heat that was starting to bubble the paint on the kitchen ceiling. The flames were already encroaching, patches on the wooden floor that joined together and then spread.

"There are people trapped in the basement," Milton said. "Three kids. I'd appreciate it if you got them out once you've done what you have to do."

"I will—you have my word."

"Thank you," Milton said. "You'd better get it over with."

Thorsson aimed the pistol at Milton's head.

"I'm sorry. This isn't personal."

"It never is."

Milton found that he was at peace. His ledger wasn't balanced, but he had done his best. He closed his eyes and waited for his successor as Number One to pull the trigger.

105

"**D**rop it!"

Milton opened his eyes again.

Fernández was standing in the doorway to the butler's pantry. He had the Peacemaker that Milton had given to Connie in both hands, and it was aimed at Thorsson.

The big Icelander was still; the only sign of emotion was the bulge in his jaw as he ground his teeth together.

"That would be a bad idea," Thorsson said.

"*Now*," Fernández said.

Thorsson raised his hands and, with a slow and deliberate stretch of his right arm, he laid the SIG on the counter.

"Get away from it," Fernández said.

Thorsson did not. "You think Milton's been helping you?"

Fernández's face crinkled with confusion.

"What? He hasn't told you his real name? What else do you think he might have kept to himself?"

Thorsson's hand was still close to the weapon, and he still had a rifle slung across his back. Milton moved quickly, fearful that he would try to fool Fernández into lowering his guard. He strode over to where the Icelander was standing, took the pistol, and held it against the back of the man's head.

"Outside," he said.

The coach led the way out of the house, with Milton marching Thorsson behind him. One whole side of the property was well ablaze, and Milton could see that there was no chance of saving the rest of it. Connie stood with the three boys, all of them looking up at the roaring flames as the snow fell all around. Fernández covered Milton as he directed Thorsson away from the property.

"Down," Milton said, jamming the side of his foot into the back of Thorsson's knees. The bigger man dropped. "Hands behind your head. Legs apart."

Thorsson did as he was asked, and Milton frisked him, pressing the gun into the small of his back as he worked his torso and then the outsides and insides of his legs. He unclipped the rifle from the strap and set it aside.

"How did you get out?" Milton asked Fernández as he worked.

"There's a coal door," he said.

Milton found a compact SIG Sauer P230 in the inside pocket of Thorsson's jacket and a small collection of zip ties in the back pocket of his jeans. Milton took one of the ties and told Thorsson to put both hands behind his back. He did, and Milton secured them.

There came another crash as part of the ceiling collapsed into the hall. The fire was spreading with frightening speed.

"I'm sorry," Milton said to Fernández.

"Forget it. The place was falling to pieces anyway. Maybe this is the excuse we need to build something decent here."

"There might be some money for that," Milton said.

Connie had led the three boys a safe distance from the fire, but now she hurried back to Milton and Fernández.

"John," she said.

"What is it?"

"You'll want to see this."

Milton left Fernández to watch Thorsson and followed her to where she had been standing with the boys. They had an angle there where they could see around the corner of the house, and Milton could see the blue and red flashing lights from half a dozen cars as they approached down the track.

"Who is it?"

"I think it might be the cavalry."

The cars stopped next to the abandoned van, and several men and women got out. One of them—a man—raised a bullhorn. He waited for the feedback to dissipate before he spoke.

"This is the FBI. Everyone inside the house, come out now with your hands raised."

Milton chuckled. Better late than never.

"What do we do?" Connie said.

"You can trust them. Just tell them what happened."

"Can't you do that?"

"Things have changed," he said, nodding in the direction of the bound Thorsson. "I think it would be better if he wasn't here when they start working out what happened."

"Why? I don't understand."

"You're going to be fine now," he said. "Just trust them and do what they say."

"What about you? Will we see you again?"

"I'll do my best," Milton said.

Connie stepped closer to him and drew him into a hug. "Thank you," she whispered into his ear.

"You're welcome."

He turned and made his way back to Fernández before she could say anything else.

Fernández nodded in the direction of the new arrivals. "The feds?"

"Yes," Milton said. "Make sure they look after them, okay? My contact is Special Agent Ellie Flowers. I doubt she's here now, but she will have set this up."

"What about you?"

He reached down, grabbed Thorsson by his shackled wrist, and impelled him to his feet. "I don't want him to be here when they arrive. Look after them. And thanks—they'd all be dead if it wasn't for you."

As if on cue, a large section of the roof collapsed in on itself with a thunderous crash, sending sparks high up into the air. Milton shoved Thorsson between the shoulder blades, and the big man stumbled ahead, his feet crunching through the crust of ice that had settled atop the snow. Milton followed, the pistol he had confiscated from Thorsson held ready.

Milton walked behind Thorsson as they trudged away from the house, their feet crunching through the snow. He held the pistol in both hands, never once allowing the muzzle to drift out of alignment with the middle of the big Icelander's back.

"What are we doing?" Thorsson said.

"I'm getting you out of here," he said.

"Seriously?"

"What? You think I'm going to shoot you?"

"It had crossed my mind."

"Ten years ago?" Milton said. "Maybe. But that was then —that's not me anymore."

"What—you've *changed*?"

There was sarcasm there, but Milton let it pass.

"Come on," Thorsson said. "We're cut from the same cloth. You can't just change."

"I regret everything that I did for the Group," he said. "Everything. Accepting the offer to join was the worst decision I've ever made. I'll never be able to scrub the blood off my hands. You might feel the same way one day. They'll ask you to do something and you'll realise that you can't do it."

He didn't answer.

"It won't be like this," Milton said. "You don't have to work too hard to justify coming after me. I'm fair game. It'll be something else. Something you won't expect. Collateral damage that you can't justify."

"What was it with you?"

"A child," Milton said.

They trudged on. Milton kept the same steady distance between them. He knew that Thorsson would not hesitate if Milton was negligent enough to present him with an opportunity, and he doubted that he would be able to take the big man out if it came to a straight fight. The Icelander was younger than he was, outweighed him by fifty pounds, and had a much longer reach. Milton was glad of the zip ties that restrained him.

They crested a hill and started the descent to the pit of the quarry. They continued, the crunch of their footsteps and the mournful call of an owl the only sounds in the icy wilderness. Milton knew that the whole area would be the scene of significant activity soon; once the agents saw the bloodshed and the money in the back of the van, they would summon reinforcements and an investigation would begin. Milton wondered whether Ellie would come out herself. He would have liked to see her, but he knew that was impossible.

"This isn't going to stop," Thorsson said. "They'll keep coming. You know what it'll be like."

"All because of Colombia?"

"I think there's more, but you know how it is—I just get the file."

Milton exhaled wearily. "Control—it's a woman now, right?"

Thorsson didn't answer.

"The reason I didn't hand you over to the FBI is because I want you to deliver a message for me. You need to tell her that the next time she sends someone after me, it won't end like this. I don't want to fight. I thought I was done with all that. But I won't just sit back and take it. I'll defend myself. You tell her if she sends another agent after me, I'll send them back in a box."

"Come on," Thorsson said. "It's just you, Milton. I know you're good, but you're on your own and you're getting older. You can't go up against the Firm—against everyone who's looking for you so that people like me can find you and put you down."

"This is the second time you've tried," Milton said.

"You were lucky tonight. And maybe you get lucky the next time, maybe you do take out one of us—the next time she'll just send two."

Milton felt his anger flicker. He kept his voice low and even. "Ask her what happened to the last team who came after me. They'll have classified the file, but you ask her about Russia and then think about whether going up against me is a risk you think is worth running. You're gambling with your life, and it's all to take down someone who has no axe to grind with London and is not a threat to them. I don't care about you. I don't care about them or what they do—I just want them to leave me alone."

"You know they won't."

They reached the edge of the quarry. It was dark, but there was enough light from the fire at their backs to see that there was a thirty- or forty-foot drop to the snow-covered rocks below.

"Stop there," Milton said.

Thorsson did as he was told. "Is this it? You going to shoot me and toss me down there?"

"I meant what I said. You get a pass today." He pointed to the east. "Highway 69 is a mile that way. Kansas City is five miles to the north. You should be able to get there by sunrise."

"What about my hands?"

"You'll manage," Milton said. "Do yourself a favour—get on the first plane home. This truce? It's only good for tonight. If I see you around tomorrow, all bets are off."

"Likewise," Thorsson said.

Milton didn't doubt that for a moment.

"Just deliver the message."

Milton started to back away. Thorsson watched him go.

"I'll see you again, Milton."

Milton raised the pistol and aimed it in the dead centre of Thorsson's chest. "Not if I see you first."

He turned and set off, walking quickly around the lip of the quarry and then turning to the east. He, too, would find transport and get back to the city as quickly as he could. He knew that he couldn't stay. John Smith was dead. The legend that had served him so well was compromised now, and he was going to have to reinvent himself. He would need assistance with that, and he knew exactly who to ask. The fact that the cobbler he had in mind lived in Bali was a fortunate coincidence; Milton had had enough of the cold and snow, and a little sunshine would be good for the soul.

He turned back, but couldn't see Thorsson. He wondered if he had made a mistake. What he had told the Icelander was true; ten years ago, he would have shot him without even thinking about it. But Milton had changed since he had left the Group, and, if that made things more dangerous for him, then so be it.

Perhaps he was naïve.

Perhaps letting him leave was a risk that he couldn't afford to take.

Perhaps.

But Milton knew one thing for sure: killing him in cold blood would have undone all of the work that he had done since he had gone rogue. It would nullify his efforts to make amends for his sins, and would unbalance the ledger that recorded the murders that he had committed in the name of his country. It would lead back to the bottle and the oblivion that alcohol offered, and he was not prepared to take himself back to that place ever again.

Thorsson would be back.

Milton knew that they would find him eventually.

He would be ready when they did.

EPILOGUE

Bobby Whitesox stared at the plain white wall on the other side of the cell. He was lying on his coat, the mattress beneath him so thin that he could feel the hard concrete and so pungent with stale urine and excreta that he had gagged the first time he had lain down on it. He had grown used to it now, and knew, despite the blandishments of the best lawyers that money could buy, that he was likely to be lying on mattresses like this for days, and perhaps weeks, to come.

The feds had arrested him at the strip club two days ago. He'd been interviewing potential new dancers—one of his favourite tasks—and the agents had burst in proffering warrants and telling him that he was being arrested on suspicion of illegal gambling, money laundering, tax evasion and multiple homicides. They had cuffed his hands behind his back and frog-marched him outside to emerge blinking into the bright sunlight that reflected back off the snow. What had followed had been a dizzying whirl of interviews with agents and tactical discussions with his lawyers, and had ended up with him here, waiting for his bail hearing.

His lawyers had acted for him before, and, although expensive, had the ethical flexibility that allowed an uninterrupted flow of information both from outside the prison to Bobby and from him to his surviving *caporegimes*. Bobby had learned of the massacre at the abandoned quarry south of the city, and knew that Sal and several of the others were dead. Antonelli had been electrocuted by a booby-trapped door handle, but, despite serious burns, he had survived and had reported back what had taken place. The man who had been protecting the Pizzolato kid had laid out a series of traps that had thinned out Bobby's men and then picked off the survivors one by one.

The van, and the five million dollars that had been hidden inside, had been confiscated by the feds. It was lost, and he knew that would attract the ire of Johnny Colombo and the Vegas mob, but that was the least of his problems. He was old, and, if the government could make the charges against him stick, he knew that he would die inside.

The lawyers said that there was a chance of exonerating him on most of the charges, but that the money-laundering rap was going to be the hardest to evade. The feds had the money, and they had the fact that Luca had been driving the van and Sal had been in the passenger seat when it had first been pulled over. Even with all that evidence against him, the lawyers thought there was at least the possibility that they might be able to say that Sal was acting on his own, and that, since he was dead, it was going to be difficult to draw a line from the van to Sal and then, ultimately, to Bobby. The feds knew that, too, and that was why they were expending so much energy in finding Patrick O'Connor. If they could find Patrick, maybe they could flip him so that he spilled about the laundering. He knew more than enough about Bobby's business to be able to bury him.

That was why Bobby knew he had to find him before the feds did.

There was a knock on the door and the bean hole—the slot through which his food was passed—was yanked upwards. A plastic tray with his dinner was shoved through. He swung his legs off the bed and looked down at the fare with which he had been provided: a hamburger, fries and a carton of milk. Bobby knew that the penal system cut corners where it could to save money, and food was an obvious way to do that. It was low cost and it tasted like garbage. He had eaten at Eddie V's the night before he was arrested and tried not to compare the lobster bisque that he had enjoyed there with the bilge he was going to have to manage on until they got him out. He looked down at the burger—a patty that would have little connection to a cow, limp lettuce and a thin bun—and rolled back onto the bed. He stared at the ceiling and reminded himself that he was going to have to be patient.

BJÖRN THORSSON WAITED in the austere anteroom that separated the bustle of the operational floor from the quiet of Control's office. He had taken a red-eye from Kansas City and had been collected at the airport by Benjamin Weaver. Control's adjutant had conducted a cursory debrief as they had been driven into the city, warning Thorsson that Control was irritated that the operation had come to an end without Milton's scalp.

There was a light above her door: it was red now, to indicate that Control was not to be disturbed, and would switch to green as the command to go inside. Weaver had gone inside first, and Björn had been left to stare at it and stew. He knew that Weaver would be reporting on the contents of the conversation in the back of the car, and perhaps offering a recommendation as to what steps to take next. Björn did not know Control's background—and didn't know anyone who did—but, given the fact that she relied upon Weaver for operational matters, he doubted that she had much time in the field.

The light flicked from red to green. Björn raised himself to his full height, smoothed down the creases in the musty shirt that he had worn during the flight, opened the door and went inside.

Control was sat behind her desk at the end of the room. Weaver had taken a seat on the small sofa nearest the door; he didn't look at Björn as he stepped into the office.

"Sit down, Number One."

Björn did as he was told, taking one of the two seats that were arranged on this side of the desk.

"Well?" she said.

"I'm sorry, ma'am."

"What happened?"

"Captain Milton is as resourceful as we suspected he might be."

"So Weaver tells me."

"There was some good luck involved, too. He had help. I was interrupted."

"I reread your report from Colombia. It seems he was lucky then, too."

"Yes, ma'am. I believe he was."

"You have to wonder," she said, steepling her fingers and staring over the top of them at him, "when good luck is being used as an excuse for something else. Incompetence, perhaps."

"I don't believe that would be a fair summation of what happened, ma'am. I had very limited intelligence, given that our source was unable to assist, and, by the time I was able to locate Milton, events had become much more complicated. The plan was for Tanner to engineer a meeting during which I would have been able to take Milton out cleanly. That wasn't possible. I was not properly equipped for what happened. I had to improvise."

"I'm just hearing excuses, Number One. And I won't tolerate them."

She left a silence for him to comment, but he decided that holding his tongue was the better option. He knew well enough that a display of temper would be unhelpful to the continuation of his career in the Group.

"I've sent Number Ten to clean up the loose ends. We don't know what Kenneth O'Connor got out of Tanner—we have to assume that it was passed on to his brother."

"Do we know where he is? I understood that he had disappeared."

"We have a lead," she said.

"What about Tanner?"

"He did the right thing in contacting us when he did. I don't have any concerns about him."

Björn nodded. He knew that Control would not have appreciated having to send agents to tidy up, but she was cautious, and there was no way that she would want to leave anything that could conceivably bring publicity to the Group's involvement.

"Do you need me to do anything, ma'am?"

"You've done quite enough, Number One." She laid her

hands on the desk. "You realise, of course, that we've squandered the advantage that we had?"

"Ma'am?"

"Milton didn't know that the Group was coming for him, did he?"

"I don't believe so."

"He does now."

Björn shifted uncomfortably.

"Weaver tells me that you spoke to him."

"I did."

"And what did he say?"

Björn shifted uncomfortably.

"Spit it out, man."

"He told me that he wanted me to deliver a message. He said that he didn't want to fight, but that if you sent anyone else after him, then he would defend himself—or words to that effect."

"Really?"

Björn watched as Control stood, turned and looked out of the window. Her office had a view of the Thames, and, to the right, it was possible to see the Millbank Tower and Thames House, the headquarters of MI5. To the right was Vauxhall Bridge and the slow, meandering turn of the river. The view would have been enjoyed by successive holders of Control's position, and Björn found himself imagining John Milton sitting in his seat, watching as *his* boss digested the suggestion that he wanted to retire. There was a connective thread that ran from that conversation to this one, and consequences still to manifest that were impossible to weigh.

She turned back to him. "Of course," she said, "that can have no bearing on what needs to be done. As far as I am concerned, John Milton has never been discharged from his service to this Group. On that basis, he has been designated a rogue agent. It is now a priority that he be found and eliminated."

DAVID TANNER PARKED the car in the forecourt of the 7-Eleven and hobbled inside to pick up emergency groceries. He had been in the hospital for three days, and what food he did have in the house had gone off. Mollie had binned it all, but had not replaced everything: he was missing limes to go with his gin and tonics and, while he was out and about, he thought he'd stock up on beer and chips. He filled his basket with the things that he needed, paid for them, and made his way back out to his car.

He opened the door, got in, and put the bag of groceries on the passenger seat. He was about to start the engine when he became aware of someone else sitting in the back seat.

"Hello, Tanner."

His heart almost stopped. "Milton?"

"Didn't expect to see me again?"

He had a small pistol in his pocket, but he knew that there was no way he would be able to reach it without Milton noticing.

He rested his hands on the wheel. "I know you'll be angry with me. I don't blame you. But I don't think I had a choice."

"I don't know," Milton said. "You could've helped me and then forgotten all about it."

"I called London," Tanner said. "My contact said the Group wanted you. I mean, they *really* wanted you. They would've found out that you'd been here, eventually, and

I've got too much to lose. *You* came to *me*, Milton. You put me in danger—me and Mollie. And that was just from the Group. I told you not to get involved with the Irish, and you ignored me. I nearly died because of it. Jack Kelly *did* die."

"And I'm sorry about that. But the kid needed my help. He would have suffered without it. And you're in no position to lecture me."

Tanner found that his throat was dry. "What are you going to do?"

"Nothing," Milton said. "I don't blame you. You're right —I put you in an impossible position, and I'm sorry about that. I should've thought it through."

"You're going to let it go? Just like that?"

"Just like that."

"Why are you here, then?"

"I want you to know that you don't have to look over your shoulder—at least not on my account. We're square." He reached for the door handle. "Good luck, Tanner."

"Wait," Tanner said.

Milton paused.

"You need to run," Tanner said. "They're coming for you."

"I know."

Milton opened the door all the way, got out of the car, and set off. Tanner watched in the mirror as he crunched through the snow, making his way to the corner of the store and then disappearing around it.

PATRICK O'CONNOR PUT his eye to the fisheye lens and looked out onto the parking lot that faced his motel room. It was quiet outside, with just a single traveller unloading his cases from the trunk of his car. The neon from the MOTEL sign above the reception bled sickly red light out over the asphalt, flickering as the tube for the *T* fizzed and popped.

He was in the Route 66 Motel in Barstow, California, an old-fashioned establishment that recalled the sense of Americana that Patrick had been entranced by as a young boy growing up in Northern Ireland. There had been plenty of choices of places to stay when he had been driving west, but he had known he would eventually be drawn to somewhere like this.

The motel had been open since 1922 and had two rows of rooms that bracketed two sides of the large parking lot. The décor was tired and the prices were too expensive for the accommodation provided, but Patrick wasn't bothered by that. He had known at once that he was going to have to leave the country, and had considered the best way to do it while he had sequestered himself here. He concluded that his first plan—to fly out of LAX—was too risky. The feds would be looking for him, and they would likely have notices posted at all the major airports. Instead, he decided that he would drive south and make his way through California to one of the minor crossings into Mexico. He had settled on Calexico and would make the four-hour journey first thing in the morning.

Patrick felt like he had passed through the seasons on his westward journey. He had left Missouri in the grip of winter and, as he had neared the Pacific, the temperature had gradually risen. His watch reported that the temperature was an unusually warm eighty degrees tonight, and the dry, air-conditioned air had given him a thirst. He checked the lens again and, happy that it was still quiet, he unlocked the door, moved the chair that he had used to block it to the side, and stepped outside.

There was a vending machine at the end of the row of rooms. He took out a five-dollar bill, fed it into the slot, and then pressed the button for a can of Diet Coke. The mechanism started, but stopped before the can could be dispensed. He sighed in exasperation and banged the heel of his hand against the glass. The can stubbornly refused to fall.

"Bad luck." Patrick turned. A woman was standing behind him. She was in her late thirties and had striking red hair that she wore in a ponytail. "Those things are, like, total frauds. You gotta give it a good shake."

The woman spoke with a Southern Californian drawl. She was pretty, and Patrick would have liked to have a conversation with her under different circumstances, but not tonight. He just wanted to get back to his room.

"Don't suppose you got a light?" she said.

"No," he said. "Sorry."

"Fair enough. I guess I'll go ask at reception."

Patrick turned back to the machine and hit it again. The can stayed where it was, resolutely refusing to drop, and, as Patrick was weighing up whether he should buy another, he saw movement behind him reflected in the glass. The woman had raised her arm and was pointing something at the back of his head. He felt a sharp impact just above his neck and then nothing at all.

THE CONCERT WAS BEING HELD at the Nelson-Atkins Museum of Art on Oak Street. Connie took her place next to the sound desk; Enzo had told her that it was always the best spot to stand when you were at an event because the sound mixer always ensured that the sound was best wherever he was. It was also dead centre and allowed her the best view of the stage. The second band of the night—a foursome who called themselves Teenage Heart Attack—were on stage at the moment, and the crowd, egged on by the kids' enthusiastic parents at the front of the room, were dancing and singing along to their cover of 'All Along the Watchtower.'

"Here you go."

She turned. Fernández had returned from the bar with two bottles of Coors.

"Thanks, Coach," she said.

"Julio," he said as he touched the neck of his bottle against hers. "Please—call me Julio."

"Thanks, *Julio*," she said.

Connie put the bottle to her lips and took a sip. It had been an interesting three days, to say the least. The FBI had taken them to the field office in the city and had then moved them to a safe house in Overland Park. There had been hours of interviews with the agent-in-charge, a man called Eric Gathers, and constant reassurance that they were safe and would be protected. Connie had felt sure that the boys would not be able to take part in tonight's concert. She had said as much to Gathers, but, after discussing it with his colleagues, he had suggested that it would be okay to come. Gathers told her that the agency's assessment was that the risk to them was lower than they might have expected. The case against Bobby Whitesox was strong, and they had every expectation that he would be spending the rest of his life behind bars. A move away from Kansas City was on the table if Connie decided that it was necessary, but, until she had been able to consider the proposal properly, all three boys had been assigned agents to watch over them. Three agents had accompanied them tonight—one was at the side of the stage, and the other two were in the crowd—and, although there was no indication that they might be necessary, Connie was still relieved that they were here.

"Excited?" Fernández asked her as the band finished their Hendrix tribute.

"Nervous," she admitted. "It's crazy—I've never heard them play together."

"I hear them practise at school. They're fantastic."

The kids were okay, for the most part. Aldo was fine, already making light of what had happened. Franny had become quiet and reserved, and Connie knew the betrayal and then death of his uncle, Luca, had been difficult for him to process. His mother, at least, seemed to have been shocked out of her negligence and had promised that she would make a greater effort in looking after her son.

Enzo had taken what had happened well. He had been frightened, as was to be expected, but he had recovered quickly and had promised her that he was okay. He had suggested that they might be able to leverage the FBI's offer so that they could be relocated in Boston, close to MIT in readiness for him to start there next year. There would be money to get them set up, he suggested, and a house where they could live together. Connie had shyly suggested it to Gathers, and he had replied that he thought that would definitely be in the cards. If it was possible to find a silver lining in what had happened to them over the course of the last week, then perhaps that was it.

There was Julio, too. He had done so much to help them, with no regard for his own safety, and Connie was grateful. Beyond that, he was a good-looking single man, and she thought that she had noticed an attraction in the way that he had been looking at her. It was not something that she was prepared to pursue right now, not while her focus was on Enzo, but in the future? Maybe. It was fun to speculate, if nothing else.

Julio took a swig from his beer. "What do you think happened to him?"

"Who?"

"John."

Connie took a drink from her own bottle. She had wondered the same thing, usually when she was lying in bed at night and trying to find sleep. He had done so much for them—he had saved their lives—and then he had simply disappeared into the night. Gathers had asked about him, and she had told him as much. He had informed her that it appeared Smith's contact had briefed the local agents, and there was no ongoing attempt to find him. Connie doubted that they would have been successful even if they had looked. Smith gave the impression that he knew how to hide and that, if he didn't want to be found, he wouldn't be.

She would have liked to have said thank you to him, though, just one more time. He had saved Enzo's life, and hers, and the others', and she wanted him to know how grateful she was. She doubted that she would ever have the chance.

MILTON STOOD at the back of the concert and watched the band on stage before Enzo, Aldo and Francesco. They were decent, wearing their influences a little too readily but still skilful and tight, and the crowd applauded generously as they concluded the third and final song of their set.

Milton was wearing a light disguise. He had bought a wig from a store in Southmoreland and had combined its unruly grey curls with a flat cap. He had purchased a pair of glasses with a heavy frame that broke up the geometry of his face, had allowed a heavy fuzz of stubble to grow on his cheeks and chin, and had obscured the scar that bisected his face with make-up. He knew from long experience that a successful disguise was more than changing the appearance of his face; today, for example, he had altered his gait by putting a piece of gravel in his shoe and was wearing a grey suit that he had picked up for twenty dollars at a thrift store. His ensemble wouldn't be enough to fool anyone who got close to him, but he did not intend to allow that to happen. He was confident that he would blend in satisfactorily as long as he merged with the crowd and kept his distance.

He had decided to stay in town for an extra few days. He was aware that there might be increased surveillance at the obvious places, especially the airport and the train and bus stations, and had delayed his departure to allow him to prepare an alternative extraction plan. The hiatus also gave him the time he needed to arrange the anonymity he suspected he was going to need if the Group were, indeed, back on his trail. It was obvious now that all of his old legends had been exposed, and, if he wanted to travel safely, he was going to need new ones. That required the services of a 'cobbler'—a specialist forger who was able to put together the documentation and background information to create a new person out of nothing—and Milton knew the perfect woman for the job. John Smith had been his *nom de guerre* for years, long before he had stopped working for the government, but now John Smith was dead. Milton would use him one final time for his flight to Denpasar, and then he would become someone else.

Connie and Fernández were standing by the sound desk. They had their backs to him, but he could see that they were relaxed and conversing happily. Milton did not give himself credit for empathy, but he had wondered whether the two of them might find a closeness through their shared experience, and whether that might, in time, become something more. Connie leaned over to say something to the coach, laying her hand on his elbow and laughing at whatever it was he said in reply. Milton hoped that he might be right; they were good people and they deserved happiness.

The MC came back out on stage and took the microphone from the stand.

"Give it up for Teenage Heart Attack," he said, encouraging another round of applause for the departing band. "We've got one more performance this evening, and it's from three young men from Blue Hills. We've got Aldo Maniscalco on drums, Francesco di Cello on bass, and Enzo Pizzolato on vocals and lead guitar. They've got three songs for us tonight, and so, without any further ado, put your hands together for Uncertain Smile."

The crowd applauded, none more lustily than Connie and Fernández, who added whoops of encouragement as the three boys made their way onstage. Francesco crossed over to a chair with the aid of a stick, picked up his bass and sat down to play it. Aldo took his seat behind the drums, and Enzo collected his guitar from a stand and looped the strap over his shoulder.

Enzo adjusted the mic stand. "Thanks for coming," he said. "We've got three songs for you. I hope you enjoy them."

Aldo tapped his sticks three times and then, in perfect unison, the three of them launched into 'My Generation' by The Who. Enzo leaned up to the mic and spat out the first line, and the crowd, immediately sensing that they were in safe hands, joined in with him.

Milton stood at the back of the room and watched, allowing himself a buzz of satisfaction in a job well done. He waited for the three of them to finish the song, lent his applause to the acclaim, then put his empty glass on the bar and made his way to the exit.

Waiting in the city a few extra days had proven to be auspicious. He had browsed Craigslist and had spotted a 1970 Pontiac LeMans. The owner had died, and the car was being sold by his son down in Labette County. Milton had hitched south to check it out. It was a two-door convertible in royal blue and was on the market for $23,999. Milton offered $20,000 cash, the vendor agreed, and Milton drove it back to the city.

It was waiting for him in the venue's parking lot. Milton had already packed his things and dumped them in the trunk. He had an appointment in Bali and had decided that he would take the scenic route to get there: he was going to drive to the border and then head south, tracing a path that would take him through Mexico, Guatemala, Honduras, Nicaragua and Costa Rica. He would finish the road trip in Panama and fly out from there.

Milton ran his fingers over the chrome on the LeMans's front end, went around to the driver's side, and opened the door. He dropped into the bucket seat and turned the key in the ignition. The 7.5-litre V8 coughed and spluttered, then settled into a steady rumble that gave Milton chills. He gripped the stick, worked it into first, and pulled out.

He could hear the thud of Aldo's drums and the throb of Francesco's bass as he rolled by the entrance to the venue. He smiled. Didn't matter if they won or lost tonight; the kids were going to be just fine.

He merged onto Rockhill Road. This would be his final journey as John Smith and, when it was done, he would become someone else. He had three and a half thousand miles of open road ahead of him, and—with the engine rumbling and the cold air whipping in through a gap between the window and the frame—the prospect of it felt *good*. Milton switched on the radio, pushed the button to jump to KCFX-FM and, with Metallica's 'Nothing Else Matters' playing out, he punched the gas and headed west.

GET EXCLUSIVE JOHN MILTON MATERIAL

Building a relationship with my readers is the very best thing about writing. Join my VIP Reader Club for information on new books and deals plus all this free Milton content:

1. A free copy of Milton's adventure in North Korea - 1000 Yards.

2. A free copy of Milton's battle with the Mafia and an assassin called Tarantula.

You can get your content **for free**, by signing up at my website.

Just visit www.markjdawson.com.

ALSO BY MARK DAWSON

IN THE JOHN MILTON SERIES

The Cleaner

Sharon Warriner is a single mother in the East End of
London, fearful that she's lost her young son to a life in the
gangs. After John Milton saves her life, he promises to help.
But the gang, and the charismatic rapper who leads it, is not
about to cooperate with him.

Saint Death

John Milton has been off the grid for six months. He
surfaces in Ciudad Juárez, Mexico, and immediately finds
himself drawn into a vicious battle with the narco-gangs
that control the borderlands.

The Driver

When a girl he drives to a party goes missing, John Milton is
worried. Especially when two dead bodies are discovered
and the police start treating him as their prime suspect.

Ghosts

John Milton is blackmailed into finding his predecessor as Number One. But she's a ghost, too, and just as dangerous as him. He finds himself in deep trouble, playing the Russians against the British in a desperate attempt to save the life of his oldest friend.

The Sword of God

On the run from his own demons, John Milton treks through the Michigan wilderness into the town of Truth. He's not looking for trouble, but trouble's looking for him. He finds himself up against a small-town cop who has no idea with whom he is dealing, and no idea how dangerous he is.

Salvation Row

Milton finds himself in New Orleans, returning a favour that saved his life during Katrina. When a lethal adversary from his past takes an interest in his business, there's going to be hell to pay.

Headhunters

Milton barely escaped from Avi Bachman with his life. But when the Mossad's most dangerous renegade agent breaks out of a maximum security prison, their second fight will be to the finish.

The Ninth Step

Milton's attempted good deed becomes a quest to unveil corruption at the highest levels of government and murder at the dark heart of the criminal underworld. Milton is pulled back into the game, and that's going to have serious consequences for everyone who crosses his path.

The Jungle

John Milton is no stranger to the world's seedy underbelly. But when the former British Secret Service agent comes up against a ruthless human trafficking ring, he'll have to fight harder than ever to conquer the evil in his path.

Blackout

A message from Milton's past leads him to Manila and a confrontation with an adversary he thought he would never meet again. Milton finds himself accused of murder and imprisoned inside a brutal Filipino jail - can he escape, uncover the truth and gain vengeance for his friend?

The Alamo

A young boy witnesses a murder in a New York subway restroom. Milton finds him, and protects him from corrupt cops and the ruthless boss of a local gang.

Redeemer

Milton is in Brazil, helping out an old friend with a close protection business. When a young girl is kidnapped, he finds himself battling a local crime lord to get her back.

Sleepers

A sleepy English town. A murdered Russian spy. Milton and Michael Pope find themselves chasing the assassins to Moscow.

Twelve Days

Milton checks back in with Elijah Warriner, but finds himself caught up in a fight to save him from a jealous - and dangerous - former friend.

Bright Lights

All Milton wants to do is take his classic GTO on a coast-to-coast road trip. But he can't ignore the woman on the side of the road in need of help. The decision to get involved leads to a tussle with a murderous cartel that he thought he had put behind him.

The Man Who Never Was

Following the events in Bright Lights, Milton and friends taker the fight to the El Centro cartel in an adventure that takes them from Amsterdam to Manchester and then jungles of Colombia.

IN THE BEATRIX ROSE SERIES

In Cold Blood

Beatrix Rose was the most dangerous assassin in an off-the-books government kill squad until her former boss betrayed her. A decade later, she emerges from the Hong Kong underworld with payback on her mind. They gunned down her husband and kidnapped her daughter, and now the debt needs to be repaid. It's a blood feud she didn't start but she is going to finish.

Blood Moon Rising

There were six names on Beatrix's Death List and now there are four. She's going to account for the others, one by one, even if it kills her. She has returned from Somalia with another target in her sights. Bryan Duffy is in Iraq, surrounded by mercenaries, with no easy way to get to him and no easy way to get out. And Beatrix has other issues that need to be addressed. Will Duffy prove to be one kill too far?

Blood and Roses

Beatrix Rose has worked her way through her Kill List. Four are dead, just two are left. But now her foes know she has them in her sights and the hunter has become the hunted.

The Dragon and the Ghost

Beatrix Rose flees to Hong Kong after the murder of her husband and the kidnapping of her child. She needs money. The local triads have it. What could possibly go wrong?

Tempest

Two people adrift in a foreign land, Beatrix Rose and Danny Nakamura need all the help they can get. A storm is coming. Can they help each other survive it and find their children before time runs out for both of them?

Phoenix

She does Britain's dirty work, but this time she needs help. Beatrix Rose, meet John Milton...

IN THE ISABELLA ROSE SERIES

The Angel

Isabella Rose is recruited by British intelligence after a terrorist attack on Westminster.

The Asset

Isabella Rose, the Angel, is used to surprises, but being abducted is an unwelcome novelty. She's relying on Michael Pope, the head of the top-secret Group Fifteen, to get her back.

The Agent

Isabella Rose is on the run, hunted by the very people she had been hired to work for. Trained killer Isabella and former handler Michael Pope are forced into hiding in India and, when a mysterious informer passes them clues on the whereabouts of Pope's family, the prey see an opportunity to become the predators.

The Assassin

Ciudad Juárez, Mexico, is the most dangerous city in the world. And when a mission to break the local cartel's grip goes wrong, Isabella Rose, the Angel, finds herself on the wrong side of prison bars. Fearing the worst, Isabella plays her only remaining card...

ABOUT MARK DAWSON

Mark Dawson is the author of the breakout John Milton, Beatrix and Isabella Rose, Atticus Priest and Soho Noir series.